"A complex case fraught with angst and danger ends with surprising revelations."

—*Kirkus Reviews*

"Debra Webb writes the kind of thrillers I love to read. Sure, there is a murder or more. Yes, a twisted mystery to be solved. Once again, in *The Last Lie Told*, her characters are fully rendered and reveal themselves authentically as her novel unfolds and careens to its stunning conclusion. *The Last Lie Told* is her best yet. Webb is the queen of smart suspense."

—Gregg Olsen, #1 *New York Times* bestselling author

Can't Go Back

"A complex, exciting mystery."

—*Kirkus Reviews*

"Police procedural fans will be sorry to see the last of Kerri and Luke."

—*Publishers Weekly*

"Threats, violence, and a dramatic climax . . . Good for procedural readers."

—*Library Journal*

Gone Too Far

"An intriguing, fast-paced combination of police procedural and thriller."

—*Kirkus Reviews*

"Those who like a lot of family drama in their police procedurals will be satisfied."

—*Publishers Weekly*

Trust No One

"*Trust No One* is Debra Webb at her finest. Political intrigue and dark family secrets will keep readers feverishly turning pages to uncover all the twists in this stunning thriller."

—Melinda Leigh, #1 *Wall Street Journal* bestselling author of
Cross Her Heart

"A wild, twisting crime thriller filled with secrets, betrayals, and complex characters that will keep you up until you reach the last darkly satisfying page. A five-star beginning to Debra Webb's explosive series!"

—Allison Brennan, *New York Times* bestselling author

"Debra Webb once again delivers with *Trust No One*, a twisty and gritty page-turning procedural with a cast of complex characters and a compelling cop heroine in Detective Kerri Devlin. I look forward to seeing more of Detectives Devlin and Falco."

—Loreth Anne White, *Washington Post* bestselling author of
In the Deep

"*Trust No One* is a gritty and exciting ride. Webb skillfully weaves together a mystery filled with twists and turns. I was riveted as each layer of the past peeled away, revealing dark secrets. An intriguing cast of complicated characters, led by the compelling Detective Kerri Devlin, had me holding my breath until the last page."

—Brianna Labuskes, *Washington Post* bestselling author of *Girls of Glass*

"Debra Webb's name says it all."

—Karen Rose, *New York Times* bestselling author

THE
NATURE
OF
SECRETS

ALSO BY DEBRA WEBB

The Last Lie Told
Can't Go Back
Gone Too Far
Trust No One

THE
NATURE
OF
SECRETS

DEBRA
WEBB

THOMAS & MERCER

Published by Thomas & Mercer, Seattle

www.apub.com

Amazon, the Amazon logo, and Thomas & Mercer are trademarks of Amazon.com, Inc., or its affiliates.

ISBN-13: 9781662508820 (paperback)
ISBN-13: 9781662508813 (digital)

Cover design by Shasti O'Leary Soudant
Cover images: © Magdalena Wasiczek / Arcangel; © KorradolYamsatthm / Shutterstock; © onair / Shutterstock

Printed in the United States of America

*This book is dedicated to a pair of very special friends:
Vicki Hinze and Peggy Webb, two ladies who have
always had my back and who are always there to lend
a helping hand—Vicki with the flashlight and Peggy
with the shovel. Twisted sisters, you are the best!*

All secrets become deep. All secrets become dark.
That's in the nature of secrets.
—Cory Doctorow

1

The Murder

Sunday, September 18

9:35 a.m.

Winthrop Residence
Morningview Court, Brentwood

This had been an enormous error.

She shouldn't have permitted the indulgence.

She should have been stronger. Need was weakness. No one knew this better than her. Trusting him had been a mistake.

She smiled. Well, perhaps she had not *really* trusted him. She'd spent so much time "in character" lately that at times it was difficult to step back. Actually, all had gone entirely according to plan.

Now it was time to finish this.

It was him or her, and it was not going to be her.

She smiled again. It was always going to be him.

Self-preservation was something she had learned at an early age. In this instance, outwitting him had not been so complicated. He was a mere man, after all. A cheater, a thief, the sort that thought only of himself when the chips were down.

She hadn't expected more from him.

The sound of water spewing from the dozen or so body sprayers in the shower abruptly stopped, leaving only the soft music from his chosen playlist and the knowledge of what must be done.

She waited and watched. Patience was essential at this pivotal moment. From her position near the door, she observed him stepping from the shower, droplets sliding over contoured muscle and slipping down tanned flesh. He reached for the towel, wiped his eyes and face first, then started the methodical ritual of smoothing the thick cotton over his body.

He adored his body. Was completely absorbed in admiring himself as he swept the towel over his skin. So much so he didn't even notice her approach. Never sensed her presence. A tragic lapse in judgment.

She was quite close behind him before he recognized her presence. Likely noticed her scent. Every woman possessed a unique scent, whether she chose to wear perfume or not. A man—especially a man who had been with her—recognized her scent.

She drew back her chosen weapon like a baseball bat as he turned, surprise marring his handsome face. She swung the weapon with all her might, twisting through her hips and driving hard into her target. The blow connected with his temple, sent vibrations along her arms, and propelled him forward. He went down. His head bounced off the tiled curb of the shower as he landed on the floor.

She stood over him to ensure the job was done . . . to witness the not-so-grand finale. He stared up at her. He didn't move. Likely couldn't. But he could see as the last moments of his life narrowed to this one unexpected instant. She wanted him to know who had ended his game . . . his life.

She smiled as the essence of him slipped from his gaze.

It was done.

Now, she drew in a deep breath and tossed the weapon aside. Time for the most important role of her life.

2

5:15 p.m.

Brentwood Police Department
Maryland Way, Brentwood

Finley O'Sullivan climbed from behind the wheel of her Subaru and fished around in the back seat for her emergency meet-a-client business jacket. Sunday was the one day each week she set entirely aside for following up on certain personal things. It wasn't a day she dressed for work.

Frankly, there were a lot of things she didn't do on Sundays that other people did. She didn't do church. She didn't do family dinners or even visit family. Finley had stopped feeling guilty for those abandoned customs more than a year ago, when her husband was murdered.

She hesitated, jacket in hand. His murder remained unsolved as far as the Nashville Metro Police Department was concerned. Her parents, friends . . . they all believed the same. But not Finley. She knew exactly who had murdered Derrick.

Proving it was the issue. She shrugged on her jacket. But she wasn't giving up. No way. She would not stop until justice was done. Which was why she typically spent a great deal of her personal time, including Sundays, tuned in to that singular goal.

As much as Finley liked having her off-the-clock time for her own purposes, working with Jack Finnegan, she had come to realize that criminal lawyers never knew when duty might call. Business hours weren't nine to five or Monday through Friday, so Finley kept a work jacket in the car. Lightweight enough for any season and black to match basically any outfit. A black jacket could elevate even an overly casual outfit like jeans and a tee to reasonably presentable attire.

Half an hour ago, her boss had called to say he was headed to the Brentwood police precinct and he needed her to meet him there. They had a new client. Finley wasn't a lawyer anymore, by choice mostly. Last year, after a great deal of pleading from Jack, she had accepted the position of investigator at the Finnegan Firm. She had never fully recognized just how important the role was to any law firm. Frankly, she enjoyed the work more than she'd anticipated. In part, she supposed, because Jack—her boss—was also her godfather. But the ability to see the case from another perspective was definitely an added perk.

She liked the view. A lot.

Finley shifted her focus to the here and now and walked toward her boss's vintage Land Rover.

Their new client's husband had been murdered, and she, one Ellen Winthrop of Winthrop Financial Consulting Group—the very same one featured in *Time* magazine last year—was obviously the prime suspect. The woman had built a Fortune 500 financial empire and operated it exclusively with the help of other women. Her history as a women's advocate and as a force to watch in the financial world was unparalleled. Sadly, with power often came other, less desirable assets and liabilities. All manner of crimes—or in this case motives—from fraud to embezzlement flitted through Finley's mind.

"Hey, kid," Jack said as she slid into the passenger seat next to him. "Sorry I had to interrupt your day." He shrugged. "Murder waits for no one."

This was true.

"No problem." Finley was well aware of the urgency involved in a murder case. Their new client would need protection from a potential murder charge. Whether the client was guilty or not, it was Jack's job to disprove her responsibility in the matter or at least to cast enough doubt to sway a jury.

The concept was a whole different ball game from Finley's days in the district attorney's office, where the sole goal was to prove guilt beyond a shadow of doubt. "What do we know so far?"

"Not much beyond the fact that Winthrop's new husband, Jarrod Grady, was murdered this morning," Jack explained. "She and Grady married just two months ago. Whirlwind-style, according to some of the gossip on social media."

Finley's eyebrows reared up. "Since when do you do social media?" This was news to her. She'd never known Jack to acknowledge any of the platforms even existed, much less to scroll the feeds. Interesting. Maybe an old dog could learn new tricks, though she had her doubts.

He sent her a sidelong glance. "I leave that unreliable and completely obnoxious resource to you, but a 'just breaking' clip interrupted my favorite rerun of *Perry Mason*. The reporter mentioned the social media buzz that had surrounded the wedding. This is one old dog with no interest in learning new tricks in that arena."

Had she mentioned he was a mind reader? Not really. She'd tossed the old-dog tag at him too many times, she supposed. Jack remained an old-fashioned-news guy. The *Tennessean* was delivered to the office every day. He still watched the news on a local cable television channel rather than streaming it.

"Have they arrested her?" she asked.

"Not yet, but we both know unless they find another suspect, it's only a matter of time before she is."

No question.

"Do you know Ellen Winthrop?" Finley imagined he did. Jack seemed to know everyone in Nashville. A woman in Winthrop's position likely wouldn't retain an attorney she'd never met for such a serious matter.

If the woman wanted the best on her team, she'd made the right decision. Jack was, unquestionably, the best. Admittedly, her godfather's reputation as a legal eagle had taken a bit of a beating a few years back, but that hadn't changed the community's awareness of his legal prowess. If anything, he was viewed as a bit more cutthroat these days—a bit more of a rogue. Who didn't love a wounded hero? He even looked the part, with his long grayish-blond hair secured at the nape of his neck and his comfortably aged vintage suit worn with the kind of confidence only a handsome, damned-good-at-his-job rogue would possess.

Jack glanced at his watch—the one on his wrist and not on his cell. Another throwback. "The detective should be ready for us now."

"Let's do this thing," Finley said, already reaching for her door. The beginning of a new investigation was always exciting. There was nothing more satisfying than taking all the jumbled pieces and putting them together one by one to recreate the picture—the story—of the crime in question.

They exited the Land Rover and headed across the parking lot. The main office was closed at this hour, but a tall figure—presumably the detective on the case—now waited at the door. Any reporters who had shown up had abandoned the hope of a statement and left at this point.

As they approached the entrance, the man in the wrinkled "it's been a long day" suit opened one of the doors. "I'm Detective Sid Ventura."

Finley stifled a grin at the thought of the pet-detective movie. Derrick, her late husband, had claimed it as his favorite. God, she'd forgotten that bit of trivia until just this moment. Strange how even after more than a year things popped back into her head with the right trigger. Somehow it always seemed to happen at the most unexpected times. Like when she was completely exhausted or when she was in the middle of work—times when her guard slipped and she couldn't push the still-raw emotions away. She exiled the thoughts. Now was certainly not a good time to drift off in the past.

"Jack Finnegan," Jack said with a nod as he waited for Finley to enter the precinct ahead of him.

"Finley O'Sullivan," she offered as she sidled in past the detective. She chastised herself for allowing her focus to slip.

Ventura gave her a nod. Once Jack was inside and the door closed and locked, the two men shook hands. The detective reached for her hand next. He had loosened his tie and opened the top button of his shirt. His strawberry-red hair was tousled as if he'd run his fingers through it too many times. Along with the light-red hair came a scattering of freckles across his nose and cheeks. His hazel eyes were bright, but the bags beneath spoke of weariness. The most telling was what Finley didn't see—that hardened bearing of a seasoned homicide detective.

"How do you want to do this?" Ventura asked Jack.

The question confirmed Finley's assessment that the guy didn't have a tremendous amount of experience with investigating homicides.

"I'll need some time alone with my client first," Jack told him.

"No problem. She's in an interview room. Follow me."

Ventura led the way through the lobby and into the inner depths of the department. Most of the offices were dark, save one where another detective sat hunkered over a file spread across his desk. He didn't look up as the group passed.

Beyond the offices were more doors and a small waiting area. Just past the small lobby, Ventura reached for the second door on the left.

"Let me know when you're ready to move forward on her official statement and the additional questions I have for Ms. Winthrop."

"You got it," Jack confirmed.

Ventura wandered back in the direction of the offices, and Finley entered the interview room ahead of Jack.

Ellen Winthrop was seated in the lone chair on the far side of a narrow beige table. The side no one wanted to find themselves on, because you were facing either the CCTV camera or the one-way viewing window so that your every response could be observed. She sat straight, shoulders square, though she looked exhausted and sad beneath the smattering of makeup that had faded over the course of the day. Her dark-brown hair was arranged in a chin-length, face-hugging style. The black pullover she wore matched the leggings that topped off black flat-heeled shoes. Both feet rested firmly on the floor, knees together. No crossed legs or overly casual positioning. A barely touched bottle of water sat on the table to her right.

The door closed, and Jack took care of the introductions. Handshakes were exchanged. The older woman's hand was cold, and her fingers trembled ever so slightly, but then she squared her shoulders once more and lifted her chin in preparation for battle. This might not be her first encounter with the police, though Finley imagined it was her first for murder. Ellen Winthrop had a reputation as a tiger in the business world; whether it would stand up in a moment like this was yet to be seen.

"Ms. Winthrop," Jack began as he and Finley took the seats on their side of the table.

"Call me Ellen, please," Winthrop suggested. Her voice was steadier than her hand and pleasantly toned.

"Ellen," Jack acknowledged, "we have a good deal to talk about, and you've had a long day already. Theories and supposition about why or how this unthinkable tragedy happened can wait. We need to nail down the details as you remember them right now, while they are freshly imprinted in your memory."

She nodded. "Of course." Deep breath. "Where would you like me to begin?"

"Let's start with when you woke up this morning," Jack suggested. "Don't leave anything out. How did you feel? Exactly what did you do?"

"Did you have any reason to want your husband dead?" Finley interjected, just to liven things up.

Winthrop blinked once, twice, her gray eyes bright with emotion. "I woke up at eight," she said, starting as Jack had suggested and avoiding Finley's question entirely. "I was stunned that I'd overslept. I'm usually up by seven at the latest. I don't have a scheduled workout on Sundays, but I do go for a nice walk, weather permitting."

She moistened her lips, glanced away briefly. "Jarrod almost always accompanied me, but this morning was different. He looked a mess and was clearly hungover. There were numerous empty beer bottles scattered around the family room."

"Why was he hungover?" Finley asked before Ellen could go on.

"We quarreled last night. He stayed up and obviously overindulged long after I exited the unpleasant exchange." Winthrop stared at Finley for one long beat. "To answer your first question, no, I had no reason to wish my husband dead."

"Good. Did you sleep in the same bed last night?" Finley pressed on, needing more specific details. As for the other comment, no suspect ever admitted to having a reason to want someone dead—at least not in the beginning.

"No." The single word was expressed firmly, almost angrily. "I needed some space. He slept on the sofa."

"What time did you go to bed?" Finley asked next. She and Jack had their strategy down to a science. He asked the primary questions, and she did the digging for the details. It served them well, allowing the clients to wear out their anger on Finley rather than Jack.

"I didn't try to sleep. There was no point," Winthrop said. "If you mean what time did I walk away from him, it was around nine."

"What did you quarrel about?" Jack asked as Finley relaxed against the back of her chair.

So far, the lady showed no outward signs of deceit. No avoiding eye contact. No nervous twitches. Direct, confident responses. No hesitating. A hint of emotion thrown in here and there. The only trouble

9

Finley picked up on so far was a noticeable lack of real, palpable emotion, which never looked good to a jury.

"On Friday I discovered a number of discrepancies in several of my personal bank accounts," Winthrop explained. "I was startled, and frankly I didn't know what to make of it. Jarrod was away on business. He wasn't supposed to return home until Saturday afternoon. I'm generally not overly patient with financial discrepancies, but this was personal. I needed time to step back and shore up my objectivity before proceeding." She drew in a fortifying breath. "Under the circumstances, I decided to wait until he returned and I had a better handle on the details of the transactions to discuss the situation with him."

"Tell us about the accounts and the discrepancies." Jack rested his forearms on the table and waited expectantly.

Another quick swipe of her tongue over her lips. First sign of nerves in response to the questioning. Understandable. Her husband was dead. If she weren't at least a little nervous at this point, Finley would be concerned.

"I have three online savings accounts to which he has—had—access, and they were almost emptied, as were both my checking accounts, along with the account I created for him. The transfers were done over a period of time, in increments just below the maximum threshold, ensuring I wasn't notified." A weary shrug lifted her shoulders. "The past several weeks have been inordinately busy with our new international endeavors at the firm; otherwise I'm certain I would have noticed."

"How much money are we talking about, Ellen?" Finley was guessing it was a significant amount. After all, Winthrop operated a financial consulting firm. No kids and not even a spouse until a couple of months ago to absorb resources. She was no doubt loaded.

Winthrop's posture visibly stiffened. "Seven point eight million dollars."

Finley and Jack shared a quick glance.

That's a hell of a lot of motive.

In Finley's opinion the most significant factor was that the husband—Jarrod Grady—had come back from his business trip. He had to understand there was a good chance Winthrop had found out about the money. The woman was a financial genius. He must have anticipated he wouldn't be able to hide what he'd done for long. Further, he obviously had no fear of serious reprisal—at least not of being murdered or even arrested right away. Was he that confident in his ability to charm his way out of trouble? Or did he believe his wife that naive? Winthrop didn't strike Finley as the least bit naive.

"Where did he go on this business trip?" Jack asked. "Out of town?"

Winthrop nodded. "Atlanta. He's . . ." Her voice trailed off. She blinked back tears, then started again. "He wanted to develop a real estate business. With property values soaring, it seemed a good move. He insisted that he wished to earn his keep." She somehow managed to maintain eye contact with Jack as she said this, though it was discernably difficult. This was the grieving widow the jury would need to see if the case went to trial.

Finley made a mental note to confirm whether Grady had made the trip as scheduled. If Winthrop hadn't been aware of his embezzling for a period of time, she likely hadn't been aware of other things.

Jack continued with the essential questions. "What time did he arrive home on Saturday?"

"Seven fifteen that evening. His flight was delayed. I wanted to send my driver to pick him up, but he'd already called for an Uber. With more than twenty-four hours since the discovery of the missing money, I'd had time to prepare myself for the confrontation. I was reasonably calm and ready to demand answers when he arrived home."

Jack waited for her to continue. The distant look in her eyes told them she was reliving those fateful minutes and hours.

"I was alone when he arrived. I didn't want anyone else there. I needed to hear his answers first." Her lips quivered, and she laughed a sad sound. "My God, I own and operate one of the top financial consulting firms in the country; how could I be conned like this?" She shook her head, battling tears once more. "The ramifications to my professional reputation stand to do far more damage than the money loss. Money, I know how to make. But recovering from this kind of scandal . . ." She bit her lips together, unable to go on.

"You grilled him the moment he arrived," Finley suggested. It wasn't a question. Winthrop had already stated that she had been prepared and waiting for him. How it had started might prove relevant.

"I did. The moment he walked through the door, he called my name. I answered from the family room, and he joined me there. I pointed to the documents on the coffee table and demanded an explanation. He dropped his overnight bag and walked to the table to view the documents. For half a minute or so, he studied the statements I'd printed. Throughout our discussion he maintained there had to be a mistake or some other explanation. We went round and round for hours. I asked him to leave, but he refused. He said he didn't want me to be alone under the circumstances." She gave her head a long, slow shake. "He went so far as to suggest that if someone had managed to break into our accounts, he wasn't sure I would be safe alone in the house."

Finley had to hand it to the dead guy—pretending to still care after swiping more than $7 million was a slick move. There was always the off chance the guy was innocent.

Doubtful. Ellen Winthrop likely wouldn't make such a mistake.

But smart women did make the occasional mistake, especially when those more intimate emotions were involved. Finley had certainly made a few. Memories of her own whirlwind marriage invaded her thoughts. She'd met Derrick, and they'd tied the knot mere weeks later. They'd lived the fairy tale for several more weeks, and then everything had shattered into a million pieces, leaving a multitude of questions and no ready answers. There were only secrets and lies . . . and mounting questions that at times overwhelmed her.

Is it possible Derrick could be innocent?

No. Anger flared, and Finley hardened herself against the memories and thoughts that dared to slip into her head during a damned client interview. There was no way to pretend he was innocent anymore. Derrick had been guilty of something. He'd lured her in with a carefully constructed web of lies, and she still didn't know the truth about him or what his endgame had been.

Yet she knew one thing for certain. The anger dissipated as quickly as it had come. She had loved him. Completely. Unexpectedly so.

Had Ellen Winthrop loved Jarrod Grady that way?

The similarities in their marriages—Finley's and this woman's—were oddly unsettling. They could be sitting here discussing Finley's life instead of Winthrop's. Though Derrick hadn't absconded with Finley's money, he'd left her with a mountain of uncertainties. Also, like Winthrop's husband, Derrick had been murdered in their home. Only Finley hadn't been out for a walk; she'd very nearly been killed as well.

Focus on the case, damn it.

Finley cleared her head and asked the question suddenly nagging at her. "Did you love your husband, Ellen?"

Winthrop blinked as if startled by the query. "I loved him. Yes."

Her eyes and the sadness that consumed her face as well as her bearing seemed to underscore her words. She was either telling the truth or the best damned poker player Finley had ever interviewed.

"What did you do when he refused to leave?" Jack prodded.

Winthrop turned to the man she without doubt hoped could save her from drowning in a painful and violent river of legal trouble. "I told him to be gone by morning. Then I went to my home office and locked myself inside. I felt safer there. It's on the ground level, and the door is like one you would find on a vault. There's a keypad with an entry code. No one was getting in unless I granted entrance. I—"

"Are you saying," Finley interrupted, "your husband didn't have access to your home office?"

"He did not," Winthrop said without missing a beat. "Perhaps in time I would have given him the code. I suppose I'm somewhat over-protective of that space."

Finley nodded. "Please continue with your story."

Winthrop took a moment to reset, then continued. "As I was say-ing, after that painful exchange I went to my office and tried to sleep, but I primarily walked the floor. At some point after collapsing into the chair behind my desk, I fell asleep there."

"But you still went for a walk this morning?" Finley was surprised she'd done so with little or no sleep, not to mention she had left Grady at the house. Alone.

"I had hoped he would leave sometime during the night, but he surprised me by daring to stay. As exhausted as I felt, I didn't want to be under the same roof with him. I told him to be gone when I came back from my walk."

"You spoke to him," Jack reiterated, "confirmed that he was alive when you left the house."

She nodded. "I did. He just stood in the center of the family room staring at me as if he still didn't understand why I was upset."

Jack studied her a moment, then asked, "Do you have any way of confirming what time you left the house and then returned?"

"I'm certain the security system will show when I left the house," she said, "and when I returned."

"Your system has cameras?" Finley hoped the answer was yes.

"Yes." A frown marred her forehead. "I'm confident the detective has already confirmed the time I left the house and the time I returned. I was gone just over an hour, from nine thirty until fifteen or so minutes before eleven."

"You returned," Jack went on, "and you found him."

"As I told Detective Ventura," Winthrop answered, "I returned to the house. The door was locked, so I assumed he was gone. Once inside, I walked straight to the family room to see if he was still loitering there, but he was not. The evidence he'd drunk himself to sleep the night before had been cleaned up."

How nice of the sneaky embezzler to clean up his mess.

"Did you search the house from that point?" Finley wondered about his vehicle. She felt confident the man had one. Probably a Lamborghini. A wedding present from his adoring wife.

"I did. First I went to the garage. His Ferrari was still there. Admittedly, this made me more than a little angry, and I stormed through the house in search of him."

Ferrari. Lamborghini. Close enough, Finley mused.

Finley waited for her to go on. Ellen Winthrop's next steps would define how this case moved forward. Could be smooth sailing or like driving over mountains of rubble.

"I checked the kitchen first. He wasn't there, and I found no sign he'd bothered with coffee, so I went upstairs to our suite to see if perhaps he was still packing." She swallowed, took a breath. "That's when I found him."

"Remember, I need to know every step, every thought, every word on your part," Jack said softly. "I know this is difficult, but it's important that we don't miss anything."

"I climbed the stairs, slowly," she said, then hesitated a moment. "By that point dread had taken hold, and I wasn't looking forward to having someone from my security service remove him. Or worse, the police. I really had hoped he would just leave." She drew in a long, deep breath. "The french doors to our bedroom were open, so I continued into the room without stopping. I was braced for battle. Determined. Frustrated." She shrugged. "Angry."

Finley held up a hand. "Think for a moment. Was there anything unusual about the room. A smell? Sounds? Anything at all?"

"The bed remained made, since neither of us had slept there." Her eyes narrowed as if she was searching her memory. "I smelled the soap he used, a leathery sandalwood scent." The features of her face tightened.

"I experienced a powerful surge of anger at that point. The idea that he would take his time, shower at his leisure, infuriated me unreasonably."

She took a moment then, seemed to gather her courage around her. "I found him in the bathroom." A beat, then two, elapsed. "At first I thought he'd slipped getting out of the shower. He was lying on the floor, his head turned so that I could see his face. I initially noticed that his eyes . . ." She gestured toward her own. "They were open. Unblinking."

She fell silent, her gaze distant, as if she were back in that bathroom staring at her dead husband.

"Take your time," Jack offered.

Winthrop blinked, his voice prompting her to go on. "There was an indentation on his left temple, as if he'd fallen and hit the edge of something. I called his name. Moved a little closer. He . . ." She closed her eyes a moment. "I crouched down . . . that's when I realized he wasn't breathing. I checked his pulse. Nothing. His skin felt cold." She shivered. "I saw the blood pooled on the floor beneath his head. I tried to draw away, lost my balance. I toppled backward onto my bottom. That's when I saw the hammer a few feet away. As if it had been tossed aside . . ."

"Did you recognize the hammer?"

Winthrop started at Finley's question. "I'm sorry. What?"

"Is the hammer one that you recognized as belonging in your home? Maybe from the garage or a tool kit you keep."

Winthrop hesitated, then said, "Yes. No." She shook her head. "It isn't that kind of hammer. One of my dearest friends, Laney Pettit, gave it to me years ago when I first made the Fortune 500. The hammer is made of titanium. She'd had it mounted in a distinctive glass case. She said it was in honor of my shattering the glass ceiling."

Interesting. Clearly the killer was aware of the personal significance of the chosen weapon. Finley wondered if Winthrop had considered that the killer might be someone in her circle. "Was the hammer on display somewhere in your home?"

Winthrop nodded. "In my office."

"The office where you slept last night," Finley confirmed, her instincts rousing to a higher level.

Another nod.

Jack said, "Did anyone besides you have access to your office? A housekeeper? Assistant?"

She'd already said only she had access, but Jack was giving her an out here. A place to show doubt . . . to produce other potential suspects.

"No."

And there it was. The reason Jack was here rather than one of the likely numerous lawyers already on Winthrop's payroll.

The police had 7.8 million motives and no other suspect besides the victim's spouse. Worse, they had the murder weapon to which only the spouse had access.

Not good. Not good at all.

"Ellen," Finley said, her gaze fixed firmly on their client, "do you know of anyone who may have had a reason to want your husband dead?"

Winthrop considered the question for a moment before shaking her head. "No one." She exhaled a weary breath, and then she laughed a sort of defeated sound. "I suppose from the perspective of the police that only leaves me."

Oh yeah. This client was on a fast track to being charged with murder, and she knew it.

3

9:55 p.m.

The Hidey Hole Tavern
Downtown Nashville

Finley nursed a beer. Had been for the better part of an hour. Their new client hadn't been arrested, which meant Detective Ventura had opted for the smartest, cleanest route for the case: he wouldn't make an arrest until the evidence was irrefutable. A good move, in Finley's opinion.

Now she was back to her usual off duty pastime: monitoring the leisure activities of one of the men responsible for tearing apart her life.

So far, he appeared to have no idea he was being watched.

For a man in his line of work, that was saying something—mostly about *her*. She had gotten damned good at this surveillance thing.

It was of course entirely possible that tonight had something to do with how much alcohol her target had consumed. Certainly, he was off his game. He had picked up a lady friend Finley had seen him with before. Generally, he showed up at her low-rent-apartment door and stayed for the night. This was the first time he had brought her along for an evening out—at least on Finley's watch. Maybe the guy had something to celebrate. Another job well done for his employer. Maybe the assassination of some poor schmuck who'd said or done the wrong thing. Life meant nothing to this bastard.

Tark Brant. That was his name. He was an off-the-record employee for Carson Dempsey, the creator of Dempsey Pharma . . . the kind of man who didn't get his hands dirty. His wealth and power rose like smoke and ash from the pharmaceutical empire he had single-handedly—or at least this was his claim—built. The creation of a new, powerful nonaddictive painkiller had been the true source of his incredible success. The rumors of bizarre side effects and his ruthless, possibly lethal tactics with the competition occasionally sprouted among the expansion cracks of phenomenal growth and threatened to damage his illustrious kingdom. But there was never any proof. Dempsey's answer was always the same: Only those who did nothing were ignored. Those who did the work to make things happen were scrutinized. He would bear the scrutiny because his work was for the greater good.

His arrogance and self-righteousness made Finley sick.

Although she couldn't prove it, Dempsey had given the order for her husband's execution.

Fury blasted through her. She wanted to nail him more than she wanted her next breath. After more than a year, one would think she would be closer to achieving that goal, but there had been complications. Like her own physical and emotional recovery. Add that to the fact that Dempsey's financial support of this city and certain leaders made him a hero. Made him untouchable. So here she was a year later, barely past square one.

Bastard. Finley's grip tightened on her beer bottle.

Brant threw back his head and laughed at something his lady friend said. A flash of memory—that broad mouth clamping over Finley's, stifling a scream—seared through her. She flinched, blinked away the rip of horror from *that* night.

She rarely allowed those unbearable moments to touch her so deeply and sharply. For the most part, after all this time, she had reached a place where she could analyze the event with an emotional distance that allowed a clearer look at the players and each moment as it evolved into the next. It was amazing the things she had missed the first thousand or so times she had replayed those seemingly endless minutes.

Her throat thickened as the fractured pieces darted through her mind like images in a rapid-fire video game. The bastard she watched tonight wasn't the one who had killed her husband. No, this piece of shit had been busy raping her as one of his pals beat her husband to death with careful oversight from the third man in the group. The three had broken into Finley and Derrick's home with one purpose: to murder Derrick and torture Finley within an inch of her life.

In the beginning she had believed her survival was a mistake. A miscalculation or oversight of some detail by one or all three. After all, these were hired killers with measurable levels of experience. But she eventually came to understand that her death likely hadn't been part of *that* night's plan. Therefore, she had lived. Barely. And not because she'd wanted to do so at the time or for many months after *that* night. There were times even now when she briefly pondered the point of going on with this hollow existence.

Then she remembered.

Payback.

It was the air she breathed . . . the heat that kept her blood warm.

Anticipation welled inside her. This was a place where Finley's situation contrasted sharply with that of Ellen Winthrop. Winthrop claimed she had no idea who had murdered her husband or why. Finley, on the other hand, knew the answer to both, where her own husband's murder was concerned.

Brant stood from his table and headed for the bar. Finley watched his long strides, the relaxed set of his shoulders. His focus was straight ahead. Get the lady another drink. Maybe another for himself. Would he glance to his right and spot Finley seated in the darkest corner of the establishment? Maybe, maybe not.

Though she couldn't hear his voice over the music filtering from the speakers, she studied his profile as he spoke to the bartender. The remembered feel of his weight on top of her pierced her with rekindled viciousness. She gritted her teeth. Reached for her beer.

The one who'd landed the fatal blow that killed her husband had gotten his recompense a couple of months ago. The memory of the scumbag's blood and brain matter spraying across her face flashed through Finley's mind. The clerk at the convenience store had put one right through his head. Finley's presence at the store, face to face with him at the time of his death, had been one of those ironies life threw one's way now and then. Though she was reasonably sure the detective investigating the shooting still didn't see it that way.

One down, two to go.

But the truth was, Finley wasn't a killer. She had graduated from law school at the top of her class. Spent four years in the DA's office as an assistant district attorney fighting for justice. Now she fought for justice from the opposite side of the aisle.

What she did on her time off notwithstanding.

Strangely enough, her work as a case investigator for Jack, more so than her previous position as an ADA, made her acutely aware of killers like the man she was watching tonight. Hired guns who existed on the fringes of their employers' world. If Tark Brant died, no one involved in his work would care. He was nothing. Less than nothing. His world revolved around getting the job done. He had one motto: kill or be killed. He truly was nothing. A piece of shit with a certain skill set. The bastard laughed at something the bartender said, probably some lame joke he'd been tossing out all night.

Finley rolled her eyes and dug for additional patience. Her primary goal in observing the two remaining assholes was twofold: to glean any potential evidence related to her husband's murder and to make sure Brant and his pal got theirs—eventually. If her little "I'm watching you" game distracted her target at some key moment and prompted an early demise, all the better.

As if she'd somehow telegraphed the words to Brant, he turned, looked directly at her. Ice formed inside Finley. For one, two, three beats he held her gaze, and then he moved.

Toward her.

She polished off her beer and set the bottle on the counter. Determination seared through her, melting the ice. She would not show fear. She refused to be frightened. Ill at ease, maybe, but never ever afraid. Tonight—like the other times—was necessary to her goal.

He leaned against the counter between her stool and the next one. Set his drinks aside and smirked at Finley. This should be interesting.

"You know"—he exhaled a big bourbon-infused breath—"I don't understand why you keep hanging on to the past. It's bad for your health, O'Sullivan. I thought you would get that by now."

Finley laughed. "Oh, I'm having way too much fun," she explained, "watching you squirm. I can't possibly stop now."

His stare hardened, black-brown eyes glaring into hers. "If memory serves, you were the one doing the squirming the last time we were eye to eye."

Outrage belted her, but she bit it back. "Does your friend"—Finley nodded to the woman waiting at the table—"know you're a rapist and a killer?"

He leaned closer still. Finley held her breath and her ground. Refused to draw away. *No fear.*

"What about you?" he snarled. "What do you know about me or the reason you're even still alive?"

She said nothing. He was baiting her. There was far more to be gained by listening even when every fiber of her being wanted to act. Patience, some claimed, was a virtue. But the true meaning of virtue had zero to do with what she felt or wanted from this man and his employer.

Her silence brought his grin back. "See, maybe you don't know all you think you know."

"Maybe not." She shrugged. "I'm just waiting." She glanced at the table he had abandoned. "Your friend is getting restless, by the way."

"Waiting for what?" he growled, impatient, without looking away from Finley. He couldn't care less what his friend was doing.

Finley smiled. This was one of her favorite things. That moment—that fleeting, infinitesimal instant—when she caught this guy or his remaining partner off guard by some action or comment. And yes, she had come to realize she might have been spared for a specific purpose. The concept was the reason these guys didn't actually scare her.

Carson Dempsey hadn't wanted her dead. No. He had wanted her to live . . . to feel the pain and agony of loss. To suffer the guilt of believing it was her fault that her husband was dead. And probably it was, at least in part. Her final case win as an assistant district attorney had been to send Dempsey's piece-of-shit son to prison. The headlines far and wide called Finley a hero and boasted the verdict was proof money couldn't buy everything. The kicker happened mere days later when Carson Dempsey Jr.—a.k.a. Sonny—ended up dead on the prison floor with a shiv in his gut. Dempsey had been understandably devastated.

Then, fourteen days and twenty-one hours after that, Derrick had been murdered.

Classic revenge motive. Finley took something from Dempsey; he took something from her.

The stare-off between her and Brant persisted. Tension visibly tightening the features of his face.

Maybe she'd get lucky and his anger would cause him to blurt out something useful. She could always hope the combination of rage and alcohol would prompt that vein throbbing in his forehead to explode. Death by aneurysm. She could live with that. Nah, she'd never get that lucky.

Her cell vibrated on the counter.

The sound shattered the intense moment. The bastard grabbed his drinks and walked away without another word.

Finley drew in a long, deep breath. She was brave, but she wasn't stupid. She was pushing the boundaries here. But then, how boring would life be if she didn't dance on the edge from time to time? She'd learned from the best. Jack was the king of pushing boundaries.

Mildly annoyed at the interruption, she picked up her cell and checked the screen.

Matt.

She frowned. Then remembered. Oh hell.

Drinks. Exciting news.

She groaned. Had totally forgotten she was supposed to meet Matt at ten.

A quick tap of the screen and she pressed the phone to her ear. "Hey, you. Sorry I'm running late. I should have sent you a text." She grimaced. Matt was her friend. Her best friend. Had been for most of her life. He was one of three people who she should never let down under any circumstances.

"No problem," he said in that smooth, deep voice of his. The one that always made her feel at peace and relaxed even when she had absolutely no right to feel that way. "I just ordered another pint," he reassured her. "I'll see you when you get here."

"Five minutes," she promised, guilt piling deeper. "I'm on my way."

Lucky for her, the Fleet Street Pub was only a few blocks away. She pointed one last glance at her target, then headed for the exit. Keeping a watchful eye on her surroundings, she hustled out to her dusty ten-year-old Subaru and climbed behind the wheel. As she rolled away, she considered it was a good thing the pub where Matt waited was casual. Since she'd forgotten their date, she hadn't bothered with a stop by the house to change after leaving the precinct. A peek at her reflection in the rearview mirror reminded her that her hair hung in a sloppier-than-usual ponytail. Three months' worth of blonde roots gave away her true hair color.

Didn't matter. Matt wouldn't care. As long as she showed up, he would be happy. He was that kind of friend.

At the next intersection she braked, then tugged her tee from her chest and sniffed herself. At least she smelled okay.

She made a right turn and scanned for an open slot. Parking was not so easy, gobbling up precious time. Downtown Nashville was like most big cities—there was never enough parking. Printers Alley was no exception. She climbed out of her Subaru and walked quickly along the alley and then down the steps to the pub's entrance. Matt waved from a table, and she relaxed. By the time she reached him, he had pushed to his feet and pulled out a chair for her.

"Sorry." She flashed a smile at him.

He brushed his cheek against hers in a quick hug. "Not a problem." He gestured to the table as they settled into their chairs. "I ordered you a Guinness."

"Thanks." She lifted the glass and savored a deep sip of the brew. She was generally a wine drinker, but beer just went better with some things, like the food served at this British-style pub. "That hits the spot."

His lips spread into a smile as he nudged a basket of crisps and french onion dip in her direction. She dug in. The spicy dip tingled on her tongue, and she grabbed another of the freshly made potato chips. Funny, she hadn't realized she was hungry. Suddenly she was starving.

This pub was one of their favorite meeting spots. The atmosphere was quiet and relaxing. When they came for dinner, the food was very good and pleasantly different from the usual fare around town.

"Don't make me wait any longer," she fussed. "What's your big news?"

Matthew Quinn worked as the liaison between the mayor's, the DA's, and the chief of police's offices—the three, or the unholy trinity, as Finley liked to call them. Talk about walking a tightwire. But he was very, very good at his work. Somehow he managed the job while maintaining a neutrality few—including Finley—could hope to achieve. If his news was work related, she hoped it was a raise.

Or maybe he'd finally met a special someone.

The idea made her heart skip. He deserved someone special. Funny how the thought made her happy for him and a little sad at the same time. A new, deeper relationship with someone else would change theirs. Finley scolded herself for the selfish thought.

"I had dinner with the governor and his wife tonight."

Finley sat back in her chair. "Wow. Sounds like someone has noticed your work."

Matt scrubbed a hand across his jaw. "His chief of staff is having some health issues and has decided to retire."

"Oh my God." Finley grinned. "And the governor offered you the position."

Matt nodded, his own grin appearing. "I'm still weighing my options."

"Shut up." Finley laughed. "You are saying yes and you know it."

His lips pressed together, and he held her gaze for a long moment, his sober. "What do you think, Fin? Is it the right move at the right time?"

She reached across the table and squeezed his hand. "It is exactly the right move and definitely the right time."

He nodded slowly. "You're right. I do think I'll go for it."

Finley motioned for the waiter. "We need another round."

When Finley had sufficiently teased him about becoming a politician, she offered, "I'm really happy for you, Matt. I'm sure your parents are so proud."

"They're on that cruise they've been talking about for years, but I'll call them tomorrow."

She'd forgotten his parents were celebrating their fortieth anniversary with an extended cruise to the Caribbean. Good for them. Finley wondered if her parents had any plans for the anniversary they had coming up. Likely not. Her mother, the Judge, wouldn't want to take the time away from the bench.

"Jack will call you a traitor," she teased, pushing away thoughts of her mother. Jack was the most antipolitical guy on the planet.

Matt laughed. "Maybe I'll change his mind about politicians."

"Don't waste your time." Another grin slid across her lips. "The trinity will go to war without you to run interference."

He shrugged. "I'm sure they'll have no trouble finding someone to replace me."

"Maybe so, but no one as good as you." She chuckled softly. "I'd love to see the surprise on their faces when they learn you're moving on up." The moment would be priceless.

"Speaking of surprises, your dad mentioned he'd accepted a position on Belle Meade's planning commission." Matt's eyebrows pulled together. "What's up with that? I thought he was taking retirement seriously?"

"I think he's bored." Finley nabbed another crisp.

Her father had retired earlier than he'd anticipated after what had happened in July of last year. *Derrick's murder.* Finley had been in the hospital and rehab for weeks. Even after she'd gone home, the rehab had continued. Still did—at least the mental part of it. Her shrink, Dr. Mengesha, believed she had needed counseling even before that horrific event. Possibly so. In her opinion, Finley had more reason than most. Growing up with Ruth O'Sullivan as her mother hadn't exactly been a walk in the park. Ruth had never really been a mother, more a boss or drill sergeant. Case in point: Finley's father had been the one to give up his career to help her through all the rehab. The Judge, of course, couldn't be bothered.

"A man should have a hobby," Matt pointed out. "Sometimes fishing or golfing just aren't enough."

Finley laughed. "And what are your hobbies, Mr. Quinn?" She knew for a fact that his were the same as hers: none. They were both completely and utterly absorbed in work. She dismissed the idea that they both shared this often-inconvenient characteristic with the Judge. Or that Finley actually had a secret obsession with watching the bastards who had wrecked her life. No one knew about that little *hobby*. Her hope was to keep that secret until she was finished.

Finished how?

Finley dismissed the accusatory little voice. She had no plans to kill anyone, only to be around when it happened.

"I have a hobby," Matt admonished.

"Name this so-called hobby," she dared.

"You," he confessed. "What better hobby could I have than spending time with my best friend?"

See, I told you the guy's in love with you.

Finley pushed her husband's voice out of her head. Derrick had sworn on more than one occasion that Matt was secretly in love with her. She was fairly certain she would know if he were. Besides—she smiled back at her friend—Finley suspected her husband simply had never had a friend like Matt.

"I don't count," she argued.

"I've been thinking," he began and then didn't go on.

Well, that couldn't be good. Anytime Matt felt compelled to beat around the bush, it was no doubt going to be a touchy subject.

Then she got it. "If the DA or anyone at Metro PD has a complaint about me or something I've done," she warned, then shook her head. Did they have someone monitoring her every move? Jesus Christ. It wasn't like she'd set out to piss off the whole world. "I swear, they can't prove anything. Jeez, for law enforcement these people are seriously oversensitive."

She might push the boundaries. She might even bend the rules, but she always pulled back before going too far—or covered her tracks when that didn't work out. As much for her boss's sake as her own. She owed it to Jack never to push too far. His reputation would be the one on the line if she screwed up. He'd done enough damage himself in the past. He didn't need any help in that regard from her.

"Fin, it's . . . ," he started once more.

Then she got it. "It's the Judge, isn't it?" A different kind of irritation sparked. The two of them had pretty much stayed out of each other's way since Derrick's death. Finley would be immensely happy if they stayed that way. Her father was the only one who wanted the whole picture-perfect-family package to include dinners and holidays. Finley tried. She really did, but she and her mother just weren't ever going to get along, much less agree.

Matt put up his hands in surrender. "Hold on, it's not the Judge or any one of the three. It's *me*."

Oh crap. Maybe he was sick. "Just tell me it's not terminal." Her chest tightened. She did not want to lose Matt to some dreaded disease.

Pain speared through her. She didn't want to lose him at all.

He laughed, a quick, short burst. "I'm not dying, and no one is currently upset with anything you've done." He frowned, searched her face. "Have you done something I should know about?"

"Absolutely not." Maybe. Hopefully.

He nodded, his expression suggesting he was not thoroughly convinced. "Anyway, I've been poking around a little in Derrick's background."

If he'd said he had quit his job and was moving to South America, she wouldn't have been more startled. Or worried. "What exactly does that mean?"

She watched his face grow more serious as he explained that he thought he might be able to find something she had overlooked, et cetera. Part of her wanted all the help she could get since she still had nothing on Derrick's history. What she had learned so far was that the vast majority of what she'd thought she had known about her husband was lies. She had no idea about his reasons for seemingly having lured her into a relationship. Or for not telling her the whole truth about himself. She was, however, reasonably confident he had loved her. He'd fought to the death to protect her *that* night.

Would a man who hadn't loved her have done that?

"No," she said flatly, the taste of beer going sour in her mouth.

"What?" Matt made a face. "Why?"

The question forced her to lie. She hated deceiving Matt. It wasn't like she hadn't done it before, but she didn't like lying to him. He and her father—and Jack—mattered most to her. Honesty counted when it came to the people who mattered. At least most of the time anyway. But there was no way out of this situation. A lie was necessary. Poking around in Derrick's past could put Matt in danger. She refused to allow that to happen.

She couldn't lose him too.

"I've decided to put the past behind me." She moistened her lips, swallowed the bitter taste of deceit. "Continuing to dig around in that part of my life isn't going to change anything. I need to move on."

Matt blinked, but not before she saw the surprise in his eyes. "That's a good step, Fin. A really good move."

It would be if it were true. *Liar.* She hated herself right now, particularly considering the hope in his voice.

"It's time," she said, turned her attention to the Guinness to wash it all down.

Keeping this secret . . . telling the lies necessary to keep it . . . would come back to haunt her one day. Sooner rather than later, most likely. She knew this better than anyone.

Changing the subject, she said, "Jack has a new, very high-profile client."

"Sounds intriguing," Matt offered, seemingly forgetting the idea of looking into Derrick's past.

Work was the best distraction.

Work kept her mind off the lies she told and the secrets she kept.

4

11:50 p.m.

The Murder House
Shelby Avenue, Nashville

Finley shifted into park and sat for a long moment.

This was home. She surveyed the small dark structure, which still desperately needed a coat of paint on the exterior. The small front porch continued to lean to one side. Definitely not Brentwood. She did a mental eye roll. She'd grown up in Belle Meade in a house that was more a museum than a home. After law school she'd come back to Nashville, landed the job as an assistant district attorney for Davidson County, and snatched up a highly sought-after condo on Woodmont Boulevard.

She'd made it, right?

The Judge had been thrilled, and her father couldn't have been prouder of her. All had been right in the world.

Then, a few years later, everything changed.

Meeting Derrick Reed had drawn her to this east-side fixer-upper. It was a dump. Truly in every definition of the word, but Derrick had assured her that he'd been working on it for months and had big plans. Several houses in the neighborhood had already been transformed. He had been so excited about doing the same with this place. Oddly enough, she'd felt more at home here than she had anywhere else. It could have been a tent, and she would probably have felt utter happiness as long as she was with Derrick. His plans and dreams had made her feel so alive. Had made her want to grab a hammer and a paintbrush and help him. Except she'd always been working. He'd insisted that she needn't worry. While she fought evil and saved the world, he would turn this dump into their dream home, he'd promised. Even now, with all that she knew, the memory prompted a tiny smile while emotion threatened to leak from her eyes.

None of those things had happened.

Finley forced the memories away. It was late. She was tired.

She pushed open her car door and got out. Grabbed her bag and shoved the door closed. Bugs flitted around the bare bulb struggling to light the front porch. As she climbed the steps, a cat scurried from under the yellow glider. The cat was fairly new. He'd shown up about a month ago, staying a night here and there. After the first week, she'd started leaving food and water out for him. Probably a mistake, but the animal had been too skinny, and she'd felt sorry for him.

The scraggly cat fit with the shabby house. *Shabby* might be an understatement. Besides the exterior being in need of paint and the grass being more brown than green, the last surviving shrub planted by the previous owners had died during the long, dry weeks of August. Week before last her dad had come over and planted a rosebush. He'd insisted the place needed brightening up.

So far, the rosebush was still alive. Part of her suspected her dad dropped by and watered it since she had a history of forgetting that part of gardening. She glanced across the street. Or maybe her flower-enthusiast, nosy neighbor had done the honors. She seemed to spend most of her time watching the place.

Finley shoved her key into the lock and opened the door. Inside she clicked on the overhead light. "Home sweet home."

You're home late. Have you eaten? The memory of Derrick's voice echoed through her.

That was Derrick. Always worried about her, always ready to help. Of course, her answer had consistently been no. Work consumed her life. She had no time to eat. If not for Matt and her dad, she would likely never eat. As for being late, she always got home late. Still did. Like tonight.

After tossing her bag on the couch, she ran her fingers through her hair and pulled her ponytail holder loose. The fresh coat of serene blue paint Jack and Matt had helped her apply to the walls, along with the clean white added to the ceiling and trim, had brightened things up inside. There was still a lot to be done. A bucket remained in the tiny hall for when it rained, since the roof continued to leak in that spot.

After what had happened—in this very house—most people didn't understand why she stayed in the unfixed fixer-upper. It certainly wasn't because she had friends who lived on the block. In fact, she didn't actually know any of her neighbors. Except for the nosy one across the street, Helen Roberts, and she didn't really know her beyond her name and strange staring habits.

After *that* night, many who lived on the block had dropped by to offer sympathy. All insisted they were there to help with anything she needed. Finley figured most were probably more curious about the murder in their neighborhood than interested in her well-being. The curiosity didn't bother Finley, since it had faded just as quickly as it had appeared.

The one thing that had stuck—at least in Finley's mind—was the moniker a local reporter had used. He had dubbed this *the murder house*. Finley couldn't think of it any other way.

Her husband had died here.

When she looked back, the part that still held an unrelenting grip on her throat was that she should have known something bad was coming.

The vague threats that had begun during the early pretrial preparations in the case against Dempsey's son had returned with fervor. Finley had recognized she was being watched. Ambiguous warnings, like a flat tire when it was time to go home at the end of the day or the front door standing open when she arrived. Not actually surprised by the tactics,

Finley had diligently reported the incidents to Briggs, her boss, and he had without hesitation or consideration dismissed her concerns. She was overreacting. He was busy.

Frankly, she had surmised from the beginning that Briggs hadn't really wanted to pursue the Dempsey case and, in the end, hadn't at all liked sharing the resulting limelight with her. Not much of a stretch was required to assume he might even have secretly enjoyed that she had to deal with some sort of repercussions. He was only human, after all, right?

Finley had her doubts on that one. Though after Derrick's death, Briggs had at least pretended to regret his dismissal of her concerns.

Too little, too late.

Finley walked into the kitchen and opened the cupboard next to the refrigerator and grabbed a bottle of wine. As was her nightly ritual, she opened it and poured a glass. When she had downed a good portion, she refilled her glass and headed back to the living room, the bottle in her left hand.

There was comfort in routine, right?

If there had been any doubt as to who was responsible for Derrick's murder, Brant, the bastard who'd raped her, had cleared those up with his harshly whispered message.

You take something from me. I take something from you.

She hadn't remembered his message until months after the hospital and rehab stays. In fact, the detectives working the investigation had grown more than a little frustrated by that point with what they'd called her lack of cooperation. But *that* night had been too fuzzy in the beginning, and she had been too damaged to allow the memories back in.

Eventually, she'd noticed the eyes watching her again. Slowly the moments from the invasion of her home and the attack had surfaced and started to clarify. She had recalled the faces of the invaders first.

When Finley was strong enough, she had turned the tables on the three bastards. She had watched them the same way they watched her.

Now there were only two.

One down, two to go.

She collapsed on the sofa—Derrick's consignment store sofa—and placed the bottle on the floor next to her. She considered turning on the television but decided against it. The news was depressing, and apparently no one knew how to make good movies anymore.

For a moment she savored her wine and considered what the hell she was doing still living here. It was the burning question in everyone's mind, right? She should move on, shouldn't she? Why linger in this dump of a house, where her dead husband's clothes still hung on one side of the tiny closet they'd shared in the unfinished bedroom. Outside, in the visibly leaning old garage, his vintage truck remained.

She could move back to the Woodmont condo. Another gulp of wine was required to swallow that thought. The tenant's lease would be coming up for renewal soon.

But she wouldn't go back. *Could not* go back.

She couldn't leave this house, because she had unfinished business here.

Derrick still existed in this place. He had touched every part of it just as he had touched every part of her. If his truck or his clothes and other stuff—or this house—could help her find the answers she needed, she had to stay close . . . couldn't let go. The fact was, all of it was evidence.

Evidence of his murder and of his lies . . . his secrets.

Derrick Reed, the man she had fallen for in record time and subsequently married without even warning her parents, had not been working on this house for months as he'd told her. She remembered vividly how he'd gone on and on about falling in love with the original floors and personally rewiring the electrical and updating the plumbing. Et cetera. Lies. Every word. He'd bought the house just a couple of weeks before the two of them met.

He had lied about everything.

She hadn't known this for more than a year after his murder.

In the beginning the physical pain of healing and the emotional pain of facing the fact that Derrick was dead and she wasn't had been all-consuming. With nothing else to do and desperately needing to occupy her mind, she had returned to work at the DA's office. Everyone had insisted that was the best thing to do. She needed to focus on something—anything—besides Derrick's murder. Bravo to her for having the courage and the strength to move forward until—in the middle of her first big postrecovery case—she fell apart.

She laughed and refilled her glass. "Fell apart?"

The term was like calling a hurricane a breeze. The diagnosed psychotic episode was a complete breakdown that had required thirty days of a different kind of hospitalization and rehab. In the end she'd walked away from her position at the DA's office and given up practicing law altogether.

Turned out it was the right decision.

Which reminded her—Finley dug her notepad from her bag and flipped to the page where she had jotted her thoughts regarding the firm's new client.

Ellen Winthrop. Finley thought of the woman who had spoken so carefully with a believable amount of emotion infused in her voice and actions here and there. Her story was precisely crafted. So exact. She could explain everything. She hadn't been in the house. Her security system proved as much. She had no idea what had happened.

This needled at Finley. It was too perfect, too detailed.

Except Winthrop couldn't explain how someone else had entered the house undetected by said security system or how they had acquired access to that titanium hammer used as a murder weapon.

The detective had pointed this out more than once during the official questioning. Winthrop hadn't wavered in her answers. Once her statement was completed and signed, she had been allowed to leave.

Finley and Jack had reached the same conclusions about their new client. They agreed that by the end of the week, Winthrop would likely be arrested for the murder unless another suspect came to light. That could happen over the coming days. It would take some time to process the scene and the evidence. There were friends and neighbors to interview. A forensic accounting of the missing money would be required. And numerous other details to confirm. The investigation had only just started.

But the bottom line was not optimal.

Jack had warned Winthrop that she should expect and prepare for an arrest.

Like Finley's mother, the Judge, Winthrop was an intelligent, powerful woman. She had run an extensive background check on her husband before they married. The Judge had done exactly that with Derrick, as had Finley. Neither she nor Finley had found anything suspicious. Winthrop said the same about her husband. She'd found nothing negative about Jarrod Grady. Finley could empathize to some degree with the idea. The part she couldn't see was Winthrop having no idea whatsoever of who might have wanted him dead. Maybe she was merely in shock and ideas would occur to her later.

Winthrop couldn't possibly have reached her current career pinnacle without making a few enemies. No matter how nice she might be, there would be bodies in the wake of her climb to the top.

Finley had other questions as well. A woman like Winthrop wouldn't leave important details like a choice of attorneys to the last minute. She had attorneys, yet she had chosen Jack for representation at possibly the most perilous time of her life. Why would a woman in her position call in an attorney she had never met or who had not been recommended by one of her trusted attorneys? Winthrop had insisted that she'd heard about Jack back in July during the Legard case. The claim was certainly possible. The high-profile murder case involving twin daughters and the death of their music-legend father had rocked the Nashville area when it happened and then half a decade later when the whole truth finally came out.

Jack and the firm had been in the news a lot back in the summer because of that case, but Winthrop's answer still didn't sit right with Finley.

It was true that Jack was an exceptional defense attorney. Finley would certainly want him on her team if she were ever charged with a crime. But this was not your average woman. This was a woman who had built a financial empire. A woman savvy in business and certainly in the law. Why wouldn't she have her personal attorney present as well?

Why turn over her fate to a man she had never met?

Finley stared at the name Jarrod Grady written across the page and then underlined.

Like her, Winthrop had never been married or engaged before.

Why the sudden marriage? At fifty it wasn't likely that she was rushing to start procreating. With all her accomplishments it didn't seem plausible that she'd wanted to impress anyone or to attain a particular personal milestone by getting married. Her life was one milestone after another according to Google.

Whatever the reason for the marriage—love, bucket list, whim— once it was done, it was an agreement. A contract. Agreements and contracts involved trust. It was possible Winthrop had learned of his deception and lost it. Killed him without really meaning to. It happened.

Finley tried to imagine how she would have felt if she'd learned of Derrick's lies while he was still alive. What would she have done? Walked out? Waged a major fight? Kicked *him* out? She couldn't see herself doing him bodily harm.

That said, she was only human. One never knew what one would do until tested by an event. Winthrop would be no exception.

There were times when even the best human could be pushed too far.

5

The Widow

Midnight

Pettit Residence
Penrose Drive, Brentwood

Jarrod was dead.

After the initial turmoil of emotions, Ellen felt oddly numb about his death.

She supposed that was normal . . . under the circumstances. Worse, she couldn't think . . . couldn't seem to grasp what she should do next. She'd been standing here, unmoving, in her dear friend's guest bedroom for half an hour.

Deep breath. *Pull yourself together, Ellen.*

Laney, her lifelong friend and considerate host, had offered Ellen wine or a cocktail, water or coffee . . . whatever she needed. Ellen wasn't at all sure what she needed.

Jarrod is dead.

She had explained to the police how her husband was not the man she'd thought he was. He had tricked her. Used her. Despite great and oddly unexpected emotional difficulty, she had provided all the necessary details.

The detective had displayed some amount of sympathy as she'd explained that she had felt entirely foolish about arriving at fifty and still having the kind of needs that ultimately rendered her vulnerable to this sort of betrayal. What was worse, she had unfortunately allowed her deep, desperate feelings of loneliness to blind her to the truth for far too long.

The stoic detective had said nothing. He'd only nodded and waited for her to go on with her story. But some degree of understanding remained in his eyes. The man had a mother. Of course he understood. Any good and kind man would. Even Jack Finnegan had seemed to soften as she told her story the second time, but whether his visible concern was real or for the detective's benefit, she couldn't say. Finnegan and his investigator, Finley O'Sullivan, were the best criminal defense team in the Nashville area. Ellen had chosen them precisely for that reason—despite her own attorney's reservations.

The step had been necessary to navigate what was to come.

Ellen's story wasn't a new one. Age, loneliness—no amount of power or money made one immune to those all-too-human weaknesses. She had first seen Jarrod the night of her ridiculously grand half-century birthday celebration. Her friends had thrown her a huge party at the Bridge Building. Jarrod had served as a member of the waitstaff. That alone made what had happened in the end all the more preposterous. No doubt people would wonder what she had been thinking.

Obviously, they would imagine, she had not been at all.

She smiled. She supposed she could live with that.

Ellen had presented the facts in the official interview at the precinct, and how could anyone doubt her? The uncomfortable questioning that followed was nothing more than a necessary step of the investigation.

Ellen had not one thing to fear.

She walked to the bed, where her overnight bag sat. Jack had driven her back to her home, where she had been allowed to gather a few things under the close watch of a uniformed officer. She flinched at the memory of yellow crime scene tape and all those markers where evidence had been flagged. The blood. She shuddered. The people still milling about in their protective gear, gathering prints and fibers. The images had been more challenging than she'd anticipated.

She wished the nightmare had not happened in her home. She'd built the house twenty years ago, when she'd closed her first multimillion-dollar deal. She'd personally selected each light fixture, every paint color . . . every single thing that went into the making of her dream home.

Now it would never be the same.

She gathered her pajamas and cosmetic bag from the jumble she'd thrown together. She crossed to the en suite. A long hot shower would help, and then she intended to have that drink Laney had offered. In fact, she wanted two or perhaps three. Whatever it took to relax her after today's trials.

She shuddered at the idea that so many reporters had gathered outside her home. Thankfully, Jack had been able to slip her away unnoticed, preventing anyone from following them here.

In the bathroom, surrounded by cool white tile and gold-tone fixtures, she shed the clothes she wore. They weren't the clothes she had been wearing that morning. The police had taken those. She'd had to remove and drop every item of fabric and jewelry from her body into an evidence bag. Her favorite walking shoes as well.

The forensic technicians would be looking for blood splatter or other evidence that she had been close to the victim when he was murdered.

Ellen knew with certainty the effort would be futile. When she had entered the house after her walk and gone in search of her husband, she hadn't moved beyond the bathroom door, although she had said she'd checked his pulse. She hadn't. There was no need. He was dead. She had known he was. Why move closer than necessary?

Besides, there had been much to do. After the initial shock of finding him, her brain had kicked into gear, and by sheer force of will she had taken care of a few unexpected loose ends around the house. Then she had called the police. The first officers had arrived in under ten minutes. She hadn't expected any less in her prestigious neighborhood.

One of the officers had escorted her to the great room and seated her out of the way of the activities that would need to take place in her home. The officer, a woman, had taken down the basic information by the time the detective had arrived.

Ellen turned on the shower, then gathered a towel before stepping beneath the hot spray. For long minutes—she had no idea how many—she stood under the water, hoping to wash away the horrors of the day.

The last words she had spoken to Jarrod, ordinary words—*good night, love you*—echoed through her. He had repeated the same to her. They hadn't slept apart as she'd stated, because she had not confronted him about his betrayal. If she had, he would have promptly left before the grand finale. She could not allow that to happen.

But it had happened. Only he hadn't left . . . he'd been murdered.

Her fingers worked shampoo through her hair, the foam slipping down her skin. As she rinsed away the soap, she struggled to analyze the feelings invading her, an odd sense of calm followed by a strange giddiness. Quite frankly, she wasn't sure how to feel just now. Hurt that someone had murdered her husband? Frustrated that she hadn't done it herself? She had no frame of reference for this particular event. She pushed the unsettling feelings aside. Strength and focus were essential now. This regrettable business had ended today as planned. Well, almost as planned.

Fortunately, Ellen was always prepared for the unexpected.

After finding him, she had quickly put away the incriminating documents and images and alerted the others not to come. Nothing she hadn't been able to handle.

Life was quite often like business. Even when your journey veered off-track, you simply recalculated and adjusted your trajectory.

Ellen had done exactly that today.

With a turn of the gold-toned handle, she shut off the water and stepped from the marble-and-glass enclosure. As she moved the towel over her body, she studied her reflection. She wasn't in bad shape for her age. She was often mistaken for someone ten or fifteen years younger. A clean diet, a steady exercise regimen, and good genes served her well. Even the lack of facial wrinkles she could chalk up to her dear mother. She'd had flawless skin when she'd passed, despite the cancer that had eaten away at her.

Today's ghastly events aside, Ellen had come a very long way from her tragic childhood. Anger trickled through her. No one was taking that away from her.

Her lips tight, she arranged the towel around her dark hair and squeezed out the water, then rubbed the length of it between the folds of thick fabric. Gray had long ago invaded her brunette tresses, but the best stylist in Nashville was at her beck and call. She deserved a bit of luxury in her life.

Ellen reached for her pajamas. The silk fabric slid down her skin. She shivered and wished she could somehow know her husband's final thought. Shock? Disbelief? Denial? How stunned he must have been to see the face of his lover as she wielded that fateful blow. Then again, Ellen couldn't be precisely sure of the killer's identity. There was, it seemed, more than one suspect—a turn of events she had not anticipated at all. Obviously, she had missed something.

Whatever the case, it was over now. There was only the matter of the cleanup details. Those would all be handled swiftly.

She had taken care of everything. She was in control.

Some said that when the heart stopped beating, a surge of utter fear spread through the motionless blood and instantly depleted it of oxygen.

Ellen hoped he had felt that incredible fear.

Renewed fury seared through her. She hoped he was in hell, where he belonged.

The rage died an instant death, and another overpowering emotion welled inside her. She closed her eyes against the tears that began to stream down her face. She wasn't supposed to feel any of this agony . . . this loss. No. No. No.

She dropped to her knees on the cold tile and wept like a child.

Jarrod was dead.

6

Monday, September 19

9:20 a.m.

Winthrop Financial Consulting Group
Commerce Street, Nashville

Before heading out for this morning's interviews, Finley had rendez-
voused with Jack at the office to hash out their agendas. He would be in
court a good portion of the day. Finley's goal was to start nailing down
the big picture and then to begin the process of homing in on the details
that spoke the loudest.

Last night she'd spent a good amount of time researching their
client on the net. Nothing had jumped out at her. Nothing unexpected
floating on the World Wide Web. Endless career accolades and achieve-
ments. Winthrop had reached a pinnacle few could hope to attain.

But no one was perfect with only great things in their history. There
was always some amount of ugly. It was only a matter of finding it.

Finding the rest of Winthrop's story started now.

Finley nosed her Subaru into a slot as close to the ground floor exit
as possible. Parking garages were always too dark, and there was never
enough security. No matter the number of muggings or assaults that

occurred in downtown parking garages, the incidents never seemed to get the attention required from the right people to change the issue.

A perfect example of not homing in on the details that mattered most.

A grin stretched across her face. Maybe Matt could put a bug in the governor's ear.

She surveyed her surroundings before getting out, then locked her doors as she walked toward the exit. Part of her was always on alert for any sign of the two thugs who kept an eye on her for Dempsey. So far, she hadn't spotted either this morning. Not that they watched her every day, more that they checked in at mostly irregular intervals. She did the same. Tracking one or both down from time to time, like last night.

It wasn't that difficult. She had studied the thugs from *that* night: Billy Hughes, deceased; Chet Flock; and Tark Brant. She had ferreted out where they lived, their preferred hangouts. The vehicles they drove. A background search had given her a good many details. The two still breathing were longtime muscle for hire. Hughes had been as well. Criminal records were lengthy but mostly ancient history. Flock, the oldest of the trio, had the least interesting criminal record. Brant, on the other hand, had a list of small-time transgressions on his rap sheet from his twenties. His thirties had proved cleaner, save a couple of assaults. At forty-one, he appeared to have learned how not to get caught. Getting caught looked bad on one's résumé. Hughes's history had looked pretty much the same. All three appeared to have been on Dempsey's personal security payroll for the past five years, at least until Hughes had screwed up and gotten himself fired. He'd fallen back into his old holdup habits, a bad decision that led to his untimely demise in a convenience store back in July.

One down, two to go.

Shifting her thoughts back to work, Finley exited the parking garage.

Commerce Street traffic was negligible at this hour, since most of the white collars who worked in these high-rises were already in their offices. She hesitated. News vans lined the sidewalk on the other side of the street. Evidently building security had kept them away from the entrance. Finley considered her options. Not that great, but she could manage. She hustled across the street in the middle of the block rather than walking to the end and using a crosswalk. She didn't move toward the building until she was parallel with the entrance; then she darted for her destination.

She had reached the glass doors by the time anyone noticed. Evidently none of the reporters recognized her, since no questions were shouted. A security guard opened the door, she flashed her ID, and she was set.

The thirty-story building had a shiny glass facade. Winthrop's offices occupied the top floor. A personal assistant would be meeting Finley and showing her around as she interviewed those closest to Winthrop in her professional world. Their client had meetings all morning and, of course, was required to be at the investigating detective's beck and call. Finley didn't consider the woman's need to work the day after her husband was murdered particularly odd. God knew Finley would have worked the day after Derrick's murder if she hadn't been in a coma. Work was essential to her survival—to her mental health. Admittedly, Finley would most likely have been working on finding those responsible for his murder, but she and Winthrop were different people from different worlds. Winthrop had never been involved in law enforcement and would instinctively look to the police to find the killer while she distracted herself with her business.

Assuming the killer wasn't her. Finley didn't have a clear picture of innocence or guilt quite yet, but she also had no reason to doubt Winthrop's story. Finley's singular task was to ensure no one else could doubt it either.

Finley showed her ID again at the security desk in the stylish lobby and was directed to the appropriate bank of elevators. Sleek concrete floors and glass walls were flanked with enough potted trees and plants to feel like a conservatory. On the top floor the car stopped and the doors opened to a smaller, more intimate lobby.

A young woman, late twenties maybe, waited for Finley. She smiled broadly, white teeth gleaming, makeup light and flawless. A pink blouse with a ruffled neckline and cuffs accented the casual yet elegant gray suit. Finley wore brown slacks and a scooped neck tee with a khaki jacket. Her version of casual didn't even get close to elegant. The wrinkles didn't help any more than the well-worn mule loafers. She should shop for new shoes. Maybe unpack the iron she was certain she had purchased a million years ago. It was in a box somewhere in Derrick's garage.

One of these days, she promised herself.

Liar.

"Good morning, Ms. O'Sullivan. My name is Tobye." The assistant extended her hand. "Whatever you need, you let me know, and I will make it happen."

Finley shook the outstretched hand. "Good morning. I appreciate your time."

"Ellen has provided a list," Tobye explained as she blithely turned and moved toward the corridor ahead, "of partners you will want to interview."

"Partners?" Finley hadn't been aware any of Winthrop's employees were business partners.

"Ellen prefers to think of all her employees as partners in our common goal of maintaining excellence. Those on your list are the senior partners."

Interesting strategy. The lobby, though small, was tastefully designed. Lots of light poured in through the glass wall that made up one side of the generous space. The layout was three specific seating areas along with an inviting reception desk. Tobye led the way beyond the space and into a wide corridor flanked by doors on either side. Even the interior walls were glass, allowing Finley to see the conference table in a large meeting room and desks in the private offices beyond. Some were darkened for privacy. Her host noted the names of the partners at each office space.

Music played in the background, but the volume was turned down to a soft level that was barely audible. The distant sound was somehow relaxing. Unlike the lobby, the floors in the corridor were softened with thick carpeting. The walls were a taupe so pale it was almost white. Very soothing environment.

Tobye paused at a door labeled *Conference Room Four*. The room beyond the glass wall was smaller and had a cozier seating arrangement than the other conference area Finley had seen. A woman was already seated at the table. She appeared to be reviewing an open notebook.

"Here we are." Tobye passed a single page to Finley. "Those are the five names Ellen provided. Jessica Lauder, first on the list, is waiting for you." She gestured to the woman beyond the glass. "If you wish to speak with anyone else, just let me know, and I'll track them down for you. Otherwise, the partners will come to you, one after the other, for a private meeting as requested." She opened the door to the small room. "I'll be in my office just over here." She gestured to the room directly across the corridor. "If you need anything at all."

"Thank you." Finley took the list and entered the conference room. "Jessica." She reached across the table. "I'm Finley O'Sullivan. Thank you for taking the time to speak with me."

The other woman gave Finley's hand a quick squeeze. "I'm happy to help. This is such a shocking tragedy." She tilted her head, her long dark hair sliding over her shoulder, and made a sad face. "I still can't believe it."

Finley wondered if she meant the missing money or the murder. She retrieved her notepad and pen from her bag. "How long have you worked with Ellen?" Everyone here seemed to use first names. Might as well go with the flow.

"From the beginning."

Lauder appeared to be in her late thirties, early forties. Finley was surprised she had been with the boss from day one.

"Then you know Ellen well." This could prove problematic. Sometimes those closest to a person were less forthcoming in a foolish effort to be protective.

"We actually attended Emory together." Lauder tucked an errant strand of dark hair behind her ear in a nervous gesture. A blush instantly tinged her cheeks. "I graduated high school at thirteen and advanced straight into my sophomore year at Emory. Ellen was a senior. I was very fortunate that she was chosen as my mentor."

Made sense considering she looked about ten years younger than Winthrop. "When did Ellen meet Jarrod Grady?" Winthrop had answered many of these questions last night, but Finley wanted each interviewee's take on those pivotal moments.

"In May—at her birthday party, actually."

"He was a part of the catering service," Finley said.

"Yes. It was the strangest thing." Lauder shook her head. "The two of them met and sparks flew." She shrugged, tapped her fingers on the notebook she'd been viewing. "Like everyone else," she went on, "I had my doubts. Ellen and I have been friends for a very long time. She has never been the type to flip out over a guy. It was as if she took one look at him and decided he was hers." Lauder laughed, the sound brittle. "You know, powerful men and women often come with that sort of reputation, but not Ellen. She is far too considerate to take advantage of anyone." Another shrug. "So, believe it or not, whatever it was, it was real."

Winthrop had a humanitarian reputation for sure, but that didn't necessarily mean she couldn't be ruthless when necessary. Few climbed to the top in their chosen careers without a cutthroat tactic or two and no doubt a skeleton or ten in their closets.

"What was the name of the catering service?" Finley prepared to make a note of it.

Lauder frowned. "I'm actually not sure. You might ask Tobye. I believe she finalized all the arrangements."

"But you and"—Finley glanced at her list—"Vivian organized the birthday celebration, correct?" Vivian Ortez was the second name. Finley wondered if there was any sort of order to the list. Oldest friend first? Closest first? Certainly wasn't in alphabetical order. Top of the food chain at the office first? Most likely to keep quiet first?

"That's correct," Lauder said. "Vivian and I basically sketched out what we wanted, and Tobye handled the details."

Finley braced her forearms on the table. Who had planned her birthday party was just one of the many questions Winthrop had answered last night. The devil was always in the details, especially in a murder investigation, and the more often you asked the questions, the more details you learned.

"What did you think of Jarrod? Once you came to know him, I mean."

Lauder reached for a bottle of water. Six bottles sat on the tray in the center of the table. "He was charming. Smart." She made a surprised sound. "Smarter than I had expected."

Finley waited, an unspoken nudge for her to go on.

Lauder downed a sip of water, screwed the top back into place as if buying time to gather her thoughts. "He appeared to genuinely care for Ellen. He was very attentive. Happy to do whatever she suggested."

She stalled there. Waited for further instructions.

Smart. Finley would have chosen the same place to hesitate.

"Did you ever see or hear the two of them arguing? Did Ellen mention any issues between them? Disagreements? Disappointments?"

"That's the really strange part," Lauder said. She, too, braced her forearms on the table and leaned closer as if what she had to say next was for Finley's ears only. "They never argued. Ever. Only a few weeks after they met, they were married. I'm confident the wedding would have happened sooner had Ellen been able to pull all the pieces together. Then on Friday she called us into her office for a private meeting."

"Us?" Finley queried.

"Vivian Ortez, Daisy Adams, Liz—Elizabeth Everson—Joanna Reynolds, and myself."

The five names on the list Tobye had given Finley.

"The five of you are . . . ?" Finley prompted.

"We've all been with Ellen from the beginning. We are her closest friends. Her most trusted partners."

Well, that explained the list to a degree. "Is the list"—Finley gestured to the names on the page—"in any sort of order? Seniority? Position held?"

"It's random," Lauder assured her. "To Ellen and to each other, we are who we are and of equal importance."

"What was the purpose of Friday's meeting?"

"She wanted us to know that she had discovered certain discrepancies in her personal accounts. She asked us to scan all the business accounts to ensure there were no similar issues. Ellen had become aware that Jarrod was moving money from her personal accounts, and she wanted to be sure he hadn't touched anything here at the office." Lauder pressed a hand to her chest. "Even the concept of a client's resources being touched that way was devastating to us all."

"What did Jarrod do here?" Finley asked. Ellen had explained that Jarrod's amiable personality and good looks made him the perfect liaison for the firm whenever out-of-town visitors were in Nashville. His reach was very limited. No access to client accounts and such. Just a limo and driver along with an unlimited credit card for showing clients a nice time in Music City.

"He was a sort of PR person." Lauder inclined her head and seemed to consider what she intended to say next. "Frankly, we were all a bit taken aback when he came on board, since Ellen has never employed a man. She—we—wanted this company to be for and about women."

"The five of you found his position unsettling?" Finley suggested.

"At first, yes, but we quickly understood the decision was for the best. Ellen felt we had accomplished our primary goal and it was time to move beyond that strict model. After some consideration we all agreed."

"Have more men been hired since revising that model?"

Lauder hesitated as if she hadn't anticipated the question, or maybe she needed to do a mental count. "No," she said then. "We haven't hired any new employees in the past two months."

Finley would be verifying the response.

"Why didn't Ellen confront Jarrod on Friday as well?" That was one of the pieces that didn't quite fit for Finley. Even if the man was in Atlanta, she could have ordered him back to the office.

"Jarrod was out of town. She didn't expect him back until Saturday afternoon. She wanted to use that block of time to ensure there were no issues with the company and that we all understood what was happening before confronting him." She gave a knowing nod. "There's something to be said for the element of surprise."

Unquestionably. Surprise was a much-desired tactic in any sort of battle. It was the personal aspect of the decision that felt odd. Finley supposed it was possible Winthrop was just really good at setting aside her personal feelings.

Don't you do the same thing?

Finley ignored the idea. "Did he go out of town alone often?" Jarrod Grady was twelve years younger than Winthrop. They hardly knew each other, and yet she seemed to have trusted him completely.

Didn't you trust Derrick completely?

Finley blinked away the question. Enough with that damned little nagging voice!

"No, he didn't actually," Lauder said. "Jarrod had arranged a meeting in Atlanta to discuss a new real estate venture. He invited Ellen to accompany him, but she begged off at the last moment." She made a skeptical face. "I'm surprised he wasn't suspicious. One never went anywhere without the other. From the moment Ellen and Jarrod met, they were together, inseparable. During office hours obviously there was some minimal time apart, but not otherwise as far as I'm aware."

"What was her reason for not going?" Winthrop hadn't mentioned this aspect of his trip.

"She had a meeting on Friday with our new British counterpart that she didn't really want to reschedule." The youngest partner turned her hands up. "Personally, I think she just didn't want to go. She hasn't said as much, but I'm sure she suspected something was wrong."

"Wrong in what way?"

Lauder blinked, her face blanked. Obviously, she hadn't meant to say as much.

"You know." Shrug number three. "Ellen is an amazingly perceptive woman. She had to feel that things were not as they should be."

Another thought occurred to Finley. "Did Ellen have someone watching Jarrod while he was away in Atlanta?"

"She didn't mention having directed anyone to watch him."

"Once she recognized the deficits in her accounts, what did she do next? Beyond bringing her senior partners up to speed," Finley asked.

"She and Liz, our head of the forensic accounting department, focused on tracking down where the money went when it left her accounts. Ellen felt they needed to have a firm handle on what was missing and from where before proceeding."

"What did forensic accounting discover?"

"The money was shuffled through several different accounts, finally landing in a bank in New Jersey. Thankfully, I believe it's still there. By the time Liz found it, there was no way to start transferring it back until opening hours today."

"Was there anyone else on the landing account besides Jarrod?" Finley saw nothing in Grady's background that made him an expert at embezzlement, which begged the question: Did he have a partner in crime?

"Not that I'm aware," Jessica said. "You can confirm with Liz."

Finley intended to do exactly that. In games like this, there was usually a silent partner or someone working from another angle.

"Vivian Ortez," Lauder went on, "our head of security, and her team worked to learn anything perhaps previously missed about Jarrod. Everyone had a role."

Finley studied her a moment, then asked, "What was your role?"

"I worked with Joanna and Daisy to scour all client accounts. It was the most important role of all."

Finley moved through a few more questions before thanking Lauder for her cooperation.

The next two interviews were basically a repeat of what Finley had learned from Lauder. The responses, even when Finley tossed out what she felt would be an unexpected question, came back the same. Same key words. Same tone in the language.

There was only one explanation for that amount of specific duplication: practice.

For whatever purpose, Ellen Winthrop's friends, i.e., partners, had rehearsed their responses to every potential question Finley might present.

Practicing so thoroughly for an event shouted there was a need to protect something or someone.

Winthrop had something to hide. Not necessarily murder but something.

Hiding incriminating information from the police was one thing, but hiding it from her attorney was another. Jack couldn't adequately represent his client without the whole truth. The risk that whatever she was concealing would come out at trial was too great.

Finley had opted to question Liz Everson, the head of forensic accounting, last. Which worked out since one of the five, Vivian Ortez, had been tied up in a meeting and would call Finley a little later.

Everson was a year older than Winthrop. Unlike her boss and friend, she didn't bother to color her gray. Instead she wore it proudly. No visible makeup and very laid-back attire. Khakis and a blue shirt. A woman after Finley's heart.

Like the three before her, Everson repeated the answers Finley had already heard. The interview with Everson needed to go further, with additional questions, in particular about the account where the missing money had landed.

"Did you discover anyone else on the account where the money landed? If so, where are you on determining the identity of the other party?" If there was a partner, he or she might very well be the one who'd murdered Grady. If nothing else, the man or woman could prove an alternative scenario for the police to investigate.

A single avenue in an investigation was never a good thing.

"There was only one authorized signatory beyond Jarrod," Liz explained. "Ellen asked me not to share this with the others until we had more information."

Interesting. "I'm certain Ellen explained that you should share whatever you know with me," Finley countered.

"Of course. The second signatory was a J. Grady. To our knowledge Jarrod has—had no family. I'm guessing the name is an alias, since I haven't been able to find anything connected to a J. Grady in Jarrod's office and Ellen found nothing in their home." Liz drew in a deep breath as if fortifying herself. "Considering what's happened, our security department has been working all weekend to determine who Jarrod Grady really was and the identity of this J. Grady—assuming it wasn't him."

"What do you mean, who Jarrod Grady really was? Is your background information on him in question?" This was new. Finley's senses perked up.

"It seems the past he had built was fabricated. Jarrod didn't exist—at least not as we knew him. And J., as I've already said, appears to be a ghost as well. At this point we're suspicious of every detail we were told about him."

"What about the money?"

"Until shortly after midnight last night, it remained in the New Jersey account, and then it moved. We haven't shared this news either."

Finley shook her head. "So, the ghost, this J. Grady presumably, took it?"

"Apparently, since no transaction was pending as of midnight last night. Any steps Jarrod took before his death would have been pending until then. We have to assume it was the other signatory."

"Where did the money go this time?"

Liz clasped her hands in front of her. "I'll let you know when we figure it out."

Finley wasn't entirely surprised that Winthrop and her security team had been duped. What could she say? It happened. Derrick had certainly fooled her.

On one hand, the news that the money was indeed gone strengthened Winthrop's motive for killing her husband, since the timing of the move confirmed he had a partner and Winthrop had discovered the second signatory before the murder. On the other, this J. Grady—or whoever was posing as the second signatory—provided the possibility of another suspect.

The question was, How much time did they have to find this potential suspect before the detective on the case figured out the money was gone, amplifying Winthrop's motive for wanting her husband dead?

7

11:45 a.m.

Davidson County Medical Examiner
Gass Boulevard, Nashville

One of the fringe benefits of serving as a Davidson County ADA for a number of years was making contacts. If you had a dead body, it was good to have a contact in the medical examiner's office. If it was someone with whom you'd attended high school and he still had a little crush on you, then it was even better.

Dennis Shafer, forensic autopsy technician, was more than happy to share his lunchtime in the building's cafeteria with the girl who'd tutored him through calculus and, as he happily reminded her every chance he got, had been a regular in his boyhood fantasies.

This was nice timing, since Winthrop's head of security, Vivian Ortez, had not been available at all for an interview this morning. Finley would catch up with her this afternoon.

"I doubt the autopsy will be done before Thursday or Friday," Dennis offered. He picked up a french fry and popped it into his mouth without bothering to drag it through the puddle of ketchup he'd made by emptying five packets onto his plate. "I can tell you a couple of things from my preliminary work, if that will help." He glanced side to side to see who had taken seats at the surrounding tables.

Finley leaned closer, resting her arms on the table. "Any information you can share will be tremendously helpful."

He smiled, then quickly shifted his face back to a more businesslike demeanor. "Surprisingly, we found nothing unexpected in the preliminary tox screen."

Finley wasn't particularly surprised on that point. The alcohol he'd consumed would likely have been metabolized by morning.

"Judging by the part of the hammer—the portion called the face—that contacted with the skull first, as well as the angle of the weapon when it made contact, it would appear to me that the killer came up behind him and swung with his left hand. Like this." He raised his left hand over his right shoulder, reaching as far back as possible and then swinging forward.

"The reason I say this," he continued, keeping his voice just above a whisper, "is because of the force behind the blow. For the hammer face to drive in at the angle it did, a right-handed person would never have been able to wield that kind of force without doing a sort of spin." He demonstrated, twisting at the waist and drawing his right hand and arm as far back as possible over his shoulder and then swooping up and forward.

Finley could see what he meant. "Would this be the same whether the person wielding the hammer was male or female?"

"The theory would be the same, yes." He grabbed another french fry. "Can I say one hundred percent your killer was one or the other?" He shrugged. "That's above my pay grade. I can say the killer was likely shorter than the victim." His face furrowed and his eyes narrowed. "The real questions in my mind after viewing the scene are, Was the water still running when he got out of the shower? Was there music playing?" He moved his hands up and down as if weighing the possibilities. "Any type of sound that would have prevented the victim from hearing his attacker walk into the room and prepare to deliver the blow?"

Very good points.

"Maybe he was singing," Finley suggested. Some people liked singing when they showered. Derrick had even belted out a tune while blow-drying his hair. The memory sent warmth flowing through her. She banished the sensation. Try as she might, she could never fully block the memories or the reactions they prompted.

Whether or not the water was running or there was music would likely be in the report made by the first officers on the scene. The two were on Finley's list to interview. If the crime scene unit finished with the house today—and they should—a look around would help her work out the scenarios more fully. She hadn't seen photos or anything else at this point.

"I do that," Dennis said with another of his wide smiles. "I sing or hum whenever I'm doing just about everything." He winked. "Even when I'm weighing organs. Kind of distracts from the reality."

"Wow." Finley stuck her fork into the bed of greens on her plate and feigned interest. Dennis had been a little odd even back in high school. Some things never changed. "Didn't I hear you'd just had number three?"

A big grin slid across his face. "I did. Another boy, Raymond. Two boys and one girl now."

He launched into a story about his oldest child's exploits. Finley smiled as much at his animated face and actions as from the stories. She had checked his social media to catch up on what he and his wife were up to. She'd had no idea they had three kids already. Where was the time going?

She suddenly felt old. And alone.

Derrick attempted to slip once more into her thoughts, but she pushed him away. She'd been doing more of that lately—the pushing-away part. The longer she put off going there, the longer before she learned more details of his betrayal.

Until recently she'd never really considered herself a procrastinator, much less a coward. But she was a bit of both lately. At least where Derrick was concerned.

Her cell vibrated in her jacket pocket, and she pulled it free just far enough to check the screen. *Boss.* "Sorry," she said to her lunch date. "I have to take this."

Finley pushed back her chair and stepped across the small dining area to the wall of windows that overlooked a well-tended garden that stood within the embrace of the building. She imagined the courtyard had once been a smoking area.

"Hey, how was court?" she asked Jack as she glanced back at Dennis, who was wolfing down his burger.

"Your mother didn't give me any grief for a change. You might want to check in with your dad and see if she's okay."

Finley chuckled. "It was probably the navy suit. That one really brings out the blue in your eyes."

He grunted. "I may have cast a few charm spells in my time, but your mother was never one to fall victim."

"I'm guessing this means we have news on the Winthrop case."

"You got it. This is the good kind of news, though. Detective Ventura says you can do a walk-through of the crime scene. Give him a call. He's available between now and two; then he has a meeting."

"Good deal." She and Ventura must be on the same wavelength. The worst part of investigating any case was the waiting for some sort of authorization. "I'll call him now."

"Catch up with me when you're done for the day," Jack said.

"Will do."

Finley put her phone away and headed back to the table and her favorite forensic tech. "That was the boss. I've gotta run."

Dennis stood. "We should do this again." He gathered their lunch remains onto his tray. "You know, my brother is single now, and he's always had a huge crush on you."

"Thanks for the lunch and your expertise," she said, dodging the comment. "Congrats again on the new baby."

Finley hurried away. Part of her had wanted to explain to Dennis that she wasn't interested in dating anyone. Just because her husband had been gone more than a year didn't mean she was ready to move on.

Outside she slowed her pace. Caught her breath. At the Subaru door she hesitated before climbing inside. Why had the idea of moving on unsettled her so? Had her running for the nearest exit?

Derrick was dead.

Derrick had lied to her.

She swallowed a wad of emotion. Because she wasn't ready to bury him—emotionally speaking—yet. She had to know everything first.

Living with the secrets wouldn't work. She could not put him behind her until she knew all there was to know.

You may never know everything.

Matt had warned her. Jack too.

They were wrong. She would. Because she wouldn't stop until she had what she wanted.

Winthrop Residence
Morningview Court, Brentwood, 1:30 p.m.

Finley parked at the curb outside the yellow tape that draped along the sidewalk and flanked the Winthrop property. She checked her teeth to ensure no lunch particles lingered, then climbed out. It was unseasonably warm, and she decided to leave her jacket behind. She tucked her cell into her bag and headed for the crime scene perimeter. She ducked under the tape and walked directly to the lanai, where Ventura waited.

Luckily the reporters hadn't drifted back to the residence. Like her, they knew the victim's spouse wouldn't be coming back to the scene of the crime for a while.

"Thanks for meeting me," Finley said as she approached the front door.

Ventura had already unlocked and opened it. He sported gloves and shoe covers. Noting her attention on his, he pulled a pair of each from his pocket for her.

"No problem," he said. "Crime scene tours are part of the job."

She slipped on the shoe covers, grateful for her practical flat mules—even if they were old. "Anything new on the investigation you can tell me about?"

He executed a tight shake of his head. "Nothing yet." He raised his eyebrows. "You?"

"Nothing yet." Finley tugged on the gloves. "Lead the way."

He gave her a nod and stepped inside. She followed.

The Winthrop home was just like the many other decadent homes around Nashville she'd had reason to visit—whether on official business or as a child growing up with a mother determined to rule the world. Winthrop's home was elegant in an understated way. Not over-the-top grandiose.

"We haven't found anything downstairs that suggests a home invasion. No sign of forced entry whatsoever."

"Any other evidence?" she asked, watching his posture, his face, as he spoke.

"Nada." He shook his head, obviously not happy to have to give that answer. "The primary crime scene is upstairs." He gestured to the staircase that rose from the center of the entry hall.

"You mind if I have a tour down here first?"

He shrugged. "Sure, why not?"

He showed her around, like a real estate agent who didn't really want to be at work today. She studied him, which was her reason for the request. Ventura was younger than she'd first estimated. Definitely under forty. He didn't look like the type who went all out at the gym, but he appeared fit. His suit was crisp today. Not sporting wrinkles like last night's attire. The reddish hair and freckles gave him a sort of boy-next-door quality. His hazel eyes were more forthcoming than the usual jaded detective's.

"How long have you been doing this gig?" she asked as they entered the kitchen, which was nothing short of a chef's dream. Lots of gleaming stainless and brass with no shortage of white stone and tile. White cabinets too.

"I started later than most," he said. His hands slid into his pockets as he assessed her. "I was thirty before I joined the department as a uni. I made detective at thirty-five. Couple years ago."

"Have you worked a lot of homicides?" She wandered across the room, heading for the family room.

"A few."

Which meant this was either his first or second one. No surprise. His inexperience could prove to their benefit, but it could also make him more dogged about coming out on top.

The sofa cushions appeared to have shifted a bit from the victim's night spent sleeping there. A throw hung haphazardly over one arm, half on the floor. A pillow sporting an indentation that could have been made by the victim's head was nestled next to that same arm. Otherwise, everything in the room, from furniture to framed photos on tables and shelves, appeared as it should.

"Did you find an abundance of beer bottles in the trash somewhere?" she asked, recalling Winthrop's description of the condition of the room where her husband had slept.

Ventura nodded. "Six beer bottles, all empty."

"Doesn't sound like enough for a serious hangover," she commented.

Ventura hummed a note of agreement. "Not for me anyway."

Who knew? Maybe Grady was a lightweight when it came to alcohol, or perhaps Winthrop just didn't recognize a real hangover when she saw one. Then again, there was always the chance that he'd snorted or swallowed a recreational drug, in which case it would show up in the tox reports. Shafer had said the preliminary screen was clean. Time would tell.

"Did you find an overnight bag belonging to the victim?"

Ventura nodded. "Taken into evidence, but I will tell you there was nothing exciting in it. Just a change of clothes and toiletries."

"Thanks."

From the family room they moved through the rest of the downstairs. The home was immaculate. Nothing askew or out of place. There had been an update of the interior in recent years. Fresh, light, and airy. Not the heavier, stuffy decor of fifteen or so years ago. Finley's Spidey sense perked up when they reached the door to the home office—the vault-style one with the keypad for gaining access.

The room sported lots of locked cabinets. A grand desk that overlooked the rear courtyard and gardens. The view beyond the window was the usual sanctuary with a good-size ornamental fishpond instead of a pool. Finley surveyed the desk, eyed the old-fashioned calendar sitting front and center. She flipped through the pages. Hair appointments. Dental cleanings. Personal stuff.

"You took the case that held the murder weapon?" Of course he had, but she wanted to know more about it.

"We did. It appeared someone had taken the box and slammed it against the corner of the desk, shattering the glass."

As he spoke, she noted the damage to the wood on the front right corner. The finish was scraped, the curved corner gashed.

"According to the housekeeper," he went on, "the display case usually sat on that shelf." He pointed to the center position of the lavish built-ins along one wall.

"Anything interesting from the housekeeper?" Finley asked as she surveyed the rest of the room.

"Nothing useful. Mr. Grady was kind and helpful. Mr. Grady was good to Ms. Winthrop. He made her happy. No witnessed disagreements. He never complained."

"Send me her name and contact info, please."

"Sure thing." He dragged out his cell and shared the info.

When her cell had vibrated with the incoming contact, she said, "I'd like to see the photos taken while the body and the evidence were in situ."

"I can make that happen."

He should have made it happen at this meeting. She opted not to say so and risk pissing him off this early in the game. So far, he was Mr. Agreeable.

"I read up on you."

She looked up. Ventura stood in the doorway, one shoulder leaned against the doorframe. "Oh yeah?"

"Yeah. You're not a typical law firm investigator."

She surveyed the blotter pad, read the notes jotted there. "More typical than you know."

"Don't play it down," he tossed back. "You're super smart. Graduated at the top of your law school class at Vandy. Made all kinds of big splashes at the DA's office." His mouth quirked into a smile. "And now you're killing it as an investigator at a top law firm." He gave a succinct nod. "But the one thing that tells me more than anything else about how good you are is that most of the detectives who've worked with you don't like you."

His assessment prompted a kick of pride. A girl had to get her thrills where she could these days.

"How do you know that?" She rounded the desk and walked toward him. Finley had had no idea she was so popular around the watercooler.

"Plenty have filed complaints against you."

She paused face to face with him. "You probably will too."

"No." He didn't withdraw from her probing glare. "I won't."

She lifted one eyebrow. "We'll see. Can we go upstairs now?"

He backed out of the doorway and indicated she should precede him.

They climbed the stairs. Marble treads. No carpet. At the top of those gleaming steps, she waited for him to provide the direction from there. He headed right. She followed. He immediately slowed his stride to ensure she caught up with him.

Give him another five years on the job, and he'd shed all the futile chivalry. He would learn that no matter how nicely he played, she and others like her would rarely do the same. Winning always got in the way.

The owner's retreat was quite large. The bed made. Everything from pillows to picture frames just so.

"There was no indication anyone slept in the bed on Saturday night?"

He shook his head. "According to Winthrop, she slept in her office and the victim slept on the sofa downstairs. Forensics is checking the hair found there to confirm."

Grady lived in the house. His hair would likely be found whether he'd slept there or not. Unless the housekeeper vacuumed daily. Maybe even then.

"Did the first unis on the scene ask if Grady was a singer in the shower?" Finding out would save her the trouble of tracking down the two uniformed officers who were first on the scene.

"There was nothing in the report about his vocal skills."

Finley drifted around the large bedroom space. Studied the framed photographs strategically scattered about. Checked the jewelry boxes and the drawers. She found nothing that didn't appear to belong. Then she moved to the en suite. The markings of a crime scene as well as a pool of dried blood marred the stunning surfaces. Lots of polished tile and glass. Big windows along the upper portions of the walls allowed light to fill the space while maintaining privacy. She walked carefully around the room. Whatever towel the victim had used was gone, as was whatever he'd slept in.

She scanned the counters. Perfumes, colognes, and other cosmetics. A cabinet towered from the counter to the ceiling between the two mirrors stationed above the matching sinks. She opened the doors and reviewed the contents of the cabinet. Band-Aids. Antacids. Vitamins. Supplements. The usual over-the-counter necessities found in most bathrooms.

"No scripts?" She turned to her guide.

"None we found."

Not particularly surprising for Grady and maybe not for Winthrop, but she was fifty. No blood pressure issues? No anxiety? Finley would ask their client.

Maybe she was like Finley and used wine as her cure-all.

Finley crossed back to where Ventura waited. "Thanks for the tour. I may want to do this again. You okay with that?"

"Anytime." He smiled. "You have my number."

Yeah. She had his number. The detective was a serious flirt.

Or maybe he was just curious about the woman who'd melted down in a courtroom and had to be restrained. And who'd survived such a brutal attack while watching her husband die.

On the way down the stairs, he asked, "Why does it matter if he liked to sing in the shower?"

Whether it mattered or not was more related to the stealth of the killer, but it was just another of the many, many details that could prove useful in any given case. "The killer attacked him from behind. Why didn't he hear the approach?"

He grinned. "I can answer that one," he said proudly.

Finley descended the final step and waited for him. "Let's hear it, then."

"The house has a killer sound system throughout. There was music playing. Not really loud, but it was playing. I turned it off after I arrived on the scene."

Winthrop hadn't mentioned the music, but if it played routinely, she might not have thought to bring it up. Finley considered that music had been playing at the Winthrop offices as well.

At the front door Finley peeled off the protective wear and handed it to the detective. "Thanks again."

When she would have turned away, he said, "You're nicer than I thought you'd be."

She shifted back to him. "No, Detective, I'm really not."

Then she was out of there. She still had Vivian Ortez to interview, and she now needed to talk to Ellen Winthrop. Being in Winthrop's house had roused questions Finley needed to ask the widow, a.k.a. the suspected killer.

8

3:05 p.m.

Winthrop Financial Consulting Group
Commerce Street, Nashville

Vivian Ortez, a member of the five, waited for Finley in the lobby of the top floor when she arrived.

"Ms. O'Sullivan, nice to meet you." She extended her hand. "I apologize for not being available this morning."

"Thank you for making time for me now."

Ortez flashed a practiced smile. "Of course. Let's make our way to my office. I hope the reporters still flocked outside didn't give you any trouble."

"Not really. Your security folks have them on a tight leash." A few questions had been shouted at Finley, but she'd just kept walking. Same old drill.

Not surprisingly, Ortez's office was the first in the wide corridor. As head of security, she would want to be situated between the lobby and the heart of the firm. The glass walls darkened as soon as the door was closed behind them.

Ortez indicated the pair of chairs in front of her desk. "Would you care for a refreshment?"

"No thanks." Finley settled into the first of the two chairs and waited while Ortez claimed her own on the other side of the desk.

Ortez was a petite woman. Five one or two, maybe ninety pounds. Lush black hair secured in a french twist. There was a time when Finley had wrangled her hair into neat arrangements and worn sleek business suits like the pale-lilac one Ortez wore. She'd stopped bothering after *that* night. In the beginning she hadn't cared whether she lived or died, which put her wardrobe well below any level of consideration. After Jack insisted she come to work for him, he paid no attention to what she wore or how she styled her hair as long as it didn't put off clients.

"As you know, I oversee the firm's security team," Ortez said, pulling Finley back to the present. "Where would you like to begin?"

"How many employees work on your security team?" Seemed a good enough starting place.

Ortez relaxed into her chair and fixed her silvery gaze on Finley. "We have three investigators and three analyzers. All six are experienced and at the top of their fields."

"You found nothing in Jarrod Grady's background to suggest he wasn't who he presented himself to be."

Ortez lifted her chin, obviously put off by the question or maybe by the reminder of the fact that she hadn't found anything. "We did not. No red flags whatsoever."

Finley wished she could demand to know how that was possible with such a top-notch team, but she really couldn't in view of the fact she hadn't found anything on Derrick and neither had her mother. If the Judge couldn't find it, it didn't exist.

Except it did. Even the best could miss something from time to time. Or perhaps it was more about the expertise of the fraudster. A good enough one could fool most anyone.

"Our team," Ortez went on, taking Finley's silence for disbelief, "is very thorough. We begin with the usual checklist: identity, employment, education, criminal record. But we don't rely solely on what we find online or on the phone. We go deeper. In-person visits with neighbors at previous addresses. We talk to former coworkers. We dig in for the long haul, Ms. O'Sullivan."

Finley got it. "How do you think Grady managed to pull off such a good cover?" She would love to know. Maybe Derrick had used a similar tactic.

"I'm afraid we don't have that answer just yet, but we are working twenty-four seven to find it. Money will only buy so much loyalty. We will find a hole in the story he wove. We won't rest until we do."

Finley recognized the motto. She operated via a similar one. *Get it done or die trying.*

Fair enough. "I toured the crime scene today," Finley said, moving on. "Is there any way Grady may have discovered the code for Ellen's home office here—at the business group's offices? Maybe there's a list of passwords and codes maintained he might have found a way to access."

"No. Only Ellen and the partners can access that information, which requires biometric and iris scans. Our people are the best at cybersecurity as well." She smiled. "Let me put it this way: I wouldn't want our team on the other side of the law. They can get in anywhere. If it exists, they will find it." She held up her hands. "That said, as with the police or any other investigative agency, we have to recognize an issue before we can find its cause."

Finley imagined they would have to be the best, considering the work done here. And she completely understood the other comment as well. There was no way to find the truth until you understood what you knew was a lie.

"No indication of some sort of code grabber anywhere in the vicinity of the lock at the home office?" Finley figured the police would have found it if there had been one, but that would depend on when it was put in place and then when it was removed.

"Nothing so far. If the crime scene unit found anything, we haven't been informed about it," Ortez pointed out.

High-end thieves used code grabbers and skimmers for all sorts of things. Locks, credit card machines on gas pumps, you name it. Wherever info was transmitted electronically, it could be captured the same way by thieves.

"Did you at any time get a sense that Grady wasn't who he said he was?" Finley had picked up on the fact that Jessica Lauder hadn't liked him at first. Her reaction to his being hired at the firm suggested as much.

"Not at all. Grady was very good at presenting himself as genuine." Ortez narrowed her eyes. "I doubt anyone would have easily seen through him. Even you, Ms. O'Sullivan."

Was that a compliment or a dig? "Finley," she countered.

"Finley." Ortez leaned forward and clasped her hands on her desk. "Jarrod Grady had his cover down to a science. His education, his previous employers—all of it checked out. A neighbor at his last residence provided rave reviews. We spoke to coworkers, even a professor from the university he claimed to have attended. Detective Ventura is still trying to determine who the victim was if Jarrod Grady wasn't his name. The truth is, we simply don't know if Grady was his real name or not."

"You'll keep me up to speed on your progress?" Finley asked.

"I absolutely will," Ortez confirmed.

Clearly the victim had gone to great lengths to set up his cover. To Finley this was very telling. An undeniable indicator that the man had very possibly done this before.

Perhaps many times.

"I'm sure you're doing everything possible to solve this tragedy for Ellen." Finley decided to shift gears. "This is devastating for her. I know from personal experience. My husband was murdered last year."

Ortez nodded solemnly. "I read about your tragedy. What you went through . . ." She shook her head. "I can't imagine, and the recovery—it speaks to your strength, Finley."

"Some days are harder than others," she confessed. "Ellen appears to be holding up as well as can be expected." Amazingly well in Finley's opinion.

"Like you, Ellen is a very strong woman," Ortez agreed. "She created this firm. You don't build an empire like this without a gift. Ellen has that gift—unparalleled focus."

"She had help," Finley reminded her.

Ortez smiled. "We all had our parts, but Ellen had the vision and she had the drive. This is her journey. We're just along for the ride. We are all very lucky to be a part of her team."

"Has Ellen always been so focused on work?" Finley asked. "Never married before Grady. No children. She appears to have concentrated her whole life on this journey."

"She has." Ortez laughed. "The rest of us haven't been so selfless."

"You're married?" Finley asked. "Kids?"

"Married twice. One daughter, who is about to graduate from Vanderbilt Medical School." She grinned. "There will be a doctor in the family."

"Wow. That's great. What about the other senior partners? Kids? Spouses?"

"Daisy is a widow. She married her high school sweetheart. He died a few years back. No children." Ortez reached for the water bottle on her desk and took a long draw. "Liz is in a long-term relationship but not married and no kids. I don't expect that will change. She's married first and foremost to the job."

"Jessica is married," Finley pointed out. She'd read as much in her bio.

"She is. Two years now. She's still weighing the idea of kids. I believe her husband is more enamored with the idea than Jessica."

A lot of career women waited to have children. For the first time Finley wondered, If things had been different, would she and Derrick have had children? The thought startled her, almost made her twitch. Finley backed away from the random notion and forced her head back in the interview. She took Ortez through the routine questions she'd asked the others. The answers were the same. Practiced. Careful. Ortez agreed there had been no new hires since Grady.

"I appreciate your time, Vivian." Finley stood. "Please let me know the minute you learn anything new on Grady."

Ortez walked around her desk. "I certainly will."

She escorted Finley back to the bank of elevators in the lobby. On the way Finley surveyed all the busy women going about their work. If there was anything negative to know about Jarrod Grady or his relationship with Ellen Winthrop, Finley had a feeling she wasn't going to learn it here.

This was a carefully constructed hive, and Winthrop was the queen bee. No one was going to fail her.

Since Winthrop had been summoned to Jack's office for another interview with Ventura, Finley wasn't able to chat with her. Ortez had answered the primary question about access to the home office that had occurred to Finley on her tour through the scene. For now, she felt no urgency to follow up with Winthrop. Although she was curious as to why Ventura hadn't mentioned requesting another interview.

Once Finley got past the horde of reporters and to the parking garage, she slid behind the wheel of her Subaru and started the engine. She adjusted the climate control and hoped it would cool quickly. It was damned hot for late September but not unusual for the South. Tugging her cell from her pocket, she checked her messages.

Nothing from Jack—always a good thing. Nothing from Ventura or any of the other detectives currently working cases that involved her in some way. Like Detective Eric Houser, who had taken over Derrick's case and occasionally poked around to keep her from concluding that no one was doing anything. Then there was Detective Ronald Graves, who still wasn't satisfied with her version of the shooting at the convenience store that had taken down the first of the three thugs involved in *that* night. Of course, Graves hadn't known—still didn't—that Finley knew the guy. The detective had his suspicions, but he couldn't prove anything.

Her cell vibrated in her hand. She snapped back to the present. Stared at the screen, then frowned. Blocked number. Oh yay. Her favorite kind of call.

"O'Sullivan," she said in greeting to the anonymous caller.

"We need to talk."

Female.

"Who's this?" Seemed a completely reasonable question.

"I'll tell you everything you need to know when we meet."

Like that was going to happen. "Sorry. I don't do blind dates."

"I'll be in that old restaurant that closed down on the corner of Twelfth and Pine at six. Come alone."

A line straight out of a bad movie. Finley rolled her eyes, glanced around the parking garage. "And why would I do that?"

"If you want to know the truth about your husband, you'll come."

Finley sat up straighter. "Who is this?"

"Corner of Twelfth and Pine. There's a downstairs entrance in the back parking lot. Be there at six."

The call ended.

Finley stared at the screen. Emotions jabbed at her. Questions hopped around in her brain like popcorn in the microwave. If this woman had known Derrick, was she a friend? Family member? Lover? Wife?

A spear of pain slid through her heart. Maybe the caller was the wife who'd been in love with the murder house—the one the previous owner had said was the reason Derrick wanted the house so badly. Maybe the caller was the one who knew all his secrets. Why he'd sought Finley out . . . lured her into a relationship . . . claimed he'd worked on the dump of a house for months when the previous owner hadn't even sold the house to Derrick until just a couple of weeks before he and Finley met.

Lies. All lies.

The burn of emotions in her eyes had fury blasting through Finley. She closed her eyes and shut it off. She had no idea who the caller was. Could be some nut trying to rattle her cage or looking for some payoff. The case had been in the news for months. Not to mention every time she and Jack won a case, there was a recap of who Finley was, as if that one night—her husband's murder—was the only story of her life worth telling.

There was always the chance this could be another ploy set up by Carson Dempsey.

Finley pushed away the distracting thoughts. Six o'clock. She would find out then. For now, she needed to speak with someone who wasn't a member of Winthrop's gang of five. Someone outside the work arena.

Laney Pettit. She was a good friend. The maid of honor at Winthrop's wedding. Winthrop was living with her while her house was in police custody. Maybe she would provide at least a different look into who Ellen Winthrop was.

Finley drove away from the parking garage. She considered touching base with Jack or maybe even Matt about the call from the unidentified female but decided she didn't want to hear how she shouldn't go alone. Instead, at the next red light she sent a text to Nita Borelli, the receptionist at the firm, who was actually the person who ran the show. Finley passed along the time and location of her appointment. It was a habit from her days as an assistant district attorney.

At least that way someone would know where to look for her body if it turned out to be a setup.

Pettit Residence
Penrose Drive, Brentwood, 4:50 p.m.

Finley pulled into the drive of the elegant home. Not bad for a woman who'd retired from teaching ten years ago at fifty-five. According to her social media page, she'd decided after the death of her last husband that she no longer wanted to be bogged down with responsibility. She wanted to spend the rest of her days digging in her garden and taking long walks on the beach. Easy to do when your third husband had been even richer than the first two—all three of whom had died unexpectedly and left everything to Pettit.

"I'm sensing a theme here," Finley muttered.

In truth, she'd checked out cause of death on the three. Two heart attacks and one stroke. Pettit was simply unlucky—or lucky, depending on how one looked at it.

So far none of the news outlets following the story had tracked Winthrop here. For Pettit's sake, Finley hoped they didn't. Having a flock of reporters camped in front of your home was not fun.

Finley climbed out of her car, scanning the expansive yard with its meticulous landscaping as she closed the door. Definitely a high-end neighborhood. Homes in the seven figures. Estate-size lots with huge maintenance price tags. Massive fluted columns and stacked stone fronted the house.

Finley rang the bell and waited.

Thirty seconds later she repeated the process. Press and wait.

When another minute ticked off with no answer, she considered her options. She could call Winthrop, but then that would tip off Pettit. Finley wanted to catch her cold. She thought of the photos of blooming gardens around a lovely patio she'd seen on social media and decided to go around back. She wandered down the walk and surveyed the high stone walls that surrounded the rear of the property.

"Aha." She spotted an arbor-topped gate very nearly concealed by the blooming vines covering it.

Finley headed that way. As good fortune would have it, the gate was slightly ajar.

Well, maybe not ajar but not locked.

It opened with ease. Finley stepped across the demarcation line that separated the sort-of-public part of the property, which was viewable and easily accessible from the street, to the part beyond an enclosing wall, which was unquestionably considered private. No barking, which hopefully meant no guard dog.

Before stepping from the shielding hedge, Finley called out, "Hello! Ms. Pettit?"

She surveyed what she could see beyond her position next to the gate. Massive green shrubs, all clipped and shorn to just the right shapes and angles. Elegant flowering trees that, though not in bloom, served as the perfect contrast to the solid masses surrounding them. Gobs of flowers in urns and beds. Stone benches and iron tables adorned the seating areas tucked discreetly around the space.

No answer. Still no barking. She might as well take the plunge. Finley started forward, the sound of water drawing her around the corner of the house. A large fountain surrounded by rows of blooming flowers and shrubs, all a perfect complement to the rest of the landscape, stood in the middle of a cobblestone patio. Music floated softly from the veranda that spanned the length of the back of the home.

"Hello!" Finley called out again. She'd already spotted Laney Pettit kneeling near a collection of blooms, carefully removing the dead petals and leaves.

Pettit held her gloved hand over her eyes and surveyed the yard. She spotted Finley and got to her feet with more spring in her step than one would expect.

"Hello." Pettit waved, then started to tug off the gloves.

Finley met her at the fountain. By then she'd removed her gloves and was reaching for her wide-brimmed straw hat.

"I'm so sorry. I didn't hear you arrive." She smiled, then frowned. "Ellen isn't home. She's still at the office."

"Actually, it was you I wanted to see," Finley explained. "I was in the neighborhood and hoped you might have some time for a few questions. When you didn't answer the door, I took the liberty of checking back here. Ellen said you could usually be found in your garden."

Actually, Pettit had said that in one of her social media posts.

"She's right, and it's definitely time for a break. Would you care for ice water or lemonade?"

"Ice water would be great."

Pettit ushered her to the veranda, where an icy pitcher of water waited. The sweat dripping down the pitcher told Finley it had been waiting there for a while now. Pettit gathered a second glass, and they settled around a small table in the pleasant shade of a massive sycamore tree.

Finley eased into the conversation by asking about her garden. Anyone who loved flowers this much would be only too happy to talk about gardening. Pettit stated proudly that she had lived in this house for fifteen years and she intended to be here until she died. The garden was her true love.

"It's very kind of you to provide a sanctuary for Ellen during this terrible time," Finley said.

"I wouldn't have it any other way," Pettit assured. "She is quite dear to me. We've known each other for eons." She laughed. "I'm much older than her, of course. I celebrated the big six-five this year."

"That's impossible," Finley said, playing the usual game.

Pettit waved her off. "I love my life, and I love sharing it with Ellen every chance I get."

Dear friends, Finley decided. "You're very close, then."

"We are." Pettit nodded. "Very close."

"Did you feel Jarrod was the right person for Ellen when she first introduced him to you?"

Pettit was silent for a bit. "Honestly, I never liked him. I didn't tell Ellen, of course. She was happy, and I wanted to support that. But I didn't trust him. Not at all."

"Have you spoken about your feelings since his death?"

She shook her head. "What's the point? What's done is done. No need to rub it in."

"Ellen seems like a strong woman," Finley ventured. "Which explains how she is holding up so well under the pressure of the investigation."

"She is strong," Pettit said. "Stronger than any woman I've ever met."

"But we all have our moments when we've had enough," Finley suggested. "No matter how strong we are."

"Well, of course. She is human." Pettit blinked rapidly. Sipped her icy water slowly as if considering how to proceed. "She was feeling a little out of sync with everything a few months back. I encouraged her to see someone." She smiled. "The most amazing therapist was recommended to her, Dr. Theo Mengesha. He was so helpful. In just a few sessions, he helped her to find her way back on track."

Finley was speechless for a moment. She and Winthrop shared a therapist? "That's great," she finally managed.

Of course Mengesha wasn't only *Finley's* therapist. He had other patients. But why hadn't Winthrop mentioned she was seeing someone? It was possible the information was irrelevant, but this was exactly the sort of thing the police would be digging for. The possibility of depression or other issues along with any prescribed medications would need to be considered.

"Yes." Pettit nodded resolutely. "It was exactly the right move. Made all the difference."

Finley set her sweating glass aside and folded her hands in her lap. "Tell me more about Ellen. She grew up in Nashville, didn't she?"

Her background had been fairly easy to research. A lot of articles had been written about her. She'd been woman of the year more than once. Countless accolades had been bestowed upon her over the years. Like the Judge, Winthrop's name was well known in charitable circles. She was one of the few who really did give back at a level reflective of her wealth. There was little out there about her childhood.

"She did," Pettit agreed, "but not on this side of town. Ellen's is a true rags-to-riches story. Her mother died when she was very young, and her father, God rest his soul, was a hard, hard man. She had no siblings." Her expression turned grim. "Her homelife was difficult. Oh, but she loved school. Everything about learning, actually. I was a brand-new teacher the first time I met her. She was a third grader and full of life and wonder. Watching her blossom into a confident, ambitious young woman was immensely satisfying."

"I imagine her tragic childhood influenced her decision not to have children of her own," Finley suggested. This was certainly not true of all or perhaps even many women who chose not to have children of their own. Spouses and children were no longer considered essential to having a full life. Many women and men chose not to go that route. The statement was an impetus for more information.

"Perhaps. She never spoke of her feelings on the matter. Not even when the rest of us were wrestling with all the usual expectations." Pettit shrugged, her gaze growing distant with memories. "The journey was not always easy for Ellen, but she never gave up and never complained."

"You mentioned her father was a hard man," Finley nudged. "Can you explain what you mean?"

Pettit averted her gaze. "She doesn't like to speak of her childhood. Nowadays her father would be jailed and the key thrown away for the treatment she suffered at his hand. But she never brings it up." Pettit shook her head. "Never talks about it or complains, as I said," she reminded Finley.

Pettit wasn't going to give those details either.

"She's an amazing woman," Finley noted. "I'm sure we could all learn a great deal from her."

Maybe more than Ellen Winthrop had bargained for when she hired the Finnegan Firm. Finley had every intention of digging up all there was to know.

Whether Winthrop understood or not, the more Finley discovered about her, the better Jack could protect her.

9

5:48 p.m.

Twelfth and Pine

Finley had parked across the street in the Turnip Truck lot, a much-celebrated natural foods store in the area of downtown Nashville known as the Gulch. She had arrived early for the appointment in hopes she could spot and identify the caller when she arrived.

The meeting location was the Two Hippies restaurant, which had closed after the extended pandemic, and so far no other business had taken over the space. The rear parking lot was empty. Didn't mean her caller hadn't arrived, just meant she'd possibly parked someplace else. Unless she was a total idiot, that would be the smart thing to do. Finley would know soon enough.

Her cell vibrated on the console, drawing her attention long enough to identify the caller.

Ellen Winthrop.

Finley had expected a call after her impromptu visit to Pettit. Winthrop liked being in charge. She liked laying out the game plan and being informed of any changes.

"O'Sullivan."

"Ms. O'Sullivan," Winthrop said, her voice tight.

"Finley," she countered before the other woman could go on. "How was your meeting with Jack and Detective Ventura?"

Frustration hummed across the line. "It was nothing more than a rehashing of what we'd already been over. I'm sure Jack will fill you in."

Finley imagined the meeting was about more than what they'd already discussed, but like Winthrop said, Jack would fill her in.

"It was my understanding," Winthrop said sharply, "that we—meaning myself and my partners—and you and Jack would keep each other informed of any updates or steps as we progressed forward with this investigation."

"That strategy is best for all concerned," Finley agreed. The woman would need to say the words. Finley wasn't going to say them for her.

"With that in mind, I'm curious as to why you made an unannounced visit to my friend Laney. I would have preferred to be made aware of your intentions, and I can tell you that Laney doesn't care for unexpected interviews. This was most disconcerting for her and for me."

Finley paused a moment to choose her words. Winthrop was their client, and it was best not to anger her any more than she already had. Better to placate her than to explain the importance of finding cracks in her story. One of Finley's primary goals was to find any potential cracks or issues before the police did. No surprises—that was the best strategy for any case, particularly one that proceeded to trial.

"Jack and I will be interviewing many people," Finley explained. "We'll be turning over countless rocks. This is what we have to do in order to keep you clear of a murder charge."

"I'm very much aware of what must be done."

Finley sighed. Her placating strategy hadn't worked. Oh well, it rarely did. She always tried. Sort of.

To hell with it, then. "In that case, you should have told us you were in therapy. It's very important that we are made aware of anything the police could potentially learn and perhaps use against you. Poking around in your personal history is essential to the right outcome."

A moment of silence.

Finley sensed the irritation building. Funny how that happened with certain clients. Usually, it was the ones who had something to hide.

"I did not kill my husband." Winthrop's voice trembled on the last. "You and Jack are my duly designated representatives. It's understandably important to me that you believe in my innocence. Somehow I'm not feeling that right now."

Surprising how a woman at the top of her career game and who all proclaimed as exceedingly strong could suddenly be so needy. Finley let it go. Why make this harder than it needed to be?

Before Finley could start placating again, Ellen threw in, "Perhaps I should speak directly with Jack on the matter."

"Jack will tell you the same thing I'm telling you. Your innocence is presumed." She didn't point out that this was the law on the matter. Winthrop no doubt was aware. "As I have explained, our job, mine in particular, is to look for what the police can find. Do you think for one second Detective Ventura is going to ask for your blessing before doing interviews? The answer is no. You can be assured that right now, at this very moment, he is scouring everything in your universe in hopes of finding a crack. A hole. A lie or a secret of any sort that might help his case."

"The evidence will support my innocence," Ellen insisted firmly.

"Having no evidence against you is important," Finley agreed. "But Ventura knows, as do I, that evidence can be manipulated, which will not permit him to stop at just the evidence or lack thereof. He'll want motive and opportunity. Sometimes a detective can't pull all three together, but most are more than happy to be able to pull together only two out of three."

"They won't find anything because I did not kill him," Winthrop repeated.

"Your adamance will not stop them from trying, particularly since they have no other suspects at this time, unless this J. Grady can be located. Take my word for it, Ellen: if there is no evidence and no other suspects, then all he has is you. The goal at that juncture will be to prove you're a liar. That you keep secrets. That you can't be trusted. That you're unreliable. Remember, all the DA has to do is make the jury doubt your credibility. Then all bets are off. Perception is a large part of the game."

More of that tense silence.

"I hit a low place," she began. "Perhaps it was the idea that fifty was looming. I don't know, but I felt off. Out of sync with myself. My friend recommended Dr. Mengesha. I attended a few sessions, and that was the end of it. I stopped going about the same time I met Jarrod. I suppose he was what I'd needed all along." Her breath caught softly. "At least that's the way it felt at the time."

"Have you or do you take any prescribed medications?" Finley asked.

"No. Nothing."

"I appreciate the clarification." Finley softened her tone and provided a reassurance she hoped would smooth over the moment. "Trust me, Ellen. I know what I'm doing. I understand how this works from both sides of the aisle. Jack and I are on *your* side. That said, and at the risk of sounding repetitive, the only way we can protect you is to find any flaws in your story first and clear them up before the police find those issues or, at the very least, be prepared to explain them away. I'm not looking for the dirty details to make you look bad. I'm looking to find whatever is out there *first*."

Speaking of trouble, a small gray sedan pulled into the lot across the street.

"You've made yourself clear," Ellen confessed. "I apologize for overreacting."

"No problem. You should call me anytime you have concerns. But while I have you on the phone, was Jarrod on any sort of medication? Prescribed or otherwise?"

"Absolutely not. Both of us took the usual vitamin supplements but nothing else."

"When I visited your home today with Detective Ventura, I noticed something I wanted to ask you about."

"Of course," Winthrop returned. "Ask anything you like."

"You mentioned that before leaving the house on Sunday morning, you noticed the empty bottles lying about from your husband's drinking the night before. Did someone clean up the mess he'd made?"

A moment of hesitation, then: "I suppose he must have picked up before going up to take his shower."

Possibly. "Thank you," Finley reiterated, her gaze fixed on the car across the street. "Remember to call me if you need anything."

Finley ended the call. She watched as the driver backed into a slot near the stairs that went down to the lower level, maybe a receiving door or employee entrance. The driver's face was turned away from Finley's location, not that it would have mattered much at this distance. Seconds later, the driver got out and headed for the stairs. Dark hair. Medium height. Slim build. Probably a woman. Jeans and a black hoodie.

Once the person in the black hoodie was out of sight, Finley rolled out of the Turnip Truck lot. She took a right, drove along for maybe fifty feet, then made a left into the far end of the restaurant's parking lot. She drove past the other car and backed into a spot several spaces away. Climbing out, she scanned the building in search of video surveillance. There was a camera on the old Two Hippies building but nothing on any of the surrounding structures. With the restaurant closed, there was no guarantee the security camera would still be active.

As she walked toward the steps, she paused to study the camera. Standing beneath its position, she recognized the camera wasn't a camera at all. It was a mount and protective hood with no camera attached. Possibly the camera had failed and had been removed with the hope of installing a new one, but then the restaurant had closed.

Finley breathed a little easier. She pocketed her cell and her keys. She kept an eye out for company until she was down the steps and headed for the double steel doors marked EMPLOYEE ENTRANCE. She steadied herself and opened the door. It wasn't dark inside as she'd expected. Dim emergency-style lighting lit the corridor. She'd made it about three good strides when the person in the hoodie sidestepped from an open door about four feet ahead on the right.

"You can stop right there."

Woman's voice. Finley did as she asked. Thankfully Finley hadn't seen a weapon yet.

The woman tugged off her hoodie, and recognition slammed into Finley. The woman from the Hidey Hole, where Finley had been watching Tark Brant. This was Brant's lady friend. Finley's senses moved to a considerably higher state of alert. A setup. No question.

Not good.

"How do you know my husband?" Finley asked.

"You mean your dead husband?" the woman taunted. "I don't. I just needed something to get you here, and I read about your husband's murder on Google. I guess it was a good plan, because here you are."

Finley wanted to be seriously pissed, but she was too relieved to muster up the anger. She hadn't wanted the caller to tell her about some other betrayal Derrick had committed. She wanted to at least be able to hang on to some tiny part of their relationship that had been real.

"Then what do you want?" The idea that Brant had used this woman to lure her into a trap was not lost on Finley. She glanced over her shoulder and then down the corridor beyond her lying host.

Finley had been pushing her luck for a while now. Until very recently she hadn't really cared. Somehow, she did now. Mostly for Jack and Matt. And her dad, of course.

"I want you to stay away from him," the woman snarled.

Finley frowned, confused. "Stay away from who?"

"Tark," she snapped. "He's mine now. He doesn't want you. Not the way he wants me. He told me he was just playing with you, but I don't like it."

Finley laughed. Couldn't help herself. The woman had no freaking idea. "You think I have a thing for him?"

"I saw you watching him. And I also saw the way he looked at you. I don't like it—whatever it is. I want you to stay away from him."

Finley held up her hands and shook her head. "This is a joke. Have a nice day."

As Finley turned to head for the door, the woman drew a weapon.

Well, hell. Finley's pulse stumbled, and her breath stalled in her lungs. Apparently, her luck had chosen today to run out.

"Don't you walk away from me, bitch."

Finley held stone still. "Trust me," she reiterated, "you've got this all wrong. I don't want—"

The door behind Finley suddenly burst open.

"What the hell are you doing, Whitney?"

Finley didn't have to look. She recognized the voice. Adrenaline rushed through her veins. *Tark Brant.*

Shit.

"I'm having a chat with this whore you been watching," the girl-friend—Whitney, apparently—sneered.

"Are you fucking crazy?" he roared, moving closer.

Finley stiffened. He was beside her now. If she turned her head to the right and tilted her face upward, she would be looking directly into his profile.

"You know what," Finley announced. The two glared at her. "This sounds like a personal issue. I'm just going to go now."

Finley started to turn away once more, and Whitney charged forward two steps, jamming the gun at Finley.

"You ain't going nowhere until I say so."

Something clicked deep inside Finley at that moment. White-hot rage rushed through her before she could hope to slow it. "What're you going to do?" she demanded. "Kill me?" She took a step closer to the woman. "You won't be the first piece of shit to try."

Whitney's eyes widened, flared with outrage of her own. This close Finley saw the fading bruises on the woman's throat. The too-large, cuffed sleeves of the hoodie had fallen away from her wrists, revealing rings of dim bruises there as well.

Why did any woman put up with that crap from a partner?

"Gimme that gun, you stupid bitch," Brant snarled.

Whitney lifted the muzzle higher, aiming directly into Finley's face. "This here's the bitch." Her lips curled back with hatred. "Maybe I will kill you."

Before Finley could open her mouth to suggest she just do it, a crushing hand gripped her forearm.

"You are fucking crazy," Brant bellowed. He glared at Finley. "You think you're bulletproof? Well, you're not. The only reason you're still alive is because someone wants you that way." He shoved her against the wall on her left. "Now get the hell out of here before I give you more of what you got last time."

Finley gasped to regain the breath that had been knocked out of her. His words whirled inside her, making her simultaneously want to vomit and want to lunge at him and tear out his jugular.

"Gimme that damned gun," he growled, turning back to his girl-friend, "or I'm going to shove it up your ass and blow your brains through the top of your head."

"Why are you always watching her?" Whitney demanded, the gun still pointed in Finley's general direction.

This was not going to end well for Whitney, Finley suspected. Or for her.

"Don't make me ask you again," Brant warned, moving one more step closer to the woman.

Not good. Not good. Finley measured the distance to the exit. Could she make it without being shot in the back?

Doubtful.

Brant moved in on Whitney, close enough to grab her by the throat, the way he'd obviously done before. His hands were hard fists at his sides, his entire demeanor poised for attack. Anger radiated off him in palpable waves.

Finley made a decision then and there. Whitney was the lesser of the two threats.

"Don't give him the gun," Finley warned. "It's the only leverage you have."

Brant glanced at her, fury contorting his face. "Shut the fuck up." He turned back to Whitney. "Give me the goddam—"

His words ended abruptly with the explosion that rent the air and sent a bullet through his chest. He looked down at the wound. Touched the blood pumping from his chest and then, lifting his face to glare at Whitney once more, he reached forward.

Whitney stumbled back.

Another explosion from the weapon.

Another wound opened in the bastard's chest, and this time he staggered. He swung in Finley's direction. She tried to sidestep him, but he toppled forward too fast, collapsing into Finley and grabbing ahold of her before she could move.

One hand swiped across her face as his full body weight slid down her, dragging her to her knees. For three beats she knelt, frozen, his weight pushing against her.

Move! her brain commanded.

Arms shaking, she pushed him off. His body landed on the floor with a thud. He lay on the cold concrete unmoving. Eyes wide open.

Finley struggled to her feet. Stared at her bloody hands and the blood streaking along the front of her clothes. *His* blood. She swallowed. Tasted his blood on her lips. Gagged.

"Is he dead?" Weapon still clutched in a firing position, Whitney stared at the man on the floor.

Finley eased back a step. Considered what to do next. Call 911? Run? Fuck! She landed on, "I don't know. One of us should see if he's still breathing."

"Don't move." The weapon swung in Finley's direction.

Shit. Shit.

"I don't think he's breathing," Finley cautioned. He hadn't blinked since he hit the floor, and she hadn't seen his chest move.

"This is your fault," Whitney accused.

Maybe. Finley had been in this exact situation before. In that convenience store two months ago . . . shit! Maybe she was crazy. Maybe she had caused all this. Fuck!

No. No. *Think. Think or end up like the guy on the floor.*

"Listen to me," Finley urged in the calmest tone she could summon. "What happened was not my fault or your fault. And right now, with this"—she gestured to the man, who was likely dead or soon would be—"you can call it self-defense. He was coming toward you. Threatening you. You were aware of his reputation, and you did what you had to do to survive. Did he put all those bruises on you?"

Whitney blinked. "Doesn't matter. I shot him. I'm fucked. But if I kill you, then there's no witness. I'm in the clear."

"They'll find you," Finley argued. "Maybe you didn't notice the camera on the building." Hopefully she hadn't noticed that it was only a camera mount and hood. "We're all three on that video. If you're the only one who leaves, then this is on you. If we both leave, I'm your witness that it was self-defense."

"I can't deal with this." Whitney shook her head. "I'm not . . . I'm not doing this." She used her sweatshirt in an attempt to clean her prints from the gun, threw it on the floor, and ran.

The door hit the wall as the woman rushed out. Her shoes pounded on the steps and then the pavement. Seconds later her car peeled out of the parking lot.

Finley didn't move for another few seconds. Her knees had locked on her, and she swayed precariously. Her stomach threatened to empty itself. She had to do something. Had to move . . .

Finally her brain got through to her body. She knelt next to the piece of shit on the floor and touched his carotid artery. No pulse. Considering the blood that had oozed from his chest and pooled on the floor beneath him, CPR would be pointless. The bastard wasn't coming back from this.

Didn't break her heart.

Gritting her teeth, she felt in his pocket for his cell phone. Ensured the device location was enabled and entered *911*. She wiped the phone using the guy's shirttail and tossed it on the floor next to him.

As she walked away, she heard the dispatcher's practiced greeting. "911, what's your emergency?"

At the door, Finley paused—shouldn't have spared the extra seconds but couldn't help herself. She glanced back at the guy on the floor.

Two down, one to go.

10

7:30 p.m.

The Murder House
Shelby Avenue, Nashville

Finley's brain was beyond estimating how long she had been sitting in her Subaru.

Five minutes? Ten?

She had pulled into her driveway and shut off the lights and the engine. Her house was dark. She was glad. No one needed to see her like this.

Her body still twitched with the receding adrenaline. He was dead. The woman—Whitney—had shot him. The bastard who had raped Finley . . . was dead. Done. Gone.

This was good. She was glad. Seeing that all three got what they deserved was her endgame, right? She'd dreamed of this moment . . .

Except . . . nothing had changed. She still didn't know anything more than she had before Brant got his.

Doesn't matter. He's dead . . . gone. That's all that matters.

A shaky inhale drew air into her lungs.

In her rearview mirror she spotted the curtain moving in her nosy neighbor's front window. Her laser-focused gaze seemed to reach all the way across the street.

Finley fought to slow the pounding in her chest.

The woman was always watching.

When she watered her flowers. When she walked her dog. When she sat on her porch enjoying a late-summer evening. And when she wasn't doing one of those, she was monitoring the street from her window.

Didn't matter. Finley had bigger issues. She closed her eyes.

The surprise and recognition that had flared when she'd come face to face with the anonymous caller flickered inside her again. What the hell had the woman been thinking?

Jealousy had driven her over some edge.

The replay of shots exploding from the woman's weapon made Finley jump. She drew in another deep, steadying breath. The stench of drying blood saturated her senses, making her gag.

She had to get out of these clothes . . .

Her fingers fumbled until she found the switch to turn off the Subaru's interior lights, allowing her to open the car door without the revealing glow. She grabbed her bag from the passenger seat and pushed herself out of the car.

She closed the door and moved forward, aware of the eyes watching her.

Ignore. Ignore.

Finley dug for her keys as she made her way to the porch. She poked one and then another into the keyhole until she got the right one. The cat peeked from under the glider and yowled up at her.

"Yeah, yeah," she muttered. The cat would have to wait.

Relief swam through her veins as she moved inside and closed and locked the door behind her.

You're home. Almost early.

Finley forced Derrick's teasing voice from her mind.

She couldn't trust anything he had said or done during their short time together.

Get your clothes off. Get in the shower.

She silently repeated the instructions until the bloody clothes lay on the bathroom floor and steam from the hot water filled the room.

Don't think. Don't think.

Beneath the spray of hot water, she closed her eyes and allowed the dried blood to be sluiced from her face . . . the stench of blood to be rinsed away. She intended to stay right here until the water ran cold, and maybe, just maybe, the steam would clear the reek of the bastard's existence from her insides.

She grabbed the bar of soap and loofah and scrubbed herself until her skin felt raw and the water started to cool. Finally, when her body started to shiver uncontrollably, she shut off the water and climbed out. She dried her raw skin and dragged on sweats and a tee.

Using plastic shopping bags as gloves, she stuffed the clothes, socks, and shoes she had peeled off into a garbage bag. In the kitchen she grabbed a Handi Flame lighter and marched out the back door. It was dark as pitch in her small backyard, but she knew the way to the make-shift firepit by heart. She tossed the bag onto the ash from all the nights she and Derrick had sat snuggled around the fire drinking wine and planning for the future.

How stupid was she for buying into his bullshit?

That future had gone up in flames, just as her bloody clothes were going to now. She went back into the house and grabbed a couple of magazines for kindling. While she was at it, she snagged a bottle of wine, was almost to the back door again when she hesitated once more. There was something she had to do. She grabbed a can of cat food and tucked a bottle of water under one arm. Back outside, she set the wine and other goods on the ground, then crumpled magazine pages until she had surrounded the bag of clothes with more-flammable material.

Once she lit those crumpled pages, the fire started in earnest. Finley collapsed onto the thick grass, screwed the top from the wine, and watched one more nightmare burn.

The cat found her, and Finley opened the can of food. The food disappeared, and she filled the little can with water. Sipped her wine. Then gave the cat more water. Drank more wine and repeated the previous step.

Vibration in her pocket reminded her that she'd stuffed her cell phone there at some point. She dragged it out and checked the screen.

Boss.

She couldn't answer. Drank more wine instead. Jack could fill her in on the meeting with Ventura tomorrow.

The flames began to die, and the wine bottle went empty. She sat motionless, numb. Her mind in an alcohol-induced fog.

The cat, sensing her foul mood, had disappeared.

Her cell vibrated again.

Somehow she managed to look without moving anything but her eyes.

Matt.

Definitely couldn't answer that one. She needed more wine.

She pushed to her feet, swayed more than a little, then staggered her way across the dinky, overgrown backyard to the door. At least she kept the grass in the front yard reasonably manicured. Not that she gave one flip. She only did it so the people who cared about her—like her dad and Matt, Jack too—wouldn't ask questions. *You okay? You're not feeling depressed, are you?*

Was she? She had dared Whitney to shoot her. A distraction, Finley assured herself. She'd known the angry, terrified woman wouldn't do it. Or Finley had thought she wouldn't, but then she'd damned sure shot her boyfriend.

Maybe Finley's instincts were failing her. Wouldn't be the first time.

Or maybe some part of her still wanted an easy way out.

She padded into the kitchen, poked around in her cupboards. She might not have a stock of dry or canned goods, but she assuredly had a wellspring of wine. There was beer too. Matt and Jack preferred beer. Most of that was in the fridge.

Derrick had preferred wine. Like her. The next door she opened revealed her stash. She reached up. The bottle she snagged slipped from her fingers and plopped none too gently onto the counter. Thankfully it didn't break.

"Oops." She might be a little more buzzed than she'd realized.

She was a lot buzzed.

A bottle of wine didn't generally have this effect on her. She hadn't eaten since . . . she couldn't remember when. She was tired. Oh yeah. She was ripe for the alcohol to go straight to her head. Damn it.

Oh well, why stop now? She opened the bottle, chugged a long swallow or two that attempted to overflow. Okay, maybe three. She placed it back on the counter, took a breath. She turned around and surveyed the shitty kitchen.

"Why the hell did you do this, Derrick?" she shouted to the walls, the ceiling, the damned original floors he had claimed to love so much.

She wobbled around in a circle as if seeing the kitchen for the first time. "What was the point?" she demanded of the places he had touched.

The wine forgotten, she tramped back to the bathroom and stared at her reflection. Hair still slightly damp and hanging in unbrushed, knotty tufts. Face flushed from the fire and the wine, not to mention the severe scrubbing.

"Why me? It's not like I'm rich." She laughed. "The Judge has all the family money. Did you hope to get to her through me?"

Finley closed her eyes and attempted to slow the spinning in her head. "Finley O'Sullivan, this is your life. Full of secrets and lies and spattered in blood."

She opened her eyes and glared at the woman staring back at her from the mirror. The blonde hair peeking past the black dye mocked her. She wasn't that person anymore. She couldn't be. Didn't know how to go back. The ache of loss welled so fast she lost her breath. She shook her head. "I don't like you anymore. Maybe I never did." Finley grabbed a jar of face cream she hadn't used in months and banged it against the mirror. Veins spread like a spider's web through the glass, casting her reflection into broken pieces.

She placed the jar back on the counter. "There." She nodded with approval. "That's more realistic."

Where had she left that bottle of wine?

Headed for the kitchen, she stalled in the living room and stared at the worn sofa she and Derrick had snuggled on so many times.

Another bolt of outrage rushing through her, she flung the cushions from the sagging frame.

Maybe she'd burn this piece of crap too. She grabbed at the cushions, hugging two to her chest, and headed for the back door.

She paused in the kitchen, felt something wrong with one of the cushions. She dropped her load. There was a lump or something. She fell to her knees and picked up each cushion, one at a time, and examined it more closely. On the bottom side of one there was something. Not really a lump but an uneven spot. Probably nothing. Maybe a knot of hardened foam. Her gaze moved over the fabric until she found the zipper. The damned thing didn't move easily, perhaps because she was inebriated; it took a slow, hard tug with much grunting involved. Once the zipper was all the way open, reaching inside wasn't any easier. The threadbare fabric was stretched tight over the foam. Both smelled far more unpleasant than she'd ever noticed before.

Ignoring the scrub of the zipper over her skin, she pushed her hand deeper inside, toward the slightly raised area.

Plastic. She felt plastic. Not hard plastic but soft, like wrap or a flimsy bag. Her fingers tightened on the plastic and pulled it toward the zipper opening.

Once the plastic was wrestled free of the fabric and the foam, she saw that it wasn't just plastic but a bag. Like a gallon-size storage bag.

Photos.

The bag contained photographs.

Suddenly sober, Finley pulled the sides of the bag apart. She watched her hand, as if it belonged to someone else, reach inside. Her fingers closed around the cluster of photos and pulled them free of the bag.

Like she was looking in a mirror, her face stared back at her.

There was a photo of her coming out of the courthouse. Another coming out of her office. Yet another at her then-favorite coffee shack.

Before. These were photos from before *that* night . . . before she met Derrick. Her hair was its natural blonde color. Her smile the one without a care in the world . . . the one she used to wear. The self-assured, well-adjusted woman in the photos no longer existed. In one the photographer had caught her midstride. The confidence in that stride. The top-of-her-game posture. All gone now.

Her throat felt suddenly dry.

Had Derrick taken this shot?

She moved on to another one. This one was of her standing on the rear balcony of her Woodmont condo. She blinked in disbelief. Judging by the angle of the shot, the photographer's lens slanted downward, he had to have been on the balcony of an upper floor and to her left.

The person behind the camera had been in the building—her building.

Heart pounding now, she moved to the next photo. She was seated at an outdoor table. Where? She recognized the place. Acme Feed & Seed, one of her top lunch spots when she was at the DA's office. She sat facing the camera, though the shot was obviously taken from some distance with a telescoping lens. She didn't need to see the face of the man at the table with her. It was Matt. His sandy-blond hair and pale-blue suit jacket were sufficient evidence.

There were more. Images taken of her before Derrick. Before *that* night.

No comments on the backs of the printed photos. Nothing.

Just moments in time captured on film for reasons she couldn't grasp.

Why? What had he been doing? Her outrage sparked. Did it matter? He was dead.

Some other emotion she refused to name kicked the outrage aside. It mattered to her, damn it.

She stuffed the photographs back into the plastic and pushed to her feet. Should she have any fingerprints she hadn't smeared by her examination lifted for evidence? Why bother? Clearly her husband had hidden the photos in *his* sofa cushion. Who else would have put them there?

She tossed the bag onto the counter and set her hands on her hips. She was tired. So very, very tired. Tired of all the questions. Tired of not having any answers. Just tired.

The emotion came from out of nowhere with such ferocity that she almost lost her balance.

Tears spilled over her lashes.

What the hell? She swiped at them.

Finley O'Sullivan wasn't a crier.

The angrier she grew, the wider the floodgates opened. Her body shook with the force of the emotions pounding her.

No. No. Damn it, no! She was stronger than this.

The surge kept coming until she had to brace herself against the counter.

Derrick had loved her. Hadn't he?

She was an idiot. How had she been such a fool?

Why the hell had she ever trusted him? Why the hell had she fallen so deeply in love with him? Because her mother hadn't approved? Had her need to go against her mother pushed her over some boundary where common sense or self-care no longer existed?

A firm knock on her front door echoed through the house. Then another.

She ignored the intrusion. She was on a roll here. How had she been so utterly oblivious to what had been happening around her?

Had the need to prove her mother wrong somehow blinded her to what was real? Damn it, she was savvier than that, wasn't she? How had she allowed her mother to hold such power over her? She was an independent woman. Every bit as full of determination as her mother was.

Except she was falling apart.

More pounding on the door.

"Fin?"

Matt.

Reality shook her. It was Matt. He was at her door.

She swiped at the tears still pouring down her cheeks. Damn Derrick. Damn her. Damn the Judge.

Finley stormed through the house and wrenched open the door.

Matt's gaze locked with hers for a long moment, and then he surveyed her. "Fin, what's going on?"

She opened her mouth to speak, but no words came out. She couldn't articulate all the feelings gushing through her.

Before she could stop herself, she flew against him. Looped her arms around his neck and held on tight. And she sobbed into his strong shoulder. Allowed the smell of him to envelop her.

She couldn't do this alone anymore.

11

The Widow

11:00 p.m.

Pettit Residence
Penrose Drive, Brentwood

"Are you quite sure you can trust her?" Laney asked as soon as the door was closed behind their departing guest.

Ellen wrapped her arm in her old friend's and ushered her deeper into the house. "We have nothing to worry about." .

Laney was a worrier, and with her ill health Ellen would have preferred to protect her from the unpleasant details. Her insistence there was nothing to worry about was perhaps a bit optimistic.

Laney turned to Ellen. "She didn't sound as confident as you and I. Are you certain this was the right move? There seems to be so much room for error. What if she can't pull it off?"

"When the police asked for a second interview," Ellen explained patiently, "this step became necessary. Sometimes the authorities don't do their due diligence, and it becomes essential to prompt their movements. Jessica can do this. She is stronger than you think."

More worry clouded her dear friend's eyes. "But she's never assumed such responsibility before. How can you be sure?"

Ellen smiled. "I've watched her for a very long time. You must trust me. She'll do fine."

Laney nodded slowly, a signal that she wasn't entirely convinced. "I should get ready for bed. I'm very tired."

Ellen gave her a hug. "Tomorrow will be better."

Her friend's worried expression relaxed into one of knowing. "You're right. Good night."

Ellen watched Laney walk away. There were people in this life who were very special. Laney was one of those people. She had given so much in her life. It was simply wrong that the damned cancer would take her from her friends and family far too soon.

Laney deserved a long and happy life. Why was it that those who didn't deserve that never seemed to be the ones stricken with cancer or some other hideous disease?

Fuck cancer.

There was nothing more Ellen could do to help her friend. She had ensured she received the very best medical care. She would see that Laney was as comfortable as possible for the remainder of her life.

The rest she had taken care of already. Ellen never left anything to chance.

She shifted her attention to the other matter. The detectives were finally on the right track. It was quite sad that nearly forty-eight hours and an additional nudge were required to put them there. Really, no wonder these cases went unsolved more often than not.

Ellen retired to her room and prepared for bed. Her fingers hesitated while unbuttoning her blouse. The memory of Jarrod helping her undress each night slipped unbidden into her thoughts.

She hadn't expected to allow him quite so close, but she was only human after all. He had made her feel so alive. His every touch had set her on fire no matter how she tried to ignore the sensations. She hadn't wanted to enjoy their time together. But she hadn't been able to help herself. He had been a master at manipulation, particularly the physical kind.

The others could never know. Ellen could never be seen as weak. Her strength was the glue that empowered the others.

She hadn't intended for this project to expand into such a brazen and provocative scheme. For the love of God, at the age of fifty, she hadn't expected to marry at all. She had lived by the adage *Who needs the frustration?* But then when marriage proved necessary to the objective, she had gotten wholly caught up in the moment. She had rationalized the fairy-tale wedding with the idea that those who knew her publicly would expect such a display.

The wedding hadn't been held in a church, though the place had once been a church. Yellow roses, Ellen's favorite, had set the theme. The bridesmaids and the maid of honor, dear Laney, had worn that same soft shade of yellow. Crisp white walls and a bow-trussed ceiling of reclaimed wood represented the perfect balance between contemporary and classic inside the venue.

It had all been the perfect, grand wedding expected for a woman of her status. The perfect illusion.

All the tiny broken pieces inside her screamed with the pain she was not supposed to feel. She should never have allowed herself to get caught up in that illusion, not even a little bit. But she couldn't change that now.

What was done was done.

Living without him required some adjustment in the short term. She wouldn't share those thoughts with the others, not even Laney. They wouldn't understand. None of them had experienced a relationship that was doomed to end with such sharp suddenness. It had been Ellen's choice, of course. She was strong. She would recover.

Ellen closed her eyes and shed her clothing of the day. She slipped into bed and allowed the memories to play with her senses. What was the harm? Surely she deserved some restitution for her sacrifice. No one ever had to know.

When she had satisfied herself, she considered that all was moving along as it should.

No need for concern.

However difficult these past two days had proved, the worst was done now. The rest would fall into place. She would in time put her mistake fully behind her.

Ellen hesitated. There was just the one anomaly. An unexpected glitch that hadn't quite smoothed out. But it would. She felt confident.

The bond of trust between Ellen and those closest to her was too strong to be undone by a mere glitch.

12

The Other Woman

11:05 p.m.

Pettit Residence
Penrose Drive, Brentwood

Jessica had known this would happen.

She had done this far too many times not to recognize the signs. Just as she had recognized them in *him*.

It was all falling apart.

Ellen was worried. Obviously, Finley O'Sullivan had proved a more than worthy adversary. So much so that Ellen had called Jessica and asked yet another favor for wrapping up this project.

Hadn't she done enough already?

Outrage simmered inside her.

Ellen had made a serious mistake with this one. This could have cost all of them everything. Now getting through the debacle was up to Jessica. She was the key. The *other woman* who would change the direction of the investigation and save the project.

She smiled. Liked the idea a little too much. Jessica had waited far too long for the others to recognize her value. She possessed assets they had long ago allowed to languish. Furthermore, she was far stronger than even Ellen or the others knew.

They would all see soon enough.

Ellen wasn't the only one who could create and pull off elaborate plans.

All Finley O'Sullivan had to do was find the carefully planted clues. She would too. She was very, very good at what she did as well. Then the stage would be set for resolving Jessica's other problem.

She smiled. Shifted her car into drive and sped away.

Her work would soon be done, and all would go just as planned.

13

Tuesday, September 20

5:30 a.m.

The Murder House
Shelby Avenue, Nashville

The house was dark when Finley's eyes cracked open.

Pain crashed into her skull.

Hangover.

Blood all over her.

Two down, one to go.

Finley bolted upright. The spinning forced her eyes closed again. Whatever was in her stomach threatened to make a reappearance. Wine. Way too much wine. When she'd calmed the roiling in her gut and her brain had reset, she opened her eyes again. Her bedroom.

Matt.

She threw back the cover and settled her feet on the floor. More spinning. One, two, three . . . up. Finley stood. A moment was required to steady herself in that upright position, and then she took a step. And another.

She found Matt asleep on the sofa. He'd tucked the cushions back into place.

Memories of him holding her in his lap, against his chest, rocking her like a baby as she sobbed, filtered through her mind. She had no idea how long he'd held her that way, and then he'd taken her to her room and tucked her into bed. She'd held on to his shirt, needing to feel him against her. Desperation had clawed at her with such ferocity that she'd been certain she wouldn't survive the intensity of the need.

Instead of climbing into bed with her, he'd sat on the edge and stroked her hair, whispered assurances to her until the craving had settled and she'd fallen asleep. She'd slept like the dead.

Tark Brant is dead.

Dread dragged at her, making her want to collapse into a depleted heap on the floor.

She was part of the reason, and . . . Finley searched her foggy brain . . . she was glad. Not for a second would she feel regret or sympathy. The crush of his body on hers . . . the feel of his hands and mouth suffocating her, tearing at her, made her stomach pitch.

Bastard. She was damned glad he was dead.

She stared again at Matt asleep on her sofa.

He's in love with you—you know that, right?

No. No, he wasn't. She'd told Derrick time and again that Matt was her friend. Her best friend. If there had ever been a question, last night had confirmed his feelings. She'd clung to him in those desperate moments, but he hadn't wanted to go there.

Regret and humiliation funneled through her.

She had behaved like an idiot.

He had been the smart one.

She pushed the memory away; there was only one thing to do now. She had to get out of here. Facing Matt this morning would be way too hard. Too awkward.

Her bag in one hand, keys and phone in the other, she slipped out of the house and eased the door closed behind her. Thankfully Matt's car was parked on the street. She slid behind the wheel of her Subaru and backed out of her driveway.

Though it was still dark, her gaze snagged on a figure standing beneath the streetlamp directly across from her house.

Nosy neighbor Helen Roberts. She was, as usual, staring at Finley. Her leashed dog at her feet, its head up, gaze following Finley just like its master's.

Did the woman never sleep?

Finley waved, the movement robotic, and then rolled forward. At the cross street she braked. Stared down at herself. She couldn't work in her sweats. She shifted her attention to the rearview mirror, thinking how easy it would be to go back home and get dressed.

No way.

On autopilot she drove the fifteen minutes to the Walmart on Powell Avenue. The parking lot was mostly empty. Who shopped before six in the morning? Only her, apparently.

Inside, stockers busily filled shelves. Finley walked quickly to the clothing department, hoping no one noticed that she wasn't wearing shoes.

Only a hangover of this caliber could send her out of the house headed to work—without shoes.

She grabbed a pair of pin-striped gray slacks. Easy enough. She moved on to another rack. Found a gray pullover that worked with the slacks. She needed underwear and shoes. With both departments close by, she quickly grabbed a bra-and-pantie set and then a pair of flat slides. Since going in the dressing room to change would be seen as an attempt at theft, she opted to pay at a self-checkout to avoid questions, then hurried back to her car.

The sun had climbed high enough to light up the parking lot by the time she reached the firm. She shut off the Subaru and stared at the old church. The lobby lights were on. Nita was at work already.

"Great."

Did the woman have to come to work this early? Of course she did. Nita Borelli never failed to be the first to arrive and the last to leave. Always. Always. Always.

Finley expelled a frustrated breath and did what she had to do. She grabbed her messenger bag and the Walmart bag and got out. Head held high, shoulders back, she strode straight into the lobby.

"Good morning, Nita." She beamed a smile that hurt her face. The bright overhead lights pained her eyes and pierced her brain. She hadn't tortured herself like this in a long time.

Nita surveyed Finley up and down, paused on the shopping bag, and then turned back to her computer. "Good morning. You have messages on your desk."

Finley moistened her lips to prevent them from cracking when she spoke next. "Thanks."

In her office, she shut the door, leaned against it, and closed her eyes. She struggled to calm the raging headache. She needed coffee. Aspirin. A toothbrush. Fortunately, the first two were available in the lounge, and the emergency toothbrush and paste were in her desk.

Forcing her eyes open again, she walked across the room and shut the blinds on her window. She searched her desk drawers for scissors. No luck. Whatever. She ripped the tags off her purchases and tossed them into the trash. The sweats hit the floor, and she swiftly pulled on the new stuff. The discarded sweats then went into the shopping bag, and Finley finger combed her hair. A rubber band from her desk drawer secured the unruly mass into a ponytail.

Good to go. Well, good enough anyway.

"Coffee." God, she needed coffee.

Her cell vibrated with an incoming call.

Matt.

She grimaced. Ignored the call. Sent a text that she was in a meeting.

Liar.

What kind of jerk lied to her best friend? The one who'd just taken care of her overnight.

Like he wouldn't know she was lying. A meeting in Jack's office this early? Yeah, right.

The rich smell of freshly brewed coffee drew her to the lounge. She poured a cup and downed half of it, scorching her tongue and throat. A refill along with two aspirins, and she headed back to her office to review the messages Nita the taskmaster had mentioned.

Nita Borelli had been with Jack for at least twenty years all told, counting the years before his big fall off the wagon and then the past five since he'd resurrected his career. Most who'd ever worked with Jack likened her to a drill sergeant. In keeping with that comparison, the woman never allowed an appointment, a message, or anything else to fall by the wayside. She kept everyone on their toes.

Back in the day, Jack would say, he'd had a large staff with several underling attorneys and their clerical support, and even then Nita had run the day-to-day operations. He could go off to court for the day or on an out-of-town deposition for several days and never worry about the office. Nita would be on top of everything.

Finley frowned. But something had happened five years ago that had upended Jack's world. Whatever it was—and even Finley and Nita didn't know the answer to that mystery—he'd fallen off the wagon. Disappeared for about six months—long enough to throw his career into chaos and to be disavowed by his partners. Even the most senior partner couldn't overcome a failure like that one. Partnerships had clauses in the contracts to cover that sort of thing.

Jack was out, and Nita was the only member of his staff who'd stood by him.

Finley had been away at law school, but she'd heard about it from her father. Her worried calls to Jack had gone unreturned. By the time she was home again, Jack had pulled his shit together and started a new firm in this former church. After Derrick's murder and Finley's own very public fall from grace, Jack had brought her on board at his new firm. She hadn't expected to be here nearly a year later. She'd expected to clock out (a.k.a. end it all), but Jack, his firm, her dad, and Matt had somehow given her the necessary motivation to go on. Even if she blurred that line from time to time, as she had last night with Whitney threatening to shoot her.

Don't look back. It happened. It's done.

Feeling considerably more human, Finley wandered back into her office and settled into her chair. The messages were from the calls she had ignored yesterday. Nita was well aware of this and had noted as much on the three yellow slips of paper.

You should answer and/or return your calls.

"Ha ha," Finley muttered.

One call was from her gynecologist's office reminding her that she'd missed her annual exam and should reschedule. She would be billed a no-show fee since she'd failed to cancel the appointment.

Finley rolled her eyes. "Whatever."

Message number two was from the public utilities company reminding her that her power would be disconnected if she did not pay her bill.

Finley groaned.

Nita had noted along the bottom that she had paid the bill and that Finley should set up autopay.

Another eye roll, and Finley was on to message number three.

Her appointment with Dr. Mengesha was at eleven this morning. Normally Finley would reschedule when in the middle of a case (and sometimes when there was no case), but not this time. Winthrop had been a patient of Mengesha's a few months back. Not that Finley expected him or anyone on his staff to tell her anything, but she would ask anyway. The response wasn't always in what a person said but in the physical reaction—the eyes, the face, the posture—when asked.

Between now and then, Finley had plenty of time to follow up on a couple of items on her checklist. So far, she had interviewed those closest to Winthrop. The women who worked at Winthrop's firm were her friends, close friends. She felt confident the women weren't entirely unbiased. Laney Pettit wasn't either. Finley needed to dig deeper.

Winthrop apparently had no friends outside work other than Pettit. No big surprise when it came to the all-work-and-no-play crowd. Ensconced firmly in that same category, Finley basically had none either. She frowned at the idea. Actually, she supposed Matt counted, since they didn't work at the same place. But he was more like family. There was the other issue with digging up details on Winthrop. She had no family. No siblings. Both parents were deceased. Finley needed to dig deeper. Someone had raised Winthrop . . . been a friend before her rise in the financial world.

Perhaps more important than what Finley didn't have on Winthrop was what she didn't have on Grady. She needed significantly more information on Jarrod Grady. Winthrop insisted she was not aware of him having any family or close friends. But she knew the name of his former employer—Imagine It, a well-known event-planning agency.

If you can imagine it, we can make it happen!

Finley checked the time: not quite eight. Since the Imagine It office wouldn't be open, she would need to try a home visit. A few clicks on the internet, and she had the owner's name and address.

Another woman.

This was good. A woman would surely be more sympathetic to Winthrop's plight. Sympathy could lead to sharing.

Finley found her toothbrush and, oddly enough, a spare hairbrush and disappeared into the bathroom long enough to make herself slightly more presentable.

Before leaving the office, Finley logged on to the utilities website and set up autopay for her monthly fees. Nita would be proud of her.

On the way out she thanked the drill sergeant for the messages and the great coffee.

At the door, Finley paused. "I signed up for autopay, by the way. Thanks for the reminder and for bailing me out."

Nita gave her a nod. "Good. You should have done it months ago."

If Finley had expected a pat on the back, she had been wrong. But Nita was right. She should have done this months ago.

There were many things Finley had fallen behind on. Guilt settled on her chest. One was thanking her friend Matt for taking care of her all the times he had since Derrick's murder. Like last night.

She owed him. She adored and appreciated him even if she didn't always show it.

But there was so much she couldn't tell him.

She slid behind the wheel of her Subaru. Like watching a man get murdered just last night. Showering his blood off her skin. Burning her bloody clothes. Not going to the police.

Finley forced away the memories.

Sharing those details wouldn't help anyone.

Unless the girlfriend ended up charged with the bastard's murder. Whitney would spew Finley's name in a heartbeat.

Worry nagged at her. Finley hoped like hell that didn't happen. Convincing her parents, her boss, her best friend—not to mention the police—that she hadn't killed anyone and that the shooting had all been as big a surprise to her as it was to them would be like trying to move a mountain with a shovel.

No easy feat.

Besides, Tark Brant had gotten what he deserved, just as his cohort Billy Hughes had.

A voice Finley had silenced about a year ago attempted to resurrect and remind her that she was—had been—an attorney, an officer of the court. She knew better. She should be ashamed of what she had allowed to happen last night . . . of her failure to report the crime to the authorities.

But she wasn't.

The reality that she had become someone else gnawed at her. She thought of the shattered mirror in her bathroom. The broken pieces of her reflection.

Her grip on the steering wheel tightened. Too late for regrets now.

Besides, there was something to be said for seeing both sides of the story. A good district attorney should look more deeply. Like Briggs was ever going to do that.

Maybe it was time someone put the good old boy out of office. Someone who lived in the real world. Someone who had actually suffered some of the sadder realities of life.

Like you?

The idea startled Finley. Had to be last night's overdose of wine.

She was never drinking that much again. Ever.

Jones Residence
Ninth Avenue North, Nashville, 8:10 a.m.

Imagine It owner Celine Jones lived in a downtown brick town house that reminded Finley of something that might be found in Chicago's Gold Coast neighborhood or Brooklyn's Prospect Park West. Fallen leaves tumbled along the tree-lined street. It was hard to believe all the big holidays were just around the corner.

Finley wasn't ready, but time just kept marching along. Her world had come to a crashing halt for her last year. When did she start moving forward again?

Just as soon as you stop living in the past.

She banished that nagging voice, parked at the curb, and emerged from her car. She grabbed her bag, surveyed the street, and started walking. The neighborhood was a quiet one. Highly sought-after properties.

A few steps along a cobblestone walk, and she was at the door. She rang the bell and prepared to give her pitch.

"May I help you?" filtered from the popular doorbell that was a camera and a speaker all in one.

Not ideal. It was always easier to talk her way in with a face-to-face situation. Not so much through a slab of wood, using a speaker box and a lens.

Under the circumstances Finley moved to plan B. She reached in her bag and withdrew her official credentials from her former employer. It wasn't a badge, but it provided the effect.

"Ms. Jones, my name is Finley O'Sullivan, and I'm here to speak with you regarding Jarrod Grady." She held up the creds, back far enough to not provide easy reading.

Hesitation. No surprise.

"I've already spoken with that detective."

"Ventura," Finley provided. "Detective Ventura and I are working together."

Liar. Liar.

More hesitation, then: "Okay."

The sound of tumblers rotating announced the lock had been disengaged.

Easier than Finley had expected.

The door opened, and the woman whose face—creamy caramel skin with dark eyes, all framed in long, lush, curly black hair—was front and center on her business website greeted Finley.

"I have a Skype meeting in half an hour," Jones warned.

Finley tucked her expired credentials away. "I only need a few minutes."

Jones stepped back for Finley to enter. Once the door was closed, she led the way to the sofa area of her open-concept living space. Big windows, lots of light. Soft, pale yellows and creams. Nice place.

They settled in seats opposite the coffee table.

"How can I help?" Jones asked.

"Tell me how Jarrod Grady came to be in your employment."

The impatience that flared in her eyes announced that she had already answered this question and didn't enjoy repeating herself.

Welcome to the world of murder investigations.

"I was short staffed as the biggest wedding season of the year approached," she explained. "I couldn't complain; we had weddings every weekend for the months of May, June, and July. Saturdays and Sundays. Birthdays and other celebrations had us sweating. Particularly the really big ones like Ellen Winthrop's. I checked in with a staffing agency I use from time to time, and they didn't have anyone available. Lucky for me, Jarrod showed up looking for work just after Mother's Day."

Just ahead of Winthrop's party.

"Did you verify his credentials?" Finley asked.

"Of course," Jones replied in a clipped tone. "I would never hire, even temporarily, anyone whose credentials weren't verified. Imagine It is my baby. I don't trust my baby with just anyone."

Okay. Finley opted not to go into the reality that credentials could be faked. Grady was a perfect example. "Tell me about your interactions with him."

"He was smart. Charming. Very handsome. A big flirt." She shrugged. "He did a great job, and clients loved him."

"How long did he work for you?"

"He was gone by mid-July." She shook her head. "Married himself a billionaire."

Ellen Winthrop.

"You never saw him speaking to or hanging out with anyone—another employee or a friend—who might have exchanged personal life stories with him? I'm looking for anyone who may have learned personal details."

"No." She shrugged. "He was very friendly, but he didn't socialize with any of the other employees. Detective Ventura interviewed me and all of my employees at length. None of us ever saw him with anyone. He kept his personal life away from work. A lot of people do, so I didn't think anything of it."

"Did he at any time do or say anything that made you uncomfortable or set off warning bells of any sort?" Finley nudged, hoping for something . . . anything.

"Never." Jones shook her head but stopped midshake. "Wait, there was this one thing I found surprising."

Finley would take it. Any new detail she could learn about Grady might prove useful.

"I was having a difficult time with this new program my CPA installed, so I called and left him a voice mail. I guess Jarrod overheard enough of the voice mail I left for him to get the gist of my issue. Anyway, he mentioned that he thought he could help."

"With accounting software?" Finley asked for clarification.

Jones nodded. "He recognized the problem immediately and took care of it for me. It was crazy, but his expertise really saved my skin that day."

Crazy for sure.

Jones checked her cell. "I really have to get ready for my meeting. Do you have any other questions?"

"Not at this time, but I hope you won't mind me calling if the need arises."

"Of course." She gave Finley a card with her personal cell number.

Finley thanked her. Next on her agenda was the Winthrop housekeeper.

14

10:45 a.m.

Mengesha and Associates
Church Street, Nashville

Finley arrived early for her eleven o'clock appointment with her shrink. A first for her. Mostly because the interview of the housekeeper had been a bust. The woman wasn't home. A call to Winthrop, and Finley had been informed that a death in the family had sent the devastated woman back home to Puerto Rico. Winthrop had no idea when she would return.

Shifting the interview lower on her to-do list, Finley had spent the next couple of hours catching up. Jack had briefed her on yesterday's meeting with Ventura. The detective had wanted to go over questions related to the interviews he had conducted with the five. Jack saw the meeting as Ventura's way of trying to ramp up the tension, so to speak, on Winthrop. A rookie move considering he had nothing real with which to back it up. Basically, Finley hadn't missed anything. Then she'd checked in with her friend Shafer at the ME's office and Tommy Hanes, her go-to CSI guy. They had nothing new from that side of the investigation—at least nothing available for sharing. But there was more, and Finley damned sure intended to find it.

There were two things she could not tolerate. The first one was easy. She'd grown up with a judge for a mother. She'd attended law school and spent four years putting criminals away in the DA's office. She hated when the bad guy—or gal—got away with it because no one could find the necessary evidence to prove the case.

Right up there next to her top pet peeve were appointments with her shrink. It wasn't that she didn't like the doc. Finley actually liked him. He was a good listener. Totally not judgmental. The man had a wicked sense of humor, even if he did keep it hidden most of the time. But that was where her appreciation for his more agreeable qualities ended.

If possible, the man was better than Finley at reading people and spotting untruths. He read her like an open book. This was not a good thing. This ability prompted other questions and a subtle pressure that she found immensely uncomfortable.

But here she was a whole fifteen minutes early, nonetheless.

The receptionist at the clinic was young. Thirtyish. Short, spiky blonde hair and bright-green eyes. Lena Marsh. She had started at the clinic not quite a year ago, and already she was a patient favorite. Two other patients had said as much while they waited for their appointments. That was another thing Finley had done today that she didn't usually do. She'd chosen to sit in the lobby rather than to wait in her Subaru until her appointment. Not that there were ever more than two or three people, and no two in the lobby were ever waiting to see the same therapist. Mengesha was not alone in the practice. There were Higginbotham and Manfred. But she hated sitting in a lobby with other people, who probably wondered what she was there for. It was like jail or prison: *What're you in for?* The covert glances and averted gazes. The scrutiny from what you were wearing to what might be wrong with your head.

Or maybe she was the only one who did that.

Luckily Finley was alone in the lobby now. The other patients had been called back. She noted that Marsh, the receptionist, was never still. Always busy with something. Her voice was soft and calm when she answered the incoming calls. All the busy and the rush vanished when the phone rang.

With a quick check of her cell, Finley stood and strolled to the elegant mahogany counter. Marsh immediately looked up, her practiced smile already in place.

"Dr. Mengesha will be with you soon," she assured.

Finley nodded. "A friend of mine is Dr. Mengesha's patient as well," she said, knowing the move was pointless, but she had to try. "Did you hear about her husband? He was murdered on Sunday morning. It's just terrible. I'm sure she'll need the doc more than ever."

Marsh blinked. Tucked away her smile and adopted a sad face. "Tragedies are very difficult. I'm sure if she calls, the doctor will work her in."

The lady was good. Not the slightest hint she recognized this particular tragedy or the patient involved.

"You started here not so long after I did," Finley said, trying a different tactic. "My husband was murdered too." She shrugged. "You probably saw that in my file."

Another sad smile. "I don't read the files, but I do remember seeing what happened on the news. I'm so sorry for your loss."

More sympathy.

Finley chuckled softly. "I guess widows have a thing for Mengesha."

Marsh glanced at the new light flashing on her phone base. "Ahh, he's ready for you."

Finley thanked her and wandered down the long cozy corridor that led to the offices. Each office had a private exit for the patients who chose to leave that way. Mengesha's was the last one on the right. He stood behind his desk, waiting for her arrival.

"Finley, good to see you for a change."

That was what happened when you canceled two appointments in a row.

"Hey, Doc." She settled into the chair she always chose. The softer one with its fluffy upholstery and low back. The wingback was too firm. Too confining. That choice likely signaled something to the doc.

He lowered into his chair and relaxed into its high back. "Let's talk about what's been going on with you since our last session."

For the next forty-five minutes, Finley weaved a story of fulfilling days at work and relaxing evenings at home, all the while dodging his digging tactics. He rallied each time and came from a different angle. She even tried her "I have a friend" approach on him to bring up Winthrop. Didn't work. No surprise.

In the end, she used the private exit to flee.

Wasn't seeing your therapist supposed to make you feel better about yourself? Finley just felt exhausted after evading his prying questions for the better part of an hour. She climbed into her Subaru and started the engine. Before she was out of the parking lot, her cell was buzzing.

She didn't recognize the number, but it was local.

"O'Sullivan."

"Ms. O'Sullivan, this is Detective Ronald Graves."

She stood on the brake for an extra few seconds even when the oncoming traffic had cleared. Ronald Graves was the detective working the convenience store shooting from back in July.

The dead guy, Billy Hughes, was one of the three who'd invaded Finley's home last year and murdered her husband. He was the first to get his.

"Detective, what can I do for you?" Finley eased into the street and headed for the office. She had a bad feeling she wouldn't be making it to that destination.

"I'd like to discuss a homicide case that landed in my lap this morning. Do you have a few minutes to stop by my office?"

That certainly hadn't taken long.

"Sure." Putting him off wouldn't help. She might as well find out what he had. "When did you have in mind?"

"Does now work for you?"

"You're in luck. I'm between appointments. I'll be there in ten minutes."

At the next red traffic light, Finley sent a text to Nita letting her know she had been waylaid by Detective Graves. She would catch up with Jack after that.

Assuming she wasn't about to be arrested.

Metro Police, East Precinct
East Trinity Lane, Nashville, 12:30 p.m.

Detective Ronald Graves kept a countdown calendar on his desk. He would retire in less than two hundred days. He had the gray hair, sagging jowls, and slightly rounded belly to prove he'd done his time in a demanding career. Had the tiny office too. Most of the other detectives were stuck in cubicles in the bullpen, but not Graves. He had what Finley felt confident had once been a coat closet.

Despite his age and the size of his office, he was sharp. He had Finley's number, and she expected he was waiting for the opportunity to prove she had lied about the convenience store shooting. Not that she had shot the guy, because she hadn't. The store's video footage showed the whole thing in vivid detail. But he understood she wasn't sharing everything. That part nagged at him. His persistence nagged at her. It was a vicious cycle.

She wouldn't be sharing anything today about the most recent shooting of a piece of shit who got what he deserved.

Sometimes the grieving widow beat down the former ADA, and the ugly came out. This was one of those times. The excuse was one that overrode much of the guilt about who she had become since Derrick's murder.

"I appreciate you coming in, Ms. O'Sullivan."

Whenever someone called her Ms. O'Sullivan, she couldn't help feeling a certain guilt that nothing seemed to override. Choosing not to take her husband's name, Reed, when they married had come back to haunt her over and over the past year. So many career women didn't change their names. Ellen Winthrop, for example. Still, after Derrick's murder Finley had felt guilty about it, because no matter that he'd said he understood, the decision had pained him a little. She'd seen it in his eyes, however fleetingly.

His lying pained you. Get over it.

She blinked away the voice. "No problem," she said to the detective. "You have something new on the convenience store shooting?"

She didn't see how that was possible. The security footage showed the store clerk shooting the man with the gun who had attempted to hold up the store. Case closed. But bringing up the older case would suggest to the detective that she had no idea about his newest case. Going straight to questions about the new case was a misstep made by many—particularly when a seemingly insignificant detail slipped out, and then you attempted to explain how you'd seen or heard it on the news. At this point, she wasn't supposed to know about the new case.

"Unfortunately, I don't have anything new on that one, but there was a murder last night. Downtown at a restaurant that's been closed for a while."

Finley made a sad face. "Violence downtown is on the rise." Then she frowned. "I didn't realize that was your jurisdiction."

It was a petty comment. She was aware it wasn't his jurisdiction. But there was an overlap in one of his cases. She knew this as well. Whether Graves could prove the connection or not, whatever detective had caught last night's shooting would gladly have pitched it to him.

And they both understood that connection was the reason he'd called Finley in for questioning. He just couldn't prove what she did or didn't know.

"The victim"—he glanced at his notes—"a Tark Brant." He looked to Finley then. "You might know him as the partner or buddy"—he shrugged—"of the man, Billy Hughes, who died in that convenience store shooting back in July."

Blood splattering across her face flashed in her brain.

Finley exiled the image and pretended to consider the possibility; then she shook her head. "No. Sorry. I've never heard of him."

Graves picked up his pen and made a note. Probably just a scribble to make her nervous. Didn't work.

"So far we've got nothing on the weapon used," he went on. "The shooter obviously wiped his prints."

His. So maybe they really didn't have anything.

Finley waited. Another of the biggest mistakes a suspect or person of interest could make was saying more than absolutely necessary. Asking leading questions out of curiosity. Never a good move. Better to say nothing.

"We're attempting to track down the victim's girlfriend, one Whitney Lemm. What we have so far is that she was seen with him most recently on Sunday night. She's a known junkie. Has a long list of arrests for prostitution. It's possible they had a falling-out that didn't end well."

No comment.

"A bartender at a downtown tavern saw her with the victim."

Silence dragged on as if he were waiting for her to say something.

There was always the chance the bartender had remembered Finley as well. If so, there was no law against patronizing a particular establishment at the same time as someone who turned up dead. It happened.

"Did you have a question that pertained to me?" If he had a point, he should get to it. She and Jack needed to catch up.

"Oh. Hazard of getting older. I get off-track way too easy."

She had no thoughts she felt inclined to share on the matter.

He reached across his desk and picked up his laptop.

A thread of uneasiness slithered through her. Had she missed a camera somewhere?

Shit.

Graves pulled up a video. Finley instantly recognized her Subaru sitting nose out in a slot at the Turnip Truck parking lot.

"Is that your Outback, Ms. O'Sullivan?"

Finley peered at the screen. "It's the same color as my car, but there are lots of cars that color on the road. Black is a very popular color."

"It's a Subaru Outback. Isn't that what you drive, a black Outback?"

"I do, but as you know, lots of people drive them. It's a very popular car in a very popular color."

Graves stared at her. He wasn't enjoying her evasiveness.

"When was this video done?" she asked as if that might help her memory.

"Last night just before six."

She made one of those overdone aha sounds. "Yes. Yes. The Turnip Truck. I shop there occasionally." She frowned. "Did this guy get shot in the Turnip Truck? That is bizarre," she added before he could respond. "I may have to stop shopping in person."

He played the video.

She held her breath.

The footage showed her pulling forward and making a right onto the street that ran between the Turnip Truck and the restaurant where the shooting happened.

The video continued for a few seconds more, but her car was no longer in view. The camera's reach only went as far as the middle of the street. It didn't show the parking lot on the other side. Relief swam through her.

"You went home from there," he suggested.

She almost said yes, but she instinctively understood this was a trick question.

"I did," she admitted. "I considered stopping at that pub a few blocks down, but I decided to go on home. Made a right on Pine."

Disappointment flared in his weary eyes. He'd known the turn shown in the video was wrong for going straight to her place on Shelby.

"You went home. Didn't stop anywhere?"

"I did. No stops." Images of bloody clothes and rivers of red rushing down her skin flashed one after the other in her brain. She shut out the memories.

Graves heaved a dramatic sigh. "This guy Brant was very much like his friend Hughes. He had a record of close calls and a rap sheet that made even a veteran like me wonder how he could still be walking the streets."

Finley kept the comment that rose to the tip of her tongue to herself.

Not anymore.

"Thanks for coming in and explaining your being in the vicinity of my new murder case, Ms. O'Sullivan."

Again. He didn't say it, but she knew he was thinking it.

Finley stood. "Happy to help."

Liar.

Graves hefted himself up. "Don't worry yourself. Although we haven't found any usable prints or other evidence just yet, I've asked the forensic techs to go over the victim's clothing extra closely. Maybe we'll get lucky and find a hair or some kind of fiber that'll give us a starting place."

Brant collapsing into her and sliding down her body zoomed into her mind.

Almost made her flinch.

"Good luck," she offered with a smile that reminded her about the headache still lingering despite the two aspirins she'd taken.

She left the dinky office and took her time exiting the building. She didn't want to be seen as rushing away.

Perception was more than half the game in these situations.

She left through the rear exit and managed to drag a decent breath into her lungs.

Then she spotted Matt propped against her Subaru. Waiting for her just like the last time she'd been called to this detective's office.

Damn Nita. She must have told him where Finley was.

Finley plastered on a smile and strode toward the man who had taken such good care of her last night.

She stopped in front of him and nodded. "I owe you big-time for babysitting me last night." Then she leaned against her car next to him. "I don't know what triggered the meltdown." She shrugged. "Maybe it was a long time coming. The upside is I saw Mengesha today. We talked it through."

Liar. Liar. Perfect timing for the appointment with Mengesha, as it turned out.

"I thought we'd catch up over lunch," Matt said rather than comment on her monologue. "Nita said you were here, and I hoped to catch you."

He would likely have heard anyway. Matt knew everything that went down in this city if it related to the mayor's, DA's, or chief of police's offices.

"Another one of Dempsey's thugs got his," she admitted.

If he didn't already, he would also soon know that she had been nearby. Damn it. But she wasn't going there until he brought it up.

"When did this happen?"

"Last night. Downtown. There's always somebody getting shot downtown." This was true. Crime—particularly violent crime—was up everywhere.

He nodded. Then he turned those piercing blue eyes on her. "I'm worried about you, Fin."

Images of last night's meltdown flashed one after the other in her brain.

She was worried about her. Emotions twisted inside her. More often than not she didn't know who she was anymore. She wasn't sure she wanted to know.

She certainly wasn't that wide-eyed defender of justice any longer.

She and Matt had started that journey together. Hurt wallowed inside her. He was still the good guy, but what was she?

Rather than say any of that, she told him part of the truth. "I'm glad I've got you in my life, Matt." She stared at the ground. "I don't know if I could get through this without you and Jack."

He slung an arm around her neck and pulled her into a hug. "When this is behind you, you can move on. And I'll still be there for as long as you want me around."

The idea was suddenly the scariest part of all. She knew he would be there. She wanted him there.

But she didn't deserve him.

Finley understood this with a new level of conviction now.

"I just want you to remember what I said about putting Derrick and any investigations into what happened with him behind you," she said, then quickly amended, "behind us. Maybe last night was about me moving on." She shrugged. "Like I said, it's time."

Matt smiled sadly. "I know what you're doing."

She hoped to hell not.

"You don't want me to worry about you, but you waste time worrying about me. We're in this together, Fin. If you're done looking back, so am I."

She drummed up a smile. "Good."

She had a very bad feeling that he understood she was lying.

15

1:32 p.m.

Metro Police, East Precinct
East Trinity Lane, Nashville

Finley sat in her car and watched Matt drive away. She'd begged off lunch with the excuse that she and Jack had to catch up.

It was true. Mostly.

She told herself to move, but she didn't.

Start the car.

She drew in a breath of hot, stuffy air and started the engine, powered down the windows to ease the buildup of heat stifling her. Graves had recognized she was lying. Just like last time. She hadn't pulled the trigger that ended the life of Billy Hughes in that convenience store back in July any more than she had the one that took Tark Brant's last night.

But she had been there. She knew things she had opted not to share. Those things were primarily irrelevant to the deaths of those men. The rest was only relevant to Finley and what those two bastards had done to her and her husband. That particular knowledge would not change the outcome of the murder investigations.

Well, admittedly the fact that Finley knew the identity of Brant's killer would make a difference, but she didn't feel compelled to share the information with Graves. Why make his job easy? The fact was, the shooting was self-defense. Brant would very likely have killed Lemm if she hadn't killed him first. Besides, it wasn't like Brant was some sort of innocent victim.

Right, Finley.

The idea went against everything the law stood for . . . against everything she had cherished before . . .

Which segued into the reality that Matt knew she was lying. This thing she was doing had gone on too long for him not to know, and the idea of it made her sick at herself.

Ellen Winthrop abruptly intruded into Finley's thoughts. Had she killed her husband for reasons she deemed justifiable?

Where was the line between carrying out the law and finding justice?

Her cell vibrated, dragging her from the dark thoughts.

Local number.

"O'Sullivan." She shifted into reverse.

This case—the similarities between her situation with Derrick and Winthrop's dead husband were undeniable. Working the Winthrop case had Finley seeing herself in a different light.

She didn't like what she saw one little bit.

"Finley, this is Jessica Lauder."

Lauder's voice sounded as if she was winded. Maybe they'd had group Pilates? "Is everything all right, Jessica?"

"I need to speak with you," Lauder urged. "It's important."

Finley merged into traffic. "I can be at your office in under ten minutes."

"No."

Finley braked for the traffic signal at the intersection. No? "Are you at home today?"

"No. I . . . I just need to speak with you privately."

A smile tugged at Finley's lips. So, the first breach in the carefully constructed wall of solidarity had happened.

That was the thing about secrets: they were only secret if only you knew them.

"Name the place."

"I can come to your office."

Worked for Finley. "I'll meet you there."

The Finnegan Firm
Tenth Avenue, Nashville, 2:00 p.m.

Jack hadn't returned from a late lunch when Finley arrived. She gave Nita the lowdown and had her send Jessica to her office when she arrived.

The youngest member of the Winthrop five looked an emotional wreck. Her hands visibly shook. Her eyes were bloodshot as if she hadn't slept.

After Finley had rounded up bottles of water, the women settled on opposite sides of her desk.

"Take your time," Finley suggested after an extended silence while the other woman sipped her water, "and tell me what's happening that has you concerned."

Jessica placed her water bottle on the edge of the desk and met Finley's gaze. "I'm very concerned about Ellen."

Finley waited for her to go on. There would be more.

"She's not herself," Jessica added. "I've never seen her this way."

"She just lost her husband," Finley reminded Jessica. "She hasn't suffered this kind of loss before; I'm sure it's a new place for her. It might be a while before she's herself again."

Jessica shook her head. "I think it's more. It's as if . . ." She seemed to search for the right words.

Finley had a few she could toss out, like *too in control, too unshaken*, but she waited. She needed to hear what this woman saw and felt.

"It's almost like she feels nothing. She carries on as if nothing happened. I don't understand." Jessica shrugged, her eyes bright with emotion. "I've known Ellen for a very long time. She's the strongest person I know, but this is not normal."

"Perhaps it's her way of dealing with the emotions." Finley stood staunchly on the "it's not normal" side, but that was just her. Her own experience was far from normal. It was the only way she had survived.

"Did she tell you he was cheating on her?"

And just like that, Finley's mean-girls radar went on alert. Was this one partner selling out another? All were fiercely competitive. It happened. "Is this something you know for a fact? Did Ellen share this with you?"

The news wasn't surprising, but it was just another aspect of the story Winthrop should have shared up front.

Jessica nodded. "It's true. Ellen told me."

Whoa. One of the five was spilling on the boss?

"Do the other partners know?" No one had mentioned even a hint of trouble in the marriage. Finley had a feeling this decision to share was about trouble within the partners or maybe just between Lauder and Winthrop.

Jessica shook her head. "The only reason I know is because he . . ." She hesitated, struggled with how to proceed. "He hit on me on several occasions. I told him I wasn't interested. I even threatened to tell Ellen, and he didn't stop. Finally, when I'd had enough, I went to Ellen."

"How did she react?"

Jessica squared her shoulders and braced herself as if what she had to say next was even more difficult than what she'd already imparted. "She wasn't surprised. She'd learned he had a history of cheating."

"Had he hit on someone else at the office?" Why the hell hadn't anyone said anything? If Ventura learned about this, Winthrop's troubles would only worsen.

Of the five, was it just Jessica, or did others have reasons to be angry with Grady? To want rid of him—the only man in an empire built exclusively by and for women. The idea these women had held out on Finley ticked her off. This was not the time.

"No. I was the only one at our office. Ellen said he had cheated with a woman who worked at her doctor's office."

"Which doctor?" This got more interesting all the time.

"Her therapist," Jessica said. "Dr. Mengesha. The receptionist. Apparently, it was a long-running affair."

Now there was an answer Finley hadn't expected. She thought of the woman she'd seen at Mengesha's office on numerous occasions. Finley had never wondered if she was in a relationship. Now she searched for any memory of spotting a wedding ring or framed photos of the receptionist with a partner or with children.

"Do you know her name?" Was the receptionist the reason Winthrop had chosen Mengesha? No, that didn't make sense, since Winthrop became his patient before she met Grady. Stated that she had stopped by the time she'd met him.

"Marsh," Lauder said. "Lena Marsh."

Definitely the receptionist at Mengesha's office with her spiky blonde hair and vibrant green eyes. Interesting.

"Was their relationship ongoing at the time of his death?" Finley asked. Ventura was no fool. He would figure this out. Finley would have to talk to Jack about how he wanted to proceed with this news. The usual strategy was to get ahead of any potential catastrophe in the making. Winthrop wasn't going to like the confrontation to come.

"Ellen was under the impression the relationship with Marsh was over more than a month ago." Lauder clasped her hands in her lap. "His inappropriate attention toward me was more recent."

"Why tell me now?" Finley asked bluntly. "Why not talk about what happened when I first interviewed you? I mean, I have to tell you this doesn't look good for *you*."

Lauder blinked, tried to conceal her surprise, but failed miserably. Moisture rose on her thick lashes. "I don't understand. Why would I be in trouble? It was him. I didn't do anything."

Shit. Now Lauder was going to cry.

"This is the sort of thing a detective or DA would see as motive," Finley explained. "I'm not suggesting this means you did or didn't do anything. I'm making you aware of how it appears."

"I explained everything to Ellen. I did what she told me to do."

Finley studied the woman. Wondered if she comprehended how that response sounded. Where the hell was this going? "What did she tell you to do?"

Lauder's eyes flared wider, as if she'd only just realized what she'd said. "She told me to avoid him . . . at first. Then she wanted me to go along with him to see how far he would take his . . . pursuit."

"How did that go?" Finley wished she could be stunned. That the idea of what Winthrop had suggested was some unbelievable concept, but it wasn't. Sometimes you just wanted to know if the husband you trusted would really make the worst decision with no care for the consequences to anyone.

Husbands weren't always trustworthy.

Finley knew this from her own short-lived marriage.

This is not about you.

"He went so far as to attempt coming up with a way we could get together." Lauder shook her head. "I couldn't continue. I told him to back off or I would make him regret his actions."

"Please tell me you have an airtight alibi for Sunday morning."

Lauder appeared taken aback. "I was at home. Relaxing. I've already gone over my alibi with the detective."

"But that was before," Finley explained, "you came forward with the news about your interactions with Grady."

She blinked. "I told Ellen, and I did what she told me to do."

Finley's door opened, and Nita poked her head into the office. She glanced at Lauder before saying to Finley, "Ms. Winthrop is here to see you."

"Oh God. I should go." Lauder shot to her feet.

"It's a little late to get away unseen," Finley reminded her. "She surely noticed your car in the parking lot."

Lauder collapsed back into her chair. She closed her eyes and shook her head in defeat. "I shouldn't have come."

"Send her in," Finley said to Nita.

There was something more than friendship and longtime work relationships going on between these women.

Was Jessica Lauder the weak link in the group? Whatever they were hiding, would she break and spill the beans?

Winthrop entered the room. Stalled as her gaze landed on her partner.

"I told her," Lauder said, breaking the silence first.

Winthrop took the final few steps into the room and sat down in the remaining chair. "I see." She turned to Finley. "I was on my way here to tell you myself."

"Is there some reason the two of you have suddenly decided to share this information today?"

"The receptionist," Winthrop explained, "called me. She was angry that you'd spoken about the case to her at the clinic. She accused me of attempting to set her up."

The idea wasn't completely outside the realm of possibility. Finley didn't know Marsh. The persona she presented at the clinic wasn't necessarily indicative of who she was outside that world.

"Why didn't you tell us about his affair and other unacceptable behavior before?" Finley asked, ignoring the allegation about her interaction with the receptionist. "Jack explained to you that withholding was not something you should do with him or with me. It always comes back to haunt you."

Winthrop lifted her chin in defiance of Finley's words, but she said nothing. She was not accustomed to being told what to do, much less being dressed down for her actions.

"The idea there was a secret this big and that sheer coincidence prompted the two of you to come out with it," Finley warned, "is unacceptable." She set her attention solidly on Winthrop. "You need to fully grasp the concept of exactly how wrong this could go if Ventura found out before Jack and I were prepared to respond."

"Very well," Winthrop announced as she pushed to her feet. "Now you know, and you'll be pleased to hear there is nothing more. We've told you everything there is to tell—at least as far as we know." She stared down at her colleague. "We've done all we can, Jessica. We should go now."

Lauder stood. "Thank you," she said to Finley.

The two walked out in a sort of strange unity.

Finley was still staring after them when Jack appeared at her door.

"Was that Ellen Winthrop leaving as I was turning into the lot?"

"Yeah. That was her and Jessica Lauder." She gestured to the empty chairs in front of her desk. "We should talk about that visit."

Jack took a seat. "Sounds like it didn't go well."

Finley explained the odd sequence of events, including her visit to Pettit, in case Jack hadn't heard about it from Winthrop already.

"We need to dig a little deeper into this receptionist," he pointed out.

No question. "Winthrop is not telling us everything, Jack." Finley considered the partners. "Whatever she and the others are hiding, they're all involved or at least aware."

"You think Winthrop wanted her husband dead. Maybe hired someone to do the deed while she was out for a walk."

Finley shrugged. "In my opinion, she's still not tracking as a cold-blooded killer. But I'm convinced we're missing something. I can feel it."

"I trust your instincts, Fin. Do what you think you need to do to find the whole story."

"Count on it." She nodded. "This morning I spoke to the event planner he worked for when he met Winthrop. He showed up at just the right time. Mid-May. She was desperately understaffed. She insists she checked his references and found no reason not to hire him."

Jack pursed his lips for a moment. "Did he make friends there? Someone he may have shared details of his personal life?"

"The owner said not. Ventura interviewed all the employees and got nothing."

Jack made a face, reached into his jacket pocket for his cell. "Finnegan." He listened to the caller for a few seconds, then: "I'll come to you."

He ended the call and pushed to his feet. "Gotta go. Ventura has more questions."

"You think he's planning an arrest?" Finley grabbed her bag and keys. She had places to go and people to see as well.

"That, in my opinion," Jack said as they walked toward the door, "would be premature. But stranger things have happened."

Outside, Finley watched her boss drive away. The relationships between men and women were complicated, some more than others. She wondered if Winthrop's marriage had been doomed from the beginning, when her family appeared to be five other women with whom she shared everything. Had there really been room for a husband?

Not to mention it seemed her husband was missing the loyalty gene. *Like Derrick.*

No, that wasn't true. Derrick had proved his loyalty when he'd put his life on the line for Finley *that* night. His issue had been secrets. About what, she had no idea.

Was there really any difference? Disloyalty . . . dishonesty. Just another kind of betrayal.

As she reached for her car door, her cell sounded off. She dug in her pocket for it and noted the name on the screen.

Dad.

She hadn't called him this week. He liked hearing from her at least every other day.

"Hey, Dad." She settled behind the wheel and started the engine. Damn, it was hot. The curse of living in the South. The heat would hang around until the freezing cold showed up. There was rarely any in-between.

"Hey, sweetheart, how's your week going?"

She smiled. Couldn't help herself. His voice made her happy . . . made her forget for a moment that the rest of her world was upside down. "Well, it's going."

He laughed. "Enough said. Listen, your mom and I feel like it's been forever since you came to dinner. We're hoping you can come tonight. I know it's short notice, but it would mean a whole lot to your old dad."

Finley swallowed a groan and dropped her head against the car seat. "Is something going on?"

Dinner with the Judge was like walking over hot coals and then deciding to sit on them just to see if the burn intensified.

"No. No. We just miss you, that's all. We're not getting any younger, you know."

And there it was, the parental blackmail card. How could she say no to that?

"I can do some shifting. See you at seven or so?"

God, she would rather have needles pushed under her nails.

"See you then, sweetheart. Love you."

"Love you too, Dad."

She could handle dinner with the Judge if Derrick were still alive—but he wasn't.

So she called Matt.

If she had to do this, he was coming with her. Matt liked the Judge. He remained in her good graces, making him the perfect buffer.

He would say yes. He always did.

Lucky for her.

16

4:55 p.m.

Mengesha and Associates
Church Street, Nashville

The office closed in five minutes.

Finley waited in the farthest corner of the parking lot. When Lena Marsh exited the building, Finley intended to follow her home. She had the woman's address, but she had no idea what her personal schedule for the evening might be. Better to follow her from here than to wait at her place and miss her.

Her cell vibrated.

Houser.

The name was one she would just as soon not appear as an incoming call. Then again, maybe he had something new on Derrick's case. Not that she really expected Detective Houser to, but this had been a strange day.

"O'Sullivan." She braced for trouble.

"Hello. Eric Houser here. Do you have a few minutes?"

She glanced at the clinic entrance. No sign of Marsh just yet. "Sure, what's up?"

"I wanted to let you know I'm still working on your husband's case. Unfortunately, I don't have anything new to share, but I wanted to check in and let you know I haven't forgotten."

Wow. Okay. What a novel idea. A detective who was concerned as to whether you were wondering what he was doing. Not likely. Nothing against detectives, but they were busy people. There was no time for speculating about what a victim's family was wondering—sadly. It wasn't about not caring; it was about being overwhelmed.

There would be a reason for his call, and it had nothing to do with what she might be thinking. "I appreciate you touching base with me."

Dead air hummed between them.

"Look," he said, kicking off whatever he intended to say next.

Here it came. The real reason he had called.

"I had a call a little while ago from Detective Ronald Graves from the East Precinct."

She should have known this was coming. Rather than make small talk, she waited for him to continue.

"This homicide vic, Tark Brant, appears to have had a connection to Billy Hughes from the convenience store shooting back in July."

"Detective Graves thinks so as well," Finley stated noncommittally.

"Graves and I put our notes together, and we're in agreement that the true connection between Hughes and Brant is Carson Dempsey."

Fourteen months, one week, and three days after her husband was murdered, the cops finally put two and two together. Amazing.

"Maybe they were involved with Dempsey's son," she tossed back. "After all, Dempsey is a mover and shaker in this city. A major contributor to all the right political campaigns. A hero in his many, many charitable works. Surely he wouldn't employ thugs."

Houser's silence warned she had hit the mark with her sarcasm.

"One of the reports I read in Derrick's file," he finally said, "was where you insisted that Carson Dempsey ordered a hit on your husband because you put his son away."

Too little, too late.

And yet, every nerve in her body pulsed with frustration. "It seemed like the most likely scenario at the time."

"I'm beginning to think you might have been onto something," Houser confessed. "I'm just sorry we didn't see it sooner."

Oh yeah. Way too late.

"Particularly," he went on, "since you were in the vicinity of both Hughes's and Brant's murders."

Deep inside, Finley stilled. "What does that mean?"

"I'm thinking," Houser went on, "these two have been following you. Keeping tabs on you for their boss. The reason eludes me, but I really feel you need to be particularly careful, Ms. O'Sullivan. In a statement you made a couple of months after your release from the hospital, you mentioned three men who worked for Dempsey. You said they had been watching you."

"I hope you finally find some answers," Finley said without responding to his comment. "It would be nice to have some sort of closure."

"Had those two men been watching you before their deaths? It's been over a year since your husband was murdered. Seems like a long time to drag out whatever point they hoped to make."

"I've seen them around." It was true. "Well, not Hughes. Not since July. But that guy—Brant—and the other one."

"Flock," he confirmed. "Chet Flock."

"Yes, that's him."

"So, they still follow you around?"

"Not like before," she countered. Not at all like before. Before they'd had the upper hand. Not anymore. Before there had been three of them. Now there was only one.

"I'm planning to bring Flock in for questioning. I'll keep you informed on what I discover."

Finley should've kept her mouth shut from there, but she simply couldn't stop herself. "What's the point? Are you going after Dempsey for Derrick's murder? If not, why bother? Why not just close the case and be done with it?"

Finley bit her lips together. Damn. She'd broken her first and most important rule. *Don't say more than necessary. Ever.*

Houser had pushed the right button, and she'd been unable to keep quiet.

Damn it.

"I won't just close the case, Finley. You have my word on that. I will find the people who murdered your husband and who hurt you."

Too late. I already did.

Lena Marsh exited the clinic.

"Thanks for the update, Detective Houser. I have a meeting."

"I'll talk to you after my interview with Flock," he said quickly before she could end the call.

She tossed her cell into the passenger seat.

"Not holding my breath," she muttered as she prepared to exit the parking lot.

Marsh Residence
Lemont Drive, Nashville, 5:30 p.m.

The neighborhood Marsh called home was a quiet one on Nashville's far-east side. The houses were small, the yards even smaller. In the grand scheme of things, it was not a bad commute to anywhere around the city, and the housing prices were fairly reasonable, comparatively speaking.

Finley parked on the street. She didn't spot any dogs, so she climbed out and headed for the front door. Inside, country music played loud enough to be heard through the walls. A press of the bell, and the volume inside immediately lowered.

The door flew inward, and Lena Marsh glared at Finley. She blinked, then made a face that suggested she was confused.

"Can I help you?"

"Ms. Marsh, I'm Finley O'Sullivan."

Her look of confusion deepened. "I know who you are. Why are you here?" She glanced right to left. "I thought my neighbor was here to complain about my music again." She rolled her eyes. "It's an ongoing battle."

"You won't get any complaints from me. I love country music." Finley flashed a smile. "I work with the Finnegan law firm, and I'm here to speak with you about Jarrod Grady."

"How did you find out where I live?" She started to withdraw. "I don't think I'm allowed to talk to you."

"I understand your reluctance," Finley assured her. "I can call Detective Ventura—the detective handling the case—and we can go to his office and talk if you'd prefer." She shrugged. "Personally, I'd rather leave the cops out of this and just talk privately. Here on your home turf."

"What makes you think I even knew him?" Marsh rallied a final counter. "Really, you people will go to any lengths to get what you want."

Hmm. Did that mean she had something Finley wanted? "According to his wife, you and he were having an affair."

Her face paled. "She's lying."

Except the woman's expression and tone suggested she was the one lying.

"For now," Finley went on, "Mr. Finnegan and I are attempting to determine whether we need to go to the police with this information. It may be irrelevant to the investigation. But we need to be sure. If you can help us come to that conclusion, then you have nothing to worry about."

Marsh drew back, opening the door wider. "Yeah, okay. We can talk here."

Finley stepped inside and waited while she closed her door.

Marsh gestured to the sofa in the small living room. "Have a seat."

She crossed to the credenza, picked up the remote, and lowered the volume of her music a little more. Finley took a seat on the small sofa. It was more a love seat, considering the room wasn't really large enough for the average full-size sofa. With no other space for additional chairs, Marsh perched on the edge of the same love seat at the opposite end from Finley.

Finley tugged her notepad and pen from her bag. "When did you first meet Jarrod Grady?"

"At a party. Dr. Mengesha's wife's birthday party back in May. He had just started working with the catering company."

"The two of you started a relationship then," Finley asked. She vaguely recalled Mengesha mentioning he'd thrown his wife a huge party for her sixtieth birthday back in the spring.

Marsh nodded. "We were both single. Why not?"

"When did the relationship end?" This was the more relevant question.

"When he got serious with Ms. Winthrop, we stopped." She picked at the fabric on the arm of the beige mini sofa. "Then about a month ago we reconnected. It was an accident, and it only happened once. I haven't seen him since."

Her gaze remained fixed on the sofa or the floor, preventing Finley from analyzing her eyes and any tells that might appear in her expression. That alone was tell enough.

"You understand this makes you a suspect in his murder," Finley said. No point beating around the bush.

"I was not even in Nashville last weekend," she argued. "I was out of town."

Finley knew the answer before she asked. "Where were you?"

"That's none of your business. I didn't come back until noon on Sunday."

"Grady was out of town on Friday and Saturday. Were you with him?"

"I was not with him." She glared at Finley then. "I don't fool around with married men." She shook her head. "That one time was a mistake." She stood, squared her shoulders. "This interview is over." To punctuate the announcement, she walked to the door and opened it.

Finley got up and joined her at the door. She tugged a business card from her bag and handed it to Marsh. "Call me if you think of something else."

"Sure."

Finley hesitated. "Just so you know, your refusal to answer more of my questions only makes you look guilty."

When Marsh said nothing, Finley walked out, and the door slammed behind her. George Strait's voice immediately filled the air loudly enough to shake the neighbor's windows.

O'Sullivan Residence
Jackson Boulevard, Belle Meade, 8:00 p.m.

Forty-five—no, forty-six minutes. Finley had been in her childhood home for forty-six minutes, and already she wanted to light her hair on fire and go screaming through the night.

"Detective Houser dropped by my office today," the Judge announced.

They were in the middle of dinner, and Finley almost choked on a brussels sprout.

"Why?" Finley stared at her mother. Houser was supposed to be attempting an interview with Flock. What the hell?

"He's concerned about you," Ruth O'Sullivan said. She patted her lips with her white linen napkin. "A man with connections to the one in the convenience store shooting was murdered, and your car was spotted in the vicinity of the shooting."

"What on earth?" Bart O'Sullivan looked from his wife to his daughter. "Fin, what's going on?"

"Houser is making something out of nothing. I was at the Turnip Truck," Finley explained. "It was a pure coincidence that someone got themselves murdered across the street."

The Judge glared steadily at Finley. Finley stared back at her. Her father nodded and went back to his meal. Matt pretended the exchange had been about the weather.

"They have good produce," Bart commented. "But I haven't shopped there since the Trader Joe's came to White Bridge Road."

"Trader Joe's is the best," Finley agreed, flashing a grin for her father. He loved Trader Joe's. But mostly she did this because the Judge continued to watch her. The Turnip Truck was equally good.

"Judge, I'm hearing the mayor may not run again," Matt said, cutting through the tension by shifting the subject.

Thank you, Matt.

"His poll numbers are dwindling," the Judge agreed. "He'll be seventy on his next birthday. He's had a good run. A politician should never expect more than his constituents have already given him. When they're done, so is he."

The Judge loved Matt. She always thawed a little when he visited.

"He has indeed had a good run," Matt confirmed. "Do you have a favorite for replacing him?" He smiled. "I'm certain you've kept your thumb on the pulse of the up-and-comers."

A rare smile—at least rare in Finley's presence—tugged at the Judge's lips. "I have my thoughts on the matter, but I wouldn't lay any odds just yet."

"My vote's going to Solomon," Finley's father said. "She has big plans for the city."

"Oh, please," the Judge argued with her husband. "She's far too soft to handle the needs of this city. We need strength." She turned to Matt then. "I'm hearing rumors about you."

Matt grinned, ducked his head before meeting her gaze. "The governor has offered me the chief of staff position, and"—he glanced at Bart before settling his full attention on Finley—"I have officially accepted."

"That's fantastic." Finley reached across the table and squeezed his hand. "You deserve this kind of opportunity."

While her parents doled out the bravos, Finley relaxed. As long as the Judge's attention wasn't on her, she might even be able to enjoy dinner with her father. And Matt. She glanced at her mother as she laughed out loud, another rarity.

Ruth O'Sullivan was a beautiful woman when she smiled or laughed. Silver strands had invaded her dark hair, adding a sophisticated air to her natural beauty. Her eyes glittered when she smiled. The same dark eyes as Finley's. Finley had gotten her blonde hair from her father. His was fully gray now. Finley's, on the other hand, was more black than blonde at the moment. During the worst days after Derrick's murder, she had dyed it black. She hadn't wanted to be blonde anymore. But recently she had started to allow the black to grow out. Currently she had black hair with about two inches of blonde roots. The look was not a particularly good one, but she didn't care. In some circles she might even be considered a trendsetter.

Maybe she should get one of those short, spiky haircuts like Lena Marsh. That would get rid of the fading black and simultaneously freak out her mother.

Finley smiled, stabbed another brussels sprout, and poked it in her mouth. It was bad enough Finley had married Derrick, an apparent nobody, but then she'd had a psychotic episode and walked away from her position at the DA's office. On top of that, the most egregious offense of all, she had gone to work for Jack Finnegan—the devil himself in her mother's eyes.

The rift between her mother and Jack was still a mystery. They'd been best friends when they were young. Like Finley and Matt. Finley had called him Uncle Jack her whole life—until they'd started working together. Five years ago, his relationship with the family had been terminated by the Judge. Jack was no longer welcome in their home, period. There had been a falling-out of which no one who knew the details would speak.

A frown dragged at Finley's face. What had happened to her family? She'd always gone head-to-head with the Judge, but after the rift with Jack and then her marriage to Derrick, it had become something more than the usual mother-daughter disagreements. Somehow their relationship had rushed out of bounds on every level. They couldn't even share a meal without knives coming out. They were broken. Now, her father, who should be enjoying his retirement, spent far too much time trying to mend things. Playing the mediator. While she and her mother studiously ignored each other.

Jack was still considered an outsider.

And Derrick was dead.

Those forty-six minutes turned into an hour and then another one. Somehow Finley made it until ten o'clock. Two hours and forty-five minutes in the Judge's presence without a screaming match or one of them walking out.

All thanks to Matt.

When they loaded into his car, she told him so. "Thank you."

He started the engine. "For what?"

"For bringing me to dinner at my own mother's house—the house where I grew up—and making it tolerable. For giving my dad a much-needed family night with little or no tension." She shifted in the seat to look directly at him. "For being you. The best friend in the world."

He guided the car to the gate and waited for it to open. "It is always my pleasure to spend time with you and your family."

And that was it. The thing that bothered Finley so much. Matt was happy to do whatever she needed or wanted. While she left him in the dark.

There were so many things she wanted to tell him . . . but she couldn't. Sharing those secrets with him would only ensure he started digging into Derrick's case. But the guilt of withholding—of lying—grew heavier all the time.

As they drove through the night headed to the murder house, she understood there was more she needed to say before this night ended. Something, anything, to lighten the guilt suffocating her. Why was that so hard for her?

"Thank you again for taking care of me last night."

He braked at a stop sign and reached for her hand. "Fin, you never have to thank me for doing what friends are supposed to do."

She turned her palm up and entwined her fingers in his. "Thanks anyway. Sometimes . . ." She hesitated. Had to be careful not to drag her friend into this thing she couldn't find her way out of. "Sometimes . . . I'd be lost without you."

"You'll never be lost, Fin, because I'll always be here."

She suddenly wondered if Matt would still consider her a friend if he knew about what had happened with Brant.

What would her father think?

Jack would be concerned, but he'd blow it off or at least pretend to. He'd toss out one of his favorite lines. *I already know I'm going to hell, kid. At this point I figure it's go big or go home.*

The Judge would officially disown her.

Finley faced forward.

Jesus Christ. What the hell had she become?

17

The Widow

9:00 p.m.

Winthrop Financial Consulting Group
Commerce Street, Nashville

The day had been a long one. Ellen had been visited by Detective Ventura and his newly assigned partner, Detective Lindale. She had summoned Jack, and he had arrived posthaste. More questions. More details. Ellen reminded herself repeatedly that patience was essential at this juncture.

It was the repetition that annoyed her.

But the day was done now. She gazed around the room at the women who made her so very proud each day. The women who brought tremendous joy and fulfillment to her life. This project had been their most difficult trial yet, but they would get through the unpleasant ordeal.

"Where are we on tracking the money?" Ellen looked to Liz to brief the group on her latest findings. The money truly was irrelevant to Ellen. But for Liz it was a matter of pride. She took herself to task for not watching more closely.

It wasn't her fault. Ellen had attempted to no avail to reassure her.

Liz was an incredible forensic accountant. If the money could be found and rerouted, she would make it happen. The others weren't concerned so much with the loss of the money but with the idea of who ended up in possession of the large sum. Ellen agreed that such a sum would prove far more useful as a donation to a worthy cause. This made Liz all the more frantic to find it.

No one had anticipated this level of talent with the manipulation of the missing funds. Yet another indicator that Ellen's worst fears could very well be true. No matter. However good Jarrod and his coconspirator were, Liz was far better.

"I have located the funds." Liz looked around the room, basking in the approving gazes of her partners. "I'm confident I will have the full sum moved to our new secure location in the next seventy-two hours."

"This is very good news." Ellen nodded, producing an approving smile. "Well done, Liz. Well done indeed."

Liz had been following the path of the money from day one. Every computer here and at home to which Jarrod had been allowed access had been loaded with the required software to trace his every move, his every keystroke. Vivian had insisted. As head of security, she'd been allowed to make the decision. A good one, as it turned out.

"What about the detective?" Daisy piped up, shifting the conversation to the more pressing matter. "I saw two of them in your office today, Ellen. The lawyer was here as well."

No doubt she and Joanna had discussed the visit at length. Daisy and Joanna were the most pragmatic of the group. They were the worriers. Whenever a kink found its way into ongoing activities, those were the two who fretted the most. But it was no surprise that Jessica was the one who appeared the most uncertain. Her silence spoke loudly of her feelings. Poor Jessica. The youngest and neediest of the five. Of those gathered around the table, she was the one who had given the most to this project. Save Ellen, of course. Perhaps, as Laney had suggested, that had been a mistake. At times the strength of these women allowed Ellen to forget that they were only human.

"The visit was expected," she assured.

"The level of personal involvement in this project," Vivian countered, "has been off putting, Ellen. We should rethink this sort of strategy going forward."

Ellen couldn't agree more. "This was a special situation," she reminded all, "but as I recall, the vote was unanimous."

No one argued. They couldn't.

Even Ellen still felt somewhat unsettled at how easily the situation had gone so far awry. On some level, she feared certain things had changed . . . forever. Soon, she hoped to more fully understand the scope of the failure.

"We've been here before." Ellen surveyed the women seated around the table where they had voted time and again on whether to proceed with their special work. "The steps are more complicated with this one, yes. Despite the unfortunate deviation from our plan, we did not miss a beat. We neutralized the unexpected and regrouped in record time. Rest assured we are right where we need to be."

Four of the five nodded, their concerns assuaged. But not Jessica. She wanted Ellen to see the depth of her dissatisfaction. Perhaps the tactic was intended as proof she was not the weak link in the group. She had performed well enough today with her added duty. Was this sudden attitude about flexing her newly gained muscle?

"Is there something you wish to add, Jessica?"

She feigned surprise, and her eyes rounded, then narrowed. "No. Of course not."

Ellen held her gaze. "It feels as if you do."

The position in which Jessica found herself was perhaps not entirely her fault. Her youth and beauty had placed her in a difficult spot. Had made her more *his* peer. Ellen had noticed that *he* noticed. When Jessica came to her, Ellen had encouraged her to allow this development to play out. It would no doubt work to their advantage.

The decision had clearly been a mistake.

Jessica lifted her chin and blurted what was on her mind. "The vote was unanimous, yes, but it was a bad decision. This—what we do—can never again be personal. It's far too important."

The others kept their attention fixed on Ellen in anticipation of her reaction. None of the others would have dared to dress Ellen down in this manner. Jessica clearly felt she had earned the right to speak out more strongly. Or perhaps the move was merely an attempt to disparage Ellen in front of the others.

Either way, it was enough. They moved forward, not backward.

Ellen stared directly at Jessica as she spoke. "We will do what we have always done." Then she glanced around the table. "Any more questions?"

There were none. They had done what they had to do.

They would always do the necessary.

Ellen's gaze landed on Jessica once more. *Always.*

Moments later, when the others filed out of the conference room, Vivian stayed behind. When the door had closed, leaving the two of them alone, Vivian turned to Ellen.

"I know," Ellen said before she could say a word. "She's forgotten her place."

Vivian released a heavy breath. "We coddled her far too long, I fear. Now she's rebelling."

It was true. Jessica was the youngest. Her life before Ellen found her had been less than optimal. Her parents had not known how to handle their child prodigy. Ellen had changed all that, but apparently, the damage had been done. Or perhaps Jessica had simply grown selfish of late. Either way, Jessica had made a mistake, and the others now waited for the other shoe to drop.

"We'll give her every opportunity," Ellen insisted. "There's still time for her to turn this around."

Vivian nodded, but the doubt lining her face was undeniable. "Good night, Ellen."

"Good night."

Ellen stayed behind for a time after Vivian was gone. She needed a moment alone.

The walls around her remained dark, giving her the privacy she needed.

She stared at the reports and photos Vivian and Liz had prepared for the meeting. Fury ripped through Ellen. She snatched at the photo of Jarrod. Ripped it to shreds, her fingers fumbling, her heart bursting beneath her breastbone.

Bastard!

She threw the torn pieces in the air . . . collapsed into her chair and fought the ache of a scream in her throat.

Yes, mistakes had been made this time. And hers was the worst.

How had she allowed him so close?

An emotional entanglement hadn't been part of the strategy. How had she allowed him to touch her so deeply?

What he had done over and over was unforgivable.

And still she had not been able to resist.

She had known. She. Had. Known. None of those he had victimized were ever able to resist him.

But Ellen had believed herself above such weaknesses.

She had been wrong.

Time was required for her to gather her wits about her. Eventually Ellen stood. She tidied the mess she had made before taking the file and dropping it into the shredder.

The first stage of the plan was complete. There had been collateral damage, yes. But that was the way of battles at times. She just hadn't expected the fight to come from within her ranks.

Ellen was not ready to give up on salvaging the situation just yet.

She cleared the footage of her momentary lapse from the security video before leaving the building. There must be no evidence of her weakness for the others to see. This was a very difficult time for all of them.

There could be no hesitation and no more mistakes.

She would see this finished . . . whatever the cost.

18

The Receptionist

11:30 p.m.

The Murder House
Shelby Avenue, Nashville

So this was where the hotshot investigator lived. Lena had seen some dumps in her day, but this one took the cake. Based on what she knew of the clever Finley O'Sullivan, it suited her. Her highly publicized big fall made this address the perfect landing.

Or maybe it was a disguise for whatever she was hiding.

Lena knew all about the things people hid. The secrets and lies. Everyone did it. And she was really good at spotting those lies. For years she had read the patient files of their targets. Oh, the lies they told . . . the secrets they kept. Life truly was stranger than fiction. All those years of experience had made her quite adept at reading those around her. Like the jerk neighbor who bugged the shit out of her. The man was a perv with nothing better to do than to watch other people's lives.

She saw through the group who worked for Ellen Winthrop too. So high and mighty. So self-righteous. Some people thought money made them better than everyone else. Lena laughed out loud. They thought they knew it all. But they were wrong. They didn't know Lena. She had recognized the trouble was not going to just go away, and she had tried to warn Jarrod. The idiot wouldn't listen. She'd even told him again when he dropped the half mil off on Saturday. He'd told his stupid wife that his flight was delayed, but that had been a lie. He couldn't exactly take the money home with him, he'd said with a laugh.

Lena had given him one last chance. Take the money and run. But he'd wanted to finish his little game. Fool. He'd always been obsessive like that. She'd had to clean up his messes before. That last one had required drastic measures. Lena was not going down that road again.

The whole situation, then and now, had escalated completely out of control.

Jarrod should have spotted this ruse a mile away. Lena had tried to tell him it was too easy. But he'd thought he was so smart, and yet he'd missed all the signs. He'd gotten them into one hell of a mess. If that weren't bad enough, he'd stupidly thought another woman—one right under his new wife's nose—was the answer.

What a fool.

Lena had recognized where the game was headed a month ago, and she'd hedged her bets. Unlike Jarrod's, her backup plan was a good one. He liked going straight to the top, going for the brass ring. But Lena had a different approach. She looked for the weakest link . . . the person who had the most to gain.

She had been right in her choice.

Honestly, when all was said and done, it was a miracle her and Jarrod's partnership had lasted this long. They'd had some good times and come out ahead every single round. Lived the good life between gigs. But she understood now that trusting him so completely for so long had been a mistake. Trusting *her* might have been an even bigger mistake. Lena couldn't be sure on that one just yet.

The twitch of a smile tickled her lips. Well, there was that little matter of the insurance policy Lena held on to. The 7.8 mil combined with the half mil equaled a hell of a lot of money.

No one would just turn their back on that kind of cash. Only J. Grady could access the money. Lena had half the necessary PIN. Without her, no one was touching that money. She and Jarrod had always shared their accounts without the worry of codes or PINs. They trusted only each other with the money.

But now it was different.

If this thing went south, there was only one thing she could do: disappear and live happily and wealthily ever after with the money she and Jarrod had stashed away over the years.

Not a hardship.

Lena might be what those bitches considered plain white trash, but she had learned from the best.

The investigator's visit to the clinic and then to her home had warned Lena she had been made. Finley O'Sullivan would figure out her game in a heartbeat. No problem. Lena knew just what to do. She would give the dogged investigator a little something to shake things up.

It was the first rule of high-stakes grifting.

Always have a backup plan to your backup plan.

19

Wednesday, September 21

6:28 a.m.

The Murder House
Shelby Avenue, Nashville

Finley woke suddenly.

She blinked, glanced at her alarm clock. Two minutes until it burst into its rude clanging.

Then why the hell was she awake?

Pecking from outside echoed through her house.

What the hell?

She sat up. Pushed her hair out of her face. Her first thought was a bird. A woodpecker maybe.

A swiping sound, then more pecking. Maybe not just one bird.

Her feet hit the floor and she stood. Someone or something was out there poking around her house.

She considered the idea of a rat invasion. Or maybe a family of birds nested in the eaves. More pecking and swiping. Damn it. There was definitely something out there.

Dragging her fingers across the bedside table, she snagged a hair tie. On her way through the house, she wrangled her hair into a ponytail. More bumping and thumping outside.

Definitely not birds or rats.

She eased to the front window by the door and peeked beyond the blinds. No one on the porch or in the front yard. Then she spotted Jack's SUV behind her Subaru.

What was he doing here at this time of morning?

At the door she slid on her flip-flops and stepped outside. She eased around the left front corner of the house. No Jack. She moved on to the rear corner and into the backyard. Jack stood in the center of her overgrown yard staring up at something. Her roof? The ancient antennae attached to the back of her house? The sagging soffit?

Worse than his oddly timed visit, he wore jeans and a tee. It was Wednesday. A workday.

Oh hell.

"Jack?"

He swung his face in her direction. "Sorry, kid. Did I wake you?"

Just then she heard the clang of her alarm clock through the wall.

She shook her head. "It was time for me to get up anyway." She noted the pencil behind his ear and the notepad in his hand. "What're you doing?"

"Your house needs painting." He pulled out the pencil and made notes on the pad. "Yellow or white, maybe. The green roof kind of limits your color options."

The roof was so old it was actually more of a dingy blackish gray than green, but he was right; color options were sort of limited.

She shook her head. "I need coffee." She hitched her head toward the house. "Come inside. We'll talk."

He followed her inside without argument. Finding her boss in jeans and a tee contemplating color options meant one thing: he was on the edge. Somewhere, probably in the Rover, would be a bottle of bourbon.

He always kept one handy when the craving hit. Some might see his need to keep his demons so close as a bad thing. It worked for Jack, and that was all that counted.

Finley popped into her bedroom and shut off the alarm before prepping the coffeepot and setting it to brew.

Jack sat down on the sofa and studied the notes he'd made. Finley pushed aside a pile of folders and notes she'd been reviewing on the Winthrop case and plopped into her fave chair.

"What's going on?" she asked, hoping it wasn't what she feared.

The case was one of those confounding ones that likely wouldn't turn out the way Jack preferred, but otherwise all was well in the world of the firm. This wasn't like the Legard case from a few months ago, when Jack had been personally involved to a degree. What had him teetering on the edge with his demons this time?

He tossed his notepad aside. "I'm worried about you, Fin."

Ah, so he'd heard about Brant. Did everyone know? "When did you hear the news?"

"Last night. The Judge called me."

Finley rolled her eyes, wished her mother would stay out of her life.

Wait. What? "She called you? Not one of her minions or my dad? *She* called you?"

Jack gave a nod. "Don't blame her," he said. He consistently gave the Judge the benefit of the doubt, no matter that she had not given him that same latitude.

"You always give her too much leeway," Finley argued.

"She has a right to be worried," Jack said pointedly. "She's your mother, and Detective Graves told her you were in the vicinity of where Brant's murder happened—in the ballpark of time of death. I checked with Nita, and she confirmed you were in the area for a meeting."

"I was at the Turnip Truck," Finley griped. "I can't help what happens nearby where I'm shopping for veggies."

"Ruth told me you lied about why you were there."

The Judge was guessing. Fishing around for a reaction, and she'd gotten the one she wanted from Jack. Damn it.

"Why do you put up with her?" Finley demanded, shifting the focus. "After a lifetime of friendship, she suddenly kicks you out of her life five years ago, and now she's bending your ear about me like she doesn't privately and publicly shun you most of the time."

"What happened back then wasn't her fault," Jack said wearily. "It was mine. I had fallen off the wagon, and she was trying to help me. I did things . . . said things, Fin. Terrible things. To her."

A full five seconds were required for Finley to fully absorb his words. "What kind of things?"

Jack never hurt anyone—except his opponent in the courtroom, and that was expected. He and the Judge had been best friends for decades.

All this time she had wondered what happened. Wanted to know. Both the Judge and Jack had stayed mum. She visually examined the sadness and defeat on Jack's face. Suddenly she wasn't so sure she wanted to know.

What if this was some awful something she couldn't unhear? There were things like that. Things you saw or heard that couldn't be unseen or unheard. Things that stayed with you forever, sucking the life out of you.

"I told her a secret I should have kept to myself."

The scent of coffee snapped Finley from her troubling musings and had her holding up a hand. "Pause right there. We both need coffee." She had a feeling he needed it worse than she did.

She hurried into the kitchen. Rinsed old coffee dregs from a couple of mugs before filling them. She walked back into the living room with two steaming mugs of coffee. She passed one to him and said, "Continue." Though she was even less sure now that she wanted him to.

His continued hesitation caused her tension to escalate even as she guzzled coffee, scalding her throat. She winced, had to stop doing that.

"I guess it's time you knew," he stated with a big sigh. "I've kept you in the dark too long." He shook his head, peered into the mug of hot brew. "I was a fool. I spent most of my younger years madly in love with her, but I never told her. That was my first mistake."

Finley almost dropped her cup. "You were in love with my mother." It wasn't a question. She'd heard him just fine. The words had somehow burst out of her, like an echo bouncing off a rock wall.

"Yeah." He tested the coffee and then downed a slug. "She loved me, too, but not that way. And it was best she didn't. I knew by the time I was nearing the end of law school that I had a serious drinking problem. She didn't need a man like me, but that didn't keep me from wanting her. When she married your father, I tried to move on. I went from one disastrous relationship to another. Nothing stuck. Eventually, I told myself it didn't matter. I had plenty of companionship, and by then I had you." He smiled at Finley. "When your mother asked me to be your godfather, I almost cried. It meant so much to me. And for a long time, it was enough. I poured my heart and soul into work. The work, mine and Ruth's friendship, and you were enough. Hell, I even grew to love Bart."

Finley managed a choked laugh. But she understood what he meant. "I'm pretty sure he loves you too."

"Which makes what I did five years ago all the worse," Jack said, the weariness or maybe sadness back. "It was late one night, and I stopped by the Judge's office to talk about a case. Everyone was gone. It was just the two of us. I'd fallen off the wagon weeks before, but I'd managed to keep it hidden. Until that night."

Finley held her breath.

"I don't know what snapped or short-circuited in my brain, but I tried to kiss her. Told her I'd always loved her. Couldn't stop. Then I crossed a line even she couldn't forgive me for. By then I was angry and shouting. I said you should have been my daughter, not Bart's."

Finley wanted to be angry that Jack would do such a stupid, selfish, disrespectful thing with no regard for the impact on her father—but she couldn't. What she felt was sympathy, sadness. Regret. For both of them. For her mother too.

"The way she looked at me." Jack stared into his mug once more. "Such pain and shock. I had betrayed her. All those years I never told her how I felt, and then I pretended to be something I wasn't. That's what she said. I pretended to be her friend and acted as if nothing had changed after she married Bart." He exhaled a big breath. "She was right. I was wrong. No matter how many times I apologized, she wouldn't let me back into her life." He looked straight at Finley then. "I don't blame her either. I'm an alcoholic. She can't trust me. She loves Bart, and she wants to protect him."

Everything Jack had just said somehow opened Finley's eyes. She'd never considered that her mother might be protecting her father in some way with this standoff. The Judge always seemed to put him in second place behind her and what she wanted.

The reality that Finley might have been wrong all this time was a hard pill to swallow. But there was one glaring question.

"Why would she need to protect my dad from you?" Finley asked. That part didn't make complete sense to her. Just because Jack cared about her mother didn't mean he would hurt her father. She refused to believe any such thing. His admission itself was disrespectful, hurtful, thoughtless, but Jack hadn't taken it further, had he?

"My opinion?" He stared at Finley a moment. "I can't say for sure, but to this day I make myself feel better by thinking that maybe, just maybe, she was in love with me too. Once," Jack clarified while Finley scrambled to catch up.

"We were both so focused on school and building our careers," he went on, "and you know how damned hardheaded we are. Anyway, I think she was in love with me back then, and she was afraid I didn't feel the same, so she went on with her life. Just like I did because I thought exactly that about her. When I drunkenly admitted this to her all those years later, I think she was angry at what we'd thrown away. At my terrible timing."

Holy shit. "You believe, even then—just five years ago—she was still, on some level, in love with you too."

He nodded. "But she wouldn't hurt Bart that way. Or you. Not to mention there was her career to consider."

Finley wasn't sure how to feel about this. Was the idea even plausible? The concept of her mother being in love with Jack seemed . . . a bit far fetched. But—she gazed at the sadness in Jack's eyes—if believing as much made him feel better, why not?

"I'm only telling you this," Jack went on, "because your mother doesn't deserve the rift between the two of you. It's time it ended."

Finley held up a hand. "I get what you're saying, but I'm not sure I can forgive her for the way she treated Derrick."

Jack nodded. "I understand how you might feel that way, but you need to try to get right with what she did. Especially if you're going to keep trying to get yourself killed."

"I didn't try to get myself killed." She held up her hands to stop him before he could argue with the statement. "The incident in the convenience store notwithstanding," she confessed. "What happened with Brant was totally out of my control. I went to the location to meet a woman who said she had information about Derrick. But it was a setup."

"Jesus Christ," Jack muttered. "You couldn't call me for backup?"

"It was stupid," she admitted. "I should have played it smarter. Anyway, she turned out to be Brant's girlfriend."

She related the details to Jack, his face going paler with each statement she uttered.

He shook his head. "You gotta have a guardian angel, kid. Damn. It's a flat-out miracle she didn't kill you."

Regrettably, he was probably right about that. Funny how sometimes the idea bothered her and other times it didn't. A smart person would share this troubling dilemma with her therapist.

Finley wasn't so sure she considered herself smart anymore.

"I need you," Jack said in his "I'm the boss" voice, "to stay away from Dempsey and his people. I swear if you'll let me, I will help you find the truth."

"No way. I'm not dragging you or Matt into this."

"Let's break this down," Jack argued. "The one who killed Derrick is dead."

She nodded.

"The one who hurt you is dead."

"Yeah."

"Then back off, and let's finish this the right way. Stay away from the third guy, and let's go about this in a way that gets the man who is actually responsible for what happened."

"The only way I will agree is if we make a verbal contract that we don't do anything without talking about it first." She didn't want Jack charging into any unpredictable situation related to Dempsey without her next to him.

"You have my word," he agreed.

"Good." She would try her best to do the same. "Now, finish your coffee, go back to your place, change, and get to the office. We need a meeting with Winthrop. We have to talk about all these inconsistencies."

He raised an eyebrow at her. "She's not going to like it," he warned.

"The trouble is, if I can find the inconsistencies, so can Ventura if he looks hard enough. It's just a matter of time. We can't properly defend her if we don't have all the details." Her boss knew this better than anyone.

Jack laughed. "The lady reminds me of you. She doesn't want to listen, but I'll give it the old college try."

Either way, Finley needed to satisfy her former-assistant-district-at-torney urges. Maybe finding answers was her addiction. Of all people, she was well aware just how dangerous secrets could be. The longer they were kept, the bigger and darker they grew.

The idea that Jack thought she and Winthrop were alike in some ways shouldn't bother her, but it did. He was right, though. How the hell had two strong, smart, determined women screwed up so badly when it came to men?

When Jack was gone, Finley rinsed their mugs and turned off the coffee maker. She got dressed and psyched herself up for the meeting with Winthrop. The part that bugged Finley the most was that if the woman wasn't guilty of any wrongdoing and her husband was the bad guy here, why all the secrets?

Why not just come clean with her defense attorney?

They were on the same side—*her* side.

Finley couldn't deny being a master at keeping secrets, but there was a time and place to come clean, as she'd done with Jack just now. Winthrop needed to recognize that time had come.

Finley grabbed her bag and keys and headed out. She locked her door and started toward her Subaru.

A crash in the garage drew her attention there. She walked in that direction, noticed the side door wasn't fully closed. She hadn't been in the garage in ages. Had Jack poked around in there while he was here this morning?

Finley pushed the door inward. With no windows, the interior was pitch dark. She opened the door wider, allowing more light inside. A stack of boxes filled with junk she'd moved out of her condo had over-turned. Thankfully the boxes were taped shut, so the contents weren't scattered all over the dusty floor. She had to go through that stuff one of these days.

"Damn it." She searched for the switch and turned on the light.

"Stay right there!"

Finley's gaze swerved to the woman who'd shouted the command. *Whitney Lemm.*

She held a shovel like a weapon. Finley knew the shovel well. Back in July she'd used it to dig dozens of holes in her backyard in search of . . . nothing, it seemed. Just a wild-goose chase her nosy neighbor had prompted with tales of having seen Derrick digging around back there before Finley moved in with him. All she'd found was the remains of a family pet that had been buried there years ago.

What in the hell was Brant's girlfriend doing here? "Whitney, you—"

"Just . . . just don't move," she ordered, her voice shaking.

"What're you doing here?" Finley figured she could get out the door before the woman could get close enough to hit her with the shovel, but her curiosity got the better of her. Why on earth would she show up here?

Lemm's lips started to tremble, and tears spilled down her cheeks. "I don't know what to do. They're going to kill me. I can't go to the police because too many of them are in his pocket."

"Whose pocket?"

She made a face. "Don't be stupid. Carson Dempsey, who else? Tark told me the kind of shit his boss does. That's how I knew he'd kill me when he found me with you. I was fucked and I knew it. Now he's dead and I'm still fucked."

Finley figured her assessment was accurate. "What you need is someone to tell your side of what happened." She needed Jack. Maybe Finley had lost her mind, but it was partly her fault this woman was in trouble. "I tell you what, Whitney. My boss is the best defense attorney in Nashville. He can help you. And I know a detective we can trust." At least she hoped she could trust him. So far, she had no reason not to trust Eric Houser.

"I'm not talking to no one unless I have some kind of protection deal."

171

Finley couldn't say she blamed her. "First, let's get you someplace where you'll be safe until we figure this out."

The woman's grip tightened on the shovel. "How do I know I can trust you?"

"You don't. But you have no reason not to trust me, either, which is more than you can say for Dempsey and his people and whatever cops you think are in his pocket."

The woman lowered the shovel and tossed it to the floor. "Makes sense."

"I have no reason to want to hurt you," Finley promised. "But I need some time to figure this out."

Whitney nodded. "Okay. So what do we do?"

"First, we get you out of here. Flock watches me the same way Brant did."

Her red and swollen eyes widened. "If he finds me . . ."

"We're not going to let that happen. We'll figure this out."

After some mental scrambling, Finley pulled her Subaru to the garage and ushered Whitney into the back seat. She stayed hunkered down while Finley drove to a motel on the far-west side of Nashville. On the way she got food since Whitney said she hadn't eaten since the shooting.

All Whitney had to do was stay in the room with the curtains closed and the door locked until she heard from Finley. She wasn't to call anyone or go out for any reason. She had Finley's number as well as the number at the firm. She would be safe as long as she stayed put.

All Finley had to do was figure out where to go from there.

Lemm could potentially corroborate Carson Dempsey's illegal activities. Maybe, just maybe, she was the break Finley had been looking for.

20

10:15 a.m.

The Finnegan Firm
Tenth Avenue, Nashville

On the way to the motel, Finley had notified Jack that she would be a little later getting in than she'd anticipated. She stayed mum about the reason to avoid making her rear-seat passenger, who'd stayed ducked down on the floorboard for most of the journey, more nervous than she already was.

When Whitney was safely tucked away, Finley drove to the office. A couple of reporters had taken up residence in the parking lot. Both shouted questions at her as she hurried inside. When she had dropped her bag in her office, she glanced out her window and spotted Winthrop's black limo navigated by her longtime driver, Amy Petropoulos, rolling into the parking lot. Finley grabbed her bottle of water and headed for the conference room. Jack was already there, reviewing his notes.

"She's here."

Jack glanced up from the top of his reading glasses. "All righty then. Here we go."

Finley stood behind her chair and Jack pushed to his feet as Nita showed Winthrop to the conference room. She'd come alone. Smart. The narrative from her side was easier to control that way. No one to abruptly blurt anything not approved for being passed along. It was a clever strategy coming from a woman who, judging by her university transcripts and track record in the business world, really was a true genius.

As always, Winthrop was dressed to perfection. Elegant, polished suit. Flawless hair and makeup. She looked sharp. Her clear, firm gaze suggested she was ready for battle. Too bad she still hadn't recognized that they were on the same side.

She and Jack exchanged greetings as she chose the chair directly across from Finley's. Finley nodded and settled into her own.

"Thank you for making time for our impromptu request," Jack said as he resumed his seat.

"Do you have news for me?" Winthrop asked with believable innocence.

"No news, which is likely a good thing," Jack said. "Of course, we all recognize the investigation is in high gear, but the longer it continues without any sort of discovery, the better for us. Bottom line, if they had something, we would know it. So obviously they don't."

Not that the police were always forthcoming in a timely manner, Finley didn't bother to add. But with a murder case, particularly one involving a high-profile family in a prestigious neighborhood, they would want to make an arrest sooner rather than later.

"We do, however"—Finley picked up from there—"have a few questions on areas of concern."

"I'm here." Winthrop presented her with a smile that showed a certain weariness around the edges. "Let's get the issues ironed out, shall we?"

"We need to ensure our response regarding the affair or affairs," Finley said, surveying her notes, which weren't notes at all, just a list of things she needed to add to her Walmart pickup order, "is consistent and as concise as possible. Less is more."

"The answer I gave you is the only truthful response. To my knowledge, Jarrod's relationship with Lena Marsh ended before he and I married. I wasn't happy to learn of his continued relationship with her once we were officially a couple, but it happened, and I was justifiably upset. That affair is the only one I know about."

Lie. It wasn't that Finley didn't want to believe Winthrop. It was simple. She recognized a lie when she heard one. It was too blunt. Too emotionless. And there was the tiny little detail of the way her eyes glazed over to control any emotion that trickled through her. The motive was easy enough to understand. What woman wanted to admit that her husband had carried on one or more affairs?

"We may encounter an issue there, since the statement given by Ms. Marsh doesn't match yours," Jack said, drawing Winthrop's attention to him.

Winthrop smiled. "I fear what we're dealing with here is a woman who sees an opportunity and hopes to gain from it. I feel confident a closer look into her background will confirm as much."

Jack gave her a nod. "We're working on a better grasp on who Marsh is as we speak."

"The more pressing issue," Finley said, drawing their client's attention once more, "is access to the murder weapon."

Winthrop flinched at the term. Good. It was important that she started acting like a grieving widow. Perception was immensely important.

Like you have room to talk.

Finley gritted her teeth. She really needed to turn that little voice off. It had become annoyingly more vocal of late.

Winthrop reached into the bag she'd placed in the chair next to her chair and retrieved a clear plastic sandwich-size bag. She placed it on the table and slid it toward Finley.

"We hired a forensic evidence team of our own. Nothing against the team from the police department, but I'm not one to leave things to chance. Our team found this hidden in a pair of Jarrod's socks."

"You hired a team," Jack said, his tone reflecting his surprise at the development, "without discussing the move with me. I should remind you, Ellen, that every step you make is under scrutiny. Leaving your legal team in the dark is not a smart move."

Well said, Finley thought but kept to herself. She and Jack should have been a part of the decision as well as any steps taken since making any discoveries.

"You'll have to forgive me," Winthrop said. "I'm accustomed to handling issues without hesitation or asking for permission."

Jack made some response, but Finley focused on the bag. She picked it up and studied the device inside. Black, fairly small. "Is this some sort of eavesdropping device?" she asked when their back-and-forth lapsed. It resembled ones she had seen before.

"When placed very close to an electronic locking device," Winthrop explained, "it copies the access code, which can be retrieved by whoever installed it."

Aha. Finley had wondered if and when such a device would be found. This could potentially rule out Ellen and her partners as suspects by proving Grady had access to the home office and had possibly shared that access information with someone else. Such as Marsh or some other partner. Like the thus-far-unidentified J. Grady.

"This could be very helpful to our defense," Jack said, still sounding annoyed, "but we'll need to prove Grady purchased it."

Winthrop reached into her bag once more and withdrew a single folded sheet of paper. She handed it to Jack.

Jack opened the document and had a look, then passed it to Finley. It was the copy of a receipt from a Nashville spy shop. Grady's signature was sprawled across the bottom of the receipt. The receipt was dated one month ago. A copy of the credit card used was included on the single page.

"It's difficult to believe we'd been married barely a month when he did this." Winthrop turned away, blinking rapidly to fight the tears shining in her eyes.

"I think," Jack said, "it's safe to say he had this planned from the moment the two of you met. I apologize for my bluntness, but this is not the time to tiptoe around the details."

Jack was right. Finley had believed that to be the case from the beginning. Grady had an agenda from the outset.

Like Derrick.

She pushed the thought away. "Let's talk about some of the things that may come up at trial," she suggested, "if it reaches that point."

"Why would it?" Winthrop asked, seeming irritated that Finley would suggest as much.

"The district attorney's office sometimes makes decisions that no one else understands." Finley turned her hands up at Winthrop's questioning look. "I was an ADA for four years. Decisions aren't always based on the seemingly perfectly aligned evidence. There are times when a hunch or a gut feeling takes precedence."

"What's your gut feeling, Finley?" Winthrop stared directly into Finley's eyes as she waited for the response.

Finley glanced at Jack; he gave her a nod. She turned back to their client. "My gut tells me you're hiding something and your partners are helping you."

Surprise flared in the other woman's eyes.

"That said"—Jack grabbed the baton and ran with it—"we will do all within our power to prevent the case from moving to trial and to defend you if it does. Our only concern is that we may be blindsided in the courtroom if you are keeping anything from us. We can only properly defend what we know."

Winthrop laughed softly. "You have my word that you have everything we know. And like this latest find"—she gestured to the device in the bag—"if we become aware of anything new, you will be the first to know." She turned to Finley. "Do you not trust me, Finley? Or perhaps you see me as a fool for having fallen for a man so much younger."

"As I've explained before," Finley offered, not wanting to elevate the tension any further, "it's my job to play devil's advocate. To make sure nothing the police find can connect our client—you—to the crime." She shrugged. "To analyze every explanation you provide for cracks a good detective can capitalize on. It's not about whether I trust you or believe in your innocence or your intelligence level. My singular motive is keeping you from a murder charge."

Winthrop nodded. "Your responses are always very specific and quite compelling, even if you didn't answer my questions."

Finley almost smiled. Touché. "I don't know you well enough to trust you, Ellen. At this point, however, I have no reason not to trust you. As for your love life choices, I'm confident, considering my own history, that you understand I am the last person who should make judgment calls in that area."

"I appreciate your candor." Winthrop held Finley's gaze a moment longer. "We've both suffered significantly at the hands of our relationship choices."

"We have." Finley decided they had reached a sort of breakthrough with this meeting. An understanding of sorts.

"Very well. I think we're all on the same page," Jack announced, closing the folder on his notes. "We will follow up on Lena Marsh, and we'll continue to prompt Detective Ventura about finding the person who murdered your husband. If you haven't already," he suggested, "you should start making funeral arrangements. Any further delay will be perceived as uncaring or perhaps guilty. The world is watching right now, Ellen. Don't give them anything to use against you."

She nodded. "Thank you. I'll keep that in mind, and yes, I have started arrangements. Something simple." To Finley she said, "Under the circumstances I've decided on cremation."

"Understandable, but I wouldn't make that public," Finley advised. "The decision could be seen as an opportunity to conceal evidence the police may not yet know to look for."

Winthrop nodded, conceding the point.

Jack saw their client out, fending off the reporters. Finley grabbed her notepad but lingered in the conference room. The morning had been intense with Jack's abrupt revelation and then the need to get Brant's girlfriend to a safe place. Finley had hardly had the time to consider the info dump about Jack and the Judge.

How had she missed Jack's true feelings for the Judge? He'd always been such a good friend to Finley's father—to the whole family. It was a shock. And the idea that her mother might have felt the same way . . .

Finley gave herself a shake. Hard to believe. Since adolescence she'd considered her mother cold. She'd wondered how her father, who was so demonstrative with his feelings, had tolerated her standoffishness.

Finley loved Jack, but she loved her father more. She wouldn't want to have to choose between them.

Had the Judge felt that way when Jack drunkenly announced his true feelings? Had she loved Jack and Bart, but all those years of marriage and having a child had tipped the scales in her husband's favor?

"You pick up any vibes today?"

Finley jerked from the thoughts and looked to Jack standing in the doorway of the conference room. "She's still not being completely forthcoming. Whether it's relevant to who murdered her husband or the circumstances surrounding his death, the jury is still out."

"You should check with the spy shop and confirm Grady bought the code grabber there."

"My next destination," she agreed.

Jack nodded. But he didn't move.

The silence twisted like barbed wire around Finley. She didn't want to feel this uncertainty . . . this uneasiness. Not with Jack. Not ever.

"We okay, kid?"

She walked toward him until they stood face to face. "Whatever happens, past, present, or future," she said, "we will always be okay, Jack Finnegan."

Spy Shop
Fesslers Parkway, Nashville, 12:15 p.m.

The low-roofed midcentury-style building sported a generic spy logo in black against tan brick. The shop was in a more commercial area on the fringes of Nashville proper. Not the sort of place one would notice while out shopping or having dinner. To find this shop, a buyer would need to have either taken a recommendation from a friend or searched the internet. It wasn't exactly on the beaten path or easily spotted.

Finley nosed into a slot right next to the entrance. She got out, grabbed her messenger bag, and pushed the door shut with her hip. She surveyed the area. The large parking lot served a number of other businesses, but none appeared to be particularly busy. The area was quiet, only a few vehicles around. There was none save hers near the spy shop, but according to her internet search, it was open.

A bell overhead tingled when she opened the door. Inside was as bland and generic as outside. Plain gray vinyl tile on the floor. Dingy white walls. Faux-wood counter spanned the middle of the retail space. Dropped ceiling with florescent lights.

A man stood behind the counter, his forearms resting on the top. A few feet down the counter, a young woman appeared to be packing gadgets. Or maybe unpacking them. Shelves behind the counter displayed a wide variety of available devices created for following, monitoring, or watching unsuspecting victims. Not that she was judging. Sometimes the results of a good spy device made all the difference in closing a case.

"Good afternoon," the man, who looked on the far side of middle age, with thin gray hair and glasses, announced. "What can I help you with today?"

"Good afternoon to you." Finley withdrew her credentials from her bag. Her current credentials. "I'm Finley O'Sullivan. I'm an investigator for the Finnegan Firm."

A broad smile split the man's face. "Jack Finnegan! Oh boy, he's the man. I see stuff about him in the news all the time. If I'm ever in trouble, I want Finnegan on my side."

Finley produced the expected smile. "That would be a good decision."

The guy laughed, glanced at his coworker as if she should laugh as well. She managed a stiff smile.

The laughing guy said, "I'm Charlie Howard. How can I help you?"

Finley produced the receipt and the bag with the bug inside. "Did this man"—she held out her phone for him to see Grady's photo—"buy this from you? The receipt is from your shop. It's dated August sixteenth."

Howard stared at the pic, his face pinched in assessment. "Oh yes, I remember him. Quiet fellow. Didn't have a lot to say. Just told me what he wanted, and that was that." He moved on to the receipt and the bagged device.

Finley watched the young woman. She pretended to remain focused on her task, but she repeatedly glanced at her boss. She was in her early twenties. Asian, perhaps. Attractive. Petite with long dark hair.

"The bug is mine. The receipt also. Bringing a photo along was smart. I like to be sure. These matters are generally quite delicate. Fact is, you never know when someone might have used a stolen credit card. Better to be sure by presenting a photo ID."

"The internet says you're open Tuesday through Saturday, nine to six," Finley said. "Do you have any other employees?"

He seemed surprised by the additional questions.

"That's right. Tuesday through Saturday. A man's gotta have time off."

"Employees?" Finley glanced at the woman down the counter.

"Oh yes," he said. "Wendy Getty."

Wendy gave Finley a nod.

"It's just the two of us," he added.

Finley really wanted to talk to Wendy without her boss. "Is there any chance your security"—she pointed to the camera in a nearby corner—"system still has the video of Grady's visit last month?"

Howard made a face. "Well, to be honest, I'll have to check. Hang on a moment, and I'll see."

As soon as he'd disappeared through the door leading to the back, Finley eased down the counter.

"Hey." She showed Wendy the photo of Grady. "Did you see him?"

She looked from the photo to Finley. "No."

"Maybe you were at lunch," Finley suggested.

Wendy gestured to a small desk behind the counter. "I eat lunch right there."

"Are you saying your employer is lying?" Finley held up the receipt. "That the receipt is bogus?"

"The receipt looks legit, but I'm saying that guy"—she nodded to Finley's phone—"never came in this shop on that day or any other day that we've been open in the past year that I've worked here."

"You're always here," Finley countered.

"If he's here, I'm here."

"Why would he lie?"

Wendy turned back to her work. "Do I have to spell it out?"

All lawyers preferred to hear the words. Finley glanced at the camera. "Are you afraid of being fired?"

Wendy paused her work and looked at Finley once more. "No. It's only video, not audio." She narrowed her eyes. "Charlie lives by a simple motto: *Money talks*. Would you like to throw a bid out there to see if yours is higher? He's always happy to change his story."

Finley smiled. "No. No. I'm good. Thanks."

"Sorry." Howard's voice rang out ahead of his appearance from the back of the shop.

Finley held up the bag and for Charlie's benefit said, "I still don't see how this stuff works."

Wendy smiled, understanding the comment was a cover for what the two of them had been discussing. "It's above my pay grade too."

"That's what I'm here for." Howard parked himself at the counter next to Wendy. "Any questions you have, I probably have the answer."

Finley forced a smile. "I'll keep that in mind when I'm ready to make a purchase. What about the video?"

"Oh yeah, that. I was thinking the video only stored for two weeks and then started over, and I was right. But really, you needn't worry." He tapped his temple. "I have a mind like a steel trap. I never forget a face."

Finley had expected as much. "Thanks for your time."

She exited the shop and considered her resources for getting info from credit card companies.

It was possible Winthrop or one of her five had paid the shop owner for the necessary documentation. It was also possible someone else had. The still-unidentified J. Grady on the bank account. Lena Marsh, the receptionist with whom Grady had an affair. Or a yet-to-be-discovered partner in Grady's scheme.

Winthrop was smart. She was savvy. But that didn't mean she couldn't be fooled on a level even she hadn't recognized yet.

Finley climbed into her Subaru and backed out of the space. Before she merged onto the highway, her cell vibrated. She answered without checking the screen.

"O'Sullivan."

"This is Lena Marsh. Can we meet? We need to talk. As soon as possible."

"I was just thinking about you." The call was definitely an odd coincidence. Maybe. Finley surveyed the traffic. "I can meet. Where did you have in mind?"

"The coffee shop on the corner near the clinic."

"I'm on my way." Finley ended the call and merged into traffic.

She had a feeling Winthrop didn't know the half of what had gone down with her husband and the other woman—receptionist Lena Marsh.

21

1:30 p.m.

Starbucks
Church Street, Nashville

Finley spotted Lena Marsh as soon as she stepped inside the door. The shop was crowded—as always—but Marsh had snagged one of the comfy seating areas in the corner near the mug display.

At the counter Finley ordered her favorite, iced caramel macchiato. A minute was required for the prep, so she checked in with Whitney Lemm. The woman answered the motel-room phone instantly. Finley had taken Lemm's cell and disposed of it so it couldn't be used to track her. If Dempsey's thug found her, she was a dead woman.

"Just checking in," Finley said, hoping to sound upbeat.

"I'm going crazy here," Lemm snapped. "When is your friend coming?"

This was the tricky part. Finley had called Houser on the way here and had finally gotten him instead of his voice mail. He couldn't meet with her until five or after. She just needed Lemm to stay calm and to stay put for a few more hours.

"I talked to him," Finley assured her, "but we can't meet in person for a few more hours, maybe five or six o'clock. Just hang on a little while longer."

"Are you serious?" More whining.

"Just stay put," Finley urged. "At the moment this is the only way I know to keep you safe."

"Fine."

The call ended. Finley stared at her phone for a moment before tucking it away. She hoped like hell Lemm was smart enough to stay hidden.

The barista placed Finley's order on the counter. She snagged it and headed for the woman waiting in the corner.

Marsh produced a smile that didn't meet her eyes. "I took a late lunch, so I only have about half an hour."

"Why don't we get straight to the point then? Tell me what's going on." Finley sipped her sweet, icy drink.

Marsh looked away for a moment. She scanned the crowd around them before turning back to Finley. "I wasn't entirely honest with you about my relationship with Jarrod."

Shocker. Was anyone honest anymore? Finley gave a noncommittal nod. "Did you tell Ellen Winthrop that I spoke to you?"

Visibly startled, Marsh stammered, "I . . . I wanted her to know I wasn't going to sit back and allow her to try and frame me for what she's done." She glanced away for a moment. "I was worried she sent you."

Reasonable response. Finley moved on. "What is it you weren't honest about?"

"Jarrod and I first met exactly like I told you—at the Mengesha party. We stopped seeing each other for a while after he married *her*." She cradled her coffee cup in both hands. "Then about a month ago we reconnected, just as I said, but it wasn't only sex this time."

Finley waited through her hesitation. When it lagged on, she prompted, "Something unexpected happened?"

"We realized we wanted to be together. He told me he'd made a horrible mistake."

"The marriage was a mistake?" Another big surprise. Grady really was a catch.

"Yes. But it was more than that—he was worried that his wife had done something really bad."

Finley nodded, her curiosity piqued now. "Define 'really bad.'"

Marsh's gaze locked on Finley's. "He thinks she had something to do with a woman's death."

There was an unexpected twist.

"Do you have proof of this allegation?" Finley was always grateful for information, but it was nothing more than hearsay unless there was solid proof.

Marsh shook her head. "No proof, but I can tell you his concerns were sincere."

It wasn't easy, but Finley managed to hold back a laugh. The man was cheating on his wife. Stealing her money. Sincerity wasn't likely one of his finer qualities.

"Her name was Nora Duncan," Marsh continued. "Jarrod found a file about her. Ellen had dug up everything on her she could find. According to her notes, she'd even started seeing Dr. Mengesha in an attempt to get information on the woman."

Not exactly the stunning revelation Finley had hoped for. "Unless you provided her information, we both know the doc didn't."

Marsh stared open mouthed at Finley, then insisted, "I told her nothing, but that didn't keep the Duncan woman from ending up dead."

"She was murdered?" So far Finley wasn't buying into the big story.

Marsh shook her head. "Supposedly she killed herself, but Jarrod was convinced, based on what he discovered, that Ellen had something to do with it. He was afraid of her. All of this happened before they met, but the idea got him digging around to see what else he could find. The more he discovered about her, the more worried he grew. He said she and her friends were psycho and he intended to get out before he ended up dead too." She blinked rapidly, but the move didn't stop the tears—whether real or fake—from crowding into her eyes. "She must have found out he was looking into her secret activities, because he's dead." Marsh leaned forward. "I'm terrified I'll be next. Someone has been watching me. Driving past my house at night. I'm certain she at least suspects Jarrod confided in me, and I don't know what to do."

"What secret activities?" This was all very dramatic, but it wasn't giving Finley much she could work with.

"He wasn't sure. Something she and the women she worked with were into."

"If what you say is true," Finley ventured, and that was a hell of a big *if,* "and he was scared for his life, why was he siphoning money from her accounts? Why didn't he just leave?"

Marsh frowned. "What do you mean?"

"Jarrod stole a lot of money from his wife. Moved it to a secret account. He didn't tell you about that?"

Marsh's expression shifted to shock as she moved her head firmly from side to side. "I don't believe you. He wanted out. He didn't want her money. He wasn't that kind of person."

At this point Finley couldn't prove what sort of person Grady had been. There were too many blank spots in his history. But the money was missing, and the receiving account did have his name on it. At least according to Winthrop's top gun forensic accountant. Could she have set the account up herself to make him look guilty? Sure, she could have. Didn't make a whole lot of sense. If killing Jarrod Grady had been Ellen Winthrop's goal, there were many far-easier ways to go about it.

"Let's go back to the Duncan woman," Finley said. "Why would Winthrop have wanted to hurt her?"

"Apparently there was a love triangle," Marsh said, glancing side to side as she spoke. "Duncan was having a relationship with someone close to Ellen, and she got jealous."

"You're suggesting," Finley said for clarification, "that prior to her relationship with Grady, Winthrop was involved intimately with someone else."

Marsh shook her head. "He didn't think it was that kind of relationship. It was a close friendship, and Ellen thought Duncan was interfering."

"I'll look into it." Ellen Winthrop was the firm's client. That alone entitled her to a certain degree of loyalty. Marsh had done nothing to deserve any sort of trust, much less loyalty. "Do you have a name for this mystery person?"

"Laney Pettit."

Now she had a smidgen of Finley's attention. "When did Grady tell you all this?" Having her repeat aspects of her story was a good way to reveal inconsistencies.

"When we got back together last month, he started sharing all his concerns." Marsh stared into her cup for a moment. "We were going to leave together."

No surprise there. Finley figured Marsh knew exactly where the missing money was.

"Were you in Atlanta with him?" If she was spilling all these truths, she might as well spill that one too.

"On Friday night, yes." She closed her eyes as if saying the next part was particularly difficult. "I came back early on Saturday. I was supposed to get ready for leaving. He told me to pack whatever I needed to take with me. I had everything ready, but he never called me. Then I heard . . ." She swiped at her eyes. "Believe what you will, but I'm telling you she killed him the same way she killed Nora Duncan."

"Where were the two of you going?" Finley had to admit, Marsh put on a believable show. But there was a little something missing. Or maybe it was just all too pat. Too carefully laid out.

"Miami. He had a contact there who planned to help us find work."

"Did he give you the name of this contact?"

She shook her head, then took a deep breath. "That's all I know. Thank you for listening to what I have to say. Telling you is the least I can do for Jarrod. He didn't deserve to be murdered."

Marsh shifted in her chair. Glanced at the entrance more than once. She was ready to leave this conversation.

"I just want to make sure I have everything," Finley said before Marsh could mention leaving. "You and Jarrod had plans to go away together. Your affair resumed about a month ago. But you had no knowledge of him planning to steal money from his wife."

"He never ever mentioned money. I'm telling you, this is her attempt to make him look like the guilty one. He was leaving her because of the things he had learned about her past and this . . . this Duncan woman. He truly thought Ellen was some sort of psycho."

The persistence in her voice spoke of more than she was sharing. "Was there something beyond his theory that she killed the Duncan woman—something specific—that set off alarm bells for him?"

"I'm sure there was. He may not have told me everything, but whatever he found in her past, including Nora Duncan, it was all connected to who she is and the things she and the others do." Marsh stared earnestly at Finley. "If you believe nothing else I say, believe this: the Duncan woman's death is pivotal to the answers you're looking for. Ellen Winthrop and those women she surrounds herself with are certified psychos."

Marsh did so like using that word. The repetition stirred Finley's instincts in spite of her attempts to remain unaffected.

"Who is J. Grady?" Finley asked.

Marsh made a confused face. "Do you mean Jarrod?"

Finley shook her head. "Maybe a brother or someone else related to him or who just happens to have the same first initial."

Marsh shrugged. "I've never heard of a J. Grady. If I had my guess, I'd say this is something else those bitches made up."

Finley wondered if this receptionist—the other woman—was dead serious or playing a deadly game.

Why come to Finley with any of this? The idea made little sense.

Marsh left the shop first. Finley took her time finishing her coffee before doing the same. She had just reached for the door handle of her Subaru when a dark sedan on the street captured her attention. The car had slowed as if the driver intended to turn into the parking lot, but he didn't.

Then Finley recognized the car. Her gaze went to the driver.

Flock.

He pointed a finger gun at her, then drove away.

Judging by the current score, he was the one who needed to be worried.

Two down, one to go.

Blakedale at Green Hills
Burton Hills Boulevard, Nashville, 3:40 p.m.

Nora Duncan had no social media presence. Her home in Franklin had been sold. Thankfully, her obituary listed her surviving family members: an elderly mother, Norine; and a cousin—one Laney Pettit.

The obit confirmed the connection to Pettit, but not necessarily the kind of connection to which Marsh had alluded.

Since starting with Pettit would have triggered a warning to the mother, Finley opted to start with Norine Duncan. She wanted completely unprepared answers. The raw truth.

The mother was a resident of Blakedale. As it was an assisted-living facility rather than a nursing home, access to the patients wasn't too complicated at Blakedale. Finley had provided her ID, and her name was checked to ensure she wasn't on a no-access list; then she was given a visitor's pass and directions to where Norine Duncan was. All the residents wore electronic bracelets that provided their positions on the property. Those same bracelets sounded an alarm if the resident stepped outside the "safe" zone of the property boundaries.

Sounded a little like house arrest to Finley, but she supposed the patients' safety outweighed any unpleasant impressions.

Finley found Norine Duncan on a lovely wrought iron bench beneath a grouping of shade trees and flanked by brimming pots of blooming flowers. The landscaping for the place must have cost a fortune. Obviously, Ms. Duncan had sufficient resources.

"Ms. Duncan," Finley said as she approached the bench.

Duncan looked up from her book and smiled. "You've found me."

Finley extended her hand. "I'm Finley O'Sullivan."

Duncan shook her hand. "Please join me, Ms. O'Sullivan." She closed her book and shifted slightly on the bench. "Do I know you, dear?"

Finley sat, easing her bag down to the lush green lawn. "We haven't met before, but I'm an investigator for the law firm representing Ellen Winthrop."

"Oh my, what an awful, awful thing." Duncan's face clouded with hurt. "Poor, poor Ellen." She sighed, then seemed to rally and asked, "How can I help?"

Now to the sticky part. "I'd like to ask about your daughter, Nora."

The older woman's face pinched. "My daughter? She passed away in April."

"Yes, ma'am," Finley assured her, "that's what I wanted to talk to you about."

"What does that have to do with Ellen or her husband's murder?"

"Nothing, I'm sure," Finley explained, "but it's my job to learn about any issues involving anyone close to Ellen. It's the nature of homicide investigations. You look at everything and everyone close to those involved. It's not pleasant, but it's necessary."

Confusion and a hint of pain lined the older woman's face, but she nodded. "All right. Anything to help Ellen."

Finley smiled. "Thank you. I'm sure she'll appreciate your support. First, can you tell me what happened to your daughter?"

Book held to her chest as if it could shield her from the pain of the discussion, Duncan nodded. "Nora had always been a bit of a wallflower. Some would have called her a shut-in, but that wasn't true. She just preferred her own company or mine. When she wasn't with me or puttering around the houses, she was with her sweet cousin Laney."

"Laney?" Finley prompted.

"Laney Pettit. The two were inseparable their entire lives. My sister, God rest her soul, and I had our daughters on the same day within a couple of hours of each other. We raised those babies together, and they were like sisters."

"I'm sure that made both of you very happy."

"It really did," she agreed. "My sister and I had our own troubles in the early years, but having our daughters changed all that. When our husbands passed in the same year, we still had each other and our girls. A true blessing."

"I'm sure Laney still comes to see you."

"Oh yes. After my sister died, Laney was the glue that held me together. She and Nora treated me like their third musketeer until I had my fall. After rehab, we all agreed that it was best if I moved here. They could visit all they wanted and still live their lives unencumbered—not their words, mine. I didn't want to be a burden. Although I'm still capable of taking care of myself to a large degree, I didn't want to wait until I wasn't. It would have made the decision far more painful for all involved."

"The choice was very thoughtful of you," Finley agreed. "I know Nora's death must have been a horrible shock to you."

Her eyes glistening with emotion, she shook her head. "I still can't believe she thought so little of herself that she allowed the loss of a man to render her incapable of going on."

Definitely not the same story Marsh had given. "She had met someone?"

"Yes." Duncan nodded, her face somber. "She and Laney never had any luck with their love lives. Laney has suffered through three marriages with men who never really loved her the way she deserved. Nora was never married, but she'd had a couple of long-term relationships. Nothing too serious. Until last Christmas. She met someone, and oh my goodness, she was so happy." She grimaced at the memories. "As happy as she was, she worried about getting her hopes up. She insisted this was why she didn't want me to meet him until she was sure it would work out. I understood. She had been down that road already. She wanted to be sure this one would take before she showed him off."

"How long did the relationship last?"

"Things were pretty good, I think, until just around Valentine's Day. 'Pretty good' might be an understatement. I think Nora was very happy. It's just hard to say anything good about that time considering what happened."

"Can you tell me what happened?" Finley needed the lady to give her all she had. If whatever had happened to Nora was somehow relevant to the Winthrop case, then maybe Marsh had been telling some element of the truth.

"He just disappeared one day. Worse, the bastard had drained her bank account. He'd stolen the jewelry my mother and I had passed down to her. Nora was devastated."

This was sounding far too familiar. "Did you know his name or what he looked like?"

Duncan shook her head. "Ned. That's all she told me. Ned this and Ned that. I never met him. Honestly, it all happened so fast there really wasn't time to bring him around to see her old mom, and once he was gone, she refused to speak of him. But her depression worsened as the weeks went by. I tried to get her to go away with me and Laney. We could have taken a cruise. Just anything to get away. Nora refused. I urged her to seek counseling. She did do that, but she'd waited too long, I guess. She'd gotten a prescription for her anxiety during the whole mess; she ended up taking too much and never waking up again."

Tears slid down her cheeks, and Finley felt horrible for having caused the fresh pain.

"I am so sorry for your loss, Ms. Duncan. Did you or Nora go to the police about the missing money?"

Duncan shook her head adamantly. "Nora didn't want anyone to know. The only ones who know what happened are Laney and me. And Ellen, of course. Ellen was fit to be tied, I tell you. She promised to find the man and see that he paid for what he'd done to my daughter."

What an intriguing promise—one that prompted an even more interesting thought. "Did you know Ellen's husband?"

"I met him at their wedding." Duncan shook her head. "Such a tragedy. Ellen was so in love with him, and he seemed like such a nice young man."

Since Duncan hadn't seen the man who devastated her daughter, the fact that she hadn't recognized Grady was irrelevant. The idea that he was this Ned was a reach but one Finley couldn't ignore.

"It's not too late to go to the police about your daughter," Finley offered.

Duncan smiled sadly. "Nora is gone. I can't go through that again. If Ellen can't find him, I just hope karma will take care of whoever was responsible for Nora's unhappiness."

In Finley's experience karma wasn't entirely reliable.

Finley opted to take a final stab at confirming Marsh's story. "Nora and Ellen got along well? Never any trouble between the two of them?"

The older woman looked put out by the question. "Certainly not. Nora and Laney treated Ellen like the little sister they never had. Nora adored her, as does Laney. Why would you ask such a thing?"

"I'm sorry," Finley assured her. "I meant no harm, but as I explained, it's important that we cover all the bases."

This visit would no doubt be related to Ellen as soon as Finley left. An attempt at smoothing the woman's ruffled feathers would be in Finley's best interest. With that in mind, she reiterated, "My job is to do all in my power to protect Ellen."

The woman visibly calmed. "I suppose I can see how you might need to ask these sorts of questions. But you can take it from me, Ms. Finnegan— Ellen Winthrop is one of the finest people you will ever meet despite the horrors of her childhood. An angel, that's what I would call her."

"Her mother died when she was very young," Finley said with a nod. Other than that she'd been poor and had a crappy father, this was about the extent of what Finley knew about Winthrop's childhood. "How sad for a little girl."

"The worst of it," Duncan said with a slow shake of her head, "was that she had no one left except her father. The man was a devil, let me tell you. I don't know how she survived his abuse."

Pettit had mentioned the abusive father. Finley thought of the strong woman Winthrop had become. "I'm sure those awful days were part of what made her the strong woman she is today." Cliché at best. Anyone who would abuse a child should die screaming in Finley's opinion. "Did her father live to see her great success?"

"No, he died when she was very young." Duncan's expression hardened. "God forgive me for saying so, but he should have been taken long before that. In the end, though, he got what he deserved, and it was a lucky break for poor Ellen."

"Heart attack?" Finley asked, prodding for more.

The older woman shook her head. "Some sort of accident. I don't recall the details. Laney took Ellen in after his death. Raised her as if she'd been her own child."

Winthrop hadn't mentioned that aspect of her relationship with Pettit. The history between the two was long and deep. Though Finley had no proof, the connection between Winthrop, Pettit, and Duncan felt suddenly important. Maybe more important than even this grieving mother knew.

"Thank you, Ms. Duncan. I appreciate your time." Finley took a card from her bag and passed it to the lady. "Please call me if you think of anything else or if you ever need any legal help. We're good people at the Finnegan Firm."

"The only thing I ask is that you take good care of our dear Ellen."

"We've got Ellen covered," Finley promised.

They said their goodbyes, and Finley made her way back to her Subaru.

She thought of her comment to the elderly woman. Were they good people? Both she and Jack had so many secrets. They pushed the envelope. Crossed lines.

All in the name of protecting their client. Surely that was good in anyone's opinion.

After putting through a call to Laney Pettit's number, Finley navigated her Subaru toward Cumberland Place. The call went to voice mail. Next, she tried Ellen Winthrop. The woman answered after the second ring. One to ID the caller and the second one to consider what she intended to say. It was a tactic Finley used all the time.

"Finley," she said rather than hello, "I hope you have an update for me."

"No update," Finley said as she merged into traffic. "But I do have questions. Let's start with, How can I reach Laney Pettit? Her cell is going to her voice mail."

Finley braced for stonewalling.

"I'm sorry, but Laney is out of town. She left for Birmingham early this morning. A dear friend is very ill and in need of assistance. Since she retired, Laney's always helping others. If you leave a message, I'm sure she'll call you back as soon as she can."

It was moments like this that made it difficult for Finley to trust Winthrop entirely. Laney being out of town was just too convenient.

"Maybe you can let Laney know I really need to speak with her as soon as possible."

"I'm happy to make a call, but in the meanwhile perhaps I can help you," Winthrop offered.

Why not? After all, Duncan would likely tell Winthrop about her visitor.

"Who was the man who stole from Nora Duncan and whose disappearance apparently prompted her suicide?"

Hesitation. Hard to believe Winthrop hadn't been expecting this call. She seemed to be one step ahead of Finley at every turn. Evidently no one from Blakedale had called to warn her about Finley's visit. Winthrop had no shortage of connections. Why not one there?

Something else she and Finley had in common.

"Oh yes. Poor Nora. Such a sad, sad situation. Laney was devastated, as was I. The two of them were like sisters. More than sisters, really. It was a terrible, terrible time."

Losing a loved one was rarely easy. "Who was the man?"

A sigh hissed across the connection. "Finley, this is a very sensitive matter. Nora's mother is fragile, and I don't want anyone doing anything that will hurt her in any way."

"I wouldn't think of it," Finley returned, tamping down the frustration that attempted to make an appearance. "But you did promise her that you'd find him and make him pay."

"You've already disturbed her with this nonsense, haven't you?"

Finley didn't respond to the question. No point confirming what Winthrop had already figured out.

"Was the man—this Ned—Jarrod Grady?" Finley asked.

Winthrop laughed, though the sound was void of humor. "Finley, I'm afraid you've reached the wrong conclusions. You see, it wasn't a man. It was a woman. Nora kept this from all of us for the longest time. I think she really wanted to see if the relationship would work out before she broke the news to us and to her elderly mother that she preferred women rather than men."

Finley braked and eased into the turning lane for Harding Place. "Who was this woman?"

"Who the woman was is irrelevant. She disappeared, and Nora decided she didn't want to ever tell her mother. It was utterly tragic. Poor Nora slipped into a deep, dark depression, and Laney and I couldn't pull her out of it. Dr. Mengesha tried to help, but I think it was too late. Nora had made up her mind, and no one was going to change it."

"If the woman is irrelevant, why make the promise to Nora's mother?" Finley asked. She waffled between being annoyed at Winthrop for sounding so condescending and being flat-out pissed off at Marsh for possibly lying to her.

More of that impatient sighing. "What does this have to do with anything?"

Finley reached for patience. "Perhaps nothing, but we need to have the facts, which means I will still need to speak with Laney when she is available."

"I want to know where this is coming from. What does Nora's tragedy have to do with my case?" Winthrop demanded. "Is it that damned receptionist?"

Before Finley could respond, Winthrop ranted on, "You cannot believe anything she says. She's only trying to make me look bad because Jarrod chose me over her. *She* had an affair with my husband."

"She mentioned secret activities you were involved in," Finley continued calmly. "Any clue what she meant by 'secret activities'?"

"She is playing you, Finley. Check your sources. For the love of God, who are you working for?"

Finley gave her a sec to ensure she was finished. "We work for you, Ellen. But if Marsh goes to Ventura with these allegations—"

"She won't," Winthrop said, her tone simmering with anger. "She's in this up to her eyeballs."

Finley braked for a stop sign. "Tell me what that means, Ellen."

For one, two, three beats, Finley held her breath. She was close to getting a piece of the truth. So close.

A horn blared behind her. Finley checked the cross street, then rolled forward.

"I . . ."

Finley didn't dare say a word.

"We believe she and Jarrod were partners in all this."

And there it was, a piece of what Winthrop had been holding back. Finley smiled and made the next turn. "What evidence do you have?"

"Nothing concrete yet," she allowed, "but Vivian and her team are working diligently to find more."

Finley nodded. "Thank you. Now we can work together toward that end."

"I'll call when we have something."

The call ended.

Finley figured she'd better update Jack in case Winthrop complained about her tactics. He preferred that she not piss off the clients, but it happened sometimes.

Sometimes the truth was messy. And that was Finley's only goal: the truth.

Was her lack of patience with Winthrop because the two of them were too damned much alike?

Maybe.

Was it possible the Marsh scenario was a dead end? Sure, but Finley couldn't not see it through.

The worst mistake a defense attorney could make was assuming anything that popped up in an investigation was irrelevant.

If it existed, it could be relevant.

22

5:00 p.m.

Marsh Residence
Lemont Drive, Nashville

Finley pounded on the front door. The car that Marsh drove was not in the driveway. And it wasn't because she was at work. Finley had stopped by the clinic, and one of the secretaries had told her that Marsh had quit—by phone and without notice. The secretary, who had been more than a little furious, hadn't known any other information. Obviously, Marsh wouldn't be getting a good recommendation.

From there Finley had driven straight to Marsh's home in hopes of catching her before she disappeared. Marsh certainly hadn't mentioned quitting her job when they'd had coffee just a couple of hours ago. But if she suspected Winthrop was onto her, she would disappear. Damn it!

Finley pounded on the door again, frustration and impatience firing through her.

"She's gone."

Finley lowered the fist poised to pound again and turned to the middle-aged man standing in the next driveway. "What do you mean, gone?"

"She came home earlier than usual. A little before three, I think. I kept hearing her car door slam over and over, so I looked out the window to see what she was doing. I thought maybe she was cleaning out her car. It kind of sounded like that. But no, she was carrying stuff out of the house and shoving it into the car. She didn't even have it in boxes or bags, just armloads."

"Did you talk to her?" Finley tamped down the mounting frustration.

"I came out on the stoop and asked her if everything was okay, and she told me to mind my own business." He shrugged. "We really didn't get along. She always played her music too loud, and I always complained."

"Do you have any idea where she was headed?"

He shrugged. "Out of here, that's all I know. Good riddance. She was one wacky bitch."

"Wacky how?" His definition and Finley's might not be the same. Right now Finley knew for sure the woman was a liar.

"I don't know." He lifted his shoulders in a half-hearted shrug. "There was a lot of coming and going. She went out a lot late at night and then came back early in the morning and then headed back out again for work. It was weird. I guess it's possible she was working two jobs."

"Did she ever have friends over?" Finley asked, stepping off the porch to move toward the neighbor.

"You some kinda cop?"

"Yeah, kinda." Finley pulled her cell from her pocket and pulled up the pic of Jarrod Grady. She showed it to the man. "Did you ever see this guy visit her?"

He nodded and made a sound that was part laugh, part grunt. "Heck yeah. I saw him plenty of times. Whenever he visited, they were either fighting or . . ." He wagged his eyebrows. "Well, you know. The walls are thin in these old houses. You can't miss the kind of rowdy sack time those two had."

Marsh had admitted the two were still seeing each other. Now the neighbor had confirmed as much. At least that much of her story had been true.

"How long has Lena Marsh lived here?"

"Since last year. September maybe."

"Had this man been visiting her the whole time, or was this a more recent activity?"

"I thought he was her husband." The neighbor scratched his head. "He lived here for a couple months when she first moved in, then just visited, then stayed full-time for a while, then back to the random visits. It was a weird relationship."

Finley's frustration shifted toward fury. Marsh had lied about how long she'd known Grady. "Have you seen him here recently?"

He narrowed his eyes as if concentrating especially hard. "Like the middle of last week, Wednesday or Thursday." He frowned. "No, wait, he came by on Saturday about five thirtyish, but he only stayed like two minutes. I don't think she was even home."

On Saturday? Grady had returned from Atlanta on Saturday. So, he'd come here even before going home. Maybe his flight hadn't been delayed after all. He just had an extra stop to make. Why hadn't Winthrop confirmed the delay? Maybe she had.

Their client had her own ideas about when and how much to share with her legal representatives. If Finley had had any doubts, their conversation just minutes ago had confirmed her suspicions.

"Are you certain about the timeline?" Finley asked as she barreled toward a pissed-off zone she rarely allowed herself to enter. What the hell were these people up to?

"Absolutely," the neighbor confirmed. "I got laid off a year ago after I hurt my back. Now I'm on disability."

Meaning he entertained himself watching the neighbors. Finley calmed herself. She needed to focus on the details. "Do you have any idea where she lived before coming here?"

"Hotlanta," he said, referring to Atlanta. "I noticed the Georgia tag when she first moved in. The guy, Jay, he was out back grilling one day, and we talked a minute. He said they were from Atlanta."

Whoa. Wait. "Did you say Jay?"

"Yeah. The guy in the picture you showed me. Jay Grady."

So the J. Grady signatory could actually be *Jay* Grady. Sounded like confirmation enough that J. Grady and Jarrod Grady were the same person. Seemed as if Winthrop's security guru should have figured this out already.

Finley pulled up a photo of Ellen Winthrop. Showed it to the neighbor. "Have you ever seen this woman visit?"

He shook his head. "Nope. That her mother?"

"Yes," Finley lied. "She's very worried about Lena. She asked me to see if I could find her and talk her into coming home. Her father is dying." Finley had always been quite good at creating profiles off the cuff.

The man made a face. "Oh hell. That's too bad. You just missed her by maybe an hour."

Finley rubbed at her forehead. "I wish I knew where she was going. Her mother will be so disappointed."

"You're a PI then," he offered knowingly.

"Yes," Finley said. Technically not a lie.

The guy eased closer. "I'll tell you a little something I know about this house." He jerked his head toward Marsh's home. "The info might prove useful to someone like yourself."

Finley waited for him to go on.

"The back door isn't locked."

He must have read the look on Finley's face, since he hastened to add, "When I saw her rushing in and out, I was worried about her. Then when she suddenly drove away, I was really confused. I checked in the windows to see if maybe something had gone down." He fixed a knowing look on Finley. "You should have a look. She left a bunch of stuff. The place looks like it was ransacked, but you might find some answers in there." He hitched his thumb toward the rear of the property. "Like I said, the back door isn't locked."

Finley didn't bother pointing out that what he was suggesting was against the law. Primarily because she had every intention of breaking it. "Thanks, I'll do that. Anything that might help me find her for her family's sake."

He shook his head. "Kids these days. They don't care about anyone but themselves."

Finley hesitated. "Would you mind helping me out?"

"Sure thing. Whatever you need me to do."

"Just keep an eye out and make sure no one gets the jump on me while I'm having a look inside."

"You can count on me. I'll just sit over here on my stoop and keep watch."

Finley walked around to the back door, and sure enough, it was unlocked. She went inside, closed it behind her. Taking this step was a minor risk. Technically nothing she found was admissible since she wasn't a cop and didn't have a warrant. For Finley's purposes it didn't matter. Finding something—anything—that would give her a clue about where Marsh had gone was the goal.

The house was small with a kitchen–dining area that flowed into the living room in an L shape. Cupboards were still stocked with canned and dry goods. Wine and milk in the fridge. Deli meat and cheese. Marsh's decision to leave certainly hadn't been a planned one. Her story about Grady telling her to pack what she wanted to take when they left together had been yet another lie. Nothing had been packed, according to what the neighbor had seen today. And Finley hadn't noticed any boxes when she'd visited, but they could have been in the bedroom. Not likely, since Marsh had carried her belongings out in her arms—no bags or boxes.

"You are looking guiltier all the time, Ms. Marsh."

Finley checked all drawers, cupboards, and floor registers in the living area. Nothing useful. Then she moved to the bedrooms. There were two small ones and a single bath. She checked the bathroom. Medicine cabinet had been emptied. Towels and soap remained under the sink. Toilet tank only held water. The furniture in the first bedroom remained. The drawers and closet had been emptied. Nothing under the mattress or under the bed.

The second, smaller bedroom was set up as an office. The top of the desk had been wiped clean; pens and paper clips littered the floor from the hasty move. The drawers were empty. No filing cabinet or other pieces of furniture. Just the small, cheap desk and a cheaper wheeled chair. Nothing in the tiny closet.

Finley knelt and examined the area beneath the desk. Nothing. She moved across the floor on hands and knees and checked under the floor register. Nothing in the metal cavity beneath it. Before leaving the room, she went back to the desk and pulled out each drawer, looking for something that might have fallen behind or under the drawers.

A piece of paper was jammed under one. Finley smiled. Maybe something, maybe nothing. She retrieved the paper and replaced the drawer. Carefully smoothing out the page, she scanned the letterhead first.

Dyson and Mekler—Psychiatric Services. Atlanta, Georgia.

Finley smiled. "Atlanta, huh?" Just like the neighbor said.

The letter was dated in February of last year, congratulating Lena Marsh for joining their team. The position—receptionist—and the salary were mentioned.

Finley pulled out her cell and called the number listed on the letterhead. It was after five thirty. She could only hope someone was still in the office.

"Dyson and Mekler."

Finley breathed a sigh of relief. "Hello, yes. May I speak with Lena Marsh, please?"

"I'm afraid she doesn't work here any longer. May I help you?"

Finley exhaled another woebegone sigh. "Oh my. This is quite the dilemma. You see, I work for an estate attorney's office, and I have a very important document I need to deliver. This is the only phone number I have for her."

"I'm sorry," the woman said. "She left in September of last year."

"Any forwarding information?" Finley mentally crossed her fingers.

"One moment."

The line went on hold, and elevator music piped through.

While she waited, a text came in from Houser. See you at 6. Your place. Finley sent him a thumbs-up.

Just over a minute later, the woman returned to the call.

"We don't have a forwarding address on file, but I do recall her saying she was moving to Nashville, if that helps."

"Thank you for checking."

Marsh and Grady had moved from Atlanta to Nashville during the same time frame. The link between the two was undeniable. Finley moved back through the house one last time to ensure she hadn't missed anything.

On her way through the kitchen, she checked the oven and the microwave. There wasn't a dishwasher. At least she had something for her breaking-and-entering trouble. Outside, the neighbor waited for her between the two driveways.

"Did you find anything helpful?"

"I didn't," Finley lied, "but I appreciate the assist."

Before leaving, Finley took the name and number of the landlord who owned the property. She thanked her partner in crime once more and headed for home. Houser would be there by the time she arrived.

She called Jack and filled him in on Marsh's abrupt departure and what her neighbor had to share.

"You're right," he agreed. "The Duncan thing may have been Marsh's way of trying to throw us off-track. That said, I'm with you on the other. If Marsh and Grady were in Atlanta together, it's a safe guess they were running a scam there as well."

"No question," Finley agreed. "It's possible the partnership goes back further, and I suspect it does, considering the level of planning and manipulation that has obviously gone into this gig."

"He may have made that final trip to Atlanta," Jack suggested, continuing that line of thought, "to follow up on a job there or for something new the two had going. Based on what we know, he was clearly on the verge of disappearing from Winthrop's life."

Exactly. "You know what this means," Finley said, making a right at a major intersection.

"You need to go to Atlanta."

"Yeah. Like first thing in the morning." Finley mentally calculated the drive. Too long for a day trip, and she didn't want to be gone two days unless necessary.

"Nita will get you on an early-morning flight down and something late evening coming back."

"Sounds good to me. Considering Winthrop was a patient of Dr. Mengesha—Marsh's place of employment—I plan to check into Dyson and Mekler tomorrow. Maybe someone there was close enough to Marsh to have learned a bit of personal information. It's possible Marsh and Grady were preying on older, lonely, rich women. What better way to find them than through their therapists?"

Jack grunted his agreement. "If your theory is right, maybe they got in over their heads this time. Or one of them wanted out."

"The question is, If Marsh wanted out, did she kill him? Or had Winthrop found out about Marsh and in blind jealousy did the deed?"

Finley thought of Marsh's comment about the secret activities. "Then again, maybe there was something going on we're missing."

"At this point anything is possible. Be careful, kid," Jack warned. "Whoever killed Grady is certainly capable of killing again. You could end up a target."

Finley agreed. But it was the other case—with Dempsey and his thug—she suspected posed the biggest threat.

If she lived through that one, maybe she really was bulletproof.

23

6:10 p.m.

The Murder House
Shelby Avenue, Nashville

Finley parked in her driveway. She was surprised Houser wasn't there already. They had agreed on six. Maybe he had been delayed by work the same way she had, except he likely hadn't been breaking and entering—not that she'd broken anything. The door had been unlocked. That part would work in her favor.

She needed to find Marsh. The answers to a couple of follow-up questions would have been nice about now. Damn it.

The pieces of the puzzle she had found today didn't all fit together neatly, but they all meant something. She needed more.

Finley thought of what she'd learned about Winthrop's early years from Duncan's mother. She grabbed her cell and started to search. It took several minutes, but she found an obituary. Luther Winthrop. Another minute and numerous searches later, and she found a brief mention of his accident. His own vehicle had rolled over him. Kind of a strange way to go. The short snippet didn't mention the circumstances, but the event had been labeled a bizarre accident. Definitely bizarre.

Finley glanced at the street. Still no sign of Houser, so she climbed out of her car, grabbed her bag, and headed for the porch. No sooner had she plugged the house key into the lock, than Houser's shiny silver sedan slowed to a stop in front of her house. She pushed the door inward, tossed her bag onto the sofa, and waited for the detective to join her on the porch.

"Sorry I'm running late," he offered.

Houser was about her age. Attractive with military-short dark hair. He wore those snug-fitting suits men his age appeared to prefer, and judging by the fabric, they wouldn't be found on a rack in just any store. Finley had done a little research on the guy. He came from money. Never married. No steady girlfriend. Had a reputation for playing the field. His parents and one sibling, an older brother, were all medical doctors. But not Eric. He had dropped out of medical school midway and applied to the police academy. Six years later he was a homicide detective for the Nashville Metro Police Department.

She expected this decision still didn't sit right with his family. This was a place she knew well. Her mother had stopped being happy with Finley's decisions when she revolted against the pink paint in her bedroom at age ten. Sometimes Jack suggested they were too much alike to get along, but Finley disagreed.

She was nothing like her mother. *Liar.*

Jack's revelation about his and the Judge's falling-out attempted to intrude, but she pushed it away.

"No problem," Finley assured Houser. "I just got here myself. Come on in." She led the way. "You want a beer? Some wine?"

"I better not." He closed the door behind himself. "Since you called, I'm assuming this has something to do with Derrick's case, which means I'm on the clock."

"Trust me"—Finley headed for the kitchen—"we're both going to need something." She grabbed a couple of beers from the six-pack in the fridge and rejoined Houser in the living room. He stood near the dumpy sofa. "Sit," she ordered. She passed a can to him. Then she popped the top on hers and settled into her chair. She would have preferred wine, but this was easier, and time was of the essence.

"Thanks." He popped the top and downed a sip.

"During the past two months," Finley began, "I've been checking up on you." Beyond his personal life, she'd done some digging into his work at Metro.

He smiled. "I've done some checking up on you as well. You'll be pleased to know my initial assessment was correct."

Finley indulged in a long drink of her beer. "That doesn't sound like a compliment."

"It's a compliment." He studied her a moment. "You're above average in intelligence. Graduated at the top of your class. Had a perfect record of winning in the courtroom."

"Not perfect," she countered. "I did lose one case."

"The last one," he said.

The infamous meltdown case. Technically it wasn't a loss. The judge had declared a mistrial. Houser said as much.

"Sometimes you can be good at one thing," Finley pointed out, "and screw up everything else."

"Your marriage," he guessed.

"I fell for a guy I thought I knew, but . . ." She shrugged, feeling damned guilty no matter that she was justified. "I didn't know him. Apparently."

"You think he was involved somehow with the trouble that took his life."

She appreciated that Houser didn't mention what happened to her. "Off the record?" She held his gaze with that question ringing in the silence. Her nerves twisted into a knot along with her emotions. But it was time. She had to do this at some point. Now was as good a time as any.

He gave a nod. "Tonight can all be off the record if that's what you need it to be."

Surprised but grateful, Finley nodded. "I'm going to tell you a story, Detective. I want you to bear all of this in mind as you proceed with the investigation into my husband's murder."

Another nod. "I can do that."

Finley squared her shoulders. "All right then. As you know, last year I brought down Carson Dempsey's only son."

"He was a rapist. A scumbag."

Finley nodded. "More so than you know. I had several other defendants but only one with evidence. Whoever murdered him once he was in prison probably didn't care that he was a rapist. I'm certain it was about his father. Someone wanted to get back at Carson Dempsey. But Dempsey blamed me for the loss of his son."

"You think he ordered the hit on your husband." Houser hesitated. "On you."

"I know he did." Finley faltered. No turning back now. She'd taken a lot of risks, and she was okay with that. But now Matt was getting involved, and Jack wanted to do the same. She would not risk their safety. "The man who murdered my husband, his name was Billy Hughes."

Houser's chin came up in an aha gesture. "The guy from the convenience store."

"That's the one."

"Then you do know the identities of the men who invaded your home that night."

She shrugged. "I couldn't remember at first. Only bits and pieces. But then I started to recall voices and images. The first time I ran into one of them, I knew it was him. They've been watching me since *that* night. Probably even weeks before that."

"You provoked Hughes." He gave a knowing nod. "Gave the clerk an opportunity to do something." Houser narrowed his eyes. "How did you know the clerk kept a shotgun under the counter?"

Finley laughed a short, brittle sound. Drank more of her beer. "I didn't know and didn't care. At the time I still had moments of just wanting someone to end it. Hughes provided an opportunity, and I suddenly wanted to take it."

Houser lowered his gaze, sipped his own beer.

"I still lingered on the fringes of a bad place."

He looked up then. "What about now?"

"Now I'm in a better place. I watch them and they watch me." It sounded surreal, but it was true. "We all know it won't last forever. I have an endgame, and I suspect Dempsey does as well."

"You believe the rumors that Dempsey's newest pharmaceutical creation is bad business? Worse as far as addiction and side effects than any that came before it."

"I don't know any more about it than you do, probably, but I know where there's smoke, there's usually a fire."

"No one has been able to prove any of those vague rumors," Houser admitted.

"Chet Flock," Finley said.

Houser nodded. "He's been avoiding my reach."

"I spotted him a few hours ago outside a Starbucks. He's still watching me."

"Damn." Houser's lips compressed with frustration. "He won't be able to avoid me forever," he promised.

"He'll try," she assured him. "Flock is the third guy from *that* night. He mostly watched, videoed parts of it, for the boss, I imagine. He's closer to Dempsey. I'm guessing he knows plenty. Turn him, and you get Dempsey."

Houser chuckled. "Remember, O'Sullivan, I'm just a homicide detective. I think you're looking for the DEA. I will gladly get the ball rolling, but I'll need help from the right source to go after Dempsey."

"If the DEA could nail Dempsey," she offered, "they would have already. If the rumors are true, Dempsey is good. Careful. He's a hero to many. A pillar of the community to most. His son's trouble put him in a bit of a bad light. Made him vulnerable for the first time, lending credibility to those vague rumors. If he isn't stopped soon, he'll bury those rumors for good."

Houser moved his head slowly side to side in disapproval. "You've already taken a great many risks, and I can understand your need to get these people. Do you have any evidence of what you're alleging?"

"I can't prove anything. But there's only one guy left now."

"Oh hell. Tark Brant," Houser muttered. His expression turned somber. "You were there when he was shot."

Not a question. "I was there."

He looked away. "Damn it, O'Sullivan. You're putting me in a tight spot here."

"I didn't shoot him."

He swung his gaze back to hers. "Tell me you can prove it."

"Can Graves prove I did?"

Houser shook his head. "He wants to, but he can't. Not unless something more comes back on forensics."

"It won't." She hoped. The memory of Brant falling against her and slipping to the floor made her gut clench.

"All right, so you didn't shoot him. Tell me what happened?"

"Brant had a girlfriend, Whitney Lemm. She spotted me watching him. Saw him watching me. She thought I was trying to steal him away from her." She made a sound that wasn't a laugh. "I didn't know her. I saw her with him a few times, but I didn't bother figuring out who she was because she wasn't relevant to my goal."

Houser held up a hand. "Are you sure you want to tell me this?"

"Off the record, right?"

"Yeah, yeah. We've gone this far." He exhaled a big breath. "What happened?"

Finley explained how Lemm had called her to a meeting, supposedly about Derrick. Then the rest.

"Son of a bitch," Houser bit off. "If Hughes was the one who killed your husband, then . . ."

Finley took a breath and said what had to be said. "Brant is the one who raped me. He passed along a message during that attack. *You take something from me; I take something from you.* At the time, I didn't know those bastards, and the only person I had taken something from was Dempsey. That's how I know it was him."

"As much as I agree with your theory, it is just a theory." Houser looked away a moment, shook his head. "Damn." He blew out a breath. Met Finley's gaze once more. "But I'm willing to go with it. So where is Lemm now?"

Relief rushed through Finley. "Someplace safe." She set her empty can aside. "She may know things that can help build a case against Dempsey. She said Brant told her things. But even if she doesn't, she may be able to lure in Flock. *He* will know things."

"You want me to help her. To . . . ?"

"Get her to the right people who can do what needs to be done."

He nodded, lips in a tight, thin line. "Okay. I know a guy. We went to Auburn together. He's actually in the DEA. He's part of the reason I decided to become a cop."

"Instead of a doctor the way you were supposed to," Finley offered.

"Yeah. I made a lot of people unhappy with that decision, but it was the right one."

"You trust him? This DEA guy?"

"Unconditionally."

"Call him. Lemm won't survive long without a way out."

"I'll call him," Houser promised. "For now, we need to be sure she's somewhere they can't get to her."

"Can you move her to a safe house?"

He nodded. "I've worked a couple of times with an agent assigned to Nashville's FBI field office. He might be able to assist with that, off the record for now."

Finley stood. "I'll take you to her."

Houser pushed to his feet. "No. Sorry, but this is where your involvement ends. You said yourself they watch you. You could lead them right to her. I'll take it from here."

Finley gave him the location. She called Lemm and described the detective coming to take her to a safe house. Lemm sounded nervous, but she agreed to cooperate. What other choice did she have?

As he was leaving, Houser paused. "The world needs more people like you, Finley O'Sullivan. Don't let what happened define you. You were damned good as an ADA. Do something big. Change the world."

With that he was gone.

Finley stood on the porch staring after him until his taillights faded in the darkness. He was right. She had allowed *that* night to define her.

Maybe the lie she had told Matt was actually the truth. It was time to put *that* night behind her. Time to do something big. Change the world.

When she turned to go inside, her neighbor stood on the sidewalk staring at her. Finley paused. Helen Roberts's dog sat at her feet, waiting for its master to continue with their walk. Dusk had settled, prompting the streetlights to come to life. The one nearest to them held the two in a gold circle, as if they were the only two characters left onstage as the play ended and the lights lowered. Finley couldn't even count the times the woman had done this. Stood in her yard or on the sidewalk and just stared. She was always watching.

What the hell? Finley stepped off the porch. "Mrs. Roberts, how are you tonight?"

"Good. And you?" Roberts said in response.

Roberts was also the one who'd called 911 *that* night. As usual, she'd been watching. She hadn't been able to identify anyone, but she'd seen more than one figure leaving Finley's house.

Finley walked across her small yard to stand at the fence. "Is there something I can help you with?" Roberts continued to stand on the sidewalk staring at Finley.

"There was someone prowling around in your backyard today."

Finley smiled. "That was Jack. My boss. He wants to paint the house." She imagined most of her neighbors would be glad to see that happen.

Roberts nodded, the move jerky. "I've seen him on television."

Finley smiled. "You probably have."

The older woman's frown deepened as if she had something more to say but couldn't recall what it was or decide whether to say it. "Him poking around back there reminded me of that time when you were in the hospital."

Her dog growled at a figure walking in their direction from the south end of the street.

Finley hesitated until she identified the man. Another of her neighbors out for an evening stroll. He said hello as he passed. Finley did the same. Roberts said nothing. She wasn't the sociable sort.

Finley turned back to her. "When I was in the hospital?"

Roberts gave a solitary nod. "After your husband was murdered. For days there were people swarming around your house."

"The police," Finley suggested. "My house was a crime scene."

"I remember those people," she said, "in their protective gear like on the television." Her forehead furrowed deeper. "But this was after that. These were men who came after the police left. After the yellow tape was gone. Men dressed like your boss was today in regular clothes."

Adrenaline roared through Finley's veins. "You're certain? This was while I was in the hospital and after the police were finished?"

216

Roberts nodded. "They came mostly at night."

Finley's heart pounded harder. "Do you remember what these men looked like? What color or make of car they drove?"

"No. No. It was dark. I never saw their faces." She shrugged. "Black cars."

Flock drove a black car. Hughes had as well.

"Thank you, Mrs. Roberts. If you remember anything else, please let me know."

Without another word, Roberts picked up her dog and walked away.

It wasn't until Finley was in the house that she allowed her anger to flare.

Had to be Dempsey's men. But why? What were they looking for? She'd dug around in the backyard after Roberts told her about Derrick digging back there. She'd found nothing, save the poor dog's remains. Maybe Roberts had gotten it wrong about Derrick and his digging. Maybe she was wrong about this too.

Finley's cell vibrated with an incoming text.

Nita.

Sent the reservations to your email.

Finley sent a thank-you and took a long, deep breath.

Whatever Roberts had seen, it had to wait. Finley needed to prepare for her trip to Atlanta.

Her cell vibrated again, this time with an incoming call. *Tad.* She wasn't sure of his last name. She didn't even know if Tad was his real first name. But he had resources for looking into credit card accounts. She'd asked him to check on the spy-shop receipt.

"Hey, did you find anything for me?"

"It's not what I found but what I didn't find that's important."

"Go on," Finley prodded.

217

"The credit card in question was only activated in July of this year, and it has never been used at the spy shop on Fesslers Parkway. The receipt is a fake."

Finley wanted to be surprised, but somehow she wasn't. "Thanks, Tad. Bill me."

"Already did. Until next time, Fin."

The call ended.

"What are you up to, Winthrop?" Finley muttered.

Not murder, Finley suspected. More likely she was covering up something else or covering for someone else.

Finley sent Jack a text with the update.

At this point both Marsh and Winthrop were on Finley's and Jack's shit lists.

His response came immediately. If we found it, Ventura will find it.

Exactly.

Whatever the game here, even Jack Finnegan couldn't keep Winthrop from a murder charge if she kept leaving such easily traced tracks.

24

The Widow

8:00 p.m.

Pettit Residence
Penrose Drive, Brentwood

Ellen surveyed the dining table and smiled. Though she would prefer to be home, Laney's was the next best thing. Large enough, understated elegance. Her friend's china was vintage, a set she had inherited from her mother, who had inherited the twelve-place setting and the matching serving pieces from her own mother. Something British from the nineteenth century. Laney had a thing for vintage pieces.

Ellen preferred new. She'd dealt with enough used stuff as a child. Used clothes—donated by people from the church her father had insisted they attend.

How else will we eat, girl? he'd demanded.

He had been right, of course. God knew he wasn't going to work, and her mother was far too frail to do anything. The church and its members were always providing for her poor family. Bringing food. Dropping off clothes.

The bastard who'd sired her had stolen what he could. When his efforts fell short of providing for his wife and child, he'd used the church to fill the gaps. Once her mother had died, he had used Ellen.

She shuddered, pushed the nightmare away. She'd never told anyone about the things he had done. Not one living soul. Even as a child she had recognized how things followed you. Kids at school made fun of her when they saw her in the donated clothes. The many harsh lessons she had experienced had been difficult, but she had learned from them. She'd made sure none of her childhood had followed her. She'd also made damned sure no other man took advantage of her. Ever.

She banished the painful memories and focused on the now.

Laney was the only part of her childhood that Ellen had kept. If not for Laney, she might not have survived. She had given Ellen a real home.

Ellen would do anything for her friend.

Laney had graciously offered her home for tonight's dinner. Aware of Ellen's need to have a private meeting with her partners, her friend had also arranged to have dinner with Norine Duncan at Blakedale. Laney knew nothing of the inner workings of the partners; she understood it was better that way.

Certainly Norine needed a good visit after Finley O'Sullivan's abrupt intrusion.

Ellen had known O'Sullivan would be a test, but she hadn't anticipated just how good the woman was. Or how relentless. Though she shouldn't have been surprised. O'Sullivan had a reputation for being dogged, and she was very, very good at her work. She, too, had lost a husband to murder. The two of them had a good deal in common.

Ellen smiled to herself. She had chosen the Finnegan Firm for that reason. She needed O'Sullivan to be very thorough. She also needed her to feel a kinship . . . to empathize. So far, so good on that count.

Liz arrived first, of course. Her internal time-is-money clock kept her on her toes and on top of all else. Ellen never had to worry about

Liz. Her abilities went well beyond numbers. Liz had a sense for the order of things.

Ellen gave Liz a hug and ushered her into the parlor, where two bottles of wine were breathing, ready for their indulgence.

Moments later, Vivian, Daisy, and Joanna arrived. No smiles tonight. They were worried. They all were. Frankly, Vivian's penchant for protection kept her worried in the best of times. It was the nature of her work. Daisy and Joanna were the best planners in the world of finance. Like builders of architectural wonders, the two could create a stock portfolio like no one else. Each had a kind of sixth sense when it came to investments.

They all had distinct skills.

Jessica, of course, arrived last.

The husband, Ellen surmised. Jessica and her husband were both hard workers. Dedicated. Ambitious. But Jessica was the shark. The marriage would never last.

"Sorry I'm late." Jessica gave her a quick hug that left Ellen feeling cold.

"No need to apologize. We've only just gathered in the parlor for wine."

There was still time for this to turn out right. For all involved to do the right thing. They had been together from the beginning. To lose one of these women would be like losing a limb. Ellen desperately hoped all would end well, but she had taken the proper steps in case it did not.

She began by pouring the wine. Tonight she served. The way these women served her at the office, this was the least she could do. Tonight was important. Tonight was pivotal.

"Why don't we move on to the dining room?" Ellen suggested.

Conversation lulled a bit as they settled around the table. Silverware clinked against china; stemware moved up and down from the table to lips.

Her friends didn't pick at their food—they ate with the same gusto with which they achieved greatness in the finance world. They were good. They had appetites. Strong appetites. Even stronger ambition.

Ellen set her fork aside first. "We've reached the stage in this project that we discussed on Friday."

All eyes shifted to Ellen. These women . . . her heart squeezed. She loved each one. Trusted . . . each one. The abrupt hesitation she felt was understandable considering what she now suspected of one.

Still, protecting them, protecting herself, was paramount.

"From this point forward we give nothing unnecessarily to anyone, not even our legal representatives. We answer only as necessary, and we stay focused on moving forward. We will not meet with Jack or with Finley alone. We meet together. All or no one."

Glances were exchanged, as Ellen had anticipated. This was a first in their many projects, and it was the sort of thing that could drive a wedge into the closest of groups. Between the most trusted of friends.

"Should we be worried?" Jessica asked, an edge in her voice.

Of course she would be the first to show fear, to throw that particular question on the table.

"No." Ellen smiled. "There is no cause for concern."

Vivian placed a hand on Ellen's as she scanned the faces at the table. "Ellen is right. There is no cause for alarm whatsoever," she repeated. "We will carry out the final steps, and it will be finished."

A moment passed, and then, once more, forks scraped china. Stemware moved to thirsty lips.

They were fine.

It would be over soon.

This was as it should be.

Ellen forced herself to swallow a bite of perfectly sautéed chicken. Some part of her had changed during the past few days. She didn't feel herself.

Still, she had no regrets.

This project had been the proper choice, no matter that certain missteps had occurred. No matter that she might yet lose more. Regrets changed nothing and wasted valuable time.

She surveyed the table . . . watched the women who had been at her side all these years.

No, there would be no regrets. But there would be pain. The idea that the missteps might have been purposely made was like a stake driven deep into her heart.

Could she trust that it wouldn't happen again?

Ellen reached for her wine, her hand shaking despite her best efforts. She could not.

25

The Other Woman

11:30 p.m.

Lauder Residence
Twelfth Avenue South, Nashville

Jessica parked in her driveway, too mentally exhausted to bother with the garage. Her idiot husband always took up more than his half of the space, which made parking problematic.

Tonight she had bigger frustrations than him. She was furious. So furious. Ellen thought she had everything under control.

Jessica would see about that.

She emerged from her Lexus and slammed the door. How dare Ellen use Jessica and then just pretend everything was fine. Ellen had no idea what was coming. All her reassurances and platitudes would prove hollow.

The others would soon see who was the most brilliant of all. Jessica smiled. How divine this was going to be.

"Jessica!"

Startled, she whirled toward the voice.

Lena.

Horror rushed through Jessica. What the hell was *she* doing here? She glanced around to ensure her husband wasn't on the upper-level patio watching. He was like that. Always in her business. Always asking questions.

"What are you doing?" Jessica hissed in a stage whisper. "You know better than to come to my home. Especially now." She glanced around again. At some point all those forensic reports were going to come back, and her new partner was going to be very surprised at what they found.

If Jessica was lucky, that information wouldn't be released until she was out of this damned town.

The more immediate issue was, How had Lena gotten here? There was no car parked along the alley. She must have parked on another street and walked over. Good God! She could have been seen by a neighbor! Jessica took a breath. She had to stay cool. Play the part.

"I took care of everything just like you said," Lena whispered, not nearly quietly enough, as she moved closer.

"You shouldn't be here," Jessica warned with another look toward her town house. Thankfully it was an end unit, so they didn't have an audience on both sides.

"I wanted to see you before I leave."

How pathetic. "You should stick with the plans we made. We'll meet in Atlanta just like we arranged. We'll fly together from there."

Lena stared at her for a long moment. Other than the lights on either side of the garage door, they were in darkness. What did this idiot hope to do or to learn by coming here at this crucial juncture?

"I need to know," Lena finally said, "that you're going to show up."

Jessica scoffed. "Of course I'm going to show up. I only have half the PIN. Why wouldn't I show up?" She was not stupid. This was about the money. What else would she possibly want or need with this person? Hello?

"It's just that . . ." Lena crossed her arms over her chest. "I don't want to be sorry I trusted you, but I've been worried since I talked to that investigator. She is figuring things out way too fast. After all our hard work to make this happen, I just need to be sure you're not going to let me down."

Jessica forced a sympathetic face and placed a reassuring hand on her arm. "You have my word, Lena. There is absolutely nothing to worry about. We're good. Everything is going exactly as planned. We'll have the world at our feet! All we've ever dreamed of and more, because I know how to turn that money into even more."

Lena nodded. "Okay. I'll see you tomorrow."

Jessica smiled, gave her arm a squeeze. "Just keep picturing drinks on the beach, baby. We are on our way."

Lena disappeared into the darkness, and Jessica relaxed. Fool. Too late for cold feet now. She turned and headed into her house. Thank God she only had to play *this* role one more night.

Whatever possessed her to want a husband?

26

Thursday, September 22

10:00 a.m.

Ritz-Carlton Hotel
Peachtree Street, Atlanta

Finley walked into the lobby and considered where to begin.

Her first stop after leaving the airport this morning had been a visit to Dyson-Mekler. The receptionist at the front desk had confirmed the photo of Lena Marsh on Finley's phone as the previous receptionist at the clinic. This was the extent of the information the receptionist would provide. When Finley had pushed, the woman called the practice manager, who had promptly but courteously shown Finley the door.

The confirmation was enough for now. It was enough to validate any further investigation would not be a waste of time and resources.

From now until her flight time, Finley intended to concentrate on whatever she could learn about Grady's visit here last weekend. Odds were, Winthrop didn't know why her new husband had made the trip to the Peach State any more than Finley understood the lies her own husband had told.

This is no time for comparing dead husbands.

Experience warned that starting with the check-in desk would be a waste of time. What she needed was an employee who worked elsewhere in the hotel.

Finley made her way to the restaurant. Breakfast was still being served for another half hour. Not that she was hungry, but she could use more coffee. The hostess showed her to a table. Before the woman could slip away, Finley flashed a pic of Grady and asked if she recalled seeing him there the week before. Ginger, according to her name tag, smiled and said she'd only started on Monday.

As soon as the hostess had floated away, another, younger woman, Dawn, materialized at Finley's table. Same coordinated charcoal-and-white attire.

Finley waited through her practiced spiel about the breakfast options. Only one other waitress appeared to still be on duty at this hour. There were just two customers besides Finley. Most people had left the hotel already, headed into their day of business or pleasure.

"I would love a bagel," Finley said. "And coffee, please."

Dawn smiled. "Anything else? We offer a lovely fruit plate. Perhaps a nice spread for your bagel."

Finley paused. "There is one other thing I'm hoping you might be able to help me with." She reached into her pocket for the two fifty-dollar bills she'd tucked there for just this moment. She placed the bills on the table and reached for her cell next. She showed Dawn a pic of Grady. "Do you remember seeing this man here last week? Maybe on Friday or Saturday?"

Dawn made a sad face. "I was off last Friday and Saturday." She moistened her lips, glanced at the bills, then across the room at the other waitress. "I'm sure Maya was here. She works the breakfast shift all the time. She's worked here a long time." She shot another look at the bills on the table. "I'll check with her."

Finley separated the two bills. "I appreciate the help."

Dawn hurried over to speak with her colleague. Maya glanced in Finley's direction. She said something, and Dawn moved on to one of the tables on that side of the room. Maya wandered in Finley's direction.

Maya was older than Dawn. Same uniform. Attractive like her colleague.

"Good morning," Maya said with a smile. "How can I help you?"

Finley showed her the photo, and Maya's smile widened. "Alex Wilensky. Yes. He was here. I think he comes to Atlanta from Chicago about five or six times a year. He always has breakfast in the hotel. Sometimes lunch. Makes it a point to say hello."

Alex Wilensky. Interesting. "Sounds like he liked staying here when he visited," Finley commented.

"Always. He said this was his favorite hotel."

It was the Ritz. Of course it was.

Finley needed more on Jarrod Grady, a.k.a. Alex Wilensky. She had a feeling this guy was more well traveled than they knew. "Was his business partner with him?"

At the waitress's look of confusion, Finley explained, "They often travel together."

Maya shook her head. "I never saw him with anyone else." She made a face. "Wait. Someone did join him for breakfast last . . ." She considered the memory for a moment. "Last Friday. It was the first time I'd seen him here with anyone."

"Must have been his partner." Finley pulled a name out of the air. "Paul Douglas. About the same age as Alex."

Maya shook her head. "No, this was no Paul. It was that attorney you see on all the buses and on the billboards around town." She rolled her eyes. "And that annoying commercial with its jingle that gets stuck in your head."

"I'm not from Atlanta, so I'm afraid I don't know who you mean."

"Lisa Lawrence," she said. "'Lisa Lawrence has got you covered,'" she singsonged.

Dawn arrived with a tray sporting a bone china plate embellished with a bagel and various condiments, along with a matching cup filled with steaming coffee. She placed each item in front of Finley.

Finley pushed the bills to the edge of the table. "Thanks, ladies. You've been a great help. I'll take my check now."

As Finley tucked the payment for her meal into the leather pouch, she downed a couple of bites of bagel and savored the coffee.

She googled Alex Wilensky and got basically nothing, at least not in the Atlanta area. So she moved on to the attorney mentioned, Lisa Lawrence. The screen filled instantly with entries. Finley scrolled through the long list on the way out of the hotel. By the time she reached the curb and flagged down a taxi, she had an address for the attorney's office, and her nerves were jangling in time with the tune Maya had singsonged.

She was onto something big here.

Lawrence Law Associates
Peachtree Street, Atlanta, 11:45 a.m.

Traffic ensured the short trip took a full twenty minutes. Now, after fifteen minutes in the lobby, Finley was escorted down the corridor to Lawrence's office. Lawrence couldn't be more than forty or forty-five years old, but she had a whole floor in a high-rise that screamed she had made it to the top of her game.

Lawrence waited in her massive office when Finley was ushered inside. The place was more like an apartment than an office. There was, of course, a grand office space overlooking the city below. Left of that was a mini conference zone, and on the right was a plush seating area of sofas, with a bar lining the wall.

"Join me," Lawrence said, indicating one of the two white sofas.

Finley offered her hand before taking a seat. Lawrence touched her palm briefly and settled onto the opposite sofa.

"First, Ms. O'Sullivan," Lawrence said, "I'll be quite frank with you. The only reason you're in my office is because I'm curious. That said, before we go any further, please give me a very powerful reason I should speak with you about Alex Wilensky. Otherwise, don't waste my time."

"If he's your client," Finley countered, keeping it in the present tense, "you wouldn't be talking to me at all."

Lawrence gave a nod. "He is not."

"But you know him. Met with him for breakfast at the Ritz last Friday."

"I know him, yes."

"Before we continue," Finley said, removing her cell phone and showing her the photo of Grady, "would you confirm that this is the man you know as Alex Wilensky."

Lawrence glanced at the photo, her face giving away her level of disgust at the image. "Yes, that is him."

Whatever he'd done, the woman definitely didn't like the guy.

"What you may not know," Finley went on, putting her phone away, "is that he's dead. Murdered."

Lawrence's expression remained neutral. "Should this news mean something to me?"

Definitely some bad blood between these two? Was Lawrence another of his victims? Damn, the guy sure had a way with very intelligent women.

Finley blocked the thought of Derrick.

"Maybe. Before his murder," Finley said, "he stole seven point eight million dollars from his new wife. We've yet to find the money."

Lawrence laughed out loud.

Finley waited for her to finish.

When Lawrence had caught her breath, she shook her head. "You'll have to forgive my inappropriate response. But thank you for sharing the news." She stood. "I'm afraid I have another appointment now."

Finley didn't move. No. No. This meeting wasn't over yet. "We have reason to believe that our client is not the first woman he's done this to."

"You would be correct." Lawrence remained standing, but she made no move to walk away.

Finley pressed on. "We also discovered a person we believe to be his partner. The man who represented himself as Jarrod Grady in Nashville and Alex Wilensky here in Atlanta is dead, but his partner is still out there. I don't want this to happen again."

Lawrence lowered back to the sofa. "A partner?"

Finley nodded. "This is why it's important that I find out anything else that connects these women. If you represent a client he swindled, I need to speak with her."

"He stole hundreds of thousands from her," Lawrence said. "She wasn't going to take it sitting down. She intended to file charges, but he used a family secret he discovered while they were together to keep her silent." Lawrence shook her head. "I urged her to go to the police anyway, but she wouldn't. This secret—whatever it was—was so humiliating she insisted and wouldn't take the risk, though I warned her he might divulge her secret anyway."

"Which means," Finley said, "that your client still isn't in the clear. His partner is out there, and she likely knows whatever he knew."

"She?"

Finley nodded. "If I can find the connection between the victims, I might be able to prove her link to Grady-Wilensky. Right now, what I know could go either way. The rub is in the proving it."

"I'll speak to her. If she's willing, I'll take you to her, and she can tell her story in whatever way and to whatever degree she feels comfortable."

"Thank you." It was the best Finley could hope for. "We owe it to these women to finish this. Bear in mind I have a flight back to Nashville later this evening."

Lawrence stepped out of her office to make her call. Finley took a water bottle from the silver tray on the table between the two sofas.

She was close. All she needed was confirmation.

Dagne Residence
Riverly Road, Atlanta, 1:30 p.m.

Since Lawrence was local, she drove Finley to her client Meredith Dagne. The client's home was grander than Winthrop's, and Finley wouldn't have considered that an easy feat. Yet here she sat in a home that better resembled a palace than a house.

Dagne was older than Winthrop as well, early sixties, and she was in ill health, multiple sclerosis, late onset.

Grady-Wilensky was a total scumbag. Fury roiled inside Finley.

"We met at a friend's anniversary party," Dagne explained. "He was with the caterer."

Sounded like the bastard stuck with a tried-and-true strategy. Or maybe food service and laying on the charm were his only business skills. No, that wasn't right. Celine Jones had mentioned his ability with accounting software.

"We dated for a few weeks," Dagne continued. "I selfishly thought I should grab on to whatever happiness I could for however long possible. Then my condition worsened, and I was forced to tell him about my diagnosis." She clutched the arms of her wheelchair. "I assumed he would disappear, but he didn't. He insisted on doing all possible to make my life comfortable and to ensure my happiness. For a time, he was like a godsend. I felt truly blessed."

Finley and Lawrence waited while she composed herself. "I gave him access to one of my accounts. I provided him with a credit card, a car. He moved into the house. And then large sums of money started to disappear. He had no idea that my accountant monitored all my accounts. I'd asked him to begin that service when I was diagnosed. I have no family, so I couldn't be certain what sort of help would end up taking care of me."

"There were a number of measures," Lawrence offered, "we instituted for when Meredith felt she would be more vulnerable."

"Lisa wanted me to press charges against him," Dagne went on. "But I couldn't. There were things I didn't want to be made public, and when I confronted him, he threatened to do exactly that."

"Which is why I met with him last Friday," Lawrence explained.

"The final payoff," Finley guessed. What a bastard.

"Five hundred thousand for his continued silence," Dagne said. "I had to consider the value of my peace of mind."

"How could you be certain that would keep him quiet?" Finley directed this at the attorney.

"It was a twofold payment. Half a million now and another half million upon her death. As long as he kept his word."

Unbelievable. Finley turned to Dagne. "May I ask you a personal question?" Everything she'd heard so far was exactly what she'd expected, but it didn't connect Marsh to Dagne.

Dagne laughed softly. "What could possibly be more personal?"

"When you met him, were you seeing a therapist?"

Dagne frowned. "I was. How did you know?"

And there it was. "Dyson-Mekler?"

Surprise flared in the older woman's eyes. "I still see Dr. Mekler."

Finley pushed to her feet and walked to where Dagne sat. She showed her a photo of Marsh. "Did you ever see this woman at his office?"

Understanding fell over the older woman's face. "Yes. Until she left last September or October, she was the receptionist. She was always so kind and helpful."

Finley showed the photo to Lawrence, then returned to her seat. "I have reason to believe this woman is his partner."

Dagne held Finley's gaze for a long moment. "And you say he is dead?"

"Yes."

Dagne nodded. "Good."

When the nurse insisted it was time for Mrs. Dagne's afternoon nap, Lawrence offered to drive Finley to the airport. If she was lucky, she could catch the earlier flight. She needed to get back to Nashville ASAP.

"What're you going to do?" Lawrence asked.

Though Finley had not mentioned their client, Lawrence was aware the firm was representing someone related to Grady-Wilensky.

"It's a sensitive situation," Finley agreed. "But you have my word I will inform the detective on the case about all that I've learned, and I'll give him your contact information." That she could do without divulging details about Lawrence's client. If a criminal case related to Marsh was opened, involving Dagne would be the detective's battle with Lawrence.

"Thank you," Lawrence said when she'd pulled to the curb at the drop-off zone. "As emotionally draining as this was for Meredith, I'm certain it's heartening to some degree for her to know she wasn't the only one who fell for him."

"I'm sure," Finley agreed. "Thank you." She reached for the door. "It was a pleasure to meet you."

"I looked you up, Finley O'Sullivan," Lawrence said, waylaying her. "I don't know the details of why you're doing this investigator gig, but judging by your record as an ADA, if you ever want to go back into practice, call me. I can always use another warrior."

Finley smiled and exited the car. The woman had no idea.

Once she'd changed her flight and tackled the security line, Finley called Jack to give him an update.

"I'll pass Marsh's details along to Ventura," Jack said. "The sooner they start looking for her, the better the chances of finding her."

Finley agreed. "The Miami destination was probably a ruse. If she headed out of town in her car, she could be halfway across the country." Nothing they could do about that. "I'll let you know when I land."

"There's been some developments here, Fin."

She didn't like the sound of his voice. "Developments?"

"That detective. Eric Houser, the one working on Derrick's case."

"Yeah," Finley said, her heart rate starting to climb. She should have called him at some point today to follow up on Whitney Lemm, but she'd gotten so caught up in her search here that she'd forgotten. "What about him?"

"He was shot last night at a dive motel over on the west side. He wasn't found until this morning. Apparently, the housekeeper went into the room and—"

"Is he dead?" Ice filled Finley's veins.

"No," Jack assured her. "He's alive. Barely. His ID was missing, so the staff in the ER didn't know who he was when he went into surgery. Obviously, he didn't show at work, and his partner couldn't find him, so he started checking in with hospitals. The partner got to the hospital and was able to see him briefly while he was in recovery. He says Houser roused long enough to say your name. It took his partner a while to figure out that Finley was you. He called here looking for you. He wants to talk to you as soon as you're back."

"What about the woman?" Finley's chest felt on the verge of exploding.

"The prostitute they found in the room with him?"

"She's not a prostitute," Finley argued, frustration joining the other emotions raging inside her. She was on her feet, walking back and forth in front of the row of chairs at the gate. "Houser went to the motel to pick her up and to talk to her. She's Brant's girlfriend—Whitney Lemm—the one who shot him." Finley's hopes sank. "She's a possible link to Dempsey."

"Sorry, kid, but she didn't make it. The setup in the room looked like Houser picked her up and things went south. The motel manager claimed he didn't even know she was in the room. It was supposed to be empty."

Outrage roared through Finley. "The fucking manager knew because I rented the room from him and took Whitney there. Houser was going to move her to a safe house and then interview her."

"Slow down," Jack said. "Explain this to me."

Finley took a breath, fought the urge to cry. What the hell was wrong with her lately? "I decided to do the right thing. I told Houser everything. He was going to help."

"Damn, Fin," Jack murmured. "You're killing me here. You have to be more careful. That could've been you dead in that room with Lemm."

"But it wasn't," she argued, renewed outrage blasting through her. "Just tell me if Houser's going to make it."

"The partner called me again a little while ago. He says the prognosis is good. But he's bugging the hell out of me about talking to you. I told him you were out of town and you'd talk to him when you got back."

"Thanks, Jack. Sorry I didn't tell you about Houser before I left."

"No problem, kid. Just promise me you'll do like we talked about and stop all these clandestine meetings with shady characters."

Finley managed a tight laugh. "Then how would I ever dig up the stuff our clients hide?"

Jack was the one laughing now. "You're right. Secrets are never hidden in safe places with nice people."

Never. They were in places no decent or sane person wanted to look.

27

5:50 p.m.

The Murder House
Shelby Avenue, Nashville

Her shabby little house had never looked so good.

Finley paid the driver and stepped out of the car, her messenger bag draped over her shoulder. Her emergency overnight bag in hand. Staying overnight had never been the plan, but these days with flight delays and cancellations, one never knew. There had also been the risk that staying overnight would be necessary if she couldn't pack all the needed meetings into one day.

Matt's car was behind hers in the driveway. He sat on her porch steps, the jacket and tie gone, shirt unbuttoned at the throat. He smiled as she walked toward him. The car that had delivered her sped away, likely headed back to the airport for another arrival.

"I would have picked you up at the airport," her friend said as he pushed to his feet. He took the overnight bag from her and moved aside for her to climb the steps.

"I wasn't sure I'd be back tonight, much less a little earlier." She unlocked the door. "You know how it is."

"I do indeed." He followed her inside, carried the bag to her bedroom. She would have tossed it on the sofa.

She needed wine. Now. "You want a beer?" She headed for the fridge. His yes had her reaching for the beers left in the six-pack she'd shared with Houser last night. She hoped like hell he would make it through this. With her free hand she grabbed the bottle of rosé already chilled and bumped the door shut with her hip.

She had called Houser's partner as soon as she landed and given him most of the story. She'd opted to start at finding Lemm in her garage rather than across the street from the Turnip Truck. She was supposed to go to the precinct tomorrow and make an official statement. She'd also called the hospital and learned that Houser's condition had been upgraded to good. Her relief at the news had been so profound she'd almost wept.

Matt joined her in the kitchen before she rounded up a clean glass. She did sometimes miss the dishwasher she'd had at her condo.

"Nita told me you'd changed your flight and what time you'd be home, so I took the liberty of ordering pizza."

The doorbell sounded just then.

"Right on time," he said with a grin.

"You're my favorite guy," Finley shouted after him as he hustled to the door.

"I won't tell Jack," he teased as he opened the door.

While Matt interacted with the pizza delivery guy—judging by his deep voice—Finley poured herself a hefty glass of wine. She downed a good portion of it and almost moaned at the promised relief. God, she had needed that. She closed her eyes and attempted to stop the whirl of pieces from this case in her head. She needed a few hours of space away from those thoughts to put it all into perspective.

"You want to eat in here or in there?" Matt called from the living room.

She opened her eyes, forced away thoughts of the case. "In there. I'm on my way with the drinks." She refilled her glass, tucked the bottle under one arm, and grabbed the six-pack ring with its remaining beers.

She joined her friend in the living room. The two of them piled onto the sofa, drinks on the coffee table. They devoured slices of pizza. Finley couldn't think about anything else until she'd finished off two. As often as she forgot to eat, she sometimes made up for it when she did. And though she appreciated Matt showing up at her door unannounced and having ordered pizza, she wasn't looking forward to whatever was on his mind. They had known each other forever, and showing up unannounced was not his MO except in an emergency, like when he couldn't reach her and he was worried. He was far too considerate and gentlemanly.

Finally, fingers greasy, wine bubbling down her throat, she listened while Matt launched into what he had to say.

"I found a connection"—he shrugged—"think the loosest definition of the word . . . between Dempsey and Derrick."

The warm, spicy pizza turned to a cold, hard lump in her stomach. "I asked you not to get involved with the investigation. Houser can handle it."

Shit. Maybe not. He was in the hospital, and God only knew what his memory of the events that had happened would be like. She should be at the hospital sitting at his side. Except she wasn't family, and with the new visitor restrictions, the chances of her getting in to see him were less than zero. Damn it.

"Maybe you didn't hear," Matt said, wiping his hands on a napkin and then reaching for his beer, "but Houser was shot last night. He's in pretty rough shape. The chief says he'll make it, but he'll be out of commission for a while."

Finley grabbed her own wad of napkins and swabbed at her mouth and then her hands. She tried valiantly to tamp down the flash of regret wrapped with intense frustration, but it wasn't happening. This . . . *thing* with Derrick was out of control. It was one thing when she put herself in danger for the sake of finding information, but putting other innocent people at risk . . . *Breathe,* she told herself. This had gone too far.

"Why do you think I asked you to stay out of this?" She threw the knot of napkins on the coffee table. "Dempsey will do all in his power to keep trouble away from his door."

Matt stared at her then. "But it's okay for you to poke that bear."

"I have no choice," she snapped before she could stop herself. Her lips clamped together to prevent any other words from slipping out.

"Because he had someone you love murdered?" Matt's jaw hardened with his own mounting frustration. "The son of a bitch almost killed someone I care deeply about. Don't I get the same privilege?"

She glared at him. "I didn't die."

"What do you want me to say?" Anger spiked in his voice. "It's okay that he did what he did because you survived? I don't want him to get away with it."

Finley closed her eyes. Fought to regain her composure.

See, I told you the guy's in love with you.

Derrick's voice floated through her, and she could barely breathe.

"Houser was almost killed because of me," she blurted, unable to hold back all the secrets and lies anymore. It had to end somewhere. "That guy in the convenience store, Billy Hughes, you saw the video. I wanted him to die." She shrugged. "Or maybe I wanted him to kill me, but I wanted all of it over."

Matt started to interrupt, but she stopped him with a raised hand. "I'm far from finished. The dead woman they found in the motel where Houser was shot and think is a prostitute, she was Tark Brant's girlfriend. She killed him. I was there. She thought he and I had a thing, and maybe we did. He was there . . . *that* night. He was the one who . . . raped me. For months I've been watching him. *I*"—she slapped her chest with her hand—"wanted him to know I was watching him. He's dead and I'm glad. But the woman—Whitney Lemm—shouldn't have had to die because of what I did. Houser shouldn't have been shot because of what I asked him to do."

Only when she shut up did she realize she was shaking. Matt moved closer, pulled her against him, and hugged her tight. She tried to push him away at first. Wanted him to understand she was dead serious about his involvement. But she was tired. Tired of pretending all that mattered was getting the people responsible for what had happened.

When in truth she was the one responsible for what had happened. She was the one who got Derrick killed. She took Dempsey's son from him, and he took Derrick from her. Fair was fair, right?

Finley couldn't cry. Until the other night, she'd thought she had forgotten how. But now, she didn't have any tears left inside her. She wanted . . . this . . . over.

She stiffened. Wait. What had Matt said?

She drew back. "What connection?" Matt's words suddenly filtered through all the crap and sank into her brain.

Matt held up a hand, stopping her this time. "You need to give me a minute to catch up, Fin. You were there when Brant was shot?"

"The girlfriend—Lemm—said she had information about Derrick. But when I got there, she just warned me off her boyfriend—Brant. Then he showed up. Based on the fading bruises Lemm was wearing, the situation wasn't going to end well. Apparently, she was aware, so she shot him." Finley exhaled a big breath and said the rest. "She was going to shoot me, too, but I talked her out of it." The whole story sounded far worse looking back. At the time it had felt like it all worked out. Not so much now.

"Does Jack know about this?"

She nodded. "Houser knows too. I told him everything."

Finley didn't miss the flash of hurt in her friend's eyes. She'd told two people, but he wasn't one of them.

"Sorry I didn't tell you too. I wanted to protect you."

The way he stared at her now, she could see that he wasn't buying it.

"I had to tell Houser in order to get help for Lemm. Jack is my boss and . . ." Jesus Christ, what was Jack? He'd always been like an uncle to her, but everything was different now. He was—had been—in love with her mother. Did Matt know?

She stared at Matt, was certain he wouldn't have hidden that information from her. But she had hidden so much from him. "Jack finally told me what happened between him and the Judge," she said. "He's . . . or was in love with her. When he fell off the wagon and walked away from his practice, he finally admitted the truth to her, and she kicked him out of her life. Our lives." Finley shook her head. "How could we not have known that?"

A moment passed before Matt said, "Sometimes we do things for the people we care about. Things that don't make sense later but somehow did at the time."

Was he giving her a way out of looking like a bad friend? That was so Matt-like.

Sadly, that wasn't Finley's excuse. "I didn't want you to know." There. She'd said it.

"Know what?" He searched her eyes. "That you wanted the truth about your husband? Of course you did. Anyone would."

"About the rest and what I had become," she confessed, unable to meet his gaze now. "A person so bent on revenge that I ignored, twisted, the law. I'd always been above that . . . but then I fell . . . and I just kept falling."

"You did what you thought you had to do," Matt said. "The only thing I regret is that you thought you had to do it alone."

His words tugged at her emotions. He made a damned valid point. "You're right. I'm sorry. I should have . . . told you."

Something else she had ignored. She'd been so focused on her own desperation to get the men involved with *that* night she hadn't realized she was pushing everyone else away.

"I told myself I wanted to protect you, but the truth was I felt ashamed. I understood what I was doing was wrong, but I couldn't stop."

"You weren't wrong, Fin," he said softly, too softly. "You were right all along. Dempsey *is* involved somehow."

Wait, wait. She needed to hear all of this. "What did you find?"

"I talked to a friend of mine. He's a security analyst for the company who takes care of Dempsey Pharma. He needed a favor, so I did a little bargaining. I did something for him, and he did something for me. He ran an image of Derrick through his system to see if he'd ever been on the Dempsey Pharma property."

A tendril of excitement or fear, maybe a combination of both, slid through Finley. "What did he find?"

"He found three different occasions when Derrick came through the gate to Dempsey Pharma. That doesn't actually prove anything except that he was on the property."

"Do you have dates?" Her heart pounded so hard she couldn't breathe.

"Two times before you met and then one more time the week before . . . *that* night."

Emotion rose so fast into her throat she put her hands there as if to hold it back before it burst out of her.

When she could speak, she managed, "Is it possible he was working for Dempsey?"

The idea clawed at her chest. Sonny—Dempsey's son—had been charged with rape the month before she and Derrick met. The case had been Finley's. Could Dempsey have hired Derrick to get close to her? Maybe to watch her? Keep Dempsey apprised of her case against his son?

No matter the lies she had already discovered . . . no matter how often she had thought she hated her dead husband for having made up the stories about the house and God only knew what else, none of it compared to this.

The defeat . . . the hurt . . . they were suffocating.

"It means there might have been a connection to Dempsey's business operations," Matt argued. "Maybe he was interviewed for a job at the company. It does not mean he was working *for* Dempsey. Bear in mind that if he was working for Dempsey, it may not have had anything to do with you."

Finley laughed, a sound that held no humor whatsoever. "Now you're reaching, Counselor. Considering what we know—or don't know, I should say"—she paused to shove back the tears crowding into her throat and eyes—"chances are it was about me. The timing says it all."

Damn it! Just as soon as she thought the tears were gone for good, they came back with a vengeance.

"It means something," Matt agreed. "We just don't know what yet, but we will find out."

Finley wrestled the hurt and anger aside, and all that remained was a kind of weary hysteria. "You do realize you probably broke at least two laws." Matt always played by the rules. He never crossed the boundaries.

"You're seriously going there with me."

"You're right." Finley scrubbed her hands over her face. "This has been the most screwed-up week."

"The case?"

Finley took a couple more deep breaths. If this was true, it only added insult to injury. The possibility of him being a spy for Dempsey to see where Finley was on the case didn't change the fact that his murder was because of her.

Just stop.

Or did it? If he'd taken the job—if he was that kind of guy . . .

Finley strong-armed thoughts of Derrick out of her head and focused on the conversation with Matt. "It's a strange case for sure." She reached for the wine bottle and refilled her glass. "So much of what I've found points to our client knowing far more than she's sharing."

The funny thing was, Finley understood Winthrop better than maybe she should. Almost respected her. And though there were moments when Finley was certain the woman was guilty of something related to her lying, cheating husband . . . how could she judge? They both wanted the same thing: the truth.

And maybe a little revenge.

"You think she may have hired someone to murder her husband?" Matt asked, jerking Finley from the troubling thoughts.

"No." She shook her head. "I don't think she would go there. I think she just wanted the truth, and maybe her methods for finding it or proving it are making her look uncaring and guilty. I'm reasonably convinced at this point that Jarrod Grady and a partner had been targeting older, lonely women of means. The team had run the scam at least once before Winthrop. Something went wrong this time, or maybe the partner decided she no longer wanted to split the proceeds. Whatever happened, it's looking more and more like the perfect how-to-get-away-with-murder plot."

"The partner would have to be a real mastermind," Matt suggested.

"My instincts are telling me that all the women involved with this case are masterminds."

"Whatever you do," Matt suggested, "try to stay out of the line of fire this time, would you?"

"I find that difficult these days." She frowned, reached for her glass, suddenly remembered last night's conversation on the street with her nosy neighbor. "You know Mrs. Roberts, my neighbor?"

"The nosy one." Matt opened another beer.

Finley nodded. "She mentioned that while I was in the hospital, there were people poking around my house."

Matt frowned. "Did she mean the cops? The forensic guys?"

"This was after the cops had finished. She said it was after the yellow tape was taken down."

"Did she have descriptions?" He sipped his beer.

"No. They were careful," she said. "She had told me a couple of months ago about seeing Derrick digging around in the backyard— before I moved in. But when I did some digging around back there, the only thing I found was a dog—presumably a family pet—that someone had buried."

"You were digging around in your backyard?" His expression said this conversation had his concern mounting.

"Not recently. It was before. Back in the summer. I thought I'd find something, so I dug around like a total maniac, and I found the dog's remains." Wait. There was something else she hadn't told him about. "And the other night—the night you took care of me—I had found a plastic baggie filled with photos of me from before Derrick and I met." She pointed to the cushion she was sitting on. "Inside the cushion."

"Like stalker photos?"

"Exactly like stalker photos." As much as she wanted to relieve herself of guilt at the idea that Derrick had been watching her for some reason, and now it turns out that reason might possibly have been that he was working for Dempsey—a stretch but entirely feasible—she still couldn't turn off the guilt. If in fact Dempsey had hired Derrick to get close to her, it would have been because of the case against his son. Any way she looked at it, it was still about her and what she was doing.

Finley forced herself to breathe, then downed more wine.

"I'm not liking the sound of any aspect of this." Matt threw back a slug of his beer. "So Roberts told you last night that back when you were in the hospital—after *that* night—she saw strangers searching or whatever around your house. Maybe inside as well."

Finley nodded. "Technically she didn't say *inside*, but once they were in the backyard, they could have come inside the house. It's not like the locks are great."

"Which means only one thing," Matt offered. "They were looking for something. This was Derrick's house. Had to be something—other than stalker photos—they presumed he might have stashed here."

"That's what I'm thinking." She just hadn't been able to look into the possibility last night, and today she'd been out of town.

"We should take a closer look." Matt shot to his feet. "You have flashlights?"

Finley was confident it would be pointless, but what the hell. "I have one. And my phone, of course."

"I've got one in my trunk. I'll be right back."

Finley was exhausted, and yet she felt giddy. The backyard was a dead end—this she knew from experience—but if Matt was game, so was she. As exhausted as she was, she needed to burn off some of these emotions.

He returned, flashlight in hand. "Let's do this."

Finley downed the rest of the wine in her glass. "Fortification."

Matt did the same with his beer. "What you said."

They laughed together, and Finley felt the first ebb of calm. Whatever happened, Matt and Jack would be with her every step of the way.

If you let them.

God, she hated that voice.

"We'll go with a grid pattern," Matt suggested, "the same way we would if we were looking for evidence at a crime scene."

"We are looking for evidence," she reminded him. "And this was once a crime scene."

"You're right. Let's get to it."

North to south, east to west, they covered the yard twice. They found exactly nothing. No indication anyone had done any digging beyond fading signs of Finley's previous efforts. No indication anyone had left anything or taken anything. Finley imagined her neighbor was glued to her window, watching the beams of light bob.

"What about the garage?" Matt asked.

The last thing Finley had found in the garage was Whitney Lemm.

She was tired and needed a shower, but another half hour or whatever wouldn't kill her. "I'm game if you are."

Inside the sagging structure, Finley flipped on the single bare bulb. Groaned at the pile of boxes. She really needed to get to those.

"Have you looked around in here before?"

"Not really." Beyond storing those boxes from her condo in here, she rarely came into the garage. All was pretty much as Derrick had left it, save for Whitney Lemm's collision with Finley's boxes. Oh, and there was the time she'd driven his truck to slip past the people watching her house during a high-profile case.

"Let's have a look," Matt offered.

They prowled and dug for the next hour or more. Picking through tools and yard implements. The boxes Finley hadn't bothered to unpack. They contained stuff from her former life . . . none of which she needed now. Except maybe that iron.

Matt, sleeves rolled up, shirt streaked with dust and grime, glanced around. "What about his truck?"

Finley surveyed the truck. "I mean, I've looked inside it. Driven it a couple of times." Or maybe just that once. She couldn't remember.

"Might as well go the distance."

Finley watched while he methodically went through the vehicle. Behind and under the seat. Beneath all the mats. Inside the glove box. He slid his hands over the headliner. Poked around under the dash. When he was done inside, he lay down on his back on the dusty concrete and had a look underneath the truck.

"Anything under there besides grease and, you know, parts?"

"Not so far," he tossed back.

Finley got down on her hands and knees and peeked beneath the vehicle to see what he was doing. He was fully under the truck now, moving from front to back.

"I think you've read too many spy novels." Finley gave up, collapsed onto the grimy floor, chin braced on her forearms. "I'm not sure I'll ever know who he really was or what . . . *we* were."

"Hold on."

Finley strained to see what he was doing. It was impossible to tell. He was reaching up, but she had no idea what toward or what for.

"Coming out," he announced.

Was that a note of anticipation she heard in his voice?

She pushed back to her feet, dusted off her clothes. Then held her breath and waited.

Matt was out and up, a small object in his hand. He opened the small square metal item. A key holder, she realized. One of those things used to hide a key under a fender or some other place in case you locked yourself out of a vehicle or house.

What Matt pulled out of the little box wasn't a key.

"Is that a thumb drive?" Did they even make those anymore?

"That's exactly what it is. Where's your laptop?"

Finley didn't bother turning off the light. She didn't care if Matt closed the door. She ran. Hit the back porch and flung herself into the house. She had her laptop open by the time Matt crossed the threshold.

He plugged the thumb drive in.

Finley's blood roared in her ears.

The device opened on the screen and immediately requested a password.

"Shit," she hissed.

"Any ideas?" he asked.

"Try our anniversary."

Incorrect.

Damn.

"Birthdays," she suggested.

Incorrect.

Incorrect.

"Damn it," Matt grumbled. "We're locked out."

"We need someone who knows a work-around." Finley's body vibrated with urgency. It was late. "Do you know anyone? Preferably that we can call right now?" The resource she had used since law school had moved to the other side of the world, literally. She hadn't found anyone as good since.

Matt nodded. "I've got a guy. But we might not be able to get him tonight. You okay with me taking this to him first thing in the morning?"

"Please do. The sooner we know what that's about, the better." Hope and worry warred inside her. What if this was it? The information she'd searched for all this time. Answers . . . the truth.

"All right then." He removed the thumb drive and dropped it into his shirt pocket. "I'll call you as soon as I have anything."

"Okay."

He grabbed his jacket and headed for the door. "This . . ." He hesitated at the door. "This could be important, Fin."

"I feel torn. Part of me wants to desperately cling to that thought, and then the other part of me wants to laugh it off as some sort of joke. There may be nothing on there but porn." The hope and worry vanished only to be replaced by fear . . . dread. Did she really want to know all Derrick's secrets? Would knowing be better than wondering?

Finley's breath stalled deep in her chest. Yes. She needed to understand. She had to know once and for all.

Matt gave her one of his lopsided grins. "Maybe, but Derrick didn't really seem like the porn type. See you tomorrow."

She laughed, a totally exhausted bark of a sound. She searched his face, shook her head at what she saw.

He frowned. "What?"

She reached up, swiped a streak of grease off his jaw. "Thanks for being you."

He hugged her hard. She relaxed into him. Needed his strength and reassurances more than anything right now. She couldn't do this alone anymore.

"We got this, Fin."

For the first time in a long time, she believed they did.

28

The Widow

9:30 p.m.

Mount Olivet Cemetery
Lebanon Pike, Nashville

Ellen never visited her mother during daylight hours. There was never time. At least this was what she told herself, but it wasn't true. She didn't want to run into anyone who might recognize her. Her history was buried far deeper than any of the residents in this prestigious cemetery. She had every intention of keeping it that way.

She never spoke of it, and she had paid a great deal of money to have her ancient history wiped from the internet. Of course, it wasn't possible to clear away everything, but she'd made it as difficult as she could to find information about her early life.

Over the years Ellen had rectified a number of wrongs from her childhood. For example, her mother hadn't been buried here in this lovely mausoleum when she'd died. No. Ellen's worthless father had turned her body over to the state for burial in a pauper's grave at the old Bordeaux Cemetery. She hadn't had so much as a marker until Ellen was old enough to get a job and pay for something small and cheap.

But all that had changed with time. Fifteen years ago she'd had her mother moved to a private mausoleum here in this much more proper setting. Ellen sat on the white marble bench she'd had installed for the rare occasions when she visited. Tonight, like the other times she felt the need, she'd contacted the senior caretaker, who gladly came and opened the gate for her. The hour never mattered to the kindly old man. He was always grateful for the nice tip.

As for the darkness, that was not a concern either. Ellen had had a solar-powered light installed when the mausoleum was built to ensure her mother never had to spend another night in total darkness.

When Ellen was a child, her father had shut her and her mother in a closet, in the dark, whenever he wanted to punish them. He'd beaten her mother so often in those days that, looking back, Ellen didn't see how the poor woman had survived. Her mother could have disappeared. Run away and never looked back. But the bastard she'd married would never have allowed her to take Ellen. And her mother wouldn't leave her. So she'd lived with the horrendous abuse until cancer stole her away. She'd suffered so much those final weeks that her death had been a relief even to a ten-year-old who desperately loved and needed her mother.

Ellen had been sure her life could not be any more miserable than it was those final days.

She'd been wrong.

Her mother was barely cold in her grave the first time Ellen's father whored out his ten-year-old daughter.

The man who'd bought her for the weekend had done things to her that no one, especially a child, should know about, much less suffer. Something had clicked inside Ellen that weekend. Changed her. Made her see more clearly.

Three years later, her father had died in a freak accident. He'd come home inebriated late one night—as usual. Evidently when he'd shut off the engine and climbed out of the dilapidated old truck, he'd stumbled and fallen to the ground. He often passed out in a drunken stupor right where he fell. Ellen would call her one and only friend, a teacher from her school—Laney Pettit. That night, Laney had come, but she hadn't helped Ellen drag her unconscious father into the house. That night everything had changed. Perhaps it was because that was the night Ellen had finally told Laney the whole truth about what her father had been forcing her to do.

Ellen would never forget the look on Laney's face.

She exiled the horrific memories. If anyone bothered to look, the police report from that long-ago night stated that Ellen's father had been so drunk that he had left his truck in neutral and failed to engage the emergency brake. The truck had rolled backward until it stalled on an object.

The object had been her father.

Thanks to Laney's selfless bravery, Ellen never had to worry about him again. Her dear friend had taken Ellen in and given her the life she'd only ever dreamed of. No one had ever been as kind to Ellen as Laney. Despite all she'd done, to this day Laney was burdened with guilt that she hadn't found a way to rescue Ellen sooner.

Ellen stood and pressed her hand to her mother's bronze marker. She wished the bastard had died sooner. Perhaps if she'd been smarter or cleverer, he would have had an accident far sooner, but she had been a mere child.

Ellen dropped her hand and walked away.

Her childhood had taught her a great lesson. There were men who lived for nothing but to cause pain, particularly to women and children. Men who used brute strength and fear to control the very people they professed to love.

It was a travesty. A blight on the human race. One that should have been eradicated long ago.

Ellen climbed into her car and closed the door.

"Home?" Amy asked.

Ellen nodded. "Yes, Amy. Thank you."

Men like Jarrod Grady were part of the blight.

Ellen hadn't dared to believe that she might be able to make a difference, but in time and with her tremendous success, the dream had sparked to life. It had started with her generous donations to shelters for abused women and children. Their stories were so often the same as Ellen's. Hearing those countless stories had ignited a new plan—one that would hit the problem at its core. In time those closest to her had joined in Ellen's efforts. For more than a dozen years, they had made a real, tangible difference.

Murder had never been part of the plan.

Certainly, Jarrod's death was no great loss to humanity, but it was a step too far. Like the others they chose, he was a repeat offender many times over. But unlike the rest, his final offense had been immensely personal. Perhaps the others were right, and the personal aspect had been the trouble from the beginning.

No. Ellen understood the problem all too well.

It was appalling enough that any woman could be so uncaring as to take part in the pain the bastard wielded. But the utterly unforgivable part was that a woman so informed and so powerful in her own right would ally herself with such a plan.

A smile touched Ellen's lips. Both should have realized they couldn't possibly hope to win.

Ellen would never allow that to happen.

29

Friday, September 23

8:00 a.m.

The Finnegan Firm
Tenth Avenue, Nashville

Finley had barely slept last night. She'd kept thinking about that thumb drive. Why would Derrick need to hide whatever data it contained? Matt's friend at the security company had run Derrick's image through the Dempsey Pharma system and discovered three instances when he'd visited the company. That alone didn't prove anything, she told herself. Yeah, right.

Matt had suggested Derrick might have gone to Dempsey Pharma for a potential job interview. But that couldn't be right either. Derrick had claimed to be a home-improvement subcontractor. He did it all, he had explained. Plumbing, electrical, carpentry work. He worked for various contractors all over the city.

She'd never questioned him about his work. Never considered he might not be telling her the truth.

Was it possible he'd gone to Dempsey Pharma for some sort of maintenance work?

She paced her small office, empty coffee mug still cradled in her hand . . . still warm from the second cup of coffee she had chugged.

Maybe he'd seen something illegal and photographed it with his phone. People did that all the time.

Finley shook her head. Why wouldn't he have told her? And even if he had, what about all the photos of her? Photos taken before they met? More likely he had been hired by Dempsey to keep an eye on her.

She stalled, took a breath. The thumb drive could be nothing.

Whoever had owned that old truck before Derrick could have stuck the magnetic key holder under there. Maybe that person had been hiding something from his or her significant other.

Nothing was ever simple in Finley's world.

It was possible, she supposed, that Derrick had been collecting data on one of his employers. Bad business went down in the construction world. There were unions and strikes. But the timing was a sticking point for Finley. Derrick had shown up in her life just before the Dempsey trial started. He had hidden those photos of her, proving that he had been watching her before they met. Dempsey's thugs still watched her after all this time.

The Dempsey connection was the only logical answer, she decided.

You're saying Derrick worked for Dempsey?

Finley closed her eyes. Hated that annoying internal voice more every day. No. She wasn't suggesting he worked for . . .

But that was exactly what the evidence suggested.

Following that train of thought, if he had been employed by Dempsey and had hidden something that someone, presumably Dempsey's people, wanted to find, that would explain her neighbor having seen people poking around her house while Finley was in the hospital.

She rubbed at the tension banded across her forehead. She had to stop thinking about the possibilities. It was driving her mad. Matt had called her on her way to work this morning and assured her that the thumb drive was safely in the trusty hands of his cyber guy. Until he got past the password, there was nothing to do.

Except wait.

The sound of Jack's voice bellowing a good morning as he arrived had Finley heading his way. She dropped her mug off in the lounge and caught him in his office. She had arrived early this morning, and thankfully, Jack hadn't been far behind her.

"Have you spoken to Winthrop this morning?" she asked.

Jack gestured to a chair in front of his desk. "Sit."

Finley wasn't sure she could be still for long, but she'd give it a shot.

"The answer to your question is no." Jack hung his jacket on the coat-tree in the corner and pulled out his chair to sit. "I called her yesterday after I spoke with you and asked her to come in today for a briefing on what we learned in Atlanta. She's going to let me know this morning what time she'll be available."

"I'm surprised she didn't demand the details last night."

Jack settled behind his desk. "She didn't ask a single question."

Strange reaction for Winthrop. She was a tiger lady. Always pushing to achieve.

"Maybe she already knows," Finley suggested.

Jack shot her a look. "We think way too much alike, kid."

True. Moving on, Finley asked, "Anything new from Ventura? Forensics should be done with at least part of the processing by now. Preliminary reports should be available."

"I left him a voice mail last night." Jack riffled through the folders waiting atop his desk. Ever-efficient Nita prepared Jack's work in order of urgency for him to review each morning.

"Based on what I've found," Finley said, "there's every indication that Grady and the receptionist, Marsh, were partners at least for the past year. I haven't been able to confirm anything beyond that time frame." Finley had started reviewing the fragments of information on this case at four this morning. She damned sure hadn't been able to sleep.

"Unless we have something that connects the two of them in Atlanta," Jack warned, "we only have a working theory."

The fact that Marsh had worked at the clinic where Dagne saw her therapist was circumstantial on its own. "I'm trying to locate a previous address for Marsh. If I can find where she lived in Atlanta, I can check with neighbors to see if Grady—a.k.a. Wilensky—lived with her or visited her regularly."

The confounding issue was that just because both had ties to Atlanta didn't mean they were partners in crime there. But Finley knew. She felt it in her damned bones.

"We need that kind of proof to solidify Marsh as a long-term partner to Grady." At her raised eyebrows, he added, "I'm confident Ventura will see the relationship here between Grady and Marsh as enough to make her a suspect in his murder, but the long-term aspect would go a lot further with fully shifting guilt from our client. FYI, Ventura has put out an APB on Marsh's car."

Finley made a skeptical sound. "If Marsh is smart, she's changed vehicles by now. She may have been the brains in their partnership. If so, she won't be easy to find." Frustration nudged her. "I can't shake the idea that Winthrop's top-notch security guru should have found this connection. It wasn't that difficult. The idea kind of makes it difficult to see Winthrop as completely innocent in all this."

Jack scoffed. "We don't have to prove she's innocent, Fin, only that she's not guilty."

Yeah. Yeah. He was preaching to the choir.

Finley had to hand it to Winthrop: if she knew all this and had worked around it toward some end—whether her plan included murder or not—she was damned good.

"Marsh's former neighbor having known Jarrod Grady as Jay Grady ties in with the J. Grady on the first bank account where the stolen money landed," Finley said.

This was another of the many pieces she had been mulling over before daylight. She didn't actually see the point of him having put his own name on the account twice, but she was sure there was a reason. She had passed the info along to Everson, Winthrop's accounting czar. So far there had been no response.

"The neighbor's statement alone suggests Marsh was at least aware of Grady's duplicity." Finley scoffed. "How could she not be?"

"I'll give you that," the boss agreed, "but does that mean Marsh was involved with the embezzling or that she killed him?"

"Maybe, maybe not, or possibly both. The one hitch for me," Finley debated, mostly with herself, "is how far she went to send me after false leads." The Duncan scenario still bugged Finley despite Winthrop's explanation. "Marsh came across as credible in her insistence that Winthrop was the one who killed Grady or had him killed. She kept calling her a psycho. She claimed Grady had dug up all this stuff in Winthrop's past that suggested she'd been involved in other murders. Nora Duncan's, for example."

Jack tapped his fingers on his desk, his face a study in concentration. "But Duncan was a dead end." He shrugged. "And we still have nothing that suggests Winthrop was the one who wielded the hammer. If we're lucky," he added, "it'll stay that way."

"But," Finley countered, "what about the fraudulent credit card receipt for the bug Grady supposedly purchased at the spy shop. That move smells of a desperate attempt to shift the focus for the purpose of protecting herself, meaning Winthrop, or someone close to her. No one else had access to her home office. Winthrop said so herself." At his skeptical look Finley held her hands palm up. "I know, I know. But whoever killed Grady had to know the relevance of the hammer, which means if not Winthrop, it was someone close to her." She blew out a big breath. "Or Grady. Winthrop could have told him the story, and he told his partner, presumably Marsh, who wielded the weapon in an effort to frame Winthrop."

They were going in circles.

Jack scrubbed a hand over his jaw. "I agree the murder weapon is the fly in the ointment where the evidence is concerned." He shrugged, his expression proof he remained unconvinced. "Equally illogical is Winthrop, an obviously brilliant woman, planning this out and choosing a weapon only she had access to. It makes no sense."

"In which case, I would go back to the theory that she's protecting someone." Finley and Jack often went back and forth like this with cases. It was the most effective way to flush out those elusive details.

"But who?" He shook his head. "One of her partners?"

"Why not?" Finley shrugged. "The five are very close to Winthrop. One of them may have thought she was helping by killing him." The memories of watching each woman in those first interviews—their actions and mannerisms—flashed one after the other through her mind, landing lastly on the one who had placed her hand on her heart to show her horror over the tragedy. "Only one is left handed, and Shafer said the killer was likely left handed."

Jack looked to her in anticipation of the answer.

"Jessica Lauder."

He grunted, a disagreeable sound. "Would she have the guts to kill a man? We didn't find anything in her background to suggest she was the violent type."

"That leaves Marsh," Finley offered.

"Why would Winthrop protect Marsh?"

"Maybe," Finley began, "she wasn't protecting her. Winthrop may have discovered not only the missing money but the other betrayal—that he was still cheating with Marsh. The news may have prompted a last-minute change of plan."

This was assuming their client was cold blooded enough to set up her own husband's murder. No one knew the hurt, humiliation, and anger of that sort of betrayal better than Finley. Was all that emotion enough to prompt murder in someone so intelligent and with so much to lose? Finley thought of the things she had done the past few months, and there was only one answer: she couldn't rule out the possibility.

"Makes a twisted sort of sense." Jack nodded slowly. "She could have decided the best way to take care of both situations with one strike was to take out Grady and set up the other woman for his murder."

"The use of the hammer only Winthrop had access to was," Finley went on, "an attempt to make it appear the other woman was trying to set Winthrop up."

Jack grinned. "The perfect imperfect plan." His grin dipped into a frown. "Then the issue was how to prove Marsh had access to the hammer. Maybe the fraudulent credit card receipt and statement from the spy-shop owner were supposed to do that. You should follow up with the employee—Wendy something—and see if she's ever seen Winthrop or one of her five or Marsh, for that matter, in the shop."

"Good idea." Finley chewed at her lower lip a moment. "It's possible Winthrop truly believes the receipt is legit and someone else besides Marsh is operating behind her back. Obviously, it would have to be someone who had access to the home office and that credit card."

Jack's expression turned grim. "And who's left handed, which brings us back to Lauder. I guess when you get down to the nitty-gritty, kid, you never really know anyone as well as you think—not even the people closest to you."

Finley nodded. Couldn't argue that point. Perfect example: the secret Jack had been keeping all these years. Jesus Christ, how could she not have seen it? Had her father noticed?

"I'll go back to the spy shop," Finley said. "Show Wendy photos of Marsh and Winthrop and those closest to her, see if she recognizes anyone."

"If she fingers Lauder," Jack said, "then we'll know we're onto something."

"And I'll track down Lauder's husband. See what he has to say about his wife."

The idea felt off to some degree. Would Winthrop really not notice one of her five—someone that damned close to her—being the perpetrator here?

You didn't notice what Derrick was doing. Or the way Jack really felt about the Judge.

Finley banished that damned voice.

Nita appeared at the door. "Ms. Winthrop is here to see you." The drill sergeant pointed a finger at Jack. "Don't forget you have that meeting with Redfield and the judge at eleven."

He nodded. "Got it. Send her in."

Nita vanished, and Fin looked to Jack. "Wasn't she supposed to call you with a time?"

"I guess she couldn't wait to hear what we'd found."

"Guess not."

Jack stood as Winthrop darkened his doorway.

Finley did the same.

"Good morning," Jack announced. "Finley and I were just discussing your case. Please, join us." He indicated the chair adjacent to Finley's.

Winthrop gave a nod. "Good to see the two of you hard at work. I have something my security team has put together that might make your job easier." She plopped a thick folder on Jack's desk. "My only regret is that we didn't have this information days or weeks ago. I truly had no idea . . ." She shook her head, her expression sad. "Live and learn, I suppose."

With that, Winthrop took the seat next to Finley and offered, "I'm sure you'll want to have a look as well. It certainly opened my eyes to how blind I've been."

Finley pushed up and rounded Jack's desk to look over his shoulder as he opened the neatly organized package.

"Our extended resources in the field finally came through," Winthrop explained. "We discovered that Jarrod and his friend, Lena Marsh, have been working together for years. It appears Marsh has used her position in the offices of various therapists in different cities and states to identify older, lonely women of means. She and Grady would choose their victims and then set up the opportunity for a meet between him and the target."

"The cases go back almost five years," Finley noted. This was comprehensive to say the least. She was impressed. And confused. Winthrop's team suddenly came through with this last-minute Hail Mary play, and she showed up as calm as a cucumber?

"They were in Atlanta before coming to Nashville," Winthrop continued. "Marsh worked for two different clinics during their tenure there. It seems a near brush with the law brought them here for a fresh start. Since Jarrod was the only one whose identity was known in the scam, his partner was able to retain her name and work references to obtain a position with Dr. Mengesha."

"They were in Nashville for several months before targeting you," Jack pointed out. "That's a considerable amount of downtime for a couple so ambitious."

"I can only assume," Winthrop said, "they had decided to lay low for a while and then possibly go for a bigger payoff before disappearing for good. The close call in Atlanta may have prompted that decision."

"Looks like you were the only one he married," Finley noted. "Making your theory logical." This report was very comprehensive. Just wow. This was . . . unexpected. But then everything about this case had been unexpected.

"I was the bigger payoff, I assume. Before me, the payoffs were under a million, it appears. As you both know, my loss was many times more."

"And this time one of the perpetrators didn't survive," Finley said, still leaning toward the idea there was more Winthrop was hiding even in light of this comprehensive package.

Their client stared at her. "I had nothing to gain by murdering my husband. Marsh, on the other hand, had much to gain. She had nothing to lose except having to share the spoils with him. I had far too much to lose to do something so foolish in my own home, however tempting the thought may have been."

Finley nodded her acquiescence. "A valid point." She studied Winthrop. "Did you suspect any of *this* before his death?"

"I only saw the report this morning."

Which wasn't actually an answer to the question Finley had asked.

"Marsh is gone," Finley said, mostly to see Winthrop's reaction.

Winthrop exhaled a weary sound. "I'm not surprised. Perhaps if my team had moved faster, we could have provided this evidence in time to catch her." She closed her eyes a moment, shook her head. "I continue to be stunned by what the man I foolishly thought cared about me was capable of doing."

As suspicious as Finley still was, she couldn't deny how painful that place could be. She thought of the stalker photos and the thumb drive and considered the idea that Derrick might have been working for Dempsey, and she felt ill with the overwhelming idea of it all. The fact was, whatever Winthrop had known before now, the final truths were rarely easy to swallow.

Jack and his client continued to discuss this shocking news. Finley listened, but one question kept nagging at her. Why, after all those years of being single and singularly focused on her career, had Winthrop suddenly married a con man? Sure, anyone could be fooled. Finley certainly had been. But this still felt off somehow.

None of it sat exactly right with Finley. Bottom line, she needed to find answers that would satisfy a jury if the prosecutor brought up this same question, and any prosecutor worth his salt would. Assuming the case ended up at trial.

Jack assured his client that he would convey this new potential evidence to Detective Ventura and go from there. Winthrop thanked them both and took her leave.

"Talk about tied up with a neat little bow," Jack said as he closed the file.

Before Finley could comment, Nita appeared again. "Detective Ventura on the phone for you," she said to Jack.

Jack raised his eyebrows at Finley as he took the call. "Good morning, Detective," he said. "I have you on speaker so my colleague, Finley O'Sullivan, can participate in the conversation."

"Good," Ventura said, "you'll both want to hear this."

Finley prepared for yet another revelation.

"First," Ventura said, "our expert discovered the Winthrop home-security-camera footage had been edited during the time frame of the murder."

Jack grunted. "Are you suggesting my client edited the video?"

"Not yet," Ventura explained, "but the edit was done remotely. She certainly could have done it during her alleged walk."

"The actual killer could have done the same," Finley countered.

"Is there a way to identify the incoming source that performed the edit?" Jack asked.

Considering what Marsh and Grady appeared capable of pulling off, Finley wouldn't be surprised at all by the possibility.

"The hacker who got in was good," Ventura said. "So far we've had no luck tracking down the source."

Finley and Jack shared an "and there you have it" look.

"We appreciate the heads-up," Jack commented.

"There's more," Ventura said. "We got lucky with the murder weapon."

"How lucky?" Jack wanted to know, his gaze locking once more with Finley's.

"We lifted a couple of usable prints. The prints were in the database from a long-ago arrest for prostitution."

Finley sat up straighter.

"A Mina Arnette. She was nineteen at the time. She uses an alias now. Lena Marsh."

Finley instantly searched her memory for one where she might have seen Marsh write something down. Memories of seeing her write messages at Mengesha's office filtered one after another through her brain. Yes! Lena Marsh, a.k.a. Mina Arnette, was left handed. Son of a bitch.

"Sounds like," Finley offered, "you've found Grady's killer and it is not our client."

"I'm not quite ready to go there yet," Ventura insisted.

While Jack argued the point, Finley motioned that she had to go.

He gave her a nod as he delved into the package from Winthrop with Detective Ventura.

Marsh was still a wild card for sure. But why kill her partner? Seven point eight million dollars was quite a large motive. Had she planned the coup all along? Or had Grady's marriage to Winthrop tripped some trigger for her?

The one snag in the theory was the meeting Finley had had with Marsh at Starbucks. Why pitch Finley the spiel about Nora Duncan? Was the story only to throw Finley off Marsh's scent? And what about the timing? Marsh had been only hours from disappearing. Why stop to throw out that bone?

Whatever the reason, Finley damned well intended to find out.

She was in her car when her cell vibrated.

Matt.

Her heart stumbled. Maybe his guy had gotten back to him already. She hoped. Needed something . . . to explain why. Why had Derrick sought her out? Was she really the reason he was dead?

Please, you know the answer to that one.

She exiled the voice. "Hey, tell me you have good news."

The silence that followed had her heart sinking.

"Sorry, Fin, the thumb drive was a bust. The only things there were those stalker photos of you."

Regret. Frustration. And then anger pummeled her. "Thanks, Matt," she managed around the knot in her throat. "I'll talk to you later. I'm on a mission for Jack just now."

She ended the call before the emotion in her voice betrayed her.

Another dead end.

Former Duncan Residence
Shadow Green Drive, Franklin, 9:45 a.m.

Nora Duncan had lived in a town house in a quiet neighborhood only minutes from downtown Franklin. Though someone else lived there now, Finley hoped the neighbors would remember her. Better still, perhaps one had known her well.

Winthrop had debunked to some extent the Duncan lead, but Finley was banking on Lena Marsh, a.k.a. Mina Arnette, having planted that seed for a reason. Either way, Finley had an obligation to follow it through.

The town houses sat in a connected row, but the facades were different, lending some amount of individuality. Finley first went to the door on the right of Duncan's former home. She rang the bell and hoped someone was home. The community wasn't a senior-living one, but those listed on Finley's go-to people-search site as Duncan's closest neighbors were retirement age.

Fingers crossed.

"Whatever you're selling," a voice said from the other side of the door, "you're not allowed to be in this neighborhood. Didn't you see the signs?"

Finley smiled in the direction of the door's security peephole. She held up her credentials—the expired ones from the DA's office. "Ms. Rantz, I'm Investigator O'Sullivan, and I need to ask you a few questions about your former neighbor, Nora Duncan."

The lock turned, and the door opened a crack, the security chain pulling tight. The woman was older, seventyish. The one blue eye Finley could see was chock full of suspicion.

"Nora passed back in the spring. Her mother is over at Blakedale if you have questions about her."

Finley kept her smile in place. "I spoke with her mother. She asked me to say hello while I'm here."

Liar.

The eyebrow over the one eye lifted slightly. "How's she doing?"

"She's doing well. She misses Nora, of course."

The door closed and the chain rattled before the door opened again. The petite blue-eyed lady looked up at Finley with curiosity. "What is it you want to know?"

"I'm looking for information on the person Nora was involved with before her death."

"You mean that Casanova she fell head over heels for?" Rantz shook her head. "I told her he was a gold digger. What young stud wants a woman more than a quarter century older than him? Please. Once we pass sixty, we need to get real. If a younger man comes sniffing around, it's about money. Poor thing, she was devastated when he left. No matter how I tried to tell her he was gone for good, she just wouldn't listen. She called him constantly. Went to his place looking for him. I swear, she'd take an Uber and just sit on his doorstep until he showed up or—if he was home—finally came out and talked to her. It was the saddest thing I've ever seen."

Finley could only imagine how awful it had been for Duncan. "Ms. Rantz, you're certain it was a man. I was told by one witness that Nora was involved with a woman."

Rantz made a puffing sound. "No way. Nothing against women who love women—I have a good friend whose partner is a woman. But I met the guy. He was all she talked about. Ned this and Ned that. Ned, Ned, Ned." She gave Finley a look. "Trust me, he was a man."

Finley pulled out her cell and showed a pic of Jarrod Grady. "Do you recognize this man?"

"That's him. Ned Beale." She pointed a finger at the picture. "Wily bastard. He should be in prison for breaking her heart the way he did and taking her for every dime she had. She just couldn't get over him. Wouldn't let go. It was like she couldn't live without him."

So, Winthrop had straight-up lied. Finley resisted the urge to shake her head. She had sensed their client was hiding something. This changed everything. Every. Single. Thing.

The little blue-eyed lady's eyes suddenly narrowed. "Why are you asking about him? Did Laney finally go to the police like I told her to?"

"No, ma'am, I don't think so," Finley said. Pettit had only gone to her friend Winthrop, who had obviously followed through on her promise to Duncan's mother. Frustration and no shortage of anger simmered inside Finley. She held it back to keep Rantz talking. "I'm here because the man in the photo you identified as Ned was murdered."

Rantz smiled. "Well, that's the best news I've heard in ages. I hope it was a painful death."

Despite her mounting irritation with their client, Finley smiled at the feisty lady. "I believe it was, for a little while anyway." She hesitated a moment, reminded herself to stay focused, and then: "Did you by chance ever see this woman?" She displayed a pic of Lena Marsh.

Rantz made a face as she studied the image. "She looks like that nurse who came to see Nora in the last couple days of her life. Maybe she wasn't a nurse. She might have been one of those delivery people."

"You only saw her once?"

"Wait. No. Twice. Yes, that's right. Twice. Maybe a week before Nora passed was the first time." She studied the photo again. "I'm sure it was her. I remember all those blonde tufts of hair. My grandson used to have one of those little troll dolls. He cut its hair really short, and it looked just like that."

Finley supposed the image was as good a comparison as any. "Do you recall the second time you saw her?"

The older woman's forehead folded into deep thought. "It was the day before or the same day Nora passed, I think. She'd gotten to the point she wouldn't even leave the house. It was just pitiful. She had everything delivered." Rantz snapped her fingers. "Wait, I remember now! She dropped off Nora's medication. I saw her go in, and then she came out about half an hour later."

Finley had a bad feeling about Marsh visiting. "Are you talking about a medication from her therapist, Dr. Mengesha?"

"That's the one. Nora knew this woman from his office." She nodded. "Yes sirree. That's right."

"Did you see Nora after that delivery?"

"Absolutely," Rantz assured her. "I went over there to check on her. Personally I don't like strangers coming inside my house. I worried about Nora letting a stranger in, especially after what happened with that turd Ned. But Nora said the woman was from her doctor's office. She'd brought her prescription. She even brought her favorite lunch from that sandwich shop she always stopped at when she went to her therapist." She frowned. "I can't remember the name of it."

Alfred's. Finley knew the place. Anticipation joined the other emotions starting to boil inside her. "Was Nora okay when you spoke to her after the woman left?"

Rantz shrugged. "I think so. She said she needed a nap, so I didn't stay long."

"She was sleepy?" Cold rushed through Finley, making her heart start to pound. If this was the day Duncan had overdosed, it seemed quite the coincidence that the event occurred right after Marsh's visit.

"She was. I helped her to bed, tucked her in, and then I came home. The next morning Laney found her . . ." Rantz didn't say the rest, but she didn't have to.

"I'm confused," Finley said, every instinct on point. "Did Nora generally need help getting to bed?"

Another moment of concentration. "I don't recall that she ever did. Before she got her heart broken and fell into that deep depression, she was as healthy as a horse. But you know, people can die of broken hearts." Rantz shook a finger at Finley. "It's true. I read about it on the internet."

Finley nodded, too focused on the theory taking shape in her brain to comment on the remark. "Do you remember the name of the medication she was taking? The one the woman delivered?"

"It was the only medication she took. Like I said, no blood pressure problems. No high cholesterol. Nothing. Just the Xanax she started taking after butthead Ned did what he did. The bastard killed her as surely as if he'd stuck a gun to her head."

Pieces of the puzzle were falling faster and faster into place. "Did you tell her cousin Laney about any of this?"

"Of course I did. Laney was beside herself. It was just awful. Laney was torn up so bad."

"Thank you, Ms. Rantz." Finley somehow managed to restrain herself from barreling toward her car long enough to give Rantz a card. "If you think of anything else you feel is important, please call me."

Rantz promised she would. Before Finley was in her Subaru and driving away, she already had Shafer at the medical examiner's office on the phone.

"Dennis, hey, it's Finley."

"Fancy hearing from you twice in one week without a second body."

Finley laughed for his benefit. "Can you check something for me?"

"As long as it isn't dangerous and doesn't break too many laws."

"You know I never break laws," Finley teased even as her entire being was pulsing with impatience.

Shafer grunted one of those sounds that could go either way but was mostly neutral.

"Nora Duncan from Franklin. She died of an overdose back in April. Can you tell me if Xanax was the drug she used? Her death may be related to this case we talked about the other day."

"Sounds easy enough. I'll check it out and get back to you."

"Thanks. Talk to you soon."

Finley put through a call to the office. "Is he in?" she asked Nita.

"He's having brunch with Redfield. Do you need me to interrupt?"

"No. It can wait. I'm heading to the spy shop over on Fesslers Parkway. When I get back, he and I need to talk."

This had just blown the neatly wrapped-up defense Winthrop had provided all to hell.

Ellen Winthrop had promised to make the person responsible for Nora Duncan's death pay.

Jarrod Grady was that person.

30

11:15 a.m.

Spy Shop
Fesslers Parkway, Nashville

The spy shop was hopping today. Maybe because it was Friday. Who knew? Whatever the reason, it was a lucky break for Finley when Wendy Getty finished with her customer first.

With Howard tied up with a couple of guys intent on buying the latest gadgets, Finley could maybe get what she needed without his interference.

Wendy smiled. "I wondered when you would be back."

Finley returned the smile. "I need something to use for keeping an eye on my neighbor."

Wendy gave her a nod and turned to the shelves behind her. While she gathered the available options, Finley pulled up a photo of Marsh on her phone.

When the gadgets lined the counter, Finley placed her phone on the side away from Howard and pointed to the photo. In a low whisper, she asked, "Did she buy the code grabber?" Then she picked up a gadget and started reading the information printed on the packaging. "This is a good one?"

"That is our top of the line," Wendy said.

When Finley met her gaze, Wendy gave her head a little shake.

"Is this the one you'd recommend?" Finley reached with her left hand and moved to the next photo.

"If audio is what you need," Wendy explained, "the range on this one is the longest."

While Finley studied the gadget some more, Wendy stared at the image on the phone.

"Well, fancy seeing you again." Howard appeared next to Wendy.

Finley almost jumped. She'd been so focused she hadn't noticed him sidling over. She set down the box, ensuring it covered her phone.

"I have some neighbor trouble."

Howard nodded. "Gotcha." He picked up another of the boxes. "You'll want video too." He turned to Wendy, who looked exactly like a deer trapped in the headlights. "Give her an extra good deal if she takes both." He grinned at Finley. "We want to keep this lady happy." He pointed at Finley. "Jack Finnegan is the man!"

When he'd drifted back to his customers, Finley turned back to Wendy. "You can ring those up for me."

Wendy nodded and moved to the register.

Finley palmed her phone. Hoped Wendy hadn't lost her nerve.

"Three fifteen," she said, looking even more nervous now.

Finley tapped her card on the payment terminal. The ding of approval had Wendy printing out the receipt.

Howard's voice as he did his sales pitch seemed to boom in Finley's ear. Why the hell couldn't he need something in the back? Or just move farther down the counter? Damn it!

Wendy bagged the merchandise and shoved the bag at Finley. "Thank you. We hope you'll shop with us again."

Finley took the bag, hesitated a moment.

The bell over the door dinged, and Wendy turned toward the sound.

Finley took her bag and walked out, frustrated more at herself than at the woman behind the counter. She had been in an awkward position. Why the hell hadn't Finley thought to pass her a card? Then she could have called.

She'd have to go back inside. She climbed into her Subaru and opened the bag. Maybe one of these gadgets had a rechargeable battery and she could go back inside to buy an extra one.

The receipt snagged her attention. Or more specifically the single word written on the receipt. Finley smiled.

YES.

Finley glanced at the spy shop. "Thank you, Wendy."

Jessica Lauder was the one who'd purchased the code grabber allegedly found in a pair of Jarrod Grady's socks. Since she had access to all security information, there was only one reason for her to purchase the device: to direct suspicion at someone else.

Either she'd been following Winthrop's orders, or sweet little Jessica was involved with the murder.

Lauder Residence
Twelfth Avenue South, Nashville, 12:55 p.m.

Since Jessica's parents had retired to Florida, that left only one option close by. Her husband.

Making a call to Wesley Lauder's place of employment and using her former position as an ADA, Finley had learned that he was working from home today.

The Twelfth South townhome was in one of Nashville's most highly sought-after neighborhoods. The perfect setting for a power couple on the rise.

Finley pressed the doorbell and waited.

Wesley Lauder was an investment banker. His roots were deep in Music City soil. His father was an investment banker, as his grandfather had been. His mother was an entertainment attorney to the biggest country music veterans in the industry. Wesley, being the only child of such successful parents, was no doubt expected to accomplish great things.

Finley doubted having a felon or possibly a murderer for a wife was on that list of accomplishments.

The door opened, and the handsome forty-year-old stood in the doorway studying Finley. "Are you the one who called my office?"

"Finley O'Sullivan." She offered her hand.

He gave it a shake. His grasp a bit on the limp side.

The man appeared to have one hell of a hangover, or maybe he'd worked all night. Either way, his eyes were bloodshot, his hair was tousled, and his clothes looked as if he'd at least tried to sleep in them.

"What can I do for you, Ms. O'Sullivan?" The pain on his face when he spoke shouted headache.

Hangover for sure. Finley knew that place intimately.

"I would prefer to have this conversation in a more private setting," Finley said.

He opened the door wider and allowed her inside.

The place was every bit as stunning as Finley had expected. Wood floors, towering ceiling. Lots of large windows and expensive furnishings. All the trappings expected in a seven-figure-income home.

Lauder didn't offer any refreshments. He just crossed to the sofa and plunked down unceremoniously onto it.

Finley took a chair across the coffee table from him. "How long have you and Jessica been married?"

"Two years." He grabbed a bottle of water and took a swallow. He frowned and gestured to Finley. "You want something to drink?"

"No thank you. Just a few minutes of your time."

He shrugged. Drank more water.

"Are you aware of the murder investigation involving your wife's employer?"

Of course he was. Finley wanted his reaction to the question.

He cleared his throat. Set his water bottle aside. "Isn't everyone?"

No eye contact. Shifting of his body as if he was no longer comfortable. Interesting. "Did you have the opportunity to meet the victim?"

"Several times." He dragged his gaze from the floor and met Finley's. "I didn't like him. I thought he was an arrogant con man."

Well said. "Did you share your feelings with your wife?"

He laughed. "I actually don't get to share much with my wife." He shook his head, stared at the ceiling for a moment. "You see, she spends all her time at work. When she married me, she failed to mention that she was already fully committed to someone else—Ellen Winthrop."

Ouch. "I take it the two of you are not in a good place right now."

He drew in a big breath, let it go. "Well, Ms. O'Sullivan, my wife is never home. She barely has time to speak to me when she is. Last night, when she finally managed to get home at midnight, she said she wanted a divorce. Does that answer your question?"

It surely did. "Do your marital problems have anything to do with the murder investigation?"

He shrugged. "I doubt it. Things weren't that good before. In fact, I can pinpoint fairly accurately when they started to go downhill." He looked directly at Finley then. "When this con man came into the picture."

"Do you believe he and Jessica were involved somehow?"

Another shrug, accompanied by an "I have no clue" face. "I honestly don't know. If she did, it was only because that was what Ellen wanted her to do." His face pinched in something like concentration. "You have to understand my wife. She has been shielded from everything her entire life. First by her vastly overprotective parents and then by Ellen. She adores Ellen. She would do anything for her. Anything," he repeated.

"Are you suggesting Jessica would kill for Ellen?"

He blinked, appeared to catch himself. "I don't know about that." He seemed to sink into the sofa. "You've come at a bad time, Ms. O'Sullivan. I'm seriously angry with Jessica right now. I wouldn't take anything I say to the bank. Check back with me when I've had more time to lick my wounds."

Finley offered an understanding smile. "I'm sure the two of you will work it all out tonight."

He shook his head. "I don't think so. She took a bag."

"She's probably planning to stay with a friend."

He laughed a bitter sound. "You mean one of her coworkers, right? Because Jessica doesn't have any friends outside that tight little group."

"Have you tried calling her?"

"She's not picking up." He stood, his shoulders slumped in defeat. "Like I said, this is not a good time for me to talk about this."

Finley pushed to her feet. "I apologize for intruding, but I do appreciate your time."

He walked her to the door, opened it, but she paused before leaving. "When she comes home, you should tell her I stopped by." No need for the visit to come back to bite Finley in the butt with Winthrop.

"I don't think she'll be back."

Finley opened her mouth to say something conciliatory, but he cut her off. "She took her passport. Ask yourself, Ms. O'Sullivan, if she planned to come back, why take her passport?"

The Finnegan Firm
Tenth Avenue, Nashville, 2:20 p.m.

"Nita made a fresh pot of coffee." Jack gestured to the carafe and cups on his desk.

"Great. I definitely need coffee." Finley poured a cup and collapsed into a chair. The frustration and anticipation had calmed to some degree, leaving her wrung out.

"You had lunch?"

Finley downed a slug of coffee and set her mug aside. "No time. I need to catch you up and bounce some ideas off you."

As if Nita had been standing at the door listening, she waltzed in and handed Finley a pack of snack crackers. "Eat," she said. To Jack, she warned, "You have a three o'clock." Then she promptly left, closing the door behind her.

Jack shrugged. "You heard the boss."

Knee bouncing the tiniest bit with renewed impatience, Finley opened the package and crammed a cracker into her mouth. As soon as she'd chewed and washed it down with coffee, she launched into the details of her interview with Nora Duncan's former neighbor Betty Rantz.

Jack listened intently. He didn't ask questions until Finley had come to the end of her story and had finished off the cheese-and-peanut-butter crackers. Maybe because she barely took a breath as she spoke. There hadn't really been a good opening.

"You're suggesting," Jack offered, "based on seventy-odd-year-old Rantz's statement, that Lena Marsh likely murdered Nora Duncan."

Finley nodded eagerly, needing him to get this the way she did. "Yes."

"Why?" He sat up straighter in his chair. "The game was over. They had her money. No one had gone to the police."

"Because," Finley said, the scenario fully formed now, "Duncan wouldn't let go. She kept calling him. Showing up at his place—wherever that was. She wouldn't stop. Rantz said so herself. How else were they going to get rid of her? If Duncan kept it up, they could end up outed."

"Valid point." Jack reached for his coffee, taking his time, as if there was something on his mind, before he met Finley's gaze once more.

"Then there's Jessica Lauder," Finley went on. She walked him through her visit with Wendy at the spy shop and then the chat with Lauder's husband. "He thinks his wife is in the wind."

Jack nodded slowly, absorbing the new information.

She wanted to shake him. He had to see what she did.

"All of this," Finley said, when he continued to hesitate, "coalesces with Winthrop. Nora Duncan died, and Winthrop promised Duncan's mother that she would find the culprit and make him pay. A few months later she marries Jarrod Grady, a.k.a. Alex Wilensky, a.k.a. Ned Beale. A couple months after that, Grady is dead. Coincidence?" Finley shrugged. "I'm having trouble with that one, Jack. If Ventura finds Marsh and connects her to Duncan, our defense is screwed. On top of that, we've got this wild card in Lauder."

Jack held up his hands stop sign fashion. "All right. You're thinking Winthrop set up this Grady/Wilensky/Beale/whatever to achieve a proper revenge for what he did to her friend Nora Duncan?"

Finley nodded. "She wanted him to know what it felt like. A real eye-for-an-eye revenge. But something went wrong. I haven't figured that part out just yet, but the plan went awry somewhere along the way. Maybe there was an actual affair with Lauder, and that turned everything upside down. Like I said, she's our wild card."

"The real question is," Jack countered, "can Ventura prove any of this if push comes to shove?"

"It wouldn't be easy." Finley considered their one, elderly witness—Rantz. Could her testimony sway a jury? Maybe. Maybe not. "As long as Marsh is gone for good, Winthrop is probably in the clear. Ventura has Marsh's prints on the murder weapon. The fact that she has taken off lends credibility to the theory. Case closed."

Winthrop would be cleared of suspicion, and that would be that.

Were they protecting a murderer? Finley didn't really believe that to be the case. Was she wrong? Maybe.

Jack shook his head. "Why marry the guy? Why not have her revenge on their first date? Why go through the whole wedding fiasco?"

"The goal," Finley reasoned, "I'm sure, was to take Grady down all the way. Though he was the target, Winthrop must have believed there was a partner. She wanted to get them both. This was personal. This was payback." God, did she understand the need for payback. Just look at what Finley had been doing for months now. Two men were dead. She hadn't killed them, but she had wanted it to happen so badly. Then there was the collateral damage like Whitney Lemm. And Houser. The thought made her sick with regret.

"Maybe the murder wasn't supposed to happen," Finley allowed, "but somehow it did, and for that they needed a fall guy. Who better than his partner to take that fall? Marsh's prints were planted on the murder weapon, and that was that."

"Marsh figured it out," Jack continued, "realized she was being set up, so she tossed us that lead before disappearing. Makes a certain kind of sense."

"I have to hand it to Winthrop," Finley confessed, not wanting to be impressed but impressed anyway. "*If* this theory is even close to right, she went to great lengths to cover every possible scenario. Whatever part she and her partners played, I'm guessing they're going to get away with it. The whole scenario played out like a well-rehearsed scene."

Was the idea a travesty of justice? Or was it simply justice? Finley examined the idea for a moment. Grady's death was not a travesty when weighed against the cost of what he and Marsh had done—maybe many times over. Against the law, yes; unconscionable, sort of; but she could see how someone like Winthrop could be pushed over that edge. Finley had been there.

Was there still—to some degree.

"You're thinking this might not be their first time avenging a wrong against women," Jack suggested.

Finley shrugged. She thought of the way every potential issue had been accounted for—covered. "Maybe I am. Look at the research that went into who Grady was and what he had done. Winthrop and her team tracked his activities back five years. Are we really going to believe work that thorough happened in the past four days? They had to know this already. Grady was maybe the latest of a long line of targets."

"That's a pretty big leap, kid," Jack pointed out.

Something Nora Duncan's mother, Norine, had said popped out at Finley. "Wait." She mulled over the conversation. "Maybe not. Duncan's mother mentioned Winthrop's father being a devil. She said he abused his little girl—our client. He finally got his, Duncan mentioned. She called it a lucky break for Winthrop. When I searched Winthrop's father, the only thing about his death I found was that it had been a bizarre accident." A final, big fat piece of the puzzle clicked into place, and a smile tugged at Finley's lips. "Really bizarre. His own truck rolled over him."

Jack shifted slightly in his chair as if wrestling with her ideas. "Now you're suggesting Winthrop—as a child—killed her own father and made it look like an accident?"

"I'm suggesting," Finley objected, "that she had help. Duncan said that Pettit took Ellen in after that. Raised her like her own daughter."

Something in Jack's expression changed. "Now you're giving me something to work with. Pettit was there to take care of Winthrop. After what Grady—or whoever the hell he was—did to Nora Duncan, Winthrop was there for Pettit."

"Yes. It was the least Winthrop could do," Finley said, the idea solidifying, "after what Pettit had done for her."

Jack leaned forward, braced his elbows on his desk, and stroked his chin. "Bottom line, what woman wouldn't want a man like Grady to get what was coming to him?" He shrugged. "To that end, Winthrop and her partners may have formed a sort of secret society like in *The Star Chamber*."

The Star Chamber. The decades-old film based on the centuries-old English court had still been late-night fodder when Finley was in law school. "You're suggesting they would ferret out these leeches and take them out of play rather than allow them to escape justice."

Jack grimaced. "The crack in that theory is that surely someone would have noticed large numbers of thieving Casanovas suddenly being found toes up?"

"Or maybe murder was never involved until this time—Winthrop's father notwithstanding." The idea was catching on fire with Finley now. "Once he was outed, what guy was going to involve the police, particularly if the group had something on him? Maybe the threat to publicly out him was enough to keep him on the straight and narrow."

"Professor Della Michaels," Jack announced, grinning as he leaned back in his chair.

"First-year criminal law," Finley said, frowning since she didn't see the connection. "She was my professor. Everyone wanted to take her class. Only a select few had the honor."

Jack explained, "I went to law school with her."

Finley held up a hand. "I don't want to hear about whatever the two of you had going."

He waved her off. "It was a note she did for law review. I'm sure it was a requirement for graduation when you graduated as well."

Finley nodded. "A make-or-break moment for some."

"Well, Michaels wrote about how the law and justice are not the same thing. She cited several cases of possible vigilantism. The victims were all men who ended up dead under vaguely suspicious circumstances; the cases were never solved. More than half a dozen cases over the course of about five or so years—at that time. Charles Whitmore. Ronald Atkins. I don't recall the other names. By graduation time I was spending a lot of time in the bottle just trying to survive. Anyway, Michaels wrote about this subject."

"These cases were all in the Nashville area?" Finley remembered Professor Michaels but not the cases Jack cited. They were well before Finley's time.

"They were. The note created a bit of a stir," Jack pointed out. "Personally, I think she wrote the piece because there were several rich, arrogant males in our graduating class. She wanted to make a point."

"I should talk to her." Finley nodded as the idea meshed with her theory. "She might be able to provide insights that would be useful to our case in the event this thing goes further south."

Or maybe Finley just needed someone to tell her that the lines she had crossed weren't so bad . . . were normal under the circumstances.

Wishful thinking.

"Fin," Jack offered, "why don't I talk to her? We were classmates. I doubt she's forgotten me, though I missed the last two or three reunions."

Finley laughed. "Like she would talk to Jack Finnegan, a self-professed womanizer."

"Ladies' man," he amended, then cleared his throat. "I suppose you've got me there."

"Besides, you have a three o'clock." Finley stood, cleaned up her lunch mess. "I'll give her a call and see if she's available."

"Keep me posted," he called after her.

"Will do," Finley called back.

She wondered what Professor Michaels would think of her now if she knew how Finley skirted the fringes of the law these days. Like going into Marsh's unlocked home. Or not reporting a homicide she'd witnessed. Well, she had reported it eventually.

Or maybe Michaels had a point—the law and justice weren't always the same thing. The debate hearkened all the way back to Plato.

As she climbed into her Subaru, her cell vibrated. "O'Sullivan."

"Finley, I have that information for you."

Dennis Shafer from the ME's office.

"Thanks for getting back to me."

"No problem. Duncan's cause of death was listed as an accidental overdose. Tox screen showed Xanax and fentanyl. The levels were just barely enough to be lethal, which explains the *accidental*. Generally, those who set out to do the job go unnecessarily overboard so as not to wake up with more problems than they started with."

Unless the person administering the dose intended to make it look that way.

She didn't have to ask him if he was sure about the fentanyl. If he said it, it was in the report. Trouble was, Duncan, according to her neighbor, had only been prescribed Xanax. Which meant Marsh had brought the fentanyl to the party.

The thought knotted Finley's gut. If Marsh had offed her partner, that was one thing, but to take an innocent victim's life—that was entirely another. If Pettit and Winthrop knew this . . .

"Do you know if the family requested a copy of the autopsy?" Some did; some didn't. But if Duncan's family had, Winthrop or Pettit would have recognized the discrepancy in the drugs.

"Hold on a sec." He hummed as he checked for the answer she needed. "Yep. A Laney Pettit picked up a copy."

And yet they hadn't pointed out the drug discrepancy to the detective investigating the unaccompanied death. With this new information, there was no backing away from this scenario. There were far too many pieces that fit. Far too many coincidences.

"Thanks, Dennis. I owe you one."

If Marsh murdered Nora Duncan, she likely wouldn't have had any qualms about killing Grady if he was in her way.

Her prints were on the murder weapon. Marsh had motive, means, and, apparently, opportunity.

Winthrop might have set out to get revenge for her friend and unknowingly provided the perfect opportunity for Marsh to rid herself of a partner she didn't need anymore. Particularly with millions of dollars at her disposal.

That would make Winthrop innocent. Of murder anyway.

Finley located Professor Michaels's number. Now all she had to do was talk her way into an appointment.

Michaels Residence
Southwinds Drive, Hermitage, 4:30 p.m.

Just over an hour after calling the professor, Finley arrived at her home for their scheduled appointment. On the phone Michaels had sounded enthusiastic and only too happy to meet with a former student. Finley hoped she would be equally enthusiastic about answering questions.

The front door opened before Finley reached it.

Michaels smiled broadly. "How very nice to see you, Finley. It's been a while."

"It's great to see you as well, Professor."

They exchanged cheek hugs.

"Please, call me Della. We're peers now."

"Della," Finley acquiesced.

Inside, Finley waited while the professor closed and locked her door. The flowery caftan she wore was a far cry from the generic two-piece business suits she'd worn in class. The scarf wrapped around her head gave Finley pause. Was this a fashion accessory or a cover for hair loss related to medical treatment?

"I've prepared a lovely peppermint tea," Michaels announced as they entered the sunroom at the back of the house. "I hope you'll join me."

"Sounds wonderful."

Michaels picked up the fine silver pot and poured two cups. While Finley had waited for this appointment, she'd called the receptionist at the Winthrop Group and asked to speak with Lauder. The receptionist explained that Lauder was not in her office today. Maybe Lauder's husband was right. She might not be coming back. Finley had then reached out to another of her sources, whose specialty was finding people's reservations on airlines and other public transportation sources. Both Lauder and Marsh could very well be long gone already, but it didn't hurt to check.

"Cream or sugar?"

"Sugar, please." Finley had never acquired a taste for cream in her coffee or the occasional hot tea.

The professor passed a dainty cup and saucer to Finley and gestured for her to have a seat. Finley settled in one of the wicker settees. Michaels chose one opposite her. Being here with one of her favorite professors had Finley's emotions reeling. She thought of how idealistic she'd been that first year of law school. So many hopes and dreams. Somehow, she'd lost all those wondrous aspirations this past year.

She'd lost herself. Something powerful and painful swelled in her chest.

How had she allowed this to happen? Leaving such a gaping hole inside her?

The professor kicked off the conversation with, "What brings you to see me? It's been quite some time since your first year of law school."

Finley pushed away the crowd of emotions. She had prepared a reasonable excuse on the way over. Now it suddenly felt trite and unimportant. "I was doing some research on vigilante cases, and I was reminded of a number of cases you mentioned in the law review your final year of law school. Whitmore, Atkins? Does either case ring a bell?"

Michaels smiled. "That was a very long time ago." She gave a nod. "The review gave me quite the reputation. My decision to be so bold was perhaps not the best decision at the time, but I survived the flurry of rumors. As for your question, there were a good number. Hall, Trask, and Price." She tapped her lips with one finger. "All appearing to be accidents, quite distinctly carried out and, in my opinion, for all the right reasons. In the end, all were labeled as accidents under suspicious circumstances, and all remain so to this day."

"As a fourth-year law student," Finley said, "you already felt strongly about the difference between the law and justice."

"I did. Still do." She drew in a deep breath. "You see, Finley, there are levels—degrees, if you will—of heinousness. Again, in my opinion."

"I'm familiar with the theory. It has been well received and used fairly broadly."

Michaels nodded. "Well, this was my belief decades before it became, as you say, well received. If you have two murders. The victims are both male. Let's say one was shot by a thief who wanted to steal whatever valuables he had in his home. The other was shot by the wife he had emotionally abused for decades. Are they the same? Should both killers receive the same sort of sentence? Is the wife even guilty of murder when weighed against all that she has suffered?"

"The real question should be," Finley offered, feeling like a student once more, "what is justice?"

"Precisely."

"Then if a person deserves to be murdered, there should be no penalty," Finley challenged, holding her breath as she waited for the prestigious professor's response.

Michaels smiled. "The circumstances make all the difference. Is it justice when a man's child has been killed by a drunk driver and he spends hours or days deliberating how to have his vengeance, eventually shooting the driver and killing him? Perhaps not. Is it justice if the same man's child is killed by a drunk driver and after months of waiting for a trial, he learns a mere technicality has caused the driver to receive only a slap on the wrist, and this man takes a gun to the driver's home, shoots and kills him? Both instances are premeditated. However, the first man refused to wait for the law to do the right thing; instead he took matters into his own hands. The second waited, gave the law time to do the right thing. When it did not, he lost control and took his vengeance.

"The answer is in the details," Michaels explained. "The killer's frame of mind, the circumstances surrounding the event. There is no one size fits all in justice, despite the way the law is written."

"But murder is murder," Finley countered.

"Are we talking about a particular case?"

Of course she would ask. "You're aware my husband was murdered."

The professor nodded. "I am. You'll forgive me if I don't recall all the details; the chemo sometimes affects my memory."

So there was a medical issue going on.

"I'm sorry to hear you're having health problems," Finley offered.

Michaels shrugged. "Too many years of smoking pot after class."

The professor laughed, the sound self-deprecating. Finley did the same, no matter that she couldn't help feeling the loss already. This woman—this incredible professor full of wisdom—would be gone.

Michaels said, "Your husband's case remains unsolved."

"Yes."

"And you're thinking of taking care of the perpetrators yourself."

Finley rode out the shock her words prompted. "No, of course not." Two were out of the way already. She blinked away the thought.

The professor smiled. "It was a reasonable question in light of the circumstances."

Finley gave a nod. "It was."

"You're working with Jack Finnegan since you left the DA's office."

Anyone who didn't live under a rock had probably seen coverage of Finley's fall from grace. "I am."

Michaels laughed again. This time the sound was deeper, richer . . . real. "That Jack. He's a pistol. Brilliant, but he had a weakness. The alcohol."

"He's been sober awhile now," Finley said, pride filling her. "And you're right. He is brilliant."

"Perhaps your research," Michaels said, shifting the subject from Jack, "is about your newest client."

"Perhaps," Finley allowed. Michaels was in ill health, but she was still on her toes, it seemed.

"Your client made a good decision. Jack is the best criminal defense attorney I know, and believe me, I know a few," Michaels said.

Finley wholeheartedly agreed. "I'm sure Jack will appreciate the compliment."

Michaels gave her a nod. "No one will ever accuse me of being anything less than blunt. I say what I think." She paused before going on. "If the research that brought you to me is related to your new client, what I would tell you to consider is that the cases I mentioned in the review were repeat offenders who got away with their evil deeds time and time again. Until someone—a victim, I suspect—caught on and decided to lure each one into a trap," Michaels explained. "Perhaps using the abuser's own selfish techniques against him."

"It's the perfect ending, some would say," Finley suggested. "The true victims are vindicated and the perpetrator is punished, all without costing taxpayers a dime or draining important public-safety resources."

"In my humble opinion, yes," Michaels agreed. "But each of us has to come to terms with what we believe to be justice. As attorneys, we are not bound by the same specificity in the law as judges are. We have some amount of leeway."

Finley couldn't argue the point. "The system never has and never will be perfect."

"This is, sadly, true." Michaels studied her for a long moment. "The downside, however, is that we must live with our choices."

And therein lies the rub.

"You were a brilliant student, Finley. An incredible assistant district attorney." Michaels sipped her tea. "I've watched you. You have the ability and the opportunity to make significant change. Grab that opportunity and don't let go. Be the person who understands that sometimes the law doesn't protect us and we have to protect ourselves. Make the difference for those who are powerless to protect themselves from the very law that should have protected them."

The words seared through Finley like fire roaring in her blood. The flow of offhanded comments District Attorney Briggs had made about Carson Dempsey, about how he was too powerful and had done too much for the community to be touched, poured through Finley's brain. Briggs was one of those people who didn't see the difference . . . who would never *make* a difference because the status quo suited him.

"You understand, Finley," Michaels went on, drawing her back to the conversation. "I know you do. Ask yourself if crossing certain lines—under certain circumstances—makes one a monster." She gave her head a shake. "I don't think so."

Finley understood perfectly. Just maybe she wasn't a monster.

31

6:00 p.m.

The Murder House
Shelby Avenue, Nashville

Finley sat in her car for a while after parking in her driveway. She'd gone back to the office and filled Jack in on the meeting, including the much-deserved compliment from the professor. Jack had news for her as well. Ventura had called to say he had officially eliminated Winthrop as a suspect and would be focusing on finding Lena Marsh. Additionally, Winthrop's personal attorney had shown up with the news that his client no longer required Jack's services.

Finley wasn't surprised by the news from Ventura. The attorney showing up with a release signed by Winthrop discharging Jack's firm from further obligation was no real surprise either. According to Jack, the guy had poured on the compliments for all their hard work.

Who was he kidding? Winthrop's team had done most of the legwork to prove their innocence beyond a reasonable doubt.

Except they weren't entirely innocent. Justified, perhaps.

A call from her source for public transportation had been a bust. No reservations for Lena Marsh or Jessica Lauder. Finley had hoped one or the other would be shortsighted enough to use her real name. No such luck.

Finley had decided at that point she needed to take the rest of the day off. She had intended to head to the hospital to visit Houser, but when she called, the information desk warned that he wasn't allowed visitors per the chief of police's orders.

Typically, Finley would not have allowed that to stop her, but just now she wasn't feeling up to a battle.

So unlike you.

God, she hated that voice.

Maybe that annoying inner voice was trying to tell her something she needed to hear and, more importantly, to heed. More likely it was her visit to Professor Michaels speaking to her.

Finley sat in the car . . . stared at the rickety old house in front of her.

What had she become over the past few months? The question had her gut clenching. When she'd left the professor, some part of her had felt vindicated, but that heady feeling had dissipated all too quickly. What she had done was no better or different, really, than what Winthrop had probably done. She couldn't view Winthrop as a criminal without seeing herself that way. The professor had basically confirmed as much.

But was this the place Finley wanted to be? This in-between place that wasn't really good or bad, where nothing was ever firm or fixed?

Deep inside, beneath the anger and the pain, it didn't feel like the place she wanted to be.

How had she fallen so far? When she'd come out of law school, everything had seemed so clear . . . so easy. So black and white.

But real life wasn't clear or easy or black and white, she reminded herself.

Derrick's murder and *that* night had damaged her ability to see clearly. To find her way through the fog.

Or was she seeing clearly for the first time?

From the DA's office her view had been the crime . . . the criminal. Getting from point A to point B with the least resistance. But now she was looking from the other side, and the views didn't properly align. There was too much gray . . . the place too fluid and rapidly changing.

She got out of her car, walked toward her front porch. The cat stuck his—or her—head from under the glider. Strangely enough, Finley was glad for the animal's sudden appearance in her life. She wasn't so sure she liked being alone anymore.

"You still hanging around?"

The cat stared up at her, didn't make a sound.

Finley unlocked the door and pushed it inward. She waited for the cat to follow. One uncertain step after another, the scraggly yellow cat followed her inside. Finley headed for the kitchen and prepared a bowl of food and a bowl of water, using actual bowls instead of empty cat-food cans.

Then she opened a bottle of red and searched for a glass.

Finley stood in the kitchen and drank. She did a lot more of that lately. But tonight she was feeling particularly nostalgic, or maybe *adrift* was the better word. She watched the cat devour the food, then lap up the water.

Lost, that was what she felt. Unmoored. Out of place. Her pulse reacted. That was it. She felt out of place . . . *adrift*.

For the first time in more than a year, Finley considered that maybe the Judge was right. What was she doing here?

She stared at the worn-out floors, the ancient cabinets with their doors that didn't quite hang right or even close.

Derrick. She nodded. "Yeah." She stayed because it was her fault he was dead.

Was it? Really? She thought of Matt's discovery about Derrick's visit to Dempsey Pharma. Did that change her responsibility for what had happened? She had no idea.

Until she understood why Derrick had sought her out . . . she didn't know one damned thing for real. It was all supposition. Theory.

Well, one damned thing was certain. If Dempsey's piece-of-shit son hadn't raped women, none of this would have happened.

Fury twisted inside her. Tears burned her eyes. She wanted to scream. She stared at the bottle of wine. Wanted to drink more, but her stomach turned at the thought. Her life was funneling out of control . . . draining away from where she was supposed to be and flying off into some place she couldn't define.

The memory of Tark Brant snarling at her before Whitney Lemm shot him rammed into her brain.

The only reason you're still alive is because someone wants you that way.

She jerked at the remembered words. Dempsey. His son. Derrick.

She had to find a way to get all that out of her head . . . to stop obsessing over the past. To start living her life again.

Houser's words seared through her.

"I will not allow this to define me anymore," she said aloud.

The cat stared up at her.

Finley took a deep breath, set the bottle aside, and walked to the bathroom. What she needed was a long hot shower, then the wine. Then a good night's sleep.

No more thinking about Derrick or the bastards who'd . . .

Stop. Stop. Stop.

She hugged herself, surveyed the shabby bathroom. Stared at the shattered mirror in the vintage medicine cabinet her husband had insisted they had to keep.

"Why can't you let this go?" she demanded, going weak again.

The questions and memories were impossible to hold at bay.

The fractured pieces of her reflection didn't answer.

There were no answers to be found in this whole damned, shitty house!

She didn't want to be here anymore. Hated this place. Rage roared through her. She grabbed the edges of the broken mirror and jerked with all her might. "I don't like you!"

The top of the door pulled loose from the cabinet.

"I hate this house! I hate you." She glared at her broken reflection before tugging again with all her might. The medicine cabinet came out of the wall, hit the wall-mounted sink before slamming onto the floor. She stumbled back, bumped the shower. Steadied herself and stared at the hole left in the wall.

"Idiot," she mumbled as she swiped the tears of anger from her cheeks.

The porcelain sink abruptly fell off the wall and crashed to the floor. Cold water suddenly spewed at her.

"Shit!" She turned her face away from the spray and dropped to her knees. She felt blindly for the shutoff valve. Closed her fingers around it and gave it a twist.

The water stopped.

She sat on her knees in a puddle of water and started to laugh.

Finley laughed until she lost her breath. Finally, she pushed to her feet and reached for the stack of towels on the shelf next to the new hole in the wall. "That was about the stupidest thing you've done," she grumbled.

She dropped to her knees once more and swabbed at the water. The sink was a goner. It had cracked. Oh well. It was junk anyway. To hell with it. Towels pushed all around the broken sink, she started to get up, but something snagged her attention, and she hesitated. Blinked. Then she looked again at the glob of white that had come loose from the sink. Didn't look like porcelain. She frowned and surveyed the underside of the sink. There were several indentations molded into the underside of the porcelain, but one had been filled with something that had fallen loose in the crash to the floor. She picked up the small clump of white. Beyond the cracks in whatever the hell it was, she could see something black. She squeezed the clump, and it broke apart. Like dried Sheetrock mud, she decided. The small dark object dropped onto a towel presently sucking up water on the floor.

"What the . . . ?"

The object she stared at right now was another thumb drive. Just like the one Matt had found under Derrick's truck. Her heart did some sort of acrobatic move that stalled the air headed to her lungs.

No. She wasn't doing this again. She grabbed the thumb drive. She should just throw it away. But she couldn't. Instead, she stared at it, marveling that it had been hidden in such an odd place. A place no one would look.

Could this one actually be something important? The something those men had been looking for? Her heart bumped hard against her sternum.

She reached for her cell. Not in her pocket. Where had she left it? She scrambled to her feet, thumb drive held firmly in her fist, and rushed out of the bathroom. Her wet feet slipped as she made the turn toward the kitchen. She barely caught herself before slamming onto the floor. She launched forward again, made it to the counter, and grabbed her phone.

It rang.

Finley started. Almost dropped the damned thing. She stared at the screen. Didn't recognize the number.

She accepted the incoming call. "O'Sullivan."

"Ms. O'Sullivan, this is Karen Segal at Vanderbilt Medical Center."

Oh hell. Finley braced for bad news. Had the Judge suffered a heart attack—assuming she had a heart? Her father? Jack? Forcing away the worries, Finley said, "How can I help you, Ms. Segal?"

"We've had a patient admitted, and you're listed in his cell phone as an emergency contact."

Finley's heart stuttered. Had to be Jack. Shit. "What happened? Is he okay?" She had been telling him for years that he needed to get into a fitness routine. If he'd had a heart attack, she was going to kick his ass.

"There was an automobile accident. He's been taken into surgery. That's all the information I have at this time. We'd like you to answer a few questions if you can. Do you know if he is currently on any medications?"

"Jack doesn't take any medications. No." Jesus Christ. Jack was the safest driver in the world. How had he gotten in an accident?

"I apologize, but we seem to have had a miscommunication. The patient's name is Matthew Quinn."

Finley's heart dropped into her stomach. "No." Oh God. She gasped for a breath. "No, he doesn't take any medication. Please, just tell me he's okay."

"I only know he's been taken to surgery. Do you know of any pre-existing conditions?"

"No. He's completely healthy. I'm heading there right now."

"Please let us know at the ER desk when you arrive, just in case we have additional questions. Drive carefully, ma'am."

Finley didn't care that she was wet from the broken sink in the bathroom. She grabbed her keys and bag and rushed out of the house.

She needed to be at that hospital. Now.

Vanderbilt Medical Center
Medical Center Drive, Nashville, 6:55 p.m.

Finley sat alone in the small waiting room on the OR floor. Matt was still in surgery but doing well. A nurse had promised to let Finley know as soon as he was moved to a recovery room. Finley had called his parents. They were on a cruise in the Caribbean and were horrified at being so far away and unable to get back in a timely manner. Finley promised to keep them closely informed. So far, it appeared Matt would come through this with every expectation of a complete recovery.

Finley refused to allow doubts to creep in. She closed her eyes and beat the dreaded thoughts back. And she did something she hadn't done since before Derrick's death. She prayed.

Just don't let him die. Don't let him die.

Finley was 100 percent certain she could not live without Matt. Life would be impossible without him.

The door opened, and Jack joined her. "Hey, kid. Any news?"

He sat down beside her in one of the less-than-comfortable upholstered chairs and reached for her. She wilted against him. Closed her eyes for a long moment and savored the feel of his arms around her.

When she could speak, she said, "Nothing more than what I told you on the phone. I'm keeping his parents up to speed on what's happening."

"Good. I stopped by Houser's room and talked to him."

"They're allowing visitors now?" She drew back, met his gaze. She would have checked on Houser already if she'd known. She'd been so worried about Matt the idea had slipped her mind. Houser was in this place because of her. Damn it.

It wasn't only her life she had ruined since *that* night . . . look at the devastation she had caused in other people's lives. She felt sick at the idea.

"He's hanging in there," Jack said. "If all goes well, he'll be able to go home next week."

She nodded. The relief she felt was beyond her ability to articulate.

"Look, Fin." Jack sagged back into his chair, exhaled a weary breath. "Houser identified the shooter as Flock."

She wasn't surprised, and yet the reality shocked her. Did Dempsey fear nothing at all? Shooting a cop? Jesus Christ. "He's probably headed to Mexico by now."

Jack's gaze shifted to the floor. "Actually, there was another detective in the room visiting Houser." He cleared his throat, still kept his eyes averted. "He had the lowdown on Matt's accident."

Finley waited, knowing deep inside that whatever was coming next would be painful to hear. "Just tell me what he said, Jack."

"The good news," he began, "is they don't have to waste any time chasing down Flock."

Did that mean they had him in custody? Had he given himself up in hopes of obtaining a deal? What the hell? Jack's somber expression told her it only got worse. Her heart sank a little lower in her chest.

"The bad news?" Finley held her breath.

"Flock is dead."

Relief flooded her. "Why is that bad?"

Three down . . . and done. Inside, she cheered.

"That's . . ." No. Reality kicked her in the face. There was still Dempsey, and Flock had been their one known option for getting to the bastard.

Finley shook her head. "I'm sorry. Go on."

"Flock was the one who ran Matt off the road."

"What? Matt was run off the road?" She'd known he'd been in a car accident but not the details. When she'd gotten the news, the details hadn't been important. She hadn't even thought to wonder . . . all that had mattered was that Matt survived.

But it damned sure mattered now.

Fury streaked through her like a bullet. "Tell me everything the detective said."

"Flock rammed Matt's car and forced him off the road, but before Flock could get back into the proper lane, a semi hit him head-on."

Not a good way to go. Finley gritted her teeth. She was glad he'd gone to hell in a merciless way. Bastard.

The jolt of anger drained out of her. "Flock did this to Matt," she muttered, then shook her head. No. *She'd* done this to Matt. She felt sicker than she had already.

"This isn't your fault, Fin."

He was wrong. Finley leaned forward, braced her forearms on her knees. When she could speak again, she explained, "We found this thumb drive hidden in the undercarriage of Derrick's truck. Matt took it to a friend who he hoped could get beyond the password lockout. And he did, but there was nothing there. Just a bunch of photos Derrick had taken of me. Maybe Flock found out somehow and started following Matt."

How the hell did those bastards know every step she made?

She should have kept Matt out of this thing. She'd intended to, and then in a moment of weakness she had let him in.

Jack leaned forward, matched her stance. "Fin, we talked about this. We've gotta get beyond this business with Dempsey."

She closed her eyes. Squeezed them tight. "How do we do that? The original three are dead now, but what do you want to bet Dempsey will have more thugs watching me? I don't think he's going to be moving on until he gets whatever it is he wants from me. One of the last things Brant said before his girlfriend shot him was that the only reason I was still alive is because someone wanted me that way."

Fury and pain roared through her, each trying to outdo the other. She thought of the medicine cabinet she'd torn out of the wall . . . the broken sink and the new thumb drive. She felt it in her pocket, small and yet somehow threatening.

A new and oddly calming realization settled over her. There was only one way this was ever going to be over. She had to find the truth. All of it.

And she had to get out of here . . .

"I should go talk to Houser." She stood. Her legs felt rubbery beneath her. She wasn't telling Jack about the thumb drive. She wasn't telling anyone. She would find a way to open it on her own. "Text me if there's an update on Matt."

Jack didn't bother trying to stop her. He knew better than to waste his breath.

Finley felt as if her movements were more out-of-body experience than her actually walking along the sterile white corridor. Derrick was dead. The bastards who'd invaded their home *that* night were dead. But other people had been caught up in this too. Detective Houser. Whitney Lemm. Matt. Jesus Christ. Matt.

She had to make it stop.

She reached the elevators and pushed the call button. This should have ended after *that* night. She shouldn't have stopped until those three bastards had been arrested, gone to trial, and been properly punished.

The elevator opened, and there was the Judge.

"Fin," her father said as he and the Judge stepped out. He threw his arms around Finley. "Any news on Matt?"

Finley felt her defenses crumbling. She couldn't do this right now. She drew back and pointed in the direction from which she'd come. "The waiting room is just down there. Jack can give you an update. I'll be back in a few minutes."

She pushed past them and onto the elevator. It wasn't until she'd stabbed the button for a floor that she realized she had no idea what floor Houser was on. As if she'd telegraphed the thought, Jack sent her a text giving her the floor and room numbers.

The elevator landed at the lobby before going back up to the floor she'd selected after Jack's text. During the lag, Finley leaned against the wall and tried to regain her composure. She didn't want to fall apart here. She had to get this done first.

The doors of the car opened, and as if the situation weren't bad enough already, she stood face to face with the chief of police. His glare warned that he blamed her for what had happened to Matt and to his detective.

What was new? There wasn't a cop in this town who liked her, except maybe Houser. But in this case, damn it, there was plenty of blame to go around. How did a man like Carson Dempsey climb to his current pinnacle without being caught?

The elevator doors slid closed. The silence was thick as the car climbed upward. The chief was apparently headed to the same destination. *Can you say* awkward?

When the elevator stopped on Matt's floor, she was grateful the chief exited. She rode onward and got out at the next stop. Houser's floor.

The uniformed officer stationed outside the room announced where she would find Houser even if she hadn't known the room number.

At the door the uni blocked her path. "I'm afraid this room is off limits to visitors."

"Can you tell Houser that O'Sullivan is here? I think he'll want to see me."

The uni went into the room to convey the message. Even through the closed door, she heard Houser's "hell yes" response, which lifted her spirits the tiniest bit.

The uni stepped back into the corridor and allowed her into the room.

Finley braced herself and walked in.

Houser looked like hell. Tubes and wires snaked from an array of machines to his body. His face was bruised and swollen. Hands swollen and busted up as well. Evidently, he'd put up a fight before going down.

"Ouch," she offered with a flinch.

He attempted to smile but only managed a wince. "Could've been worse. I thought I was a goner for a minute."

Finley moved to his bedside. "I'm sorry I dragged you into this," she confessed. "I should've stuck with my initial strategy."

"You did the right thing, O'Sullivan," he said, his voice taut. "You can't—you shouldn't take on something like this alone. You carried that load all by yourself for too long as it was."

"You might be one of the few who sees it that way." The chief hadn't spoken to her. The Judge had stared at her without saying a word.

"I heard about Quinn," he said. "He's gonna be all right, isn't he?"

"We think so." She drew in a big breath. "I should get back there and see if there's an update. I just wanted to see for myself that you're hanging in there."

"I'll survive." He made a sound that wasn't a laugh but tried valiantly to reach that level. "The bastard got his, which always makes the pain a little easier to bear."

Finley summoned a smile for him. "I'll check in on you again tomorrow."

She paused at the door and wiggled her fingers at him. He lifted his hand and gave her a salute.

Every ounce of resolve she possessed was required to restrain her emotions as she walked away.

Finley boarded the elevator once more and headed back to the waiting room on the OR floor. If luck was on her side, the Judge and the chief would be gone by now. Her poor father. Finley felt guilty for wishing her mother away, which inevitably meant less time with her father.

If Matt was okay, she could deal with anything else.

Jack, the Judge, and Finley's father were seated in the waiting room. For the first time in her life Finley looked at the three and wondered how they could be in this room together with all the secrets and pain that stood between them.

Who was she kidding? She was as guilty as any of them.

She'd understood when she decided to work with Jack that she would be on a different side of the aisle in the courtroom. Sometimes she was certain she could do the most good there.

Other times, like now, she wasn't so sure. Maybe all the good in her was gone.

Her chest squeezed. She no longer knew this person she had become. As much as she loved Jack, even he had crossed certain lines because of her that he never would have crossed before.

They all stared at her now. Maybe because she'd been standing there for about thirty or so seconds without speaking, her gaze fixed on them in the same way theirs were fixed on her now.

She uttered the only thing she could manage: "Any news?"

"He's in recovery," her father said.

"The surgery went well," Jack followed up. "The ruptured spleen has been repaired. He has a grade-three concussion but no skull fractures or other injuries to the brain."

"Good." Finley's legs felt stiff as she made the short journey to the collection of chairs. Then her legs gave out, and she folded into the seat.

She was next to Jack. Her father and the Judge were seated directly across from them, maybe three feet away. Her chest felt tight again.

"Are you all right?"

The question came from the Judge. How was it, Finley wondered, that the Judge's tone was always the same? Always. Perfectly modulated with no hint of emotion. Finley, on the other hand, wanted to scream with indignation. She wanted to rant at the injustice of it all.

And just like that, all those years of expensive education vanished.

There was no reason in any of this. There damned sure wasn't any justice.

And no, she wasn't all right. But that wasn't what mattered. What mattered was that Matt was in recovery from life-threatening injuries. Houser was a few floors away after having been beaten, shot, and left for dead, but he, too, would survive.

"No." Finley shook her head. "I'm not all right."

"We should get coffee." Jack stood. "You up for a stroll to the cafeteria, Bart?"

"Sure." He rose from his chair. "We'll bring coffee," he said to his wife and daughter. His eyes urged the two of them to remain calm.

Finley might never feel calm again.

The two men were out of there faster than either one should've been able to move in light of their ages.

The thumb drive in Finley's pocket seemed to sting her skin through the fabric of her slacks. She had to find a way to open it, assuming it required a password as well. "Dempsey got to Matt."

The Judge stared at Finley, her face clean of emotion. "Jack explained what happened."

Finley struggled to hold back the emotion threatening to explode from her. "It was one of his hired guns. Dempsey's. One of the three who broke into my house and killed Derrick . . . and raped me."

Her mother flinched. "If what you say is true, you have my word Dempsey will not get away with it."

Finley suddenly felt more helpless than she ever had in her life. "You don't understand. He already got away with it, and now he'll get away with what he's done to Matt and to Detective Houser. He won't ever stop."

Not unless Finley stopped him.

The door opened and a nurse appeared. "We have Mr. Quinn in a room now, and he can have one visitor."

Finley shot to her feet. She turned back to the Judge. "I'll be back soon so someone else can see him."

The Judge nodded. "Go. I'll let your father and Jack know."

Finley followed the nurse down the seemingly endless corridor and to the elevator. One floor up, and they were in another long corridor.

The nurse paused at a door. "He's still drowsy. He may go in and out on you, but that's normal."

Finley nodded her understanding. "Thank you."

She stepped inside. The sight of her dear friend made her breath stick deep in her lungs. His eyes were closed. There was a repaired cut on his forehead. Like Houser, he was attached to the machines monitoring his vitals and keeping him hydrated and hopefully out of pain.

Finley moved closer. For a long time she stood there staring at him, terrified to touch him. She'd never seen Matt look vulnerable or fragile. When she had been recovering after *that* night, he had sat at her bedside night after night. Whenever she opened her eyes, he would be there. Sometimes reading to her. Sometimes just smiling at her.

She needed—wanted—to do that same thing for him.

Nothing could have stopped the tears. She didn't even try. She just stood there and cried like a damned baby.

When the tears finally stopped, she squared her shoulders and did what needed to be done. She leaned down and kissed his cheek, then walked out of the hospital and to her Subaru. She climbed behind the wheel and sat for a long time. Minutes, maybe a half hour. Then she picked up her cell and made the call to the only person she knew who had the necessary expertise to help her with no questions.

"Finley," Winthrop said, "I'm surprised you called."

Finley licked her lips. "I need your help."

There was a distinct moment of silence.

"How can I help?"

The words poured out of her. She couldn't have stopped if her life had depended on it.

When she finished, there was no hesitation. "I understand. I'm sending someone to you now. When we have the thumb drive unlocked, I will notify you."

"Thank you."

Finley ended the call.

Desperate times called for desperate measures, and right now Finley was way past desperate.

32

10:30 p.m.

Winthrop Financial Consulting Group
Commerce Street, Nashville

Finley parked on the street. She climbed out of her Subaru and stared up at the towering glass building where Ellen Winthrop waited on the top floor. If someone had told Finley five days ago that she would be here meeting their latest ex-client for help with her own husband's murder, Finley would have laughed.

It was surreal.

Go big or go home.

Finley wasn't going home. She was desperate, and Winthrop had the resources she needed.

Thankfully there were no reporters loitering about. Jack and Ventura had released statements earlier in the day. Winthrop was no longer a lead item for the news.

A security guard opened the front entrance and allowed Finley inside. She walked straight to the bank of elevators and climbed inside a waiting car. Her chest tightened as she moved upward. The likelihood that this thumb drive would be nothing, like before, was great. But Finley had to be sure.

The elevator doors slid open, and Winthrop was there, waiting for Finley. She stepped off the elevator, and the doors closed with a whoosh behind her.

"Thank you." Whatever she was about to learn, Finley appreciated her help.

Despite their differences, this one thing—a dead husband, one who had betrayed them—bonded the two of them in some strange way. More likely it was all the shit they had done related to their dead husbands that really tied them together.

"Don't thank me," Winthrop said, "until you've seen the files. No one has gone beyond the gate. Whatever is inside, I made sure all understood that it was for your eyes only."

Fighting that damned hurricane of emotions again, Finley followed the older woman to her office. Dim lighting beyond all the glass walls showed the empty offices and conference rooms. By the time they reached Winthrop's office, Finley's pulse was hammering. An open laptop sat on the conference table. With monumental effort, Finley restrained herself from rushing to it . . . to what Derrick might have left there, if anything. Instead, she stood in the middle of the other woman's office, oddly at a loss for words.

"I like you, Finley," Winthrop said.

When Finley met her gaze, she went on, "I'm aware you know things that could change the course of my husband's homicide investigation."

Finley took a deep breath. This was completely off the record. The Finnegan Firm no longer represented Winthrop. It was late, and Finley cared only that maybe, just maybe, she was about to find some answers.

She shrugged. "I know you didn't kill him."

Winthrop's eyebrows lifted in surprise. "How can you be sure?"

Finley shook her head. "I know a cold-blooded killer when I interview one."

"You're that sure, are you?" Winthrop countered.

"I am." Finley inclined her head. "But you did protect the person who killed him, and I don't think it was Marsh. It would have been too risky for her to come into your home and carry out the act. She would have chosen more neutral, safer territory unless she was doing you a favor, and I'm guessing that isn't the case."

"But her prints were on the murder weapon," Winthrop challenged, her face clean of tells.

Finley laughed. "We both know how easily that can be done."

Really there was only one possibility beyond Marsh. Only one partner who was left handed. Finley and Jack had discussed this scenario; it made the most sense. As it turned out, they had been right.

Winthrop opted not to comment.

Finley figured she might as well say the rest. "You expected better of her, but she let you down. All those years you kept her close, took care of her, and still she betrayed you."

Ellen assessed Finley a long moment. "When did you know for certain?"

"An employee at the spy shop confirmed it was Jessica who bought the code grabber." This was the part that had sealed it for Finley. "When you discovered it was Jessica who'd purchased it—and you must have—and planted it in your husband's sock drawer, did *you* realize she was the one who'd killed him?"

That truth must have cut to the bone.

"I did." Ellen drew in a heavy breath. "At that stage I wasn't completely convinced she and Marsh had formed an alliance of sorts. Not until Ventura found Marsh's prints on the murder weapon. Obviously, Jessica used Marsh to get what she wanted—a scapegoat for her big exit."

Finley mulled over the idea. "And disappearing was her endgame? Take the money and run. Away from a handsome, well-bred husband and an enviable career by anyone's standards. It just wasn't enough. Or maybe it was too much."

Winthrop dipped her head in acknowledgment. "I couldn't protect her from herself. Sometimes when that level of brilliance blooms at such a young age, it comes with other issues. Jessica never learned to play well with others. Jarrod should never have continued to play with Marsh while he toyed with Jessica. It was a destructive combination for all involved."

"How long do you plan to continue protecting her?" Apparently, Finley hadn't completely snuffed out her former ADA self. She was interrogating the woman like the star witness for the defense. "According to her husband, she left, took her passport with her. Should we expect Marsh's body to show up anytime now? I can't see Jessica sharing the money with anyone."

"You and Jack needn't worry. I am very, very good at tying up loose ends," Winthrop assured her. "As for Marsh, Jessica will toy with her as long as it suits her."

Finley smiled with the realization of what Winthrop was telling her. "You know where they are, and you have a plan."

"You really should have higher aspirations, Finley. No offense to Jack, but you are capable of so much more."

She'd heard that a lot lately. Except she didn't feel all that capable right now.

Winthrop gestured to the table where the laptop waited. "Make yourself comfortable. If you have any questions, I will summon Vivian. She's working late tonight."

Finley moistened her lips, hated that her pulse was suddenly tripping. "Thanks."

Winthrop left her office, closing the door behind her.

Finley stared at the laptop only a few steps away. Surely if the thumb drive had contained nothing, Winthrop would have said as much.

This could be it.

The moment Finley had been waiting for all these months.

With a deep breath, she moved to the conference table and sat down. She tapped the space bar, and the screen lit up. A barrage of unopened files and images filled the space. She flinched. So it wasn't empty.

"Okay," she murmured. Her fingers hovered over the keyboard. A lump had settled in her gut, and her chest felt so tight she couldn't get a breath. "Just do this."

She opened the first folder and scanned the contents. Lists of dates and locations. Names. Images and more images. All regarding Dempsey and his company. Numerous meetings with a South American drug lord were listed. Finley sat back, stunned. "Holy hell."

She kept going. This drug lord, Ivan Orejuela, was one of the primary sources of heroin in the illegal drug world. The information Finley was staring at suggested Orejuela also represented a significant source for Dempsey Pharma.

"Jesus Christ. What the hell were you doing, Derrick?"

There were detailed documents and research studies about the issues with Dempsey Pharma's newest miracle painkiller. The rumors were right, and Finley was looking at the evidence. Deep inside, she started to shake.

Derrick had been collecting this information for months before his death.

Finley's hands fell to her lap, and she leaned back once more, away from the screen. She felt as if she'd just run a marathon. Out of breath. Her heart pounding. Her muscles quivering. The only reason for Derrick to have been collecting this sort of evidence was if he'd worked for the police or the DEA. Some law enforcement group.

She bit her lips together and squeezed her eyes shut to hold in the emotion. *No damned tears. Keep it together.*

Was it possible that he was one of the good guys?

She forced her eyes open and placed her fingers on the keys once more and opened the final file icon. The file opened and revealed a video. Blood roaring in her ears, fingers trembling, she adjusted the volume, braced herself, and hit play.

Derrick's face appeared on the screen.

Finley's heart stumbled.

"Finley, if you're watching this instead of hearing it straight from me, then I'm probably not around, and you or someone has found the evidence I stashed." He smiled, a pale version of his usual broad grins, and still every fiber of her being reacted. "Sorry about that," he said. "I wouldn't have left you like this if I had a choice in the matter."

Finley swiped at a damned tear that escaped despite her best efforts to hold it back. His face . . . his eyes . . . the sound of his voice . . . it all seeped into her. Made her weak. God, she had missed him so.

"Six months before we met, I managed a feat no other agent before me had been able to do. I found my way into Carson Dempsey's dark world. Not the world the public knows about but the one he operates behind that facade."

Finley held her breath. So he had worked for the authorities. Agent, he'd said. The trembling that had started in her fingers spread through her limbs. She fought to steady herself.

He looked away from the camera for a moment. "When it became clear you were going to be successful in taking his son to trial, Dempsey asked me to get close to you. He wanted me to watch you, to keep him informed of your every step." Derrick cleared his throat. "It wasn't a hardship by any means." He smiled sadly. "The trouble is, I didn't do a very good job of pretending." He stared directly into the camera, his eyes bright. "I fell in love with you, Finley, and this made me vulnerable. Not your fault." He shook his head. "I'm not telling you this to make you feel guilty. You got that? None of this is your fault."

A fat plop fell against her hand, and she realized the tears were pouring down her cheeks. She didn't care. She reached out, touched the screen, bit back a sob.

"I've been copying data for months now. Every time I think I'm done, the powers that be want more. I guess they just need to be sure it's enough to take this son of a bitch down." He shrugged. "Anyway, I've learned how to get beyond the security system and how long to stay before the anomaly is spotted. I don't think it will be long now. I have to admit I'm getting a little nervous at this point." He looked away a moment. "I wanted to make this video for you just in case something happened." He smiled and her heart lurched. "I'm sorry about all this, Finley. I had hoped when my assignment was done that we could have a real honeymoon and maybe start a family."

A sob escaped her lips. She pressed a hand to her mouth and rocked back and forth in her chair for what could have been. For the man she had been right to love and trust.

"If something unexpected happens to me and you find this thumb drive, you should turn it over to Scott Langford, DEA. He'll know what to do. I've been keeping this copy hidden because . . ." He exhaled a big breath. "I'm kinda worried that the agent I've been working with, Wayne Bates, is up to something. I hope I'm wrong, but this is my insurance. So you be sure to give it to Langford, not Bates." He recited the agent's email address, then managed another sad smile. "I love you, Finley, and just know that I wouldn't have missed loving you for anything. I'm only sorry that my timing sucked."

He looked away again, silence filling the video, then said, "Whatever happens, you deserve to be happy. Forget about me, and be the amazingly wonderful and happy woman I fell in love with."

For a moment he stared into the camera, saying nothing.

Then . . . "Bye, baby. I love you."

The video ended.

For a long while Finley couldn't move . . . couldn't even breathe. Derrick hadn't lied to her to hurt her. He hadn't set out to betray her. He had loved her. She swiped at more of those confounded tears. A couple of deep breaths were required before she could pull herself together enough to act.

"Think, Finley," she ordered her soggy brain. She needed that email address. She ran the video back and listened to the Langford guy's email address again. She entered it into the notepad on her phone. Then she prepared to forward the files via Winthrop's internet server. Finley doubted there was a more secure one anywhere in the city. The combined files were too large to send in a single email, so she pieced them out, sending numerous emails to Langford, to Matt's work email, and to Jack. Whatever happened, at least those three would have the evidence Derrick had collected.

She still had questions, but for now, the answers she had were enough. Derrick hadn't been trying to betray her. He had loved her.

Finley dug through her bag until she found a single, probably used tissue. She dabbed at her nose and eyes. Before closing the laptop, she closed the file and removed the thumb drive. She stood, steadied herself, and tucked the thumb drive into her pocket. Deep breath. Then another. Finley exited the borrowed office.

Winthrop waited at the elevator. She didn't ask any questions, just pressed the call button as Finley approached with her red, puffy eyes. They rode down to the main lobby in silence, then exited the building.

On the sidewalk, Finley hesitated. "Thank you." She felt the need to say more, but somehow the words wouldn't come.

Winthrop gave her a nod. "It was my pleasure."

Finley took a breath, told herself to go, but somehow her feet just wouldn't get going. "You know," she said, needing a subject change to pull herself together and still curious about all those loose ends this woman claimed she'd tied up, "I can't help wondering where those two will end up."

Winthrop laughed softly. "I can tell you that Liz is following the money. I suspect they'll both be found where the money lands."

Finley gave an eyebrow flash. "They say it's the root of all evil."

Even split two ways, 7.8 million was a hell of a lot of money.

"You know, Finley," Winthrop said, "there are two things in life we cannot do. Once we've flown the coop, we can never really go back. Home and the people there are never the same as what we recall. Not to mention, all one's old secrets remain buried there."

Very true. "What's the other thing?" Finley asked.

"We can never bite the hand that feeds us and walk away without consequences. I remind the women who work with me of this often."

Well said. "Good night." Finley turned to go but hesitated again, couldn't help herself. "I looked for past cases like this one—with and without murder involved. I didn't find anything." She studied Winthrop for a time. "Jack and I are fairly convinced this isn't the first time your group has taken down someone like Grady."

Winthrop smiled. "Often lessons can be taught and learned without legal action. Certainly, without physical harm. Murder would never be the proper ending. A simple presentation of what will happen if one decides to make the same mistake again is far more comfortable for all involved. It works every time. In fact, we believe what we do makes our little corner of the world a better place. This most recent disaster notwithstanding."

"You should watch that going forward," Finley suggested.

"Good advice," Winthrop allowed. "Good night, Finley."

Finley loaded into her Subaru. Winthrop watched, her own car and driver waiting close by. As far as Finley and Jack were concerned, the Winthrop case was closed. Finley drove away without looking back.

Derrick had loved her. She grinned, feeling as if a dump truck had been lifted from her chest. He hadn't betrayed her. She wanted to get back to the hospital and share the news with Matt.

After what he'd been through, he deserved to be the first to know. When he was home and recovered, they were going to celebrate. She pressed the accelerator a little harder.

"Make the next right."

Finley jumped. Swerved sharply before righting the car. Her gaze flew to the rearview mirror. She didn't recognize the face there. Didn't need to. All that mattered was the weapon aimed at the back of her head.

Fear banded around her rib cage, but she ignored it. "Where are we going?"

"No questions. Just follow my directions."

She slowed, made the right turn. Her fingers tightened on the wheel. Did she keep driving? Make a sudden, jarring stop in hopes of throwing him forward?

The gun could go off, and since it was aimed at her head, that wasn't a good idea.

Think, Finley! This wasn't the first time she had been in a precarious position like this one.

She had known there would be others. Did he have to show up now? Damn it. Anger blasted through her. She was sick and tired of these bastards hounding her.

"Left at the light."

She did as he ordered, her rage building. She should be scared, but by God she'd had enough. She was not going down without a fight.

Hell no!

"Left at the stop sign."

The turn told Finley where they were going.

The murder house.

How fitting. The place she should have died more than a year ago.

A new surge of outrage belted her. The bastard was too late. At this point, she had no intention of dying. Matt needed her. Her parents and Jack needed her. Derrick wanted her to be happy.

Besides, she had plans now. Damn it. She intended to make a difference. Houser's words echoed in her head. She intended to change the world.

"Pull into the driveway."

She did as he asked but not before she spotted Helen Roberts peeking out her front window. Hope gave her a boost. *Please let her be her nosy self and notice that something is wrong. Please let her call the police.*

"Shut off the engine."

Finley complied. What now? Should she open the door and make a run for it?

Scream at the top of her lungs?

No. No. She couldn't do either of those.

Wait until they were outside the car and turn on him? Kick him in the balls?

"We're going inside," he growled. "As long as you behave, no one else will get hurt. You scream and a neighbor rushes out, they're dead."

"Got it." Finley opened her door and climbed out. Her body felt oddly disjointed and numb. Putting one foot in front of the other was no easy task. *Keep going. Wait for the right moment.*

"Move." He nudged her with the gun.

She hadn't even realized she had stopped.

The bastard followed her to the porch. Too bad she hadn't left on a light. She dug for her key, taking her time. She had to do something soon. Say something . . .

"You're wasting your time," she told him as she dug around in her bag, buying time, wishing she had pepper spray. "I've already emailed the files and images Derrick collected to the DEA."

"He knows and he'll deal with that," the man assured her. "This is about all the trouble you've caused." He laughed, an ugly, ruthless sound. "You should have stopped while you were ahead."

Finley's hand closed around the house key, allowing the long end to stick out between her fisted fingers. She could do this. *Don't think . . . just act.* "What can I say—I have issues letting go."

"Too bad for—"

She steeled herself, whirled around, and stabbed at his face, aiming for an eye.

He swore loudly, stumbled backward. "Bitch!"

Finley kicked him in the balls. Turned and started to run.

The gun fired. The bullet flew past her left ear. Shit! Her heart lunged into her throat. She dived to her right. Hit the ground just beyond the edge of her porch. She rolled. Got to her hands and knees to scramble away.

"You are dead!" he roared.

Finley lunged forward, trying to put distance between them, went facedown into the grass.

A loud clangy thud echoed in the darkness.

Then another. She scooted farther across her little yard, staying low in case he fired his weapon again.

The sound came a third time, and she twisted around to see what was happening.

The man lay motionless on the ground. Helen Roberts stood over him, staring down at him, a shovel in her hands. 'I don't think he's going to try getting up again."

Finley clambered to her feet. Searched for the gun. The bastard was out cold.

Lights had come on, and neighbors were pouring out of houses. Good. Someone would call the police. Where the hell was her phone?

She found the gun. Trudged to the porch and collapsed on her steps. She held the weapon clenched between her hands, aimed toward the ground. Roberts remained standing over the man, shovel in hand.

Something touched Finley's side. She jumped. The cat yowled, then rubbed against her. Finley laughed, but in spite of the reaction, tears were rolling down her cheeks. Who laughed and cried at the same time?

Didn't matter. She was alive. By God. She was still alive.

33

Saturday, September 24

4:30 a.m.

Vanderbilt Medical Center
Medical Center Drive, Nashville

Jack and her parents had long ago gone home, and Matt was sitting up when Finley arrived. Well, *sitting up* was a bit optimistic. The bed had been raised, and he was in a more upright position. But that was progress.

"You look almost ready to go home," she teased.

She reached for a nearby chair to pull closer to his bed, but he wrapped his strong fingers around her arm and pulled her toward him.

"Lower the bed rail and sit by me." He patted the mattress.

When she'd finagled the bed rail down, she eased carefully onto the bedside. "Why are you still awake?"

She had never been so exhausted in her life, and still she might never sleep again. It was over. She had the truth she had been searching for. It had taken hours to sort out the situation with the police who arrived, lights and sirens blazing. Every single person on her block had come out to help.

"I was waiting for you." He stared up at her, his bruised face making her heart ache. "Jack said you were coming right back."

She smiled. Yeah, that had been like six hours ago. "I had to take care of a few things. But I'm here now. How are you feeling?"

"Like I was hit by a Mack Truck."

She rustled up a laugh that sounded raspy and kind of pitiful after all the crying she'd done. "Nah, that was the other guy."

Matt laughed, then winced.

She took his hand—the one not inundated with needles and IV lines—in hers. "I found another thumb drive."

He searched her face. "You did? Why didn't you call me? I could have called my guy."

And he would have. Finley knew she could always count on Matt. "I took care of it." Her lips trembled, and for a moment she couldn't speak. As if he understood, Matt waited for her to go on, his own eyes bright with emotion.

"Derrick worked for the DEA. He was collecting evidence against Dempsey. The bastard was buying some of his drugs from a South American drug lord. There are FDA rules against that sort of thing. He'd somehow blocked numerous research studies warning about the potential ill effects of his miracle product. Basically, from what I could tell, he's in pretty deep shit."

Matt grinned. "This is good news, Fin."

"Derrick had infiltrated Dempsey's organization before he met me."

"Which means," Matt pointed out, "that nothing you did put him in Dempsey's path. He was already there."

She nodded. "It was another agent. He sold Derrick out."

She wanted to say more but couldn't find her voice again. Matt understood. He held her hand. Didn't ask questions. Just let her be.

She decided not to tell him about the thug Dempsey had sent to take her out when she left Winthrop. No need to bother him just now with how she'd called her friend in CSI, Tommy Hanes. He'd come right over and helped her search the house. He had found four bugs in her house and two in her car. Dempsey had been listening all this time. This was how he so often knew her next move. Bastard. At least he hadn't been able to get to her phone, or he might have inflicted far more damage.

Eventually, she said, "The DEA has everything. I sent a copy to yours and Jack's emails too. Seems like it's over. Done. At least my part." The burn of tears was back, and Finley wanted to scream. She had lost so much and could have lost more. And she was so damned tired.

Matt reached over, swiped away a tear. "No crying." He pulled her down next to him, hugged her to his battered body. "You did it, Fin. You solved the case and you beat that bastard."

She rested her head against his shoulder and closed her eyes. She didn't want to think anymore. Definitely didn't want to cry anymore.

Matt was right. She had beaten that bastard and survived. She'd helped to finish what Derrick had started. Just as important, she had cleared his name.

"Fin, you know you're my hero, right?"

She peered up at her friend. "I'm no hero, Matt." He knew the things she had done. Whatever hero material she'd possessed was long gone now.

"You're one of the strongest people I know. You were the best damned ADA Davidson County has ever seen. And you never gave up on finding the truth for Derrick. What else would you call that except a hero?"

She didn't answer. Couldn't answer.

"Jack and I talked about you while you were MIA all those hours," Matt went on.

"Should I be worried?" Speaking of Jack, he was not going to be happy when he found out she had taken the thumb drive she hadn't told him about to Winthrop. Ended up with a hired gun in her back seat. It really was a miracle she'd survived.

She would never ever again get annoyed at her nosy neighbor. If anyone in all this was a hero, it was Helen Roberts.

Life was full of ironies.

"Jack feels you're not reaching your full potential at the firm."

Finley drew back. "What? Is he firing me?"

Matt laughed. Winced. "No. He's not firing you. Jack and I believe you should go for the brass ring, Fin. Get out there and do big things. Make the Judge proud."

Finley rolled her eyes. "There you go, ruining the moment."

He lifted his hand, touched her cheek, prompting her to look at him. "Fin, you mean the world to me. I want you to be happy. I want you to do all the things we talked about back in law school. I want you to be you, and I want to be able to watch you shine."

She smiled, remembering all those fierce conversations and debates before and after exams. All the wine and beer and cramming. "You mean the world to me too, Matt. You are the smartest, most—"

He pressed a finger to her lips. "Just listen."

She nodded, her lips suddenly on fire. Maybe she was just too tired to think straight. Had to be the problem.

"I don't want you taking any more crazy chances or driving yourself crazy about the past. I need your word on that."

"I swear."

"Good."

He smiled, held her gaze with his until she was certain he would kiss her.

"So when Jack and I were talking," he went on, breaking the tension, "we discussed the fact that Briggs is up for reelection next year. You should throw your hat in the ring and go for it."

Finley put her hand to his forehead. "Are you okay? Should I call a nurse?"

"I'm serious," he insisted. "And so is Jack. Just think about it, Fin. Think about the difference you could make. The change you could effect."

"No promises," she warned, "but I will think about it."

Matt regaled her with the story of how a nurse had given him a sponge bath and Jack had been so jealous. She listened and laughed and thanked God a thousand times that her dear friend was okay.

She had loved Derrick with all her heart, but Matt was right. She couldn't keep looking back. Derrick wanted her to be happy, and she intended to give it her best effort.

When Matt drifted off to sleep, she watched him until she could no longer hold her eyes open. Matt was her best friend. She adored him.

She loved him.

He's in love with you—you know that, right?

Yes. She did know.

34

The Other Woman

1:00 p.m.

Seven Mile Beach
Grand Cayman

The weather was amazing, exactly the right temperature.

The sun, the sugary-white beach, and the sparkling water, all the things Jessica had longed for. But her husband never wanted to take a vacation. Ellen never wanted to leave the office for more than a weekend.

Jessica was still young; she wanted more, and kids were not part of those desires. Let her husband find some other broodmare. This was her happy place. She reached for her cute little exotic umbrella drink and savored a long sip before placing it back on the table next to her.

She was never leaving.

Coming here had been a very good idea. Jessica glanced at the woman relaxing in the chaise next to hers. Lena looked beautiful and happy. Jessica was glad. She wanted her to enjoy these precious moments. There weren't many left.

Jessica smiled, closed her eyes. Only a little while longer, and it would be finished.

She had spent her entire life under someone else's thumb. First her overbearing parents, who insisted she be perfect at every little thing. Just because she was a genius didn't mean she didn't want to attend the same parties other kids her age were enjoying. She hadn't wanted to study and test all the time.

It wasn't until she was away from them at college that she found hope. Ellen had taken her under her wing and shown her how much of the world could be hers. A frown tugged at Jessica's face. Except then Ellen had changed. She'd wanted to accomplish great things, and Jessica had been part of her plan. Life returned to all work and no play.

Jessica had hated it. Nothing she did, even marriage, had changed the way she was viewed. Her husband wanted more money, a larger house in a more coveted location. He nagged at her about asking for raises. Hounded her about having kids before her eggs all dried up. She was nothing but a means to an end.

Then Jarrod had entered the picture. Charming. Relaxed. Handsome. He'd started flirting with Jessica right from the beginning. That was when her plan took shape.

Getting involved with him had been the best thing to happen to her. He'd thought he had her fooled and that she knew nothing of his past. But she had known everything. He was the one who had been fooled. Their tight little group had gone after him for what he had done to poor, tragic Nora Duncan.

Jessica smiled to herself. He had chosen the wrong woman to take advantage of when he picked out Nora. Taking down men like Jarrod was Ellen's one and only hobby. They had dug and dug until they had uncovered all his scams. Though Ellen and the others enjoyed their little side job immensely, they were always very careful to choose only those who deserved to fall the most. No one ever died, of course. Or even went to jail. How boring was that.

But this time had been different. This time Jessica saw an opportunity. Her little affair with Jarrod had shown her there was more to life than work and ambition. She'd wanted more. She'd wanted to escape. So she'd made him see how taking a measly little million or two was simply poor form. That would never have been enough for Jessica. She had played him perfectly, and Ellen had hardly suspected a thing.

But there was Lena, Jarrod's longtime partner.

Jessica cut her a look from the corner of her eye. She was attractive in a plain sort of way. Leading her along had been relatively easy. She'd grown tired of Jarrod and his scams. He'd changed, Lena said. After the Duncan ordeal she'd wanted out. Jessica had shown her how they could escape together. The memories twitched her lips. She'd shown dear, unsuspecting Lena how the good life really looked. She'd wanted it, would do anything for it . . . even kill the man in their way.

She'd done it before. But it hadn't been necessary in this case. Jessica had wanted to do it herself. But she'd made sure the world would believe it was Lena. In fact, Jessica had dug up every single one of Lena's secrets. Like how she'd escaped to Grand Cayman at nineteen. She'd lived right here in paradise for six years before meeting Jarrod, who had arrived with one of his targets on his arm. Lena had been a waitress with a gorgeous tan and long blonde hair. They'd made the perfect pair. She was smart and could learn any skill. He had the charm and plenty of skills of his own, primarily the sort that made lonely, rich old women want him.

Yes, coming here had been the perfect plan. Lena knew all about the islands, and she had a deeply buried history here. She'd worked as a high-end prostitute for a man named Kenneth Dart. Dart had been quite the scumbag, taking advantage of the women in his stable. Lena had said he treated them like slaves rather than business associates. Not a single one seemed to know what had happened to him when he disappeared. Lena had reveled in telling Jessica all the dirty details. Where she'd hidden his body and the murder weapon she had used. Every little thing.

Lena thought she had once again found in Jessica the kind of female bond she'd had with those women all those years ago. She could come back here and enjoy the good life. She had a new identity. All the money she could ever want. No one from Nashville or any of the other cities where she and Jarrod had worked their scams could touch her in this place. And she had a new friend with the same aspirations.

It was the perfect escape.

Except it was all just an illusion.

Jessica wasn't sharing with anyone. Jarrod and Lena had been fools to trust her. Jarrod had given Jessica the full PIN when he added J. (Jessica) Grady to the account. He'd wanted to dump Lena, and he and Jessica would get married and live happily ever after.

Like that was ever, ever going to happen.

A shadow suddenly blocked the sun.

Jessica smiled. She turned on her side and watched as Lena's eyes fluttered open.

A man in a white uniform stood over her. Not the waiter who had been so attentive to their needs.

"Mina Arnette?"

The look of sheer horror on Lena's face was priceless. Jessica shivered with excitement just watching.

Lena sat up and removed her sunglasses. She glanced at Jessica, who shrugged, then stared up at the man, who was a local police officer.

"I'm afraid you've made a mistake," Lena argued. "My name is Lena Marsh."

She glanced at Jessica again, and Jessica of course pretended to be agog with shock.

The policeman reached into his pocket and removed a paper. Took his time unfolding it and then turned it around for her to view.

"This is you, is it not?"

How cute, Jessica thought. *Not.* There was Lena with her formerly long blonde hair, all decked out in whore garb. Pathetic.

"That isn't you," Jessica argued, then turned to her pretend friend. "Is it?"

Lena stared at the mug shot. "Well, she certainly looks like me, but it's not me."

The policeman didn't believe her, of course. Jessica had made sure there would be no question as to who Lena Marsh really was.

Suddenly more uniformed men appeared.

"Mina Arnette, you are under arrest for the murder of Kenneth Dart."

Lena shook her head. "No. You're mistaken. I—"

Hands grabbed at her.

Jessica watched the struggle. Shrugged when Lena called for Jessica's help. Too bad her temporary friend would be spending the rest of her life in prison.

Jessica lay back on the chaise. All that money was hers now.

Life was finally perfect.

Her cell pinged, and Jessica reached for it. An alert from the bank appeared on the screen.

She sat up, drew her sunglasses away so she could see the screen better.

The alert was a warning that her balance had dropped. Heart racing, fingers fumbling, she quickly opened the app. There had to be a mistake.

Her hopes sank.

Balance zero.

The money was gone. The phone rang. The bank. Her hopes dared to resurrect. Perhaps there had been a mistake.

"Hello." She held her breath, hoping for good news.

"J. Grady?"

"Yes, yes, this is she."

"This is Carl Wettig from Trident Trust. We need to have a meeting regarding certain issues with your account. Are you available now?"

Jessica ended the call. No! No! No!

Another ping of her cell sounded. Jessica checked the screen. A text. She tapped the screen.

Never bite the hand that feeds you.

"Ellen," she snarled, "you bitch."
Jessica threw her phone across the white sand.
What the hell was she going to do now?

35

2:30 p.m.

Harpeth Hills Memory Gardens
Highway 100, Nashville

Finley sat in her Subaru for a long while.

She had only been here once. She'd been too hurt . . . too angry to come back.

Her father had picked the cemetery and made all the arrangements. Finley had been in no condition to make those decisions. When she was released from the hospital, her father had brought her here, and then she'd started her physical rehab and never returned.

The agent Derrick had told her about, Langford, had provided Finley with Derrick's personal information. Derrick Reed was his real name. He'd grown up in Mobile. He had no immediate family. His parents had died when he was a kid. A lot of what he'd told her was true. Somehow that made her happy. She liked that he'd shared his real self with her.

Knowing the truth—knowing that what they had shared was real—meant the world to her.

With a big bolstering breath, she climbed out of her car and headed for the cemetery gate.

Dempsey had been picked up and questioned. The goal was to find a way to hold him until the evidence could be sorted out. The fear was that if given the opportunity, he would disappear. His bank accounts had been frozen, his passport seized, but passports could be bought on the black market.

A few minutes ago Detective Ventura had called to say there was news in his investigation. Lena Marsh, a.k.a. Mina Arnette, had been arrested for another murder in Grand Cayman. Jessica Lauder had been with her and was now under investigation for fraud by one of the major banks there.

Sounded as if Winthrop had come through and ensured all the loose ends were tied up. Finley wasn't surprised. Her respect for the woman grew a little more.

Finley planned to take some time now to decide what came next. For the past fourteen months she had been fighting an uphill battle to find the truth about Derrick. Now it was time to let herself really grieve his death. She had some healing to do for sure. She also had some catching up to do with her father. There were a lot of things she had put off for far too long.

But she wasn't going to wait long before making other decisions. Career decisions. As much as she loved working with Jack, she did want to do something more . . . something that would make a real difference. She wasn't entirely sure what that would look like, but she was toying with Matt and Jack's idea of running for the office of Davidson County district attorney. She wasn't perfect and certainly not innocent, but she knew how to ferret out the truth beyond and among secrets and lies maybe better than anyone. Being squeaky clean wasn't a requirement of the position. She just needed to do the job without bias and without the possibility of being bought.

Finley wasn't for sale in any capacity.

She found Derrick's grave. The headstone surprised her. She hadn't seen it. She vaguely remembered her father mentioning that it had arrived. He'd ordered it. Black granite. Simple but elegant.

Perfect.

She sat down on the ground and plucked an overgrown sprig of grass away from the headstone.

"Sorry it took me so long to come back." She'd always thought talking out loud to a dead person was dumb, but here she was. "I watched the video. Langford has all the evidence you collected. Dempsey is in deep shit." She laughed every time she said the words. The idea made her immensely happy. "Just so you know, the others—the ones who came *that* night—got theirs. And the bastard who gave you up, former agent Wayne Bates, is under investigation. He retired right after you . . . died. But he's not going to get away with what he did. I'll make sure."

She pulled her knees up and propped her chin there. "Matt and Jack helped me paint the inside of the house. Jack is there today starting the exterior painting. The Judge thinks I'm crazy for staying, and maybe I am. But I couldn't go until this was done. I needed to be close to you. Now I just want to stay. It's where *we* were, and I don't want to leave. Not yet anyway."

Her neighbors, particularly Helen Roberts, had gone above and beyond. How could she leave such a great neighborhood?

Then she told him her potential career plan. She talked it out at length, mostly for her own benefit. By the time she was ready to go, she had cried some more and laughed plenty.

She dusted off her jeans and said her goodbyes. When she made it to the gate, the Judge's car was waiting next to hers.

"Did you like the headstone?" she asked as Finley approached.

She nodded. "Dad did a good job."

"I picked it out."

Her father hadn't mentioned her mother being involved. Probably hadn't wanted to open a can of worms.

"It's perfect. Thank you. Exactly what I would have selected."

The Judge nodded. "I'm sorry," she said, the two words coming out like rocks being pushed through a straw. "I misjudged Derrick, but when you have children of your own, you will understand how I felt."

Wow. An apology from the Judge. Finley wanted to pretend indifference, but she couldn't. The words touched her.

"Thank you," she admitted and propped a smile into place.

"We've always had our differences, Finley. I hope for your father's sake that we can work through those in the future."

"I think we can figure out a way to do that." This time her smile was real. "Jack says the reason we don't get along is because we're too much alike."

The Judge made a distasteful face. "He may have a point."

Finley laughed, felt a burst of freed tension. But there was one other thing she needed to make right first. "I have one condition," Finley said, "regarding our efforts going forward."

Her mother studied her a moment. "What condition is that?"

"Forgive Jack. Forgive yourself, and let's get back to being a family, Jack included."

The Judge appeared taken aback for about two seconds, and then she took another couple to consider the request. "I'll work on that."

Finley nodded. It was the best she could hope for . . . for now. "I have to go. I'm picking up Matt at the hospital."

He was going home today, and Finley intended to take care of him the same way he had her.

O'Sullivan Residence
Shelby Avenue, Nashville, 4:00 p.m.

Finley hurried around to the passenger side of the car. Matt had the door open, and she gave him a hand climbing out.

He groaned. The doctor had said he would be sore for a while but recovery should be smooth sailing. Either way, Finley had brought him home with her. His house was a sprawling three stories with his suite on the second floor. Her house was all on one floor. Closer to downtown and work.

Thankfully Jack and one of her neighbors had gotten a new bathroom sink installed.

Helen Roberts, her dog in one arm, the water hose in her other hand, watched from across the street.

Finley waved at her neighbor, and Roberts waved back. Not only did she wave, but she smiled. Finley smiled in answer. The lady had probably saved her life last night. Finley would forever be grateful to her.

As she and Matt made their way up the walk, Finley noticed the buckets of paint. She had no idea what color Jack had decided on. She had left it up to him. He and her father were going to whip the place into shape, Jack had told her. She liked that the two of them would be working together. Two of her favorite people.

In the house, she settled Matt on the sofa. He was her other favorite person.

"The Judge called as I was driving to the hospital. She insisted on bringing over dinner tonight. I hope you're up for that."

"She's coming here?" Matt looked surprised.

He was no more surprised than Finley. She wasn't sure how they would get back to a normal mother-daughter relationship, since they'd never really had one, but she was willing to take it one step at a time. "She is. Dad too. And Jack. He's bringing dessert."

"Okay, now I'm worried," Matt said. "Are you sure the doc didn't say I was dying?"

Finley laughed. "I'm positive."

He grabbed her hand and pulled her down to sit beside him. "This has been a lot to take in. You sure you're okay? You're working things out with the Judge. Putting the Dempsey business behind you."

"I'm also considering your suggestion, Mr. Chief of Staff in the Governor's Office. I might just look into running for DA. I can't have you getting so far ahead of me."

He smiled. "That's awesome. And I might just be able to wrangle an endorsement from the governor. He talks a lot about fresh blood." Matt searched her face, his concerned. "You know, you can take this a piece at a time. No one will think less of you if you don't go so fast."

"No." She shook her head firmly. "I'm not wasting any more time. I want to get on with my life. I want to make a difference. And I want the people I care about with me."

"I hope that includes me."

"You're right at the top of my priority list." She wasn't sure how to tell him just how much he meant to her.

He stared at her for a long moment, and Finley wondered if he wanted to kiss her as badly as she suddenly wanted to kiss him.

But that was one fresh start she intended to take very slowly. Her relationship with Matt was far too important to risk acting prematurely. She had finally found closure on the past fourteen months. The horror of *that* night, losing Derrick, living with the guilt. She was putting it behind herself and moving forward. She wanted Matt with her every step of the way. Not just as her best friend but as the man she loved so, so much.

They talked and laughed until Matt dozed off on her. She tucked a pillow beneath his head and pulled a throw over him. She walked to the front window, smiled at the cat curled up on the glider. She'd have to come up with a name for the little guy. Or girl.

She made a conscious decision not to call this place the murder house anymore. Yes, Derrick had been murdered here. But it was home now, and she was fairly certain Derrick would be good with the change.

Somewhere in the distance she heard the wail of a police car.

She smiled. *Watch out, Nashville. Finley O'Sullivan is about to shake things up.*

ACKNOWLEDGMENTS

I come from a long line of very strong women. My mother was a tiny woman but as fierce as a giant. When my grandmother was born, women did not have the right to vote, but that changed when she was a young woman. She lived through the Great Depression, saw the first woman elected to Congress, and rooted for Rosa Parks when she refused to give up her seat on a bus in Montgomery, Alabama. Both my mother and grandmother cheered when the Equal Pay Act was signed into law by President Kennedy. These women witnessed many firsts and shattered glass ceilings of their own before the phrase was coined. I am so grateful for the strength, courage, and determination of the women in my family. My grandmother and my mother gave me the courage to believe that a girl from a farm in Nowhere, Alabama, could write a book and have it published and read by people all over the world. Women really are amazing!

ABOUT THE AUTHOR

Photo © 2019 Jenni M Photography LLC

Debra Webb is the *USA Today* bestselling author of more than 170 novels. She is the recipient of the prestigious Romantic Times Career Achievement Award for Romantic Suspense as well as numerous Reviewers' Choice Awards. In 2012, Webb was honored as the first recipient of the esteemed L. A. Banks Warrior Woman Award for her courage, strength, and grace in the face of adversity. Webb was also awarded the distinguished Centennial Award for having published her hundredth novel. She has more than four million books in print in many languages and countries.

Webb's love of storytelling goes back to her childhood, when her mother bought her an old typewriter at a tag sale. Born in Alabama, Webb grew up on a farm. She spent every available hour exploring the world around her and creating her stories. Visit her at www.debrawebb.com.